Graeme Hague
in Queensland.
nates between being a professional musician
and working as a technician in live theatre.

Also by G. M. Hague in Pan

A PLACE TO FEAR
VOICES OF EVIL

G.M. HAGUE

GHOST BEYOND EARTH

PAN
Pan Macmillan Australia

First published 1993 by Pan Macmillan Publishers Australia
Pan Macmillan Australia Pty Limited
St Martins Tower, 31 Market Street, Sydney

Reprinted 1996

This edition published 2001 by Hinkler Books Pty Ltd
17-23 Redwood Drive, Dingley, Victoria 3172 Australia

National Library of Australia
cataloguing-in-publication data:

Hague, G.M.
Ghost beyond Earth.
ISBN 1-865-15633-7
I. Title.
A823.3

Typeset in 10.5/12pt Plantin by Midland Typesetters
Printed in Australia by Griffin Press

Acknowledgements

Writing a novel requires, for me, a lot of rather selfish time and patience, so thus I've accumulated a correspondingly large amount of 'thank yous' that must be said. Without giving them an order of preference or importance, I'll start with my family, meaning my mother who's silently waited for me to achieve something—anything, in fact. My new wife who accepts that my staring out the window for hours is actually working. Brothers Stephen and David, helping with computer software and hardware, and putting up with my microchip illiteracy which means I have to call them every second day and ask why 'it's not working *now*'. Dale Kennedy comes into the same category, freely supplying phone answering machines, CD players and headphones for keeping the world at a distance. The rest of the 'pub night' crew for encouragement and a lot of laughs. The other members of The Sheep, Tony, Avon and Steve, the best damn rock band in the land, helping me pay the bills. Likewise the folks at the Entertainment Centre, past and present, accepting me as the most permanent casual you could get, giving me work when I needed it. Peter McLachlan, for his help and expertise. And my friends in the West, some now scattered around the country—you know who you are—who've stuck by me for many, many years.

And of course, my agent and new friend, Selwa Anthony, whose advice and guidance are invaluable.

Thanks, everyone.

G.M. Hague
1993

For Phillipa

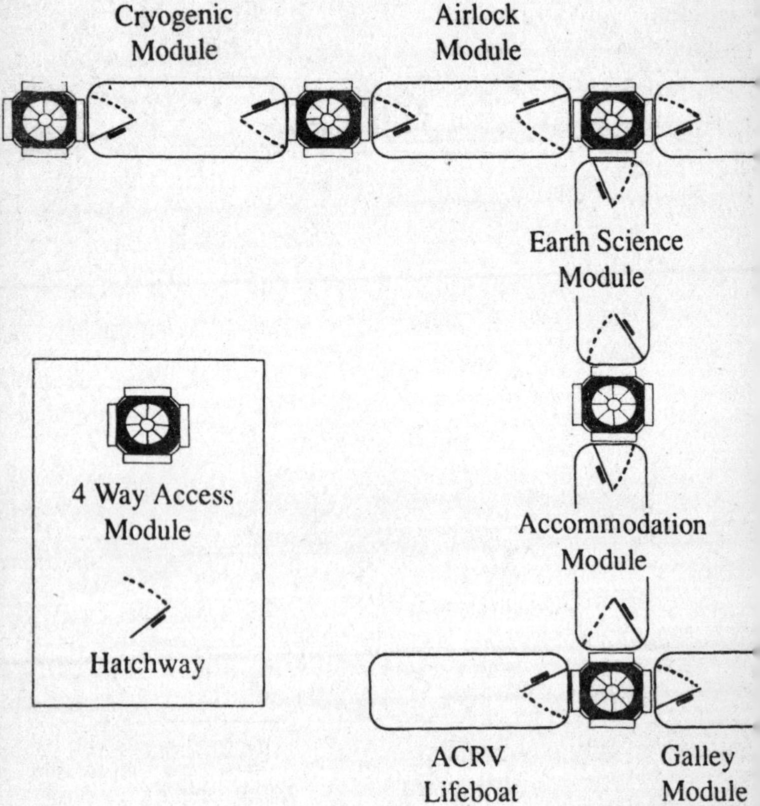
Cryogenic Module
Airlock Module
Earth Science Module
Accommodation Module
ACRV Lifeboat
Galley Module
4 Way Access Module
Hatchway

Space Stati

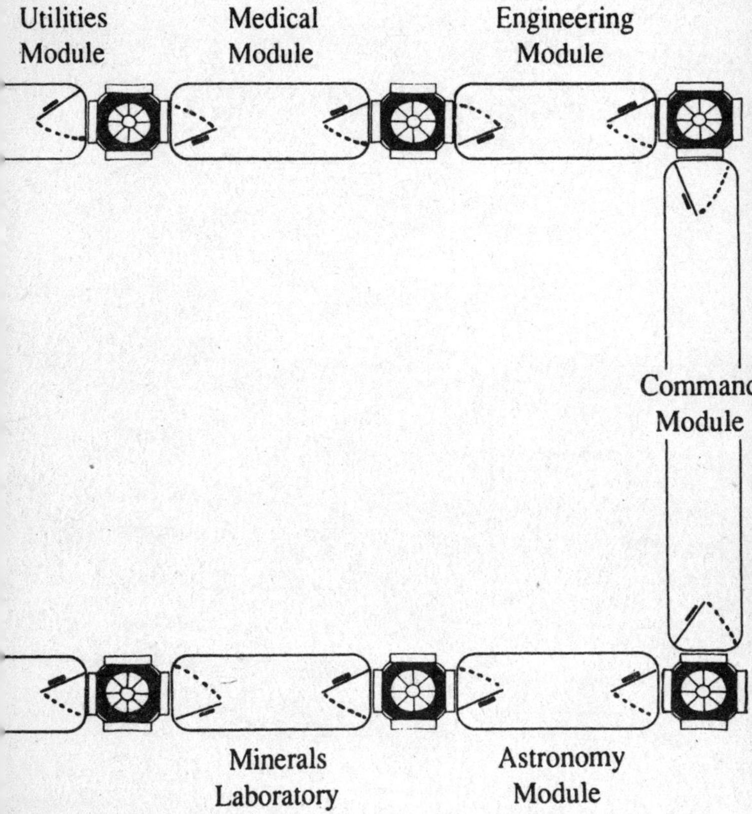
Utilities Module
Medical Module
Engineering Module
Command Module
Minerals Laboratory
Astronomy Module

on *Freedom*

1

MAJOR JOHN QUANTEY SHOULD have felt utterly alone.

He was imprisoned in a spacesuit drifting nearly two hundred miles above the Earth's surface. True, he was holding on firmly to one of Freedom's lateral struts and there were another seven astronauts inside the space station. And before stepping into space he had gone through the usual lengthy preparations. But once outside, he was on his own. It was a high-risk situation. Anything might suddenly malfunction and Quantey was the only crewmember in a position to do anything about it. It would be a rare malfunction which allowed him enough time to get back inside or for one of the others to suit-up and come to his aid.

That was why an EVA—Extra Vehicular Activity—always made him feel particularly alone. Vulnerable.

But never nervous. (*Or scared*, an inner voice whispered.) Never on edge, like he was now.

Crawling over the superstructure of a space station in Medium Earth Orbit was not a logical place to be looking over your shoulder. Yet the only thing stopping him from doing just that was the spacesuit, which required Quantey to roll on to his back to properly see behind him.

So instead, Quantey tried hard to shrug away the creeping tension between his shoulder blades.

Gently he pushed himself towards the next strut. All around him the perfect, inky blackness of space contrasted sharply with the brilliant stars. He was working in the shadow of one of the laboratory modules. When he pulled himself back into the sunlight his facemask would instantly darken in the bright light and the sun would blot out the stars.

Quantey cursed silently as a bead of sweat began to trickle down his forehead. It ran into his eye, stinging and making him blink.

'Get the job done and get the hell back inside,' he told himself.

The space station always suffered a wastage of its artificial atmosphere. The pressure inside was high compared to the almost total vacuum outside. There was no such thing as the perfect seal—not after nearly seven years of operations. Freedom was made up of twelve separate modules, all interconnected by hatchways and each with a ring-seal protecting the married access tunnels.

They leaked. Not a lot, but they leaked.

Quantey was supposed to check how *much* they were leaking—or rather, ensure they weren't seeping too much. The only accurate way of testing the seals was to check them from the outside. That meant an EVA by someone, and it was his turn.

He could have used the Wheelchair, an elaborate backpack the astronaut practically sat in. Small jets propelled it in any given direction. It was even fun, but the set-up was too cumbersome to be able to get close to the seals and run the detector correctly around the rim.

Quantey wasn't happy about doing the job. It wasn't a popular one with any of the crew. But it had to be done, and done well. He managed a grim smile. They all agreed that running unexpectedly out of air would have serious implications.

He chose to haul himself around the ladder-tracks of Freedom's girder network with the seal-tester clipped to his belt. He also discarded the Umbilical, a line carrying power and communications, and used the smaller self-contained life support system. He figured the trailing cord of the Umbilical was more of a hindrance than a help when moving around as much as he needed to. All but one of the astronauts operated the same way. NASA frowned on the practice, but often found out too late to do anything about it.

Celia Hereson's voice crackled in his helmet. 'Time for a break, John.'

'I'm okay,' he replied, reaching for the next girder.

The sigh was audible through the communications link. 'You know it doesn't work like that,' she warned. 'Stop right now and have a rest. Enjoy the view.'

'I've seen it,' Quantey grumbled, but he did as he was told and stopped. He grinned again and thought about Celia.

Twenty-seven years old, blue eyes, blonde hair cropped short. A fantastic body, he decided. Nice, too—if a little too professional and uptight. Celia didn't relax very often.

'Are my Vitals showing anything interesting?' he teased. 'I'm thinking we could take a shower together after I come in.'

They often joked about the lack of privacy space station life forced upon them and the possible, personal relationships that might arise as a result, although they were strictly forbidden. This time, Quantey knew, he was asking for trouble, because Celia had no time for humour or tomfoolery during exacting operations like EVAs. But it took his mind off the curl of apprehension in his gut.

'Settle down,' she said, sharply. 'We don't want any more stupid press.'

'No one can hear us.' His voice sounded tinny and harsh over the radio. He made a conscious effort to stop his eyes from flicking nervously around the grid system. He had no idea what he was looking for.

'There're at least ten guys on Earth who reckon they listen to everything we say on EVAs,' she reminded him.

'Bullshit,' he snorted. 'Can I move on now?'

'No. Another thirty seconds.'

Celia listened to his impatient breathing. EVAs were hard work. It was easy to overexert yourself and get into serious trouble. That's why the 'walker' was always controlled by someone inside.

'Okay, go,' she commanded, checking her wrist-watch.

'About time,' Quantey muttered. Through the microphone Celia could hear the crunching of his spacesuit as he began to move.

The eight astronauts on Space Station Freedom shared a demanding schedule. The multitude of experiments they were expected to perform, in addition to the necessary housekeeping of the space station itself, meant they all worked at least twelve-hour shifts. The remaining hours of the day were supposed to be spent resting and exercising.

Exercising came first. Zero gravity didn't promote muscle building. In the weightless environment the astronauts literally 'swam' around the space station, pulling themselves along by any convenient handhold. Back on Earth they'd been trained to move this way in a large watertank, the underwater conditions being the best available simulation of zero gravity. However, space didn't provide the resistance of the water mass around them, so movement on Freedom was even easier. Monitoring of the crew's muscle atrophy was important to avoid problems.

Relaxation and sleep came far down the list of priorities. Everyone was accustomed to a feeling of mild exhaustion, but the crew had been chosen because they could work well under pressure.

In the Minerals Laboratory Module, Hugh Lyghtson toiled to finish a handwritten report. He could have typed it straight into the computer, but his typing was lousy. It would take him twice the time and besides, he liked to think of himself as one of the last bastions of handwritten communication. So many people grew up with a computer keyboard under their fingers, he thought. The finished report, absorbed and recorded by the computer's touchpad, would go straight down to his department head in NASA.

The ML Module was a confusion of analytical machines, computer terminals and racks of experiments. Hugh floated comfortably in midair, pressing the touchpad against a cleared section of aluminium bench. Whenever he flicked back through the pages to check any previous observations the pen he used stayed where he let go of it, conveniently suspended by the weightlessness. He'd once noted in his diary that nothing ever rolled off your desk onto the floor in zero gravity.

He signed his name with a flourish, but instead of being satisfied, he clicked his tongue in annoyance. The completed report served merely to remind him just how far behind his program was getting. He compared it to the dog-eared list taped to the wall. It wasn't his fault, he told himself. There was so much to do and so little time in which to do it.

'John,' he muttered aloud, then pulled a face. Most of his facial expressions were hidden by his thick red beard. 'My turn next. Maybe I can get Celia to take my place. She seems to like it out there. Give me some extra time in here.' He gestured at the array of experiments.

A noise came from the end of the module, from the inside. Someone was coming.

Each of Freedom's modules was a separate container, connected to the others by Access Modules. These were actually four-way intersections which allowed for further expansion in the future, but because the space station had yet to progress beyond a two-dimensional square configuration, the modules instead created short tunnels between the sections, with the unused hatchways blocked off to each side. Only the Earth Science and Accommodation Modules had three-way intersections, while each end of the Command Module used only two, but in a ninety-degree fashion.

'You'll have to stop talking to yourself,' Lee Wynn called, floating gracefully through the access tunnel. Lyghtson noted, not for the first time, how well she'd adapted to zero gravity.

She pulled herself to one of his computer terminals and tapped a few keys.

'Damn,' she muttered after a moment.

'What's up?' Lyghtson tried to look over her shoulder.

'I want to access some research files which I know are in Boston General Hospital. I can't get them.'

'They're a long way away.' He smiled. 'Anything might be stopping you.'

'No. I mean—' Lee stopped and shook her head. Her brown, shoulder-length hair wafted slowly around her scalp. She tried another command on the keyboard, then let out a grunt of disapproval. 'At first I thought it might be my terminal, you know? That's pretty stupid, I realise, but I thought I'd try yours anyway.'

'So what's the problem?'

'I can't seem to get outside our own network.' She gestured, palms up, at the computer. 'I can get any of our own stuff, no problem, but when I try to go beyond to a private outfit, I get a brick wall.'

'Maybe there's a problem coming out of Canaveral?'

'I don't have to go through the Cape. I tried a few other avenues and got the same story. It's like a network problem of our own.'

Lyghtson cocked his head to one side and pondered for a while, stroking his beard with the end of his pen. 'Pass,' he decided eventually. 'Why don't you call and ask?'

'Trust you to come up with a logical, straight-forward idea,' she answered, smiling. Lyghtson smiled back, a stir of longing in his heart. She was attractive both physically and in personality, always laughing, joking and willing to help anyone out. 'I was actually quite content abusing the computer, but I guess I'd better go to Command and get a visual link.'

Lyghtson watched enviously as Lee nimbly launched herself back towards the access tunnel. She was responsible for Medicine and Life Science, and she was keeping her program on target. Wynn would be invited on a second tour of Freedom for sure, whereas Lyghtson would most likely return to Earth with an unfinished portfolio and a recommendation that he not return to the space station.

He shrugged. He wasn't so certain he would miss the place anyway.

The Command Module was almost twice as big as the others. Originally, cuts in funding for the space station program in the early nineties caused major changes in design. The modules were made smaller, so they could be lifted into orbit in one piece by NASA's shuttle fleet. Later, an ease in world tensions and subsequent cuts in defence spending allowed NASA to quietly pare away money from the defence budgets towards its own programs. The go-ahead for a larger Command Module came through and it was raised into orbit in four sections by Heavy Lift Launches. Piecing it together in space, so that it was in working order and connected to Freedom's existing modules was a feat regarded as a major achievement in space technology.

Lee pushed herself into the Command Module in time to hear Celia say, 'John, I don't like some of the Vitals readings I'm getting here. What are you doing?'

Lee laughed. 'Is he fooling around again—?'

Celia cut her off with a hard look. Lee wasn't offended. The women liked each other and enjoyed their time together, so Lee realised immediately that Celia was troubled, concentrating hard on something.

Quantey's voice came through the monitor speaker. 'I'm fine. Only three more seals to do and I'm back inside.'

Celia consulted a readout again. 'Your temp's up a little and your heart's playing the bongos.'

'I'm *okay*.' They could hear the snap in his voice.

'Well, humour me,' she tried, lightly. 'Take a break.'

‘I just had a break. I’m not due.’ Now he was sounding defensive. His breathing was becoming more rapid.

Worried, Celia glanced at Lee. She took a breath and became resolute. ‘Take a break, John. I’m not fucking around here. I mean it.’

Lee blinked at Celia’s language, but said nothing. There was a long pause before Quantey answered.

‘Okay,’ he said shortly.

The two women listened carefully. From Quantey’s microphone came the rustle and crackle of movement. Distant, muted by the fact it came from a simple communications device in Quantey’s ear, came the beep of the tester.

‘He hasn’t stopped,’ Lee said, surprised. ‘What’s wrong with him?’

Celia made sure her own microphone was off before asking, ‘Can you go and get Alex? I could page him on the intercom, but I want him here fast and I don’t want to alarm the others.’

‘Where is he?’

‘Cryogenics.’

‘Shit!’ It was the furthest possible point from the Command Module. ‘Why don’t you page him like normal and I’ll head towards him and hurry him up?’ Lee suggested.

‘Good idea.’

As Lee left the module Celia made the call, then switched her headset mike back on. ‘You’ve still got another thirty seconds, John.’ She knew it was pointless.

‘Yeah, right,’ Quantey came back. It didn’t sound as though he cared.

He cared, all right. Quantey wanted to finish the job and get back inside the space station as fast as he could. He didn't know what was happening out there. He just knew he didn't like it one little bit. The feeling that he wasn't alone had grown to a certainty he was being *watched*, which was insane. He briefly wondered if there was something wrong with him. Perhaps a bad breathing mixture, or a reaction to weightlessness built up over the weeks.

Whatever it was, he would deal with it once he got back inside. Two more seals to go. He wasn't going to cop out now. Someone else would have to come out and do them if he quit.

A flicker of movement caught his eye. There was something moving between the girders on the far side of Freedom.

Impossible, he told himself shakily.

Do the job.

Quantey pressed the detector to the outside of the next seal and pulled himself around the circumference, keeping the detector in contact. Measurements in micro-units flashed up on the readout. Nothing alarming.

Except the feeling that someone was out there with him.

Quantey paused and waited for Celia to tell him his thirty seconds was up. It would make him jump if he wasn't listening for it. After nearly a minute he decided she wasn't going to tell him.

Colonel Alex Seerey was the Mission Commander. This was Seerey's third stay on Freedom. Initially his program had been to study radiations from the sun and deep space. He dabbled in weather observations as well.

On this third tour he still specialised in these areas, but it was generally recognised that his experience and abilities as Mission Commander were far more valuable than any scientific data he might provide.

A short, stocky man possessing a tanned pate with just a ring of distinguished grey hair, he was closer to fifty than he cared to admit. Still, he was very fit and strong, and despite the lack of gravity made sure he stayed that way.

Seerey pulled himself quickly into the Command Module, followed by Lee Wynn. Celia immediately saw the edge in Seerey's manner, the quiet authority in his eyes. He was a gentle, soft-spoken man whose confidence and ability were usually all he needed to get things done. He wore no badges to display his seniority. Like the others, he was clothed in a blue overall-style garment made of tough, but very lightweight, cloth. NASA emblems were printed on the shoulders and utility pockets were sewn into the chest, hips and legs. He managed to tread the fine line between friendship and command with the others. The crew both liked and respected him.

Before anyone could say anything, another speaker barked into life. 'Freedom, this is Ground Control. You have an EVA in progress?'

Celia leaned over, touching a button. 'Yes, Ground Control,' she said impatiently, knowing what was coming next.

'Our relays show your bird is having some

problems. Are you aware of it?'

'Yes, Ground Control. We are attempting to deal with it now.' *And piss off*, she almost added. 'We'll keep you posted,' she said instead. She turned the volume down on the system before anything else could come through.

'What's happening?' Seerey asked briskly. A muffled squawking still came from the Ground Control link. They both ignored it.

'John's doing the seal EVA. He's been out nearly an hour.' Celia tapped two readouts with the tip of her fingernail. 'His temp's high and his heart-rate's over the moon.' She hesitated before going on. 'I've ordered him to take an extra break, but I think he's ignoring me.'

'Can we get one of the cameras on him?'

'Jesus, of course we can.' Celia was disgusted with herself. Why hadn't she thought of it before?

She quickly glided over to a bank of monitors and started flicking switches. Choosing a camera, she used a toggle lever to start it panning in a slow arc. Stars slid by, then the screen flared as the lens came close to capturing the sun, the automatic filters slow to react to the brightness. The flaring faded to reveal the stark white girders of the space station meshed together and holding the modules like fat, pale insects caught in a spider's web.

'There he is,' Wynn said breathlessly.

Celia zoomed the camera. Quantey was straddling one of the seals and concentrating on his task. Seerey scooped the headset off Celia's head and pressed it on his own. Leaning over her shoulder he punched the switch to cut in the voice actuation circuit.

'Quantey? This is Alex. You're supposed to be taking a break.' Seerey's voice was firm, nearly harsh.

'I am,' Quantey came back, after a surprised silence.

'We've got you smack in the middle of camera four,' Seerey told him drily.

The spacesuit was no medium for body language, but to the three astronauts in the Command Module Quantey seemed to sag, like a child caught in the act.

'I just want to get the job done,' Quantey rasped. 'Get off my back and let me do it.'

Lee and Celia exchanged an alarmed glance, waiting for the reprimand. Seerey surprised them.

'How many seals have you got left?' he asked.

There was another pause, followed by a grunt from Quantey. 'Just finished this one. One more to go.'

'Leave it. Come inside.'

'No way. It's got to be done. You know it does. One more won't kill me.'

'No, forget it,' Seerey ordered him firmly. 'Come inside now. If you want to be that damn conscientious, we'll do an interior pressure-drop test later.'

'They don't show anything except major leaks,' Quantey countered. He began to move. The three watching in the Command Module could see he was heading for the last seal.

'God damn it, don't piss me off!' Seerey snapped. 'Quantey, get back inside this minute!' The commander was in the difficult position of being leader of the mission, but having no real authority. For instance, he couldn't threaten Quantey with any punitive action. There was none.

'We'll all feel better if every seal is checked,' Quantey was saying. 'Only another five minutes and I'll be—' His voice cut off. After a long silence they heard a hoarse whisper.

'Oh my God!'

The words stunned the listeners in the Command Module. Celia reacted first, hitting her thigh with a clenched fist and snarling, 'Jesus! I *knew* something was going to happen. I could feel it.'

Seerey ignored her, narrowing his eyes as he tried to see more detail on the camera screen.

'What's the problem, John?' he asked calmly, though he felt far from calm inside.

Quantey didn't reply. Over the monitor speaker his breathing came in harsh rasps.

'His heart's gone almost hyper,' Celia reported clinically. 'I think he's under a great deal of stress.'

Seerey just looked at her.

An icy hand of fear closed over Quantey's heart. As he'd moved away from the completed test and up onto the laddertrack for the trip to the last seal, something had revealed itself on the other side of the module.

It was his father.

Edward Quantey stood upright, his scuffed shoes touching the metal skin of the module as though it was the most natural place for him to be. He wore the same suit his son had seen him wear a thousand times. The frayed edges, the faded check pattern and the missing last button on the jacket that he stubbornly believed no one would ever notice. He'd only owned the one suit. He wore it everywhere. Even to John's pilot graduation ceremony. His father had always insisted his son would never amount to anything. That day the sneer on his face had told John that he now hated him for proving him wrong. For proving he was a far better man than his father had ever been.

Two years ago, his face had worn that same sneer the day before he died—the last time John saw him.

The image confronting Quantey in space sneered at him now, the old man's eyes burning with the familiar contempt.

John Quantey blinked, but his father didn't disappear. And then, shockingly, his father spoke.

'*I told you you'd never amount to anything.*'

The voice was dry and dead, like fallen leaves stirred by a chill winter wind. The words were the echo of a lifetime's misery—John Quantey's lifetime. Quantey's father had despised his son's natural intelligence, his ambition and ability to succeed. If Edward Quantey had been able to force his son to fail, he would have. It would have made *him* feel better—and that's all that mattered.

'You're—you're not fucking real,' Quantey choked, his senses reeling. 'You're not *there!*' The sight of the human figure, standing unprotected in space, clashed absurdly with the stark clean lines of the surrounding space station.

His father answered him with a mocking, humourless chuckle. It had always amused him, Quantey remembered, that his son—despite being younger, smarter and faster—could never cope with his father's scorn.

John closed his eyes, counted three deep breaths and opened them again. If anything, the sneer on his father's face had grown.

'This is impossible,' Quantey said aloud. He could feel the sweat pouring down his face. 'I'm imagining this. It's all in my fucking mind. I've been out here too long—' His control snapped. '*What do you want?*' he cried.

Inside the Command Module Seerey, Wynn and Hereson exchanged frantic, puzzled looks as they listened to Quantey's voice.

'Who's he talking to?' Celia asked.

'No one,' Seerey snapped. 'He must be hallucinating.' Raising his voice he called, 'John! Take it easy, will you? What's the problem?'

Quantey couldn't hear him. His father's soft laughter filled his mind.

'*I just want to hold your hand,*' the ghost whispered. '*We never used to hold hands like other fathers and their boys. But we can start now.*' His father chuckled again.

Quantey's voice broke with the strain. '*No!* You're dead, you bastard. I know you're dead. Leave me alone.'

Edward Quantey's spirit suddenly looked sad, then the expression turned to one of hurt.

'*Please, John. Just take my hand.*'

John's father stretched out his right hand and began to walk slowly across the surface of the module. Quantey watched with growing horror, then his willpower—his refusal to believe what he was seeing and hearing—shattered.

'*Stay away from me!*' Savagely he pushed himself away from his father's advancing figure. Instantly he was free in space and tumbling away from the space station.

'Oh Christ!' Seerey exploded as the camera showed Quantey falling from Freedom. Celia and Lee both let out cries of alarm.

'He's moving down! Towards Earth!' gasped Lee.

'And he's tumbling!' Celia said, appalled.

Seerey was reaching, flicking the general intercom switch. 'Scott! Wherever you are, our EVA's adrift. Suit up and get in the Wheelchair *now!*'

Scott Dawkins was the same age as Celia Hereson. He possessed a magnificent physique from constant, heavy exercising. His portfolio on Freedom was the study of weightlessness and its effects on the human body over long periods of time. This was his second tour on Freedom and his experience with EVAs was only second to Seerey's. His strength also gave him an edge when it came to struggling into the bulky spacesuits.

Forever in good spirits, his cheerful, resigned reply came through moments later. 'Okay. I'll go and fetch the man.' In the Command Module they could hear the laughter beneath his voice.

EVAs going wrong—it had happened before in Freedom's history and Dawkins had been the rescuer on one occasion. Both times the luckless astronaut had simply drifted beyond the reach of something solid and been stranded, hardly moving, but incapable of propelling himself back.

Seerey used the intercom again to tell Dawkins

that this was different. 'Scott, it's Quantey and he's moving away fast—and I mean damned fast!' He didn't listen for a reply. Seerey turned his attention back to the stricken astronaut.

Celia was panning the camera, trying to get a picture.

'John,' Seerey called. 'Can you hear me?'

There was a moment's silence, then Quantey answered, 'Yeah, I hear you.' His voice was devoid of any emotion. Dead.

'John, Scott's coming out in the Wheelchair to get you. Just hang on, okay?'

Quantey managed a bark of laughter. 'Hang on? A bit late for that. Tell Scott not to bother.'

'Don't be stupid. He's coming.'

'Why? I'm moving too fast. I'll bet you know that already. By the time he suits up and gets the Wheelchair out here, I'll be too far away. He'll never catch up in time.' Even calling his own death sentence Quantey was totally calm.

'Don't give up so fast,' Seerey told him, but Lee saw a cloud pass across his eyes. They both knew Quantey would be a good judge of how fast he was moving and the consequences.

Seerey put a hand across his headset mike. 'Lee.' He jerked his head at a bank of instruments. 'See if you can get a result on the DeeMor.' The Distant Moving Object Radar was a very narrow beam designed to track anything of any substance moving within the inner solar system.

Lee moved to the control terminal. 'I'll have to adjust the software to track something so close and so slow. It'll take a minute.'

'Jesus,' Celia whispered, grabbing their attention. She'd managed to lock a camera onto Quantey. His white, tumbling form was already almost lost against the background of the Earth below. 'God, he's moving fast.'

They stared in dismay at the screen.

Dawkins broke the spell by announcing over the intercom, 'I'm suitin' up as fast as I can.'

'Okay,' Seerey acknowledged.

An alarm began to sound.

'Shit,' Seerey growled. 'I wondered when they'd think of that.'

It was Ground Control employing a device designed to do exactly what it was doing—alerting the astronauts to the fact that Ground Control was being ignored. Seerey cancelled the alarm but, well aware the controllers could reactivate it whenever and as often as they wanted, he turned up the communications link. On the screen an angry Mission Controller was waiting for someone to answer him.

'Be quick, Jack. We've got troubles up here,' Seerey said sharply. As an afterthought he killed the headset mike, which would have relayed his side of the conversation to Quantey.

Jack Hitchcock was not so easily put off. 'What the hell's going on up there, Alex?' He was nearly shouting. 'What's happening to your EVA? We're getting all sorts of panic down here and you people aren't talking to us, for Christ's sake!'

'We'd better go code,' Seerey told him, leaning forward and dialling in the 'scrambler' with a keyboard. When Hitchcock's voice came through next it had a metallic quality, a result of the system.

'This is obviously not going to be good news,' he said heavily.

'Quantey had some problems—we don't know what,' Seerey explained rapidly. 'It looked to me like he backed away from something. A reaction. He didn't stop to think of the consequences. Anyway, he pushed himself away from the station and now he's heading towards a lower orbit and re-entry all by his damned self. To make matters worse, he's moving very fast and tumbling.'

'Backed away? Backed away from what?' Hitchcock's confusion was clear. 'Alex, are you saying you're going to lose him?'

'I don't know, but it doesn't look good.' Seerey held up a hand, gesturing Hitchcock to be patient. Hitchcock would see it. Ground Control could view most of the module. Seerey could only see his controller's head and shoulders. 'Leave me alone, okay? I can't deal with anything and talk to you at the same time. I'll leave the comm-link open. You'll hear it all.' He turned away. Lee was trying to get his attention.

'It's very bad,' she told him gravely. 'Quantey's moving at close to eleven feet a second. The tumbling makes it a give-or-take figure, nothing that matters though.'

'*What?*' Seerey frowned. 'What the hell did he do? Throw himself off the grid?'

'It almost looked like it, didn't it?'

A new voice interrupted them from the intercom. It was Judith Cianta, the third female astronaut aboard Freedom.

'I'm helping Scott suit-up and get in the Wheelchair,' she called. 'The damn thing's only half-gassed. I need an executive decision.'

'For God's sake!' Seerey said, angrily. 'Who

used it last? No, forget that. I don't give a damn at the moment. Scott, I'm going to send you out as you are. There's no time to gas up.' He didn't wait for a reply. 'Do you know how fast that thing can go?'

It took a moment for a surprised Dawkins to digest the question. 'Oh, four miles per hour is about tops, or you can't manoeuvre accurately. But in theory I can go as fast as I want in a straight line. I just keep the hammer down.'

'Wait,' Seerey ordered.

At the other end of the intercom Dawkins and Judith Cianta looked helplessly at each other. The Airlock Module, housing the spacesuits and Wheelchair, also provided a storeroom and the main plant of the Closed-Loop Life-Support System. But the primary function of the module was the airlock itself, a double-door system with a small holding chamber like those used by underwater complexes, which allowed a safe transfer out into space without jeopardising the atmosphere inside Freedom.

Dawkins was already strapped into the Wheelchair. His helmet hovered above his head, waiting for Judith to lower it. She was slim, olive-skinned and thirty-five years old. The mission's agriculturist, she experimented with life-sustaining plant-types in zero gravity.

Judith floated near Dawkins' right shoulder and looked dubiously at the cylinder of propellant in her hands. It was unheard of to send the Wheelchair outside without it being one hundred per cent fully serviced.

'Something really bad's happening,' she said.

'Quantey must be in big trouble,' Dawkins agreed. 'Put my lid on, babe. I'd better get out there.'

'Alex said to wait.'

'I'll wait outside.'

Judith snapped his helmet on, then pushed herself to the airlock proper. She expertly undogged the locking mechanism and swung the door open. Only the outer door operated electronically. There was no point in wasting valuable kilowatts on something that could be done with underused human muscles.

Dawkins steered the Wheelchair through, its propellant jets hissing at absolute minimum. Judith reached in and slapped him on the shoulder before closing the door.

In the Command Module Seerey was puzzling over the calculations. He figured Quantey's speed against the Wheelchair's safe operational maximum, and the added factor of the time elapsed. He cursed his indecision, especially since, in the end, he knew he was always going to make the attempt. He stabbed the intercom switch.

'Judy? Send Scott out now.' Then he switched on his headset mike. 'John? Still hear me? Scott's just about on his way.'

'Look, Alex—' Quantey stopped, but his mike circuit stayed in. It would cut out after ten seconds of silence. His breathing was now ragged, but his voice remained flat and emotionless. 'Alex, don't send Scott out. He won't reach me for sure. I've been working it out. I'm starting to feel sick, too.'

'Sick?' Seerey looked at Lee.

'It's the tumbling, probably,' she guessed quickly. 'The sight of everything rolling past could affect him. He won't be *feeling* anything without gravity, of course. Tell him to close his eyes.'

'Close your eyes, John.'

'And miss the last minutes of my life? You've got to be kidding. No way.'

'Stop thinking like that. Scott's coming out and you're going to need some pretty smart work for him to snatch you.'

'Yeah, right.' The deathly sarcasm cut through the electronics.

'Alex,' Lee called quietly. 'Scott's going to have to travel at three times what he considers the Wheelchair's optimum working speed just to catch John within the next twelve to fifteen minutes. That's just to *catch* him, right? Then he's got to stop him, turn them both around and come back.'

Seerey desperately did some more sums in his head. 'Shit, that's going to put them over two miles away from the station. That Wheelchair's never been more than thirty fucking yards away—not that it would stop Scott from trying.'

'Don't forget, Quantey's already been out there nearly an hour,' Celia added. 'He was on the last seal.'

Seerey groaned and put a hand over his eyes. 'Okay, that's something I haven't thought about. So—what's that give him in airtime?' He tried to make the question sound casual, as if the answer hardly mattered. They all knew better.

Celia's reply rang in their ears like steel off an anvil.

'Twenty minutes. Thirty at the most, if he controlled his breathing.'

They were silent for a moment.

'Too late,' Lee whispered. She gestured at the speaker. 'Listening to his breathing there, I'd say he's already cut into that twenty minutes.'

Crackling from the speaker, Dawkins' voice startled them.

'I'm out! I'm ready to go. Where the hell is he?'

'Forget it,' Quantey's voice came softly. 'There's no point.' Dawkins was now on the same network.

'Shut up, John,' Seerey snapped. 'I don't want to hear any more of that shit. Scott? He's about one mile away directly towards Earth. If you head that way we'll use the DeeMor to home you in closer. But you're going to have to do eight or nine miles an hour to catch him in time.'

'He's a mile away?' Dawkins was shocked. 'Jesus! Okay, but I'm going to lose a couple of minutes lining up on his bearing.'

'This is stupid,' they heard Quantey say.

Jack Hitchcock's voice came over loud from the comm-link. 'Alex? Listen to me. You can't do this.'

'Can't do what?' Seerey said, glaring at the screen.

'An engineer here says operating the Wheelchair at that sort of velocity would be suicidal. The steering jets aren't designed for it. There's every chance when Scott tries to alter course that he'll throw himself into a spin—or even a tumble like John's.'

Seerey stared helplessly at the screen. The other

astronauts held their breath. He was faced with the possibility of losing a second life in a futile attempt to save the first.

'About another thirty seconds and I'll be on a rough bearing,' Dawkins called. No one answered him.

Seconds crept away. Seerey looked from the comm-link screen and Hitchcock's grim face to the DeeMor display. Quantey was represented by a small, flashing dot. He was no longer visible on the camera screen.

The stricken astronaut's unnaturally calm voice entered the module. 'Don't do it, Alex. There's no point. I'm gone.'

Still nobody said anything.

'I'll call it, if you like, Alex. I can do it anyway,' said Hitchcock through the screen.

'No!' Seerey answered immediately. He took a long, last look at the DeeMor display. It was as if he were trying to stare Quantey in the eyes. He finally called to the astronaut.

'John? God knows I don't want to do this, but I don't think we can help you,' Seerey said, sickened by his own words.

Dawkins drowned out any response from Quantey. '*What?*' he yelled. 'We can't just leave him! We have to give it a try. I'm ready to go! I'm clear of the station.'

'Stay where you are!' Seerey ordered, his voice catching. 'Ground Control says we'll lose you too, unless you take it slow.'

'So? I'll take it a bit slower. Big fucking deal!'

'John will run out of breathing mix before you even get close,' said Seerey bluntly. To him it sounded as though he was decreeing Quantey's execution.

Dawkins was often quick to anger, but he was also capable of bringing himself back under control. Now he didn't answer. His despairing silence told Seerey he understood the hopelessness of the situation.

Instead, Quantey spoke. 'It's okay, Scott,' he said, still quiet and unemotional. 'I knew how it was the moment this started. Maybe sooner. I think it was meant to happen.'

'What the hell's *that* supposed to mean?' Lee asked. Tears ran down her cheeks.

Seerey waved her to silence. He closed his eyes and gently punched the control panel in despair. 'What can we do, John? What can we *say?*' he asked, suddenly close to crying, too.

'You can't do anything. There's nothing to say.' If anything, Quantey sounded even calmer. 'Tell my wife I love her, and I'm sorry. Things haven't been too good at home for the last two years. It's my fault.'

Seerey nodded, then realised how stupid that was. 'I'll tell her,' he promised. Next to him the two women were quietly crying. Seerey wished he could break down himself.

Quantey fell silent. Every few seconds the space station slid across his vision, giving him a tantalising glimpse of safety and rescue. So close, yet so far away—and getting smaller with each rotation. It felt incredible to be dying like this. So comfortable, breathing good air and bundled up warm in the spacesuit like a child wrapped in its blanket. Watching the stars, Earth and Freedom tumble around him like toys suspended above a crib to rock him asleep.

For eternity.

Then he began to talk. Across the uncaring vacuum of space he spoke of things he'd never discussed with anyone before. His childhood, his college days, his love life and his marriage. He mentioned the kind and patient woman his mother had been until her early death from leukemia. He didn't speak of his father. He said several times he had no regrets.

Seerey could only make noises, letting Quantey know he was still listening. He didn't have the courage or heart to interrupt. After several minutes he was startled to realise Quantey had begun speaking in short bursts, in between periods of laboured breathing. Of the twenty minutes Celia had offered as his remaining life span, only nine had elapsed.

Quantey might have read Seerey's mind. 'Air's getting a little thin,' he said, breaking a monologue about his selection for astronaut training.

'You're talking too much,' Seerey said. 'Take it easy.'

'What's the point?'

Seerey didn't answer that. 'You'll go down as some sort of hero,' he said, stupidly, immediately hating himself for saying it.

Quantey tried to laugh, but didn't have enough breath. The effort seemed to exhaust most of his remaining air. His next words came harshly interspersed with rattling breaths.

'Be . . . careful. Just in . . . case . . . it wasn't . . . me,' he said, his voice now a hoarse whisper.

'Easy, John,' Seerey told him, softly. 'It wasn't your fault.'

'No . . . no, I mean . . .' Quantey's words faded away.

'He might be hallucinating,' Lee tried to explain through her tears. 'Lack of oxygen—like a drowning man seeing his life pass before his eyes.'

'John, don't worry,' Seerey called.

He was answered by a long, drawn-in breath. A few seconds later Quantey's voice activation circuit, deprived of any substantial signal, cut the astronaut's microphone.

Only a faint hiss of static came through the Command Module's speaker.

Frantic thoughts entered Seerey's mind. Ideas of prompting 'last words' or, in turn, offering solace that might ease Quantey's last minutes alive. By the time he found the courage to utter the half-formed words in his head, he knew it was too late.

'He—he must have blacked out,' he said aloud.

The others stared back at him. The moment had arrived—it had been coming for some minutes. Still, they weren't ready for it. Seerey realised they would never have been ready for it.

'What the hell did he see? Why did he jump?' Lee sobbed.

'We'll never know,' Seerey answered.

'God rest his soul,' Celia murmured shakily.

No one offered an Amen.

2

IF JOSEPH KING HAD been in the Command Module as Quantey died, he may have offered the doomed man some comforting words from the Bible. His Bible. King was a very religious man.

In fact, he secretly believed he might talk to God very soon. In person.

King was the eighth crewmember aboard Freedom—a crew now numbering seven. First and foremost he was an astronomer. Freedom had three telescopes and King used them all daily. He took photographs, recorded data and made observations that were impossible on Earth because of the restrictive blanket of the atmosphere. He had many critics. Those who decried his work, claiming it did not justify the enormous cost of lifting him into orbit and placing him on board Freedom. But the astronomical societies argued that they'd donated their fair share of funds to Freedom's building and maintenance—they'd earned the right to make use of Freedom. NASA agreed.

So King was included in the thirty-eighth tour of Freedom, employing extra equipment lifted with him as well as the permanent telescopes previously used for little more than impressive public relations photographs. His program alone kept him busy. But King made sure he found time for some extra studies. Work no one else knew about.

Joseph King was trying to make contact with God.

King was a devout Christian who believed there was an all-seeing, all-knowing being who watched over and influenced his every moment. How else, he reasoned, could he have come so far? All his life, he'd prayed for the things he wanted. And he'd got most of them, which was more than many people could claim. He'd learned the power of prayer early, when his grandfather had taken him into his care and showed the youth what could be achieved with belief.

His teachings were so clever, so subtle, that the young Joseph didn't see that his grandfather's beliefs were so different from others'. He had already been exposed to many diverse religions and beliefs. Every day he saw Jews, Hindus and Muslims, to name a few, displaying their different forms of worship with their dress, their speech. His grandfather's quiet and cunning way of teaching Joseph his own brand of dark, evil religion—still within the parameters of the most widely accepted

Christian doctrine—seemed pale by comparison. But quickly it became too late, and he didn't question anything. The prayers were twisted, distorting good with evil until one became the other. When his grandfather died, he left behind a potent legacy of his teachings—the young man was a true believer.

King realised his beliefs could lead to a lot of trouble—professional trouble. Strong religious convictions of any sort these days were regarded with suspicion rather than tolerance. Among the smart people of the world, anyway. King's doctrine would have horrified them. And while a vast majority of the Earth's population still embraced one religion or another, very few believers lived within the scientific community—the people who were responsible for putting men and women into orbit and keeping them alive for indefinite periods, the people King dealt with each day of his professional life.

So he kept his beliefs to himself. It was better that way. It didn't mean, however, that he couldn't practise his religion in the fleeting moments of privacy Freedom provided.

The space station's living quarters took up one module. Because of the staggered hours the astronauts worked it was impractical to black out the quarters for sleeping at any one time. Instead, the narrow bunks were each enclosed by a thin roller-door. Some crewmembers found it too claustrophobic in a work environment undeniably close and constricted at the best of times. They simply learned to sleep in the light.

The bunks overcame the sleeping problems encountered during early space flights. The astronaut slipped into a lightweight sleeping bag which was stuck to the surface of the bunk. It remedied the psychological barriers of weightless slumber and prevented unwanted drifting in zero gravity.

Each bunk had a small writing desk at its foot. The owner could sit on the foot of the bunk and use the desk for writing notes or studying. Strangely, despite the zero gravity which allowed a book to float conveniently in front of a person's face, most astronauts found it disorientating to read without some sort of solid surface beneath the book. Jotted notes, of course, required an unmoving surface, though writing letters home was almost unheard of—a visual communications link was installed in every astronaut's home. Contact with the families was arranged at frequent intervals.

Joseph King used the flat surface at the end of his bed for something different.

He used it to read his Bible. But it was not like other Bibles. It was bound in worn black leather. A gift from his grandfather, who'd migrated to the USA from a corner of eastern Europe, it carried messages different from those normally found in the Testaments. Good messages. Messages that showed a believing man the truth. A different truth. A better truth.

While John Quantey died the slowest of deaths King prayed. He didn't hear the intercom. It was a distant, muted sound which failed to intrude on his concentration—which had never been so *intense* before. So complete. It was as though, at last, he was finally going to *touch* someone. Someone important.

Someone like God.

For the first time there was a feeling of *contact*.

Through his initial shock a sense of jubilation grew. He'd always believed it could happen in orbit, away from the clutter of the theological strivings of Earth's massed living souls. Two hundred miles into real space, within the Heavens humans had looked towards since the dawn of religion, King accepted it might be possible to talk to God. It never troubled him that his grandfather's God might be quite different from the benevolent deities embraced back on Earth.

Thirty minutes before, while Quantey still felt confident and unworried on what should have been another routine seal check, King had rolled down his privacy screen, flicked on a small reading light and pulled his Bible from the bottom of his sleeping bag. He placed it on the writing desk. Next he pulled out a blank piece of paper. Settling himself comfortably took some effort; his tall thin frame was unwilling to bend as he pushed his feet into the two restraints beneath the desk. He opened the Bible at a marked page and started to read. The soft light reflected off his sallow skin and made dark shadows in his sunken cheeks. King's brow furrowed with concentration. After a few paragraphs he took a pencil from his top pocket and drew a symbol on the paper. He read some more. A second symbol was sketched. A Swiss army knife came out of another pocket, the sharp blade was used to fine the lead tip of the pencil. He continued to scan the pages until, a few minutes later, a total of five shapes were neatly drawn on the paper.

What followed was something he had not tried before. King took the army knife and deliberately sliced open the ball of his thumb.

He waited until an appreciable amount of blood had welled out, then began to dab the cut on each of the drawn symbols, at the same time muttering a litany. Though he was carefully watching the placement of every smear of blood, his eyes had glazed over.

When the contact came it was so sudden, and so totally unexpected, it made King gasp with shock. Yet it wasn't a real contact, like a solid connection of minds. It was more a tenuous grasping after something he knew wasn't a part of himself nor a creation of his own imagination. It was like holding a handful of fine sand, which he couldn't prevent from slipping between his fingers.

He saw images he didn't recognise. Unfamiliar people and places. Time passed, but he had no impression of how long. He began to hear voices, but only some of what he heard made sense.

He wants to hold my hand, he understood, a shiver of anticipation passing through him.

Then the contact broke, like the snapping of a thread.

King let out a small cry of surprise and disappointment, jerking back from the desk. The foot restraints stopped him from tumbling about the bunk enclosure.

It brought him back to reality. He was breathing heavily, a sheen of sweat coating his face. He looked down at the writing desk and absently folded the paper, placing it inside the Bible and closing the leather covers. He suddenly felt exhausted, and pushed himself backwards until he lay on the bunk, his feet still in the restraints. He closed his eyes and fell asleep almost immediately. He didn't dream.

The intercom woke him, calling all crew to the Command Module. King blinked, knowing instinctively he hadn't slept for more than fifteen or twenty minutes. After taking a few moments for consciousness to return fully he flipped up the privacy screen. Rolling into the passageway he saw the Bible still on the desk. He calmly picked it up and stuffed it back into the sleeping bag. The action caused the ball of his thumb to sting. Making his way to the hatchway he absently sucked at the small cut, licking away the blood. He frowned. He couldn't remember hurting himself.

The Command Module was crowded with the six people gathered there. Seerey watched grimly as they settled themselves. He remained tight-lipped after telling them to wait for Dawkins, who had returned inside, unsuited with Judith Cianta's help, then gone quickly to wash himself and change into clean clothing.

'What's happened?' Lyghtson asked, seeing Celia's and Lee's stricken faces.

'Wait for Scott,' Seerey told him gravely.

Lyghtson looked to the others for a clue. Only Joseph King seemed completely surprised by the meeting. Another thought jarred into his mind. *They were waiting for Dawkins, but not John Quantey. Quantey had gone adrift during his EVA, but Scott had gone to get him.* He'd heard that much over the intercom. *Surely Scott had brought him back—hadn't he?*

A glance at the faces of the women crewmembers made his heart sink. Judith, who hadn't been in the Command Module, looked distraught too.

Of course, he realised. *She knew Scott had come back alone*.

'Dear God,' Lyghtson breathed, understanding. Seerey glanced at him. Hugh didn't notice a confused, troubled stare from King.

Dawkins pulled himself into the Command Module. He nodded sombrely at everyone, his eyes lingering on Seerey's for a moment. Inside, Seerey felt a rush of gratitude. The look told him Scott had come to terms with his decision, acknowledging that it was the right one to make.

'For those of us not quite in the picture, let me explain,' Seerey began gruffly. 'We just lost John Quantey. He went adrift during his EVA—adrift in a big way—and he ran out of oxygen before we could bring him back.' He coughed into his hand, clearing his throat. 'Perhaps I'd better clarify that, because there's bound to be an inquiry when we get back. In fact, I stopped Scott from making the attempt to save John because I believed he would be risking his own life with no chance of success anyway.'

There was a long silence. Only King appeared totally startled by the news. The others either knew or had guessed.

'Why did he go adrift?' Judith asked shakily.

'We really don't know. Our best guess is that he began to fit or hallucinate. He appeared to try to get away from something and his movements propelled him away from Freedom.'

'Get away? Get away from what?'

'I'm not suggesting for a moment there was

anything *there*,' Seerey told her. 'It must have been in his head. What I want to do is put *our* heads together right now and try to work out what happened, and what we're going to do about it. It's important that we look at it while we still have events fresh in our minds, painful as that may be. So, any suggestions?'

He looked around. Everyone seemed too upset to try some serious thinking.

'Come on, people!' Seerey snapped. 'We cannot afford the luxury of feeling sorry for John or ourselves. We need some ideas.'

It took a moment, but Celia reluctantly offered, 'A bad breathing mix?'

'Maybe. It's a start,' Seerey nodded. 'It's a good example of why we have to come up with some answers, because we're breathing the same stuff right now.'

There was a ripple of concern.

'But that's the argument against a bad mix,' Dawkins pointed out. 'We're breathing it now, no problems. And I was on the same tank mix outside as John. I didn't feel anything wrong.'

'How about a contaminated Life Support Unit?' Hugh asked.

'Possible, but it sounds a little thin,' Seerey replied. 'I guess everything we come up with is going to sound pretty thin.'

'How about solar activity?' Lee tried.

'Ah, no,' King said, startled because the question came within his field. 'None of the bells went off.' He referred to an alarm system announcing any unusual solar events.

'No malfunctions? Have you checked?'

'I only just found out about the bloody accident!' he retorted. 'Besides, it's got three backups.'

'Okay, just checking.' Lee was surprised by his reaction.

'Take it easy, folks,' Seerey warned. 'Lee, John wasn't on any medication we should know about?'

'No, I would've mentioned it by now,' she answered, suddenly weary.

Seerey sighed. 'Any other suggestions?'

He was answered by silence.

'All right.' He looked at them all again. 'This isn't going to sound the greatest, but we have no other choice. We have to continue on as normal, okay? I know money isn't everything, but NASA and their sponsors paid a lot of dollars to get us up here. No matter how we all feel right now, we should still deliver. Besides, personally, I think some hard work will keep my mind off John's loss.'

Seerey didn't mention that most of his 'hard work' over the next few hours would be a detailed report and analysis of Quantey's death. All hell would break loose on Earth when the news broke, especially in the press. He would need some smart answers up his sleeve. NASA would expect them.

'So are you saying we should just leave here and forget all about it?' Dawkins asked, a little angry.

'No, of course not! I'm saying we should try to not let this tragedy interfere with our work. Quantey wouldn't want it, either.'

'Well, I wish we could do something,' Dawkins said, frowning. 'We can't just carry on like nothing's happened.'

'But what? It would be a farce if one of us

attempted some sort of religious service—is that what you mean?'

'I don't know—I guess so,' Dawkins shrugged. 'No, I don't know.'

'We could arrange something on the comm-link,' Celia suggested quietly. 'Any of us who wanted to could meet here.'

'Okay, that's a good idea. I'll talk to Jack Hitchcock.' Seerey rubbed a hand across his tired eyes. 'Let's try and deal with this as best we can. But try and get some work done.'

Reluctantly, as if they were also dismissing Quantey's memory, they began to move.

Lyghtson stopped them with a last question. 'What—what about John? Will we ever retrieve his body?' The question showed Hugh was more of a minerals scientist than he was an astronaut.

'Hugh, John's body will eventually re-enter the Earth's atmosphere and burn up to nothing,' Seerey explained, his face blank.

'Oh. I didn't realise he went that way.' Lyghtson looked uncomfortable, almost embarrassed. 'I'm sorry. I should have known. I—I thought he might find his own orbit, or something.'

Instead of being annoyed at his ignorance Seerey sounded wistful. 'His own orbit? That would be some sort of memorial, wouldn't it? But no, he fell towards home. He'll accelerate as he gets closer, too.'

Lyghtson nodded. He was the last of the procession of astronauts to leave the module.

Seerey found himself alone with Celia.

'Can I say something?' she asked carefully.

'Sure? Why not?' Seerey had his eyes closed and was taking slow, deep breaths.

'I think you've handled the whole thing really well. No one else could have done it better. I sure as hell couldn't.'

Seerey looked at her, not knowing what to expect. He discovered she was genuine, her words intended as both praise and comfort. She wasn't looking for any favours.

'Thanks,' he said, after a moment. 'I think Ground Control would've done it for me anyway. No big deal in the end.'

'I don't think so,' she smiled sadly.

'So, what are you doing here?' he asked, changing the subject.

'Nothing. My EVA's over,' she added wryly.

'Nothing to do?'

'Cryo check.'

'Damn. I was down there before, doing a line trace on some electricals. If I'd remembered it was due, I could have done it while I was there. Now I've got these reports to do before I head back that way. I'll be a while. Will you be all right?'

She shrugged. 'The place gives me the creeps,' she said, then managed a laugh. 'After a million dollars' worth of training and education, a bunch of frozen dead people still makes me feel weird. I'll get used to it, though.'

'Between you and me, I think it's a complete waste of our time.'

'I think everyone here has said that to me at one stage or another. It's a good money spinner, though. Pays the bills, I suppose—a cargo of billionaire corpses waiting for a second chance. Crazy really though, don't you think?'

'No doubt about it.' Seerey looked at the blank

comm-link screen. 'Well, I've got some explaining to do.'

'I'll leave you to it.' As Celia pushed past she gave Seerey's shoulder a squeeze. 'It wasn't your fault, Alex. You did everything you could.'

'Yeah, I know.' He patted her hand. 'Thanks.'

The Cryogenic Module was the last in a line of modules, attached to the end of the Airlock. While Hereson managed to greet some of her fellow crew on her way through their respective work areas, there was an entire empty module between her and the other astronauts—as long as no one was working in the Airlock/Storeroom Module. At the moment there wasn't anybody in there. Celia noticed a 'danger' tag stuck to the Wheelchair as she passed through. Dawkins, she knew, would be doing tests on his body, trying to detect any adverse reactions to his brief spacewalk.

Everyone called the Cryogenic Module 'The Morgue', with good reason. Four gleaming steel 'coffins' lined each side of the module. Although they weren't the traditional coffin shape or adorned as such, their square, six-foot-long configuration suggested nothing else. Only six were occupied. Above each container a computer screen displayed the current status of the corpse. Inside the containers the controlling computers had to maintain a temperature within very narrow tolerances. A probe inserted into each body monitored the preservatives and kept a check on the content levels. Several other facts and figures were important too, but the astronauts only knew what numbers were good and what figures constituted a failure of some kind. They didn't understand what those figures represented.

Like almost everything aboard Freedom, the computer systems were integrated with alarms. If any data were deemed unsatisfactory by the computer, the alarms were triggered. But such systems had been known to fail and as, theoretically, human life was involved, a manual check was scheduled every five days.

Celia took a clipboard from one corner of the module and moved to the first container. She knew many of the figures by heart, but used the chart anyway. It was a list of acceptable readings.

She scanned the screen, occasionally referring to the clipboard. There were no names anywhere. After paying millions of dollars for their slim chance at a second life, the cryogenic 'patients'—as they were known by the more optimistic supporters of the program—were kept strictly anonymous. Still, Celia couldn't block out of her mind that the numerical figures written dispassionately on the screen represented a cold, dead human being.

After she was satisfied with the computer readings, there was one more test. Celia preferred to leave this until last and do all the containers at once, so she moved to the next one, repeating the process.

While checking the fourth container an icy chill stole down her spine, raising goose bumps on her arms.

'Go away,' she said out loud, shivering a moment. It had happened before. The place just got to her.

Five minutes later she completed the last of

the computer comparisons. It was time for the final checks. She hated them.

Each container had a sliding panel which, when drawn back, revealed a square of thick plexiglass. Lying beneath the glass was the corpse's left hand.

It was, quite logically, the best way of checking whether any manner of deterioration or decomposition was taking place. Unfortunately, it wasn't enough simply to slap the panel back and make sure the hand was still *there*. Celia had to peer at each one for several seconds, looking for flaking skin, blackening fingernails or a loss of condition.

The fourth 'coffin' contained a woman, Celia believed. She held a firm rein on her distaste as she studied the lifeless hand. The fingers were long and slim, the nails showing evidence they'd been manicured all their lives, despite being cut short now. As in all the patients, the skin was a sickly white, framing dark bulging veins. Celia knew that this was the effect of the preserving fluids, which were resistant to freezing even at incredibly low temperatures and much darker than blood. She also knew all the hair had been removed from the bodies to avoid infection. The astronauts were supposed to report any indications that body hair was growing back—an occurrence which seemed highly unlikely to Celia.

With a grimace she closed the panel and moved on to the next one. This patient was different, too. The hand wore a heavy ring on the middle finger. It was the only body wearing any visible jewellery, which said to Celia that this person still got their own way about *something*, even after death.

Her musings were interrupted by a noise. Something about it made her senses become electric. The goose bumps returned.

Freedom was an intricate piece of technology—and thus made a variety of unexpected noises. There were literally miles of pipes pumping coolant throughout the station. They creaked and groaned occasionally. Electrical circuit breakers cut in and out too, automatically supplying power where and when it was needed. Sometimes sounds the other astronauts made were transmitted through the hull.

Why then, Celia asked herself, *did that last noise make you jump out of your damn skin?* Because it sounded as though it came from the *outside*, as though there was an EVA in progress and someone was moving across the module's outer skin.

Celia knew that wasn't possible. EVAs would be suspended. Anyway, an EVA would have an ongoing sound, and now everything was quiet again.

She closed the panel. The click of meeting metal coincided so closely with another noise that one masked the other. It still made Celia draw in her breath with a sharp hiss and hold it, her body tense.

It sounded, for all the world, like the beeping of the seal-tester coming through the hull.

'Now I *know* I'm going crazy.' Celia hoped the sound of her own voice would comfort her. Instead, the shake in it frightened her. Motionless, she waited for the noise to come again.

There was no sound, but in its place came a sudden, overwhelming conviction there was someone *inside* the module with her. Someone bad.

With a small cry she twisted around violently, looking along the length of the module. Of course she was alone. Except for the six corpses.

'Fuck you. You can rot, for all I care.' Celia dropped the clipboard, which just floated where her hand left it, and moved to the hatchway. Fingers of fear touched her back as she pulled herself through. Then she turned and closed the hatch after her—something no one usually bothered to do. Her hands trembled as she dogged it closed.

'I must need some rest,' she told herself. Her voice still didn't want to work properly.

As she started towards the Command Module, reason took over. Her fears began to ebb away, leaving behind an uneasy embarrassment and a certain amount of guilt, because she hadn't actually completed her task. The further she got away from the cryogenics the more she convinced herself she'd overreacted in a silly way. The noises had been just *noises*, nothing more. It wasn't even worth mentioning to anyone.

Despite this, it helped to know that the hatch to The Morgue was locked closed.

3

SOMETIMES HE TRIED TO convince himself it had always been just a dream—or a nightmare. But that was ridiculous, because he knew it had all been very real. Something peopled by real characters still alive now—or some of them were. The house was probably still standing too, somewhere in a depressed and crowded Melbourne suburb. Matthew Kindling could never quite remember the address. He didn't want to, really. It was strange, though, considering he recalled everything else with such stark clarity.

Now when the memories came, he dwelled on them, let them roll through his mind like an old movie, instead of trying to shut them out. This way, he hoped, some sort of catharsis might occur.

She had been the epitome of a struggling, middle-aged housewife. In the clarity of his mind's eye he could see the forty-odd years of hardship worked into the lines of her face. He could see her dreams had never come true. She wasn't particularly poor or even unhappy, as a rule—just resigned. Her dreams hadn't come true. She'd accepted it now. It was too late to change or hope differently.

Kindling saw himself walk past the woman into her hallway. The watery sunlight coming through the front door made little impression on the gloom. Other footsteps followed behind him. Faithful to the memory, as so many times before, it was Father Stewart Andrews. It had been his idea for Kindling to come.

Mrs Williams' timid voice echoed in his mind. 'First door on the left. Just go on in. Don't mind anything he says.'

It was a small lounge room, darkened by curtains. A television glowed in one corner, the picture snowed by bad reception. Something gleamed in the flickering blue-white light. The chrome fittings of a wheelchair. A crumpled figure occupied it, side-on to Kindling and facing a blackened fireplace. His head lifted as the three entered.

Mr Williams' face was withered, drawn by age and disease, his eyes deep inside sunken sockets. They fixed on his wife with naked contempt.

'You've brought the priest back, bitch?' His voice was shockingly harsh. 'And he has a friend—a *priestling*.' He let out a vicious bark of laughter. 'Tell them to fuck off.' With deft movements he swivelled the wheelchair around a few degrees so he could face them.

'Please, Allen, try to be nice for once. They're trying to help you.' She flinched from his anger.

'Hello, Mr Williams,' Kindling said, keeping his voice carefully neutral. 'How are you today? My name is Father Matthew Kindling.'

'Shut your pious mouth,' Williams snapped, turning his burning gaze on him. The man's look was like a slap in the face.

'Your wife is concerned about your health. So is Father Stewart. He asked me to come and see you. Perhaps I can help.'

'I'm as healthy as a pig,' Williams said flatly. Suddenly his eyes glazed over and he began painful, heaving motions with his chest and stomach. A bubble of vomit spilled out of his mouth and down his chin. There was enough to form a small pool in his lap. He cackled with laughter again. 'See? See that?'

'Oh, Allen,' his wife cried, moving forward and picking up a roll of paper towelling. The two priests kept their composure. Williams watched his wife approach, waiting until she leaned forward to wipe his lap.

'Fuck off, bitch!' he shouted, lashing out with the back of his hand. He caught her squarely on the cheek, one of his rings breaking the skin. She fell back with a whimper, clutching at her face.

Kindling moved to help, but Father Andrews stopped him with a hand on his arm.

'No, don't go any nearer. That's what he wants.' Andrews was a short, slightly tubby man. His voice was disproportionately high-pitched.

'She's hurt,' Kindling protested.

'Stay where you are,' Andrews insisted, his face hard.

Mrs Williams staggered to her feet and brushed past them into the passageway. They heard her crying as she slammed a door closed.

'Stewey knows, don't you?' Williams said in a sing-song manner. 'Even for a gay, he's quite smart. How young are your little boys now, Stewey?'

Father Andrews ignored him, keeping his attention on Kindling. 'Have you seen enough?' He waited.

Andrews believed in all the things Kindling thought had strangled the church for centuries. The traditions, the basic concept of Heaven and Hell, good and evil. Devils, too. The world was full of them now—more than ever before, but while Andrews could see in some an embodiment of the true Evil, the greatest and eternal enemy of the church, Kindling only believed in a sickness of the times. They were a symptom of the sorry state in which the world now found itself. Kindling's church was, in reality, centuries distant from Andrews'. The younger priest didn't even particularly accept the existence of One God. Quietly, he thought the subject was open to debate.

So Kindling sighed and lowered his voice, saying patiently, 'The man is obviously very sick, both mentally and physically. How long has he been crippled?'

'About four years. An accident on his own back steps. He became increasingly depressed from the very first—no insurance or anything like that. He's paralysed from the waist down. These are classic conditions for possession—a long history of depression and physical weakness.'

'I can hear you!' Williams taunted. 'Hey guys! Look at this!'

Unwillingly, they turned towards him. Williams stroked a large lump in the crotch of his pants. He leered at them. 'Don't tell the bitch I've got this. She'll want it. She's been wanting it for about four fucking years. I'm still not going to fucking give it to her, though.'

Deliberately not reacting, the two men turned their backs slightly, denying the cripple his audience.

'See?' Andrews whispered. 'He's supposed to be paralysed. He's certainly not supposed to be capable of any sexual behaviour.'

'You just can't tell.' Kindling shrugged. 'Paralysis is a big mystery too, in many ways. Anything can happen. Apart from some possibly . . . remarkable *medical* situations here, I can't see anything to suggest something—well, abnormal.' He stopped and thought for a moment. Unnoticed behind them, Williams muttered darkly to himself.

'The deranged mind is capable of many things,' Kindling continued. 'The vomiting is not uncommon. There's plenty of cases involving worse—self-mutilation, for instance.'

Father Andrews glanced briefly at Williams. 'This one's different. That's why I wanted to show you. I believe he won't be the first you'll see.'

'I'm sorry, but I'm not convinced in the slightest. I don't mean to be difficult.'

Andrews opened his mouth to reply, but stopped. His eyes widened. Kindling turned to follow his gaze, at the same time hearing a humming noise.

The wheelchair hung suspended nearly thirty

centimetres above the carpet. Williams grinned across at them with maniacal glee. The wheels of the chair were spinning at a tremendous speed.

'Brrmm! Brrmm!' he cried, laughing again.

'Dear God,' Andrews croaked, crossing himself and backing away.

'No, it's not Him!' Williams screeched with delight.

Kindling could only stand there, transfixed by the sight. He felt utter despair. It didn't occur to him to be afraid. He'd confronted too many terrors on the city streets too many times to frighten easily.

But the despair was like a wave crashing down, swamping him. He could see his New Age beliefs, the scientific bedrock of his modern religion, lying in ruins at his feet. He was going to be the church of the future. Now, suddenly, he knew how wrong he'd been. In only a fraction of the time it had taken him to build these hopes, a nightmare from the past had shattered them. His religion never allowed a place for the demons and Hell of the past millennium. There was goodness and God, but no Satan or evil—except in the minds of men and women themselves. No Devil, no horned demon to tempt you to sin.

Nothing essentially bad.

Now the truth was being forced down his throat. He wasn't looking at 'kinetic energy released by an unbalanced mind', or a 'natural paranormal event caused by as-yet-unknown forces'. The trite phrases arrayed themselves mockingly in his mind. He knew so many of them.

He was watching an old man being manipulated—*tortured*—by a mad, malicious spirit.

It finally occurred to Kindling he should be very frightened indeed.

As Williams howled with joy, the wheelchair crashed to the floor. It landed unevenly, the spinning wheels shooting it forward and askew. It rammed into the stone fireplace, catapulting Williams from his seat. He hit the stonework headfirst with a sickening thud, then collapsed back into the wheelchair.

Blood spurted from a wide split in his forehead, quickly running down his nose and cheeks. Instead of being stunned or knocked unconscious, however, Williams turned back towards his visitors. His teeth shone whitely from the mask of blood. His tongue slipped out, licking the corners of his mouth.

'That tastes good,' he said, and giggled insanely. Then his expression turned serious, his eyes filled with insatiable greed. 'I think I want you,' he growled at Kindling. 'You look ripe for plucking.'

Kindling turned and ran from the room.

The moment he ran from the house was the instant he left the church as well. He never went back. Father Andrews came to visit him a few times, but Kindling wouldn't change his mind. As a young man he'd joined the church to help people, seeing religion as a means to move comparatively unhindered among the destitute and the wild, rampaging street kids. It was a noble and very rare ambition. Kindling wanted to change things, to make a better world. He was only twenty-two, young enough to really believe he might make a difference. His widower father, an ageing social worker fast succumbing to cancer, didn't have the heart to offer his son the truth.

Kindling found acceptance in a splinter group that called itself a New Age religion. Here, God came a subtle second to a message of caring, help and a social conscience. There were no devils, no menacing, pervading darkness. Only the things Kindling wanted to do.

Until, eight years later, Father Andrews took him to a small house where a crippled old man in a wheelchair showed him a true demon. Perhaps the Devil himself.

Williams' eyes, filled by someone—or something—else, had looked into Kindling's. Recognised him. *Marked* him.

Terrified him.

In the darkness Kindling blinked. The real world around him pushed away the last shreds of the memory. He was back in his one-room apartment. The place smelled of his sweat. Neighbourhood noises filtered through the thin walls. A baby cried, a man further away yelled obscenities. Underneath them all came the chatter of televisions, the clinking of crockery and metal pans.

Outside, the angry bustle of peak-hour traffic had abated to a smoother evening murmur. The apartment's single window changed colour in response to the surrounding neon lights.

He sighed, swinging his legs off the bed onto the floor. Standing, he groaned and slapped a hand to his lower back. Kindling had a strongly-built figure, slightly shorter than most men giving him a powerful, squat appearance. He'd always believed in keeping his body fit and his mind alert, and often allowed himself a slightly vain feeling of pride that he was still in better condition than many people ten years younger. This morning he wasn't so sure anymore. The previous day's work had obviously—and unexpectedly—taken its toll. Kindling had done many things since leaving the church over a year before, but being a brickie's labourer was a first. It hurt, he decided. The others had watched him with barely concealed amusement, waiting for him to crack and chuck his hand in. The looks turned to near pity as Kindling plodded grimly on. In the end there was grudging respect, a friendly slap on the shoulder and advice to buy a good pair of gloves the next day.

At least the job had an early start and early finish. Kindling had time to buy a few groceries on his way home. When he got to his apartment the rigours of the day overwhelmed him and he collapsed on the bed.

As usual the dreams came licking at his mind as soon as he began to relax. Kindling wasn't even sure *what* they were any more—dreams, nightmares or simply memories. He couldn't be certain he actually slept.

The questions nagged at him, too. Why did they come back? Why did they keep returning to trouble him? He'd seen worse things in his life. Things much more worthy of a lifetime of nightmares, even if they hadn't been instilled with a terrifying touch of the unknown, such as he'd seen in the Williams' house that day. Kindling remembered the pitying face of Stewart Andrews when they met weeks after the incident.

'Leaving the church isn't the answer,' Andrews

had said, the gravity of his words somehow enhanced by the dark rings of fatigue under his eyes. It was to be the last time Kindling saw him alive. He would be dead two weeks later.

'It's not my church anymore,' Kindling had replied, without conviction. 'Now it's a thing of—of . . . God knows what. I don't understand, or even begin to comprehend it. I can't cope with it.'

'You're scared, and you've every right to be,' Andrews told him softly. 'Because now you know something others of us can only unwillingly believe—they are never given the opportunity to *see*. Now *you* know, and *I* know that there has always been an "other side", just as surely as we've always taught there is a God. To believe in one and reject the other is illogical. And for you this is only a beginning—something you must come to terms with.' Andrews' voice had become harsh as Kindling started to shake his head.

'This is not the reason I joined the church.'

'Maybe not. Nevertheless, it is the reason you must stay.' Andrews' tone became imploring as he urged the younger man to understand. 'It's like a gift, but a terrible gift. Other men have been exposed to the like of what you saw that day, but the demons don't always reveal themselves. We don't know why. This one revealed itself to you—or God showed him to you. I believe it's His way of choosing us, selecting those of us strong enough to seek out the Evil in this world and fight it.'

Kindling was shaking his head again. 'It's too fantastic. I joined the church to help people, not fight ghosts and demons like somebody in a damned B-grade movie. Besides, you know it's still possible the man was ill. Look, there have been cases cited of—' Kindling stopped, his desperate attempt to console himself, *convince* himself, grinding to a halt. He was no longer able to come out with the sterile, comforting rationalisations. They'd lost their meaning.

'No, Matthew,' Andrews touched his arm sympathetically. 'It's fated to be your work. I can tell you that with the utmost authority.' A sad smile played across his lips at the formality of the words. 'It's unfinished business, Matthew.'

The knock on his apartment door made him jump. It was a confident knock—the sound of authority or strength, not someone selling wares.

'Just a minute,' Kindling called warily. He looked down at his bare feet and thought better of bothering with shoes. He doubted he would be letting anyone in. His wasn't a bad neighbourhood—not as bad as some, anyway. It didn't hurt to be cautious after dark, though. Kindling straightened and walked to the door, his face pained as his back twinged alarmingly.

'Who is it?'

'The police, Father Kindling.'

Matthew winced at the use of his defunct title. The door had a peephole and he leaned forward, pressing his eye against it. The smudged, concave lens showed him two serious-looking men. They were casually dressed and stood patiently in the hallway.

'Oh,' Kindling was momentarily at a loss. 'Have you got any identification? Do you mind?'

There was a scuffling and a plastic card appeared under the door. Kindling picked it up. The card identified the holder as a member of the Special Branch. He realised wryly he wouldn't recognise a bogus ID from a real one anyway. He hadn't even known Australia *had* a Special Branch.

Kindling reluctantly shot back some of the door locks, irrelevant thoughts about the unmade bed, and his bare feet and unkempt appearance going through his mind. The door opened less than ten centimetres, stopped by two heavy security chains. He regarded the men through the gap. They looked back impassively.

'Father Matthew Kindling?' one of them asked. Tinges of grey in his close-cropped black hair suggested he was older than the other man. Both were solidly built and looked fit.

'It's not "Father" any more,' Kindling explained, still off-balance. 'I left the church some time ago.'

'Yes, we know.' The man seemed completely unconcerned he'd got it wrong. 'Can we come in? We'd like to talk to you.'

Kindling glanced at the card in his hand. It didn't tell him anything more. 'I suppose you'd better.' Pushing the door closed, he unlatched the chains, then opened it again. His visitors gave him grateful glances as they walked past into the apartment. Kindling locked the front door again after them.

'Please, sit down.' He gestured at the only lounge chair, a battered two-seater. He looked guiltily at the unmade bed.

'Thanks.' The older man sat, but his companion stood near the window.

'My name's Detective Fraser. This is Detective-Constable Austin.' Fraser put his hand forward, meaning to take back his ID. Kindling mistook the move and awkwardly shook the outstretched hand before self-consciously giving back the card. He glanced at Austin, who contented himself with a polite mock-salute from the distance.

'Well, what can I do for you?'

'Father, to be honest—'

Kindling cut him off. 'Please, I'm not "Father" any more. I told you.'

Fraser bowed his head, then scratched reflectively behind his ear. 'I'm sorry, Mr Kindling.' There was a pause. 'To be honest, we can't tell you how you can help. We're simply running an errand here. We don't actually *know* what's going on. In fact, we've only been asked to give you a ride into town. There's somebody there who would like to speak with you.'

Kindling raised his eyebrows while his stomach did a loop. 'You're arresting me?'

'No, nothing of the sort. It just means even *we* aren't entrusted with the details of this matter.' A trace of rancour crept into Fraser's voice. He obviously didn't like being an errand boy.

'I have no idea what that might be,' Kindling admitted. There was an uncomfortable silence. 'On that basis, I'm not sure I'm willing to come with you.' The words sounded braver than he felt, but Fraser only nodded and looked at Austin, who stepped forward and reached into his top pocket.

'Mr Kindling, this is authorisation for you to call this gentleman and ask him anything you want.

He'll tell you enough to convince you that we're genuine and official.'

Kindling took the paper. On it was the name of a current government minister.

'There's something else,' Fraser said. 'That man is in his office right now. You couldn't call him through the switchboard, because the night switch will be operating, but you can call the building's security, which is twenty-four-hour, and ask to be connected. They're aware of the possibility of your calling.' Kindling looked confused and Fraser explained. 'It means you can find the number in the telephone book. You don't have to use the one we've given you there.' Again, a trace of acid crept into the policeman's manner as he recited what he considered to be the overelaborate precautions taken on Kindling's behalf. He thought it would have been simpler to just grab the man and apologise later, if need be.

'I see.' The room filled again with a strained silence. Kindling began to feel like a trapped animal. 'It's all a bit overwhelming,' he said.

'Exactly.' Fraser couldn't stop the sarcasm.

'When am I supposed to go?'

'Now, of course,' Fraser frowned.

'Sorry—of course.' Kindling looked around helplessly, as if some explanation might be written on the walls for him. 'I haven't a clue what this is about,' he repeated.

'Well, there's only one way to find out,' Austin said, showing his impatience and earning a warning glance from Fraser.

'You'll be perfectly safe,' the other detective offered flatly. 'I can understand this is a little worrying. Be assured, there's nothing to worry about.'

'It is a bit,' Kindling nodded. Despite the unexpected nature of events Kindling was quick enough to realise that he probably didn't have much choice in the matter. The polite requests would eventually turn insistent if he didn't agree.

Kindling had come into contact with the authorities many times during his years with the church, mediating between them and some of the more wayward members of his congregation—if he could call the street youths of his neighbourhood that. At that moment he believed Fraser and Austin *were* police, and he knew he had nothing to hide.

He shrugged and came to a decision. 'Can I take a moment to shower and change?'

'Sure.' Fraser relaxed. 'No real rush.'

Twenty minutes later Kindling was in the back of an unmarked car gliding through the city. Neon lights slid past, crowded on top of each other in the quest for optimum exposure. The sidewalks were crowded too. It was still early enough for people to be out wining and dining, or late night shopping, before the streets were given over to more sinister nightlife. In the front seat Fraser and Austin indulged in small talk, not bothering to include their passenger.

Kindling realised they were heading for the city centre, with its bland public buildings and glaring security floodlights. After a few quick turns down some narrow alleyways the car entered a small courtyard and pulled up behind a darkened building. The unusual approach tricked Kindling. He didn't know where he was.

'Just follow us,' Fraser told him, opening his door.

Their footsteps echoed off the surrounding concrete. Stopping at a nondescript doorway Fraser inserted a plastic card into a metal slot. The door opened, and an oblong of light spilt out over the bitumen. Fraser entered, and Austin motioned for Kindling to go in.

The interior of the building was as anonymous as the outside. Polished corridors between offices and glass cubicles offered little to Kindling to suggest where he had been brought. There were few people to be seen. An overalled maintenance man cleaning the floor didn't even lift his head as they walked past him.

The three shouldered together into a small elevator. Kindling suffered the slight swoop in his gut as the floor started to rise. As the entire lift began to vibrate badly, he couldn't help looking dismayed.

'Hasn't fallen yet,' Austin told him, obviously enjoying his discomfort.

They got out at the fourteenth floor. Here the hallways were carpeted, the walls painted in softer pastel colours. Kindling felt the chill of air conditioning. Fraser waved him through an ornate doorway, where he found himself in a pleasant lounge room.

The lights were dimmed. Deep carpet covered the entire floor, over which expensive rugs were scattered haphazardly. One wall boasted a well-stocked bar, while on another, long windows offered a panoramic view of the city. Six leather chairs dominated the centre of the room. Three were taken.

Their occupants stood politely as Kindling and his escort entered.

'Mr Kindling.' A large, self-assured man with a friendly smile but steely eyes stepped forward, his hand extended. 'Michael Lay,' he said, as they shook hands. 'And these two gentlemen are Evan Wiley and John Smith.'

They clasped hands and exchanged greetings. Kindling thought he detected an accent, and it was confirmed when Smith said, with an amused twinkle in his eye, 'You'll have to take my word on the "John Smith". It's my real name.'

Kindling picked Smith for an American or a Canadian—he could never tell the difference. He guessed Wiley to be the same. They were both tall and dressed well in tailored suits. Wiley was in his fifties and balding. The younger Smith made up for this with a thick head of hair heavily gelled into good behaviour.

Lay looked at the detectives. 'Do you guys want to slip next door and have a drink? We'll call if we need you.'

'Okay,' Fraser nodded, and gestured for Austin to follow. He managed another suspicious glance at Kindling before the door snicked closed behind him.

'Please, take a seat.' Lay pointed to the armchairs. 'Would you like a drink?'

'Just a light beer,' said Kindling. He sat down, the soft leather capturing his body with luxurious comfort. The Americans sat opposite him, smiling. Drinks were on a small table near them.

'I suppose you're wondering what this is all about,' Lay called from the bar as he poured Kindling's beer.

'It is all rather a . . . surprise,' Kindling agreed.

'Yes, well—' Lay walked over and handed him the beer. He waited until he seated himself before continuing. 'Where to begin? That's the question, hey?'

'At the beginning, perhaps,' Kindling said drily, his confidence slowly returning.

'How about the name Anton Vasta?' Lay asked. 'Do you remember him?'

There was a silence, then Kindling answered. 'Yes, I remember him.' He kept his voice steady, but inside a spark of anger ignited. It was history now—it should be left alone. A moral judgement Kindling had made and had been condemned for ever since. It was still a sore point in his conscience—a matter left unresolved because the man was gone. But it didn't deserve to be dragged out into the open again.

'How would you describe Vasta?' Lay asked softly.

'Dead, of course.'

'Of course,' he nodded. 'But apart from that?'

'Look, is this some sort of game? What's the damn point?'

'Please, Mr Kindling.' Wiley held up a hand. 'Humour us for a moment—believe me, you're not in any sort of trouble here.'

Kindling let his anger run for a moment longer, then relented. 'Vasta was a businessman. By all accounts he wasn't a very honest one, but that wasn't my concern.'

'No?' Wiley raised his eyebrows. 'Does modern religion overlook sins such as murder, extortion and embezzlement?'

'That's exactly the sort of rubbish I had to put up with for years from people like you,' Kindling said, starting to snap again. 'For a long time I had police on my doorstep almost every day, accusing me of all sorts of collusion, aiding and abetting—and God knows every other crime too, all because the man's wife came into my church once a week and he occasionally came with her. So we talked! We discussed the damn weather. What of it? The police figured I was arranging every bloody drug deal in the city. I got sick of it then, and I'm sick of it now. Don't you people know the truth when it's placed in front of you? You're supposed to.'

'Take it easy, Matthew,' Lay waved a hand. He neither apologised nor asked for the use of Kindling's first name.

'So, what was the truth?' Wiley asked, unperturbed.

'Vasta came to me privately a long time before anybody took a lot of notice of him. He even explained what he was—what he did. Then he asked if I would supply a place of worship and religious teaching for his wife and family. He assured me they had no part in any of his illegal dealings. They were totally innocent. Vasta himself didn't expect me to tolerate him inside my church, but I invited him anyway. He sometimes accompanied his family.'

'And you believed him? About his family?'

Kindling shrugged. 'Why not? His wife was a lot younger than him. One child was six years old, the other about four, I guess. Hardly criminal material, don't you think?'

Lay looked thoughtful. 'But you were well

aware of Vasta's activities? You knew what he was?'

'Apart from what he said in our first meeting, I only knew what I noticed in the newspapers—which was very little, really.'

Lay turned to the Americans. 'Vasta was very good at keeping his hands clean. He stamped very hard on press linking him to any crime, even if it was common street knowledge that he was involved. He managed to sue once.'

'Sounds like he knew his stuff,' Wiley observed.

'So?' Kindling asked. 'Now *you* tell *me*. What's all the fuss? He's been dead nearly two years.'

The other three men exchanged meaningful glances. Then Wiley spoke carefully.

'Matthew, what would you say if Vasta were alive today? What would your attitude towards him be?'

Again, Kindling shrugged. 'If he'd lived and not changed his personal wishes, and if I'd stayed in the church, then I don't see why my feelings would have altered much. That's a lot of if's, though.'

'True,' Wiley nodded slowly. 'But what if he came back from the dead?'

'I don't see the point of the question. He won't.'

'Okay, I'll be more specific. What if we were *to bring him back to life?*'

Kindling looked at them all, trying to figure out the joke, or decipher the meaning behind the questions. They looked back calmly, completely serious.

'There must be something you know that I don't,' Kindling said finally. 'Otherwise, this conversation doesn't make sense.'

'Right,' Smith agreed, speaking for the first time. 'Okay, what do you know about Space Station Freedom?'

The change of subject threw Kindling for a moment. 'Not a lot. It's not something I'm interested in—wait a minute. Didn't they have some sort of accident there a few days back? Somebody died?'

'That's correct, but it's not what we're concerned with here.' Smith became stern. 'I'm going to tell you something about Freedom that's classified. That means you're not allowed to mention it to anyone, unless it's someone we security-clear beforehand, do you understand?' Kindling blinked at the thinly-veiled threat. 'Freedom has a cryogenics section already operating in orbit. Are you familiar with cryogenics?'

'Cryogenics? Ah—yes, just a minute. Let me think.' Kindling rubbed his eyes, which suddenly felt tired. 'It's preservation in extremely low temperatures. I think they've been experimenting with sensitive medicines, plants—even precious documents and artefacts. Something like that. I read it in *Time* magazine a while back. Am I right?'

'As always, Mr Kindling. You're far too intelligent a man to be carrying bricks for a living,' Wiley said.

Kindling bristled. 'It's none of your business how I earn a living.'

Smith forestalled any further argument by going on smoothly, 'Did the *Time* article mention people? Preserving them, I mean.'

'Well, yes,' Kindling turned back to him. 'But it was more a novelty than anything. It mentioned a few famous people—Walt Disney was one of them, I think. Nobody seemed to take the idea seriously.'

'On the contrary, Mr Kindling, some people take it very seriously,' Smith told him. 'There are six bodies in hermetically sealed containers aboard Freedom right now.' Smith didn't need to add the touch of drama. There was a silence while Kindling digested this information.

'*What?*' After the initial surprise, Kindling's first reaction was an urge to laugh. *Crazy Americans*, he thought. *Wasn't anything sacred to them?* 'Why? What's the point in it?' He smiled. 'Nobody thinks it can work, do they?'

'Anton Vasta is one of those corpses,' Smith said gravely.

Kindling's smile faded. 'Vasta? Impossible. I presided over his burial myself.'

'You buried what we refer to as a "John Doe". Vasta's body was nowhere near the cemetery. In fact, he was already being transported by special arrangement to the US.'

'Now hang on a minute! What are you talking about? And why wasn't I told?' Kindling was angry again. 'You're saying I conducted a funeral and a burial service over the wrong body? Do you realise what that means to me?'

'There are many obvious reasons why the authorities don't want this program to be public knowledge,' Smith said. 'Not just Vasta's inclusion. Except for those within a certain security clearance, nobody knows the facilities exist. Otherwise everybody from the Pope to the President of the United States would be pressuring us to bring someone back to life—anyone, so we can ask them all the big questions. It's been a very, very tight package, Matthew, and not hurting your feelings or insulting your religious ethics was the least of our worries. It was considered you didn't need to know about the cryogenics project. Now we're allowed to tell you it does exist.'

Kindling found himself groping blindly for his drink, which he located and raised to his lips. It was already flat, but he didn't notice. 'I don't believe it,' he said finally, but without conviction. The others watched him, waiting for him to say something more.

'There's a simple enough explanation,' Wiley began. 'I'll give you some of the facts. You might find it a bit more believable afterwards.' He paused and sipped his drink. 'One of the problems with human cryogenics is sedimentation. The body is purged of blood and pumped full of preservatives, then frozen—although the temperatures involved make "frozen" sound a little inadequate. The preservative doesn't freeze—' he held up a finger, '—it's designed not to. But there is still a problem when it settles, as blood will, to the lowest parts of the body—that's sedimentation. No matter how careful the doctors are, there will always be some parts unaffected by the preservative solution. These will become irreparably damaged over the years.'

Smith took up the explanation. 'But not in zero gravity. Not in orbit, understand? The solution doesn't settle, because there's no gravity to affect it. That's why scientists believed a cryogenic storage unit in space might succeed.'

'Sheltered from direct sunlight, it's easier to

maintain the low temperatures, too,' Wiley added. 'Everything's extreme up there.'

Kindling held up his hand. 'All right, I can see all that.' He shook his head, struggling to keep up. 'I believe there's a—a unit of some sort up there. But Vasta? How did that happen?'

'He planned it,' Wiley said simply. 'He knew through his contacts in the States that the program existed. He bought his way into it.' Wiley sounded almost as if he was apologising for the system. 'It's sort of an exclusive club, considering it costs fifty million to join.'

'*Fifty million?* Vasta had fifty million dollars?' Kindling was stunned.

Lay pulled a face. 'He was involved in a hell of a lot of illegal activities. Profitable too, when you're controlling them.'

'But—my God! I didn't know he was that big.'

'Do you remember how he died?' Lay asked.

'He was diagnosed with bowel cancer. It came on very quickly.'

'It didn't even get a chance to take hold,' Lay said. 'Oh, it was there, all right. Big enough to paint a fatal picture. But Vasta suicided before any real damage was done. He had a walk-in meat freezer installed in his home, then he drank himself into a stupor inside it. He froze himself to death.' Kindling looked at him in amazement. 'It didn't quite have the desired effect, because he still went through all the normal processing at the local hospital and morgue, before they released his body—he'd contacted the Trust and told them exactly what was happening.'

'Didn't they try to stop him?'

'They couldn't. He was already dead. He used the different time-zones between here and the States and a fax machine to deliver his suicide message several hours after he started. When his wife found him frozen to death in the freezer it was the beginning of a tragedy for her, but in fact the mechanisms for transporting his body to America had been in action for some time. He took care of everything before he killed himself. He left nothing to chance and avoided any delays.'

Wiley spoke. 'By all accounts Vasta still got what he wanted. The experts say he avoided the usual decomposing for some time *before* the cryogenic principles are applied.'

'I'm utterly amazed,' Kindling admitted. Then realisation burst into his mind like a bright light. 'And you're talking about bringing him back to life? Now?'

'The cancer he suffered from was unique, because of his own rare blood type. Someone has come up with what looks like a cure. They want to attempt reviving Vasta and administering the drug.' Wiley made a 'who knows?' gesture, palms up.

'After two years.' Kindling shook his head again. 'After the man's actually been dead for more than two years, you want to bring him back to life.' He whistled through his teeth. 'God, anything could happen. Then again, if it works, Vasta couldn't possibly be more than a human vegetable. I can't believe he would be normal.'

'Vasta believed he would be,' Lay said, walking back to the bar. 'More importantly, the scientists running the project believe that, after a certain period of adjustment, he will lead a normal life.'

Wiley leaned forward, looking intent. 'Vasta is almost the perfect subject to be brought back. Apart from the way he killed himself, making him the healthiest corpse we've got,' Wiley's lips twitched, 'there's the way he *lived*. He was a criminal who bought his way into the program with dirty money. If anything goes wrong, who's going to care? If he were one of the world's great benefactors, we might worry more—but he's not. If something goes bad, the scientists can learn from it and stick him back in his damn coffin, or whatever it is they're keeping him in. No one's going to feel particularly upset about it.'

'And what if it works?'

'Then we'll keep him for as long as we want. Study him. He's hardly in a position to complain.'

'And will he ever be set free?' Kindling was surprised to find he was slightly disgusted by Wiley's clinical approach, even if Vasta had been as criminal as they claimed.

'That's not my concern.'

There was pensive silence. Kindling thought he could already guess what they wanted of him. It was time to ask.

'So what's my concern in all this?'

Smith accepted a fresh drink from Michael Lay. 'The Cryogenic program attempts to cover all the possibilities, Matthew. One of them is that Vasta will need some sort of—religious guidance. As such he was required to nominate a suitable person to fulfil this duty. Since he entrusted you with his family, you were the obvious choice. It's your name on the form, at least. We are bound to recognise that and, of course, the cryogenics people want to deliver him into the most stable of environments—people he'll know. As few strangers as possible.'

'Guidance!' Kindling laughed. 'If he comes back in one piece, he'll be the one telling *me* about the afterlife.'

'Yes, that's possible too. However, we just don't know.'

Kindling was cynical. 'How am I supposed to supply this guidance? Where will he be?'

'He'll be revived inside Freedom,' explained Wiley. 'He *won't* be brought back to Earth first. Then he'll go to a special institution in Canaveral, where the shuttle will land, weather permitting.'

'You'd fly me to America? Just for this? I'm flattered,' Kindling said drily.

Wiley's response was just as dry. 'We try to give Vasta value for his fifty million—no matter where it came from.'

Sitting back in his chair, Kindling had to shake his head. 'You're forgetting. I left the church over a year ago. I'm not in the business anymore.'

'That's not the point. He asked for *you*. And besides, that makes you even more suitable,' Lay replied. 'You've still got the knowledge, the religious education, but without the—ah, constraints, the possible moral objections, of a man still in the church.'

'I see your point,' Kindling admitted ruefully. They didn't say anything more, and Kindling realised they were waiting for him to make some sort of decision. 'Look. It's a lot to throw at me in the space of half an hour. I really don't know what to say.'

'Of course, you'll be extremely well paid,' said Smith.

'I wasn't even thinking of that,' Kindling replied truthfully. But now that money had been mentioned, it became a major factor. Since Kindling's last days in school, his life had always been aimed at joining the church. Now, having left it, he was like a man who'd lost his trade. At thirty years of age he felt strangely old—especially as he was having so much trouble letting go of his old life. He'd wrapped himself into a cocoon where he didn't think about anything—except his next tortured night's sleep. His future looked bleak, and he was only human. A large injection of cash could help.

'What would I be expected to do? Now, I mean.'

'There's a communications network in this city linking with NASA's codes into Freedom,' Smith told him. 'We'll give you access to that, where you can keep tabs on progress. It'll take three weeks to bring Vasta's temperature up to a point where they can try to revive him. In that time we expect you to read some files on the process, so you have a better understanding of what's going on.'

Lay interrupted. 'I'll give you some files, too. On Vasta and his family. You should know everything about him. I doubt whether you'll like much of it.'

Kindling picked up his drink again, using the time to think. In the end only one thing made him nod his agreement.

He wasn't considering the morality of it all, nor was he too concerned about how Vasta might be treated—both issues which might have made him refuse to be a part of it, given time to think them over.

They were secondary concerns. Deep down Kindling believed it couldn't work. Bringing a man back to life who'd been dead for over two years, bringing him back normal and healthy, was too fantastic to accept. It had to fail.

So, despite feeling he was being rushed, he decided to play along. Do what they asked and take their money for as long as they wanted to pay him.

As Wiley suggested, it would be better than carrying bricks for a living.

It was nearly midnight by the time they dropped Kindling back at his apartment. The two detectives drove away promising to collect him the day after next. Kindling had asked for a day to tie up loose ends.

Back in his flat, sleep was out of the question. Everything he'd been told whirled through his brain. Kindling turned on his old television, but the images flickered unseen as his mind kept going back over the evening's events. Eventually he fell into a fitful sleep on the lounge chair.

He awoke just before dawn, the looming orange glow barely discernible, blocked by the city skyline. The moment Kindling opened his eyes he knew what he was going to do. Perhaps he'd dreamt it. At the same time he didn't want to consciously think too deeply about it, or give commonsense a chance to overrule his instincts.

He dressed quickly and drank a cup of coffee. In the car park his battered Nissan was coated with gleaming silver frost. Kindling's breath made thin clouds of vapour in the early morning chill. The car started the first time, which was rare. Kindling looked worriedly at the fuel gauge for a moment. It didn't move off the red line. He decided to risk it. It wasn't far and the traffic would be light.

He still wasn't sure why he was going. Maybe, he thought, there simply wasn't a *why*. He was following a gut feeling. The radio gabbled early morning cheerfulness and Kindling grimaced, changing to an all-classical station. This sounded morbid and funereal, which should have been fitting, but he snapped the radio off.

The traffic lights were kind and he made better time than he expected. When he arrived the sun was still trying to climb above the skyline, throwing long shadows. Kindling didn't bother locking the car.

He pushed against the cemetery gates and discovered they were still chained. It didn't matter. Kindling easily swung himself over the low stone wall. After a few steps the headstones crowded around him like a miniature city. Some were tall and ostentatious, topped with trumpeting concrete angels and ornate crosses. Others gleamed with gold and silver lettering set in pristine, ageless marble.

Their last attempt at immortality, Kindling thought, as he trod carefully between the graves. *Probably a better investment than Vasta's fifty million.*

Kindling had his views on death and remembrance. That, he suspected, was one of the reasons his instincts had brought him here. People came to remember their lost ones through the headstones, the etched lettering in the marble. They soon stopped thinking of the thing beneath the soil. The corpse itself quickly became something unimaginable, rotted beyond recognition. It had no place in cherished memories.

He came to Vasta's grave. It was completely white: a white headstone, with a white marble border and the top covered by fine, white pebbles like gravel. The epitaph was in deep black lettering: *Anton Vasta. Born 1961. Loved and missed by his family and friends.*

Kindling had never noticed before that the headstone gave no date of death. He stared at the grave, thinking of the man whose name marked the stone—not the poor, nameless wretch who lay buried there.

What are you trying to do? Who do you think you are? God? he asked the uncaring tomb.

Kindling began to understand fully why he was there, standing in the cemetery in the chill, early daylight. While he'd accepted Wiley's offer, content the whole thing was harmless and doomed to failure, another smaller voice warned it just *might* happen. Visiting the grave was like a rehearsal, a dry run of what he could say to a man who might have all the answers.

Even practising, Kindling felt uncomfortable.

What are you going to say to us? What have you seen? Everything? Have you met God? Or did He know you were coming back and deny you everything, put you in limbo?

Most of all—do you want *to come back? Now?*

Then Kindling kept his mind silent. Around

him the city was coming slowly awake. He looked at the headstone and hoped something inspirational would come to him. Nothing. Instead, he noticed a feathery green creeper taking hold amongst the white pebbles, ruining the otherwise immaculate grave. He bent forward, grasping the weed between his fingers to pull it loose.

Another hand burst from the pebbling on the grave and gripped Kindling's wrist.

It was bloodless-white with black dirt under the broken fingernails. A gold ring gleamed on the middle finger. The hand held him with a fierce strength. Kindling cried out and pushed himself backwards, but the hand stopped him. He stared at it incredulously, fear clamping down over his heart. Desperately he looked around the cemetery for some kind of help. The scene that met his eyes made him almost faint with fear.

Everywhere there were ghosts. Some were tall, ethereal figures standing by their graves. Others were lifelike facsimiles of the living person they once were. Many had an air of calm patience and Kindling knew instinctively that they were waiting for their loved ones to join them. But a few spirits sent out vibrations of deep sorrow and anger. A hint of blackness smeared their images and these filled Kindling with a hopeless fear. A scene in the distance mesmerised him. A soldier, dressed in a uniform over a century old, lay grappling with another man, who looked just as terrified as Kindling felt.

He's alive, Kindling realised, then understood more. *But it's not happening now. I'm seeing the past—or even the future. God, I'm seeing everything!*

Suddenly the hand let go of his and disappeared.

Kindling toppled backwards onto the frost-covered grass. He sat, legs sprawled, and looked at the grave with wide, frightened eyes. The surface appeared untouched. Even the weed was still there.

At first he couldn't believe it had happened. An ache in his wrist told him otherwise. His mind was numb and he couldn't decide whether the grasping hand was trying to pull him down—or expected Kindling to pull him *out*. Both thoughts made him shudder. A sick sensation filled the pit of his stomach.

A voice came into Matthew Kindling's mind. At first he couldn't tell if he was actually hearing it or if his memory was playing tricks on him. It was a familiar voice, but it offered no comfort. Kindling could almost see Stewart Andrews' wry smile.

It's unfinished business, Matthew.

4

RHIANNA STATION WAS NAMED after Daniel Littlewood's great-great-grandmother, Rhianna Feaney, who had run the sprawling cattle property single-handed after her new husband disappeared into the mud of Flanders during the Great War. In those days the homestead's isolation was complete. Using her wits and charms as well as the Remington shotgun from under her bed, she dealt with everything: the vicissitudes of Mother Nature, attacks from natives, amorous hired hands with visions of marrying into landed wealth—and fickle bank managers. The latter, she claimed in her finely-written diary which Daniel never tired of reading, always regarded her with suspicion. Even in the best years, a succession of waistcoated pen-pushers sat behind their bankers' desks and drafted Rhianna letters of thinly-disguised concern that she didn't *really* know what she was doing.

She proved them all wrong, surviving floods and droughts, and seeing the good times, too. Her heart finally softened for a leading hand called Joe Littlewood who, even when Rhianna looked as if she'd been rolling in the nearest mudhole, still took his hat off and called her 'ma'am'.

They married and had four children, ensuring the property would remain a family concern.

Now, almost a hundred years later, Littlewoods still owned and ran the station. Daniel and his wife even slept in Rhianna's wrought-iron bed, although, as Georgina pointed out whenever her husband waxed lyrical on the family history, they used a vastly improved mattress. Having an antique was one thing, she claimed, but it was no damned good if you couldn't get to sleep on it.

For a while, this was about as close as Georgina came to humour, and even that was an improvement on the past. She was getting better. They both were. But the scars of the Littlewoods' personal tragedy were taking a long time to heal.

Three years before, their middle child, Ellen, was diagnosed with advanced kidney disease—in both kidneys. It was too late to do anything. At the last moment, like a miracle, a donor became available, but Ellen's body rejected the organ for reasons which became academic as she quietly lost her fight in the early hours of a winter morning.

The tragedy had drawn the family closer—Daniel and Georgina and their eldest child Peter and seven-year old daughter Susan. They got on with the business of running the property and waited for the pain of Ellen's death to fade.

One morning Georgina felt something new in the air. It was her day for cleaning the house. Any other day of the week might find her helping the men out on the land, but she insisted on having a day devoted to the homestead, which she kept spotless. Peter often teased her about it, reminding his mother the nearest 'neighbour' who might drop in unannounced would need to travel over one hundred and fifty kilometres. Georgina ignored him or, if he pushed his cheek too far, she gave him something to clean, too.

Georgina was dusting around her knick-knacks. The television was tuned to a current affairs channel, courtesy of the gleaming satellite dish behind the house. It meant their programming fare was predominantly American, because Australia had only two such channels, both of which heavily emphasised sport. When her mind was only occupied with menial tasks Georgina preferred to have the television on, in case something interesting came up.

Susan was in her room taking her third class of the day via an audio-visual computer link. Everyone called Susan 'Rainy', because her first attempts at saying her middle name, Rhianna—another tribute to the old matriarch—had come out just like that. The name stuck.

Picking up a fine crystal glass Georgina inspected it for smears. These small possessions were very important to her. They made her house a home and forged a link with the years in which she had travelled in her youth. She felt the glass tremble in her fingers and she frowned. After a moment a possible reason came to her. She put down the glass and hurried outside.

The last few years had been kind to Rhianna Station. The wet season rains arrived regularly, while the summers that followed were comparatively mild. The sight greeting Georgina as she stood in her front garden, hands on hips, would have warmed the heart of any farmer. Abundant, tall grass, polished a golden brown by the months of sunshine, rippled in the gathering breeze. The scene stretched away to the horizon, in every direction except in the east, where Daniel had recently grazed the Brahmans. There the grass was cropped close to the soil.

Georgina was a strong woman, her muscled arms and legs tanned a deep brown, her hair kept sensibly short. She shaded her eyes and looked out across the land. Eclipsing even the abundance of feed and the rich colours of a property in prime condition, something else brought a smile of pleasure to Georgina's lips.

The first thunderstorm of the year, a blackened and boiling mass of cloud, was coming from the southeast. Overhead Georgina saw smaller puffs of vapour scurrying directly towards the storm, being sucked into its low-pressure maelstrom. A faint rumble carried across the kilometres, more a vibration in the air than a sound.

She revelled in the sight of the approaching storm for a few moments more, then reluctantly went back inside.

Georgina knocked on Susan's door before opening it. Rainy looked up in surprise. It was unusual for anyone to interrupt her lessons. In front of her a video monitor displayed brightly coloured charts, while an electric pointer accompanied by a female voice explained the details.

'What's up, Mum?'

'Looks like we're getting our first storm. You'd better warn Miss Hasker,' Georgina nodded at the screen.

'Great!' Rainy smiled widely. She punched an override command and her teacher's face immediately replaced the diagrams.

'Yes, Susan?'

'Mum says we might have a storm coming,' Rainy told the clear image.

'Okay, make sure you shut down, before it gets too close. Let me know when you're ready.'

Rainy glanced slyly at her mother, who was expecting it.

'But not a moment too soon, young lady,' she warned sternly. 'It's a good few hours away yet.'

''Course not, Mum.' Rainy managed to look hurt. Georgina kept the smile off her face until she closed the door behind her.

There were things to be done. The storm might veer around them completely, or just brush a grey tail of cloud across the station, teasing them with droplets. On the other hand, if it hit, the homestead could expect a brief period of high winds. Georgina carefully made a circuit of the house, picking up several gardening tools and other odds and ends that might be thrown in a gale. She decided to leave some sheets of iron until Daniel and Peter returned, which she was sure they would before the storm got too close. She left bringing in the washing until last.

Inside, it was a matter of closing windows and drawing curtains. If the storm stayed around until nightfall the lightning would scare Rainy, as it always did. As Georgina walked past her daughter's room she heard the mutter of Rainy's voice. Doing her lessons until the last moment, after all, she noted with motherly pride.

There was one door next to the main bedroom at the end of the hallway that she didn't need to check. Beyond it, the windows were always closed, the curtains permanently drawn.

It was Ellen's room. Exactly as it had been, clean and tidied, on the day they'd started the final trip to the hospital. For some time after her death each member of the Littlewood family had found comfort there, sitting alone in her bedroom as though it were a shrine, trying to talk across the bridgeless gap of mortality to their little girl. It was a way of remembering. Even Rainy spent some hours in there, lightly touching her sister's possessions and talking to Ellen as if she were in the room herself, alive and listening.

Georgina had cried a thousand tears in that room.

No one had been in there for a long time, another sign the family was coming to terms with the tragedy. Only Georgina regularly put her head around the door to make sure the dust wasn't settling too thickly. Those occasions, she thought guiltily as she passed, weren't quite as regular as they used to be, either.

But now the door was open.

The realisation stopped Georgina dead in her tracks, one hand on the doorknob of the main bedroom. The other door was only open a crack—any less and the latch would snick into place.

'I wonder how long—' she started to muse aloud, before she decided it could have been that way for a while. It was only the need to shut up the house that had caused her to notice it.

As the sky darkened with the approaching storm, Georgina saw something else, too. The light in Ellen's bedroom was on.

She sucked at her teeth, a habit of hers when she was annoyed. The unattended light might have drained the solar batteries completely. She went to enter the room, but again something stopped her.

Strangely, it was like a bad feeling. She could almost swear a cold chill ran down her arm as she touched the metal of the door-handle. Suddenly, she didn't feel good about going into Ellen's old room.

'God, what am I thinking?' she asked the house around her. 'Why should I be frightened of anything in *this* room?' Determinedly, she pushed her way through.

Georgina was upset but not alarmed at what she found. The neatly-made bed was now badly rumpled, as though someone had stood on it and bounced. More distressing, however, was a book lying open on the floor. Ellen had kept a small bookshelf filled with cuddly toys, a few dolls and, of course, her favourite books. One of them had been taken out and read, but not replaced.

Georgina picked it up and read the cover before

putting it back. It was called *The Man in the Moon*, an advanced children's novel. It must have been Rainy, she thought crossly.

She smoothed the bedding, her earlier guilt causing her to take particular care. Twitching the curtains aside she confirmed that the windows were closed, but was surprised to see that the sky was now a solid grey. As she watched, a jagged line of lightning speared to the earth near the horizon.

At the door Georgina turned and had a last look, her hand on the light switch. She promised herself and the memory of her daughter that she would take greater care of the room. She would have to tick off Rainy for being so sloppy too, but it could wait until after her lessons.

She clicked off the light and closed the door firmly.

The house secure, Georgina made herself a cup of coffee and sat on the verandah, watching the storm approach. The clouds bore down on the homestead, filling the sky. The thunderclaps were getting closer and after several loud booms in a row Georgina called out to Rainy to shut down her equipment.

Rainy emerged moments later and looked in wonder at the storm. Georgina opened her mouth to mention Ellen's room, but the joy on her daughter's face made her pause. It would be a shame, she realised, to spoil the moment.

Rainy lifted her head and smelled the rain on the wind. 'It's going to be a beauty,' she decided.

'Yes. Your father should come tearing home any minute now.'

'Where was he?'

'East Forty—hey, you want to do something for me?'

Rainy's pretty face fell. 'Oh, come on, Mum. I just finished classes! Give me a break.'

'You poor overworked thing,' her mother mocked. 'Don't worry. It won't kill you.'

Rainy sighed, resigned to her fate. 'Okay, what is it?'

'Go to the shed and fire up the generator. Just run it for a few minutes and make sure it's okay. Peter'll probably disconnect the batteries when he gets home.'

Rainy was instantly happier. 'Wow! All right, I'll go now.' She ran from the verandah, her fair hair flowing behind her.

'That's what I had in mind,' Georgina murmured, amused.

Anything mechanical intrigued Rainy, but because of her age, she was expected to keep her distance from most things. Any excuse to circumvent this rule was gladly welcomed.

Over the last four years Daniel had invested in some modern technology for the homestead. Almost everything electrical now ran off a row of solar panels near the house. At the same time power was bled off to recharge a bank of batteries which supplied the electricity at night. The generator was mainly for backup when, after a succession of cloudy days, it was possible to overextend the solar system. Also, because the sheer voltage of a lightning strike at the wrong place could destroy the batteries, Daniel made it a practice to completely isolate them during storms. Again, the generator took over supply.

A few minutes later Georgina heard the generator kick into life. As if on cue, large drops of rain began to plop onto the iron roof of the house. They steadily increased, creating a staccato drumming noise, which lulled her into a peaceful reverie.

Her peace was soon shattered by the arrival of a flat-bed truck pulling up noisily at the front. Two young kelpies barked at her from the tray, announcing their return; an older dog, mother of the two, came from behind the house to investigate.

'Hey! How's it going?' Daniel Littlewood climbed down from the driver's seat and closed the door with a healthy slam.

'What do you think?' Georgina shouted back, smiling and waving.

Peter dashed out from the other side of the truck. At sixteen he was a younger double of his father. Tall, lean and hardened by his outback life. As he passed his mother he swept off his hat and planted a quick kiss on her forehead.

'Hi, Mum. Any cold drink left in the fridge?'

'Of course,' she replied over her shoulder, well aware he hadn't stopped to hear her reply anyway. Daniel flopped down in the seat next to her and kissed her cheek. He smelled damp and dirty.

'Back in business again,' he nodded at the rain.

'We're having a good run,' she agreed carefully, unconsciously touching the wood of her chair to keep fate at bay.

'How's your day?'

'Well, I went to the supermarket, popped over to visit Gran's, then I went to the races and had a bet on the Melbourne Cup,' she told him, her face deadpan.

'That's a good day,' he raised his eyebrows. 'All I did was mend a few fences.'

'Actually, I lied,' she admitted. 'I didn't go to Gran's. I went straight to the races. Blew a lot of money, too.'

'Never mind,' he said, standing. He pointed at the sky. 'I'm going to celebrate this anyway, with a beer. Do you want one?'

'No thanks, I've just had a coffee.' Daniel went to walk inside, but she reached out and touched his arm. 'Oh Dan, I forgot. Those sheets of iron are still around the side. Do you want to move them, in case it blows up?' Georgina had to raise her voice. The rain was really pounding the roof now.

'Damn, I suppose I'd better,' he looked disappointed. Looking at the truck gave him an idea. 'I know, I'll load it on the truck, tie it down and chuck it off in the morning.'

'Good thinking.'

Daniel started to run back to the truck, but he slowed and then stopped, turning to face her. 'Shit, why not?' he shouted. 'It does you good to stand in the rain once in a while. It's nearly a tradition! Would you like to join me?'

'I'm too old to go dancing in the rain.'

'Too old! Forty next birthday and you're an old lady, is that it?' He laughed.

The laughter died on his lips as a guilty look passed between the couple. For so long it had seemed wrong to laugh. The rain brought a change of season after months of dry weather. Was it also bringing a change of mood? Daniel had laughed so rarely since Ellen's death.

Georgina broke the awkward tension. 'It's okay

to laugh, Dan,' she called, softly. 'It's been long enough. We should both try to laugh a little more.'

He managed to smile, but it was a sad, lopsided smile. 'Yeah, I know. Don't worry, we're getting better. It's all downhill from here.'

He spun around and climbed into the truck. The engine roared, its muffler long since rusted to uselessness, and the truck pulled away with a splash of mud.

It rained most of the night.

The next morning was an early start for everyone. Because of the rain, they needed to check the riverbeds and waterholes for any stock that had bogged themselves in the new mud. As usual, Daniel and Peter would take the flat-bed and assign themselves the more distant and inaccessible areas. Georgina would take the smaller Toyota four-wheel drive on her own. The paddocks she would check were populated by younger cattle. As long as she could get a rope over the head of any stricken animal and attach the free end to the bull-bar, she would be able to pull it free with the vehicle. If not, there was the radio to call for help.

Rainy would look after the homestead and, much to her disgust, attend to her lessons. Station life had matured her early. Her parents had no qualms about leaving her alone.

Daniel was finishing the last of his coffee. 'You sure you'll be all right?' he asked Georgina, who was packing herself some sandwiches.

'Of course. I've done it before, remember?'

'Got that new rope?'

'Yes, Dan. Peter loaded it in for me a few minutes ago.'

'Make sure you check the radio—regularly, too.'

'*Yes*, Dan.'

Georgina hadn't been 'born on the land', as Daniel thought of it. He'd brought his young bride from the city, where he'd been attending a business management course. Eighteen years later he still worried.

Peter came inside from the yard. The open door behind him showed a tinge of pink creeping across the sky. 'You're all fuelled up, Mum.'

'Thanks. There's an esky of sandwiches and drinks for you both.' She pointed.

'Great. Time for another coffee?'

'Nope.' Daniel put his cup down firmly. 'It's time we went.'

Peter rolled his eyes, but picked up the esky and hefted it through the door, calling goodbye to Georgina as he went.

'Be careful,' Daniel told Georgina, kissing her on the cheek.

'I'll call if I have any problems,' she assured him.

Once he was gone she finished her own preparations. Another small esky, a water bottle filled with iced cordial and a second water container for emergencies. She threw a tube of block-out cream and some insect repellent into a satchel.

Finally, she scribbled some instructions for the evening meal on a scrap of paper and stuck it on the refrigerator, where Rainy couldn't miss it. Rainy was still asleep—one advantage of staying behind.

Outside, the eastern sky was beginning to glow.

The air smelled fresh and washed clean. Georgina loaded the back of the four-wheel drive and sloshed through a puddle to the driver's side door. The motor started after a few protests and she pulled away, the headlights sweeping across the wet yard.

She concentrated for the first few minutes, watching carefully for mudholes in the track and for the first of two gates. At the second gate a young bull caught in the headlights looked at her mournfully.

'You're never bloody happy,' she told it, shooing it away so it couldn't bolt between the gateposts as she drove through.

Back in the car she glanced in the rear-view mirror, automatically checking the gate was closed properly. By chance, the mirror reflected an image of the homestead. Something she saw made Georgina brake hard and twist around to see better.

It was still quite dark. The house was silhouetted by the early dawn. The homestead was a long, low structure which had grown over the years as successive generations added more rooms. Tall trees grew close around it, offering shade most of the day. The roof's extra-wide eaves kept the walls in deep shadow and gave the house a hooded, brooding look. Georgina knew its shape, its every corner and angle, as well as her own face. The kitchen window glowed brightly, where she'd left the light on in case Rainy awoke. Further along the black outline another light shone, not so clearly, as if it were trying to escape drawn curtains. The distance and darkness might have been confusing her, she tried to tell herself—but in the pit of her stomach Georgina knew which window was lit.

It was Ellen's room.

Georgina frowned, pressing her lips together. She pushed away a flicker of emotion before she would have to admit it was actually fear—something unexpected. There was nothing to be scared of, she knew. Just something to *get to the bottom of*, as Dan would say. That sounded much more innocent—and less threatening. Obviously Rainy was starting to sleep in Ellen's room. Who knew why?

It was too far away and too late to worry about it now. The sun would rise soon, switching the power supply to the solar cells, so the bedroom light wouldn't be draining the batteries. As for Rainy, Georgina would confront her when she got home that afternoon.

Georgina had a good day. She only bogged her vehicle once, and then a convenient tree allowed her to easily winch herself free. Only two beasts needed hauling from the fresh mud. The first was quick and easy, while the second wasn't entirely to blame for its predicament. A section of fencing around one side of a waterhole was down. It had been put there precisely because part of the bank of the small dam became treacherously soft after any decent rainfall. An older animal had blundered through the broken wire and sunk to its stomach in rich, red mud.

'Silly bastard,' Georgina said aloud. She nosed the four-wheel drive close, then got out and retrieved the rope from the back. The noose was still there from the last rescue. She shook it open as she approached, the beast watching her warily. After a few steps into the mud Georgina realised she was putting herself at risk trying to get close enough. She retreated back to the vehicle and tied the free end first, giving herself a lifeline.

The mud came to past her knees before she could flick the noose over the animal's head. Georgina grimaced as she clambered back to solid ground, the mud caked to her skin. Scraping it off with a stick helped, but not much.

'Oh well,' she sighed, climbing back into the four-wheel drive and smearing muck everywhere. 'It'll be a good cleaning job for Rainy.'

As she backed the vehicle away, the rope slowly tightened on the bull's neck. When it became taut the beast panicked for a moment, pulling against the Toyota.

'No, you stupid bastard,' Georgina gritted her teeth. She gunned the motor a little, gently adding more pressure.

Suddenly it all came together, the animal flailing at the mud and breaking the suction, pulling free with a rush.

Afterwards, she spent some time jury-rigging the fence up. Without new materials it was little more than a token barrier, but it was better than nothing. Daniel would have to take care of it properly later.

Georgina's first priority was a shower. The clinging mud had dried and hardened, mostly cracking and falling from her clothing and skin, but still leaving her pores choked with dirt. Perspiration from driving through the heat of the day was making her feel sticky, as well. After calling to Rainy that she was home, and getting a muffled reply from the bedroom, Georgina headed straight for the spare shower in the laundry.

She took her time, washing her hair and scrubbing every inch of her body. When she finished she wrapped a towel around herself and padded through the house to the bedroom for some clean clothes. Seeing the door to Ellen's room reminded her of the morning.

This time she didn't wait for any misgivings to stop her. She opened the door. There was no need to look hard. For Georgina, it was bad.

Again the bed was rumpled, but more so. Another book was out too, except this time it lay open on its back. Pages had been savagely ripped out, leaving jagged edges sticking up from the binding. The loose sheets were scattered over the floor. What was left of the book was scarred by crazed red crayon marks. Some of the lines ran off the paper and extended across the floor.

'Oh God,' Georgina whispered, shocked. Her tears came quickly. A small part of her was surprised at how much the scene affected her, but it wasn't really hard to understand.

It was as though someone had desecrated Ellen's grave.

She walked slowly into the room and bent over, picking up the book. The crayon lines were meaningless, just angry slashes. As meaningless as the torn pages.

Anger suddenly rushed over Georgina, too. It had to be Rainy. It was all so childish. *What was wrong with the damn girl? Had she lost her mind?*

Georgina spun on her heel, with the book in her hand, intending to walk straight into Rainy's room and demand an explanation. A distant voice of commonsense made her pause. Rainy would be still doing her lessons, and it would do no good to disturb them. It would have to wait until they were over.

Tears of anger and sadness fell on the blanket as she straightened the linen for a second time. Then she gathered up the torn pages and put them between the book's covers. She clasped it to her chest and left the room for her own to get dressed.

Later, Georgina sat on the verandah as she had the evening before, waiting for Rainy to emerge. Another storm was beginning to fill the sky, but she didn't really see it. Instead of relaxing, her anger was building up like the storm. Georgina realised that she was getting unreasonable, but she couldn't do anything about it. Whatever Rainy had been trying to do or say, she'd gone about it the wrong way—in a *hurtful* way. The memories of Ellen were too close, too *precious* to be used like this.

Rainy's footsteps echoed through the house.

'I'm finished, Mum. How'd you go?'

Her mother turned. Rainy was standing just behind her. Georgina didn't wait, but pulled the ruined book from her lap and shoved it under Rainy's nose.

'What's the meaning of this?'

Rainy recoiled, stung by her tone. 'What? What is it?'

'Take a good look. I think you'll recognise it.'

The girl peered at the torn pages. 'Hey, it's one of Ellen's books.'

'Correct,' Georgina snapped. 'What have you done to it?'

'Oh, it's been ripped!' Then Rainy realised she was being accused. 'What do you mean?' She reached out to take the book, but Georgina snatched it back.

'Well? Answer me!'

If Georgina hadn't been so angry she might have registered the look of utter bewilderment on her daughter's face.

'What? I didn't do it!'

'Then who did? Me? Your father? No doubt you'll say it was Peter.'

Her brother's name died on Rainy's lips. It wasn't that she wanted to incriminate him—they were too fond of each other. He was simply the only alternative.

'I—I don't know,' she changed her mind. Everything was happening so fast—so unexpectedly.

'Are you telling me you didn't do it?'

'No! I mean—yes! It wasn't me.'

Georgina couldn't control her anger.

Thinking she was going to be struck for the first time in her life, Rainy flinched as Georgina flung out her arm to point. 'Go back to your room until you learn not to lie to me, girl!' She felt herself trembling, out of control. Deep down she knew she'd waited too long to deal with this, letting her anger grow. *God, were Ellen and the memories still so strong?*

Rainy burst into tears and fled. Again Georgina failed to see that her tears weren't because of her punishment. Rainy was crying because her mother didn't believe her.

Dinner that evening was a subdued affair. Rainy sat sullenly playing with her food, her face flushed from crying. Georgina's face was like stone. The two men suffered both, exchanging puzzled glances.

Later, when Peter went to his room to work on some lessons and Rainy had skulked away, Daniel asked Georgina what had happened.

She explained, adding, 'She lied to me. We can't have that, Dan. Not out here. We've only got each other.'

Daniel didn't question that, but his eyes were troubled.

It was enough to make Georgina think again.

What's happening? Do we have a daughter with behavioural problems? How do we deal with something like that out here? Then she began to feel guilty. *Was I unfair? Did I overreact?*

They all went to bed early after Peter came out and asked for an explanation, too. His glum response didn't shed any light on Rainy's behaviour.

Later that night another storm rolled over the homestead. Rain lashed the roof and a high wind moaned in the eaves. Peter was the only one who woke up and he lay there for some time, listening. Eventually he decided that a visit to the toilet and a drink of water might settle him and let him sleep again. He slipped quietly out of his room, glancing back along the hallway to see if his parents' bedroom door was open, which would prevent him from turning on a light.

But there was a light on already. In Ellen's old room.

'Jesus, Sis. You're a glutton for punishment,' he whispered, shaking his head. Still, he thought, it might be an opportunity to see what she was doing. Maybe they could talk. Sort things out.

As he tiptoed along the hallway a strange feeling began to creep over him. His nerves tingled. It was such an alien feeling, so unexpected in his own home, that it took a moment for Peter to recognise it.

It was dread. He was afraid to look in Ellen's room.

'Don't be stupid,' he told himself. 'Rainy's probably crying her heart out in there.'

Silently he turned the door handle and slipped inside. The bright light in the bedroom dazzled him for a second, leaving him blinking. Then he saw his sister sitting cross-legged on the floor next to the bookshelf, her back to him. Her head bent, she appeared to be reading a book on the floor in front of her.

When Peter quietly spoke, his voice was filled with sadness and pity. 'Hey, Rainy. What are you doing up at this time of night. Are you okay?'

Slowly, she looked over her shoulder at him—and he saw it wasn't Rainy at all.

It was his dead sister Ellen.

Peter was so struck with terror that he couldn't move or make a sound. A scream burned in his chest, locked there by paralysed muscles.

It wasn't just the presence of her ghost. It was the look on her face. It was still Ellen's face, but its expression of hate and contempt made her look ghastly. Old, and withered like a witch.

Evil, Peter understood through his horror.

Her face twisted with wrinkles of age and bitterness as she opened her mouth, laughing softly at his terror. The sound seemed to chill his very soul. When she spoke, her voice was guttural and mocking. Her eyes glittered insanely.

'Hello, Peter. I'm coming back. Did you miss me?'

5

'THEY'RE ACTUALLY GOING TO try it,' Seerey announced to the crew meeting in the Command Module. Some of them were reminded of the last time they had all met there. Memories of Quantey's loss were still strong.

'Try what?' Celia asked for all of them. 'An inquiry into John's death?' She shrugged wearily. 'We've been expecting that, haven't we?'

'Nothing to do with Quantey,' Seerey said tightly. 'I'm talking about our passengers in the Cryogenics Module. Our "patients". They're going to try and revive one of them.'

There was a stunned silence.

'Which one?' Dawkins eventually asked.

'Number Five.'

'With the ring,' Celia murmured absently.

'I don't fucking believe it,' Dawkins shook his head. 'They can't be serious, can they?'

'They've *always* been serious,' Lyghtson said.

'I didn't think they would *ever* try and bring one back,' Celia half-laughed. 'Unless it's a joke. Is it a joke?' she asked hopefully.

Seerey looked wry. 'No one downstairs thinks we're ready for jokes yet.'

'No, I guess not.'

'Fascinating,' Joseph King ventured, but no one paid any attention to him.

'Oh well, if the stupid bastards want to try playing God, it's not really our problem,' Dawkins said, sounding slightly disgusted. 'So what do we do? Wrap him up and send him back in the shuttle?' He spread his arms, the gesture mocking the whole idea.

'This is where it gets a bit unreal,' Seerey said gravely. 'We're going to revive him up here.'

Everybody started to speak at once. Seerey held up his hand for silence. 'I know, I know. It doesn't make a lot of sense, but that's the way it's going to be.'

'But why? What's the point?' Lee looked to the others for support. 'For starters, the guy'll spin out when he realises where he is.'

'In theory he's supposed to *know* where he is—or at least expect it.'

'Still in space? Was that the original plan?'

'C'mon, Lee,' Dawkins prompted. 'You don't really believe this guy's going to pop up out of his coffin and say, "Where the hell am I?"?'

'Isn't that what they want?'

'Yeah, maybe. But I can't see—' Dawkins stopped and just shook his head again.

Lyghtson cleared his throat. 'Okay Alex, tell us. Why up here? It doesn't *really* make sense, does it?'

Seerey sighed. 'Apparently they don't think the body will survive the change of environment. Temperature is critical, and they can't promise adequate insulation from the re-entry heat. Even an increase of a few degrees might make all the difference.'

'Sounds like bullshit to me,' Dawkins snorted.

'Well, possibly,' Seerey conceded. 'There's also the fact we have the reviving capability up here, and they don't have it on Earth.'

'In other words, they were never meant to be revived anywhere except up here,' Celia protested. 'I don't remember *that* in the contract!'

'I don't think *any* of us took much notice of the fine print in that clause. None of us ever thought it would come to this.'

'It was in there,' Lyghtson nodded soberly. 'Something about having to perform any duties requested by the correct authorities, including revival techniques. I remember I got quite a laugh out of it. It doesn't seem so funny now.'

Everyone took a moment to think about it. Celia spoke first. 'Christ, so we wake him up. Then what do we do with him?'

'Then we send him back on a shuttle,' Seerey replied.

There was more silence as the tension built inside the module. Some of the astronauts exchanged uneasy glances.

'Can somebody tell me why I've got an unhappy

feeling about all this?' Judith Cianta asked. 'I mean, apart from the "waking-someone-up-from-the-dead" bit. There's something else, and I don't like it. Nothing seems *right* about it, somehow.'

'I know how you feel,' Seerey told her. 'But it's probably just John's death unsettling us all.'

'But why don't they make a special mission of it? Can't it wait? Get some experts up here?'

Seerey shrugged. 'So who's an expert? It's never been done before.' Secretly, he had his own ideas on that one. Between Lee Wynn and Scott Dawkins, they probably *had* the best people available on the spot. And while Seerey wasn't one to blow his own trumpet, he was considered the best mission commander currently flying. Perhaps their assignment to this tour wasn't quite so coincidental after all.

'Well, I still don't like it,' Judith grumbled.

'I can't imagine any of us are over the moon about it,' Seerey said, giving her a look. 'But the fact is, we're supposed to be able to cope. We all signed that contract, remember?'

Judith pulled a face. 'I don't think I even *read* the damn cryogenic clause. Did anyone, apart from Hugh?'

A few of them laughed, easing the tension.

'Okay,' Seerey said, relieved. 'Let's get down to some basics. A Remote Lift Vehicle is due tomorrow, as long as the weather at Canaveral stays fine enough for a lift-off. On it is a spacesuit—custom fitted, I'm told—' He paused long enough to raise his eyebrows at the thought. '—along with the serum expected to cure the poor bastard from whatever killed him in the first place, plus a few other bits and pieces that go with the whole process.

Mail and supplies are in there too, of course. Until then, there's not much we can do. I suppose we'd better check him, make sure he hasn't rotted away on the eve of his resurrection.' Seerey smiled grimly. 'Any questions?'

'Only the obvious one,' Celia said immediately. 'Exactly who are we talking about? Who's the lucky corpse?'

Seerey nodded at one of the computer terminals. 'I'm expecting a full biography any moment, but right now I don't even know his name.'

'Who gets to do all the work?' Hugh Lyghtson asked. 'We can't all get involved. We'd get nothing *else* done—and I'm far enough behind as it is.'

'Are you?' Seerey looked interested. It was the first time Lyghtson had mentioned having problems with his program. The worried edge in his voice told Seerey that Hugh was already more than a little behind schedule. The commander made a mental note to check this out. It was his responsibility in the end, after all.

'Okay, look—bringing people back from the dead is obviously a medical proposition,' Seerey said. 'That makes Lee and Scott our best candidates for the job.' Lee and Scott groaned and Seerey tried to placate them by adding, 'Don't fret, you two. I'll make sure you get released from enough of your other work to give you extra time.'

'That's not what pisses me off,' Dawkins said, but didn't bother to explain further. Lee rolled her eyes at him in agreement.

'One last thing,' Seerey announced. 'There's total secrecy on this subject. In fact, they don't trust us anyway. If you try to communicate anywhere outside of NASA's network you'll come up against a dead end. We've been cut off—which I know won't help some of our existing projects.' He held up his hand again to forestall any protests.

'That explains it,' Lee said, turning to Lyghtson. 'Remember the other day?' He nodded.

'Okay,' Seerey sighed, dismissing them. 'Scott, would you do the honours of the cryo check? You might as well get used to working in there. Celia's only recently done one, I know, but let's play it safe. The rest of us carry on as normal, while we can. I promise to keep you as well informed as I can.'

Dawkins was surprised to find the hatchway to the Cryogenic Module dogged closed. *It's not as if anyone's going to try and get out*, he thought. He spun the locking mechanism free and opened the round metal door. He noticed that the opposite end of the access tunnel was left open.

Like everyone else, he had no love for this section of the space station. The rest of Freedom had an almost homely appearance, with funny, scribbled notes and photographs of loved ones stuck everywhere. Elsewhere, too, the equipment was scratched, sometimes grimy and even dented from the years of use.

The Cryogenics Module was nothing like that. The astronauts rarely went there unless they had to, and then they didn't stay. There were no cartoons taped to the bulkheads, no worn keys on the computer keyboards. In fact, the module still gleamed with newness and cleanliness.

Just like its namesake—a fucking morgue, Dawkins decided, not for the first time.

'Hello, patients,' he said out loud. 'It's time for your regular check-up from Doctor Scott. Say "ah".' He reached automatically for the clipboard and was surprised to find it missing from its usual place. He looked around and found it floating near a computer monitor.

'Tut, tut, Nurse Hereson.' He shook his head. 'Very unprofessional.'

He quickly went through the computer comparisons, finishing each by casually flicking open the inspection panels and adopting a bored expression as he studied the lifeless hands. He lingered on container number five, really noticing the gold ring for the first time. Its metallic gleam mocked the pallid skin and bulging, blackened veins of its wearer.

'Personally,' Dawkins told the hand, 'I don't reckon you're going to get much better.' He stopped, a sudden thought occurring to him and he glanced back at the previous container. Dawkins, too, figured the slimmer and softer-looking hand must belong to a woman. 'Maybe you two are married? Is she going to be next?' He shrugged to himself and slapped the inspection panel closed.

It wasn't a strange question, but what prompted it would have frightened Celia Hereson, had she been there to witness it.

The golden ring was now on the corpse's wedding finger.

Lee had already scheduled herself a few hours' sleep. Now, with the prospect of the next few days being very busy indeed, she was all the more determined to get them. Making her way towards the Accommodation Module, she paused long enough to locate Seerey on the intercom and let him know her plans, adding a request for a wake-up call six hours later, if she needed it.

In the crew quarters she found herself alone, which made it an excellent time to have a shower. The frosted plastic shower cubicle offered complete privacy, but you had to undress outside. NASA didn't expect their astronauts to be modest, but naturally Lee wasn't entirely comfortable disrobing in front of the men. Not that it happened that way, because everyone made efforts to respect each other's privacy. But you never knew when someone would come unannounced through the access tunnel.

The shower was an ingeniously simple design. Instead of a normal drainhole in the floor—useless in zero gravity—a similar-looking hole provided a mild suction, drawing loose droplets of water down to be recycled. A corresponding amount of air was flushed in through the ceiling. The cubicle was necessarily airtight.

The hand-held shower rose also had a suction cap. When Lee was clean and rinsed she stopped the water and used the suction to dry herself. Then she went carefully over the entire cubicle, removing any remaining droplets.

Then she peeked through the door and saw she was still alone. Feeling daring, she gathered up her clothes and floated quickly across to her bunk, pulling the privacy screen down after her. She didn't mind the shut-in feeling when it allowed her to sleep naked.

Lee could also rest without the restrictive sleeping bag. She wasn't affected by the sleeping disorders others suffered. She composed herself on her back, hands on her stomach, luxuriating in her nakedness and the feel of the cool, still air all around her. Relaxing almost immediately she reflected idly on her future plans.

Another tour of Freedom would set her up perfectly. Maybe she could start an elite medical practice in Washington, perhaps combine it with a health club and gymnasium. Scott Dawkins might be interested in joining her in that one. She liked Scott. Her mind nearly drifted completely into sleep when a familiar clunking sound brought her back. It was someone closing the hatch at one end of the module.

Lee frowned. It was unusual for anyone to close hatches in this part of the station. In the early years of Freedom it had been standard procedure to keep each compartment sealed from the others in case of emergencies, but those rules had gradually slackened. She supposed it must be one of the other girls heading for the shower, looking for some privacy as well.

Her mind began drifting again as she listened to the whispering, knocking sounds of somebody pulling themselves along the module.

Hearing the other hatch close woke her fully.

Privacy was one thing, but sealing the module was going a bit far. Perhaps, she thought, everything was being sealed? Was there a problem? She hadn't heard any alarms.

'Hello?' she called. 'Who's that, please? Is anything happening?'

Nobody answered, but again she heard the unmistakeable sounds of someone moving around the module.

'Hey, c'mon! Can you hear me? What's going on?'

Again, no reply. More noises. It was as if someone was deliberately moving up and down the compartment to upset her.

Suddenly Lee became very aware she was nude and leaned down to make sure the lock on her screen was secured. Twisting nimbly within the confines of the bunk area she found her clothes and awkwardly began pulling them on. 'Whoever's out there, don't play games,' she called, fighting against the weightless clothing. 'I'm not in the mood for jokes.'

The answering silence began to scare her. Still there came the sounds of someone moving around.

'You wait, arsehole,' Lee muttered, trying to find some anger to smother her growing fear. Finally she got her flying suit on. 'Right, now we'll see who's a funny bastard.' She reached down, flicked the lock off and tried to sweep the screen upwards.

It was stuck tight.

'What the—' she began, then pulled harder. The screen wouldn't move. 'Jesus! Who *is* this clown?' She stopped to listen, hearing the moving sounds again. A feathery touch of fear ran down her spine.

'Oh, come on!' Lee snapped, slapping the screen once, hard. 'This is not funny any more! Open the damned screen.' After another silence, she closed her eyes and cursed under her breath—and became aware of something different.

A thin cloud of steam came from her lips. The temperature in the module was falling fast.

Very fast.

'Something's wrong,' she said to herself. 'Damn wrong.' Lee slapped the screen twice again. 'For Christ's sake, let me out, you fool! Something's going wrong with the Climate Control System. Can't you feel it? *Let me out!*'

No answer. Just the whispering of something moving up and down between the bunks.

Immediately Lee felt herself begin to shiver with the cold. She hugged her arms to her shoulders and was startled by the sudden sound of her teeth chattering. The temperature was falling incredibly fast—but then she knew it could in space. Her breath began to create clouds of vapour inside the bunk. She thought about getting into the sleeping bag, but instinctively didn't like the idea of being so restricted. Instead, she unstuck the bag from the bunk and wrapped it around herself. Her shivering became violent as the temperature plummeted.

'Oh God, what the fuck's happening?' she said aloud. Lee couldn't even guess any more. The cold had already sapped her strength and numbed her mind. Her fear and uncertainty were threatening to overwhelm her. Alarms should have been going off all over Freedom, but they weren't. It was hard for her to understand, because while the space station was always a hazardous place with little room for error, there was also the huge support and back-up system. Very little was supposed to happen on Freedom—right or wrong—without someone or something knowing it. The extreme cold, the jammed screen, even with the lack of alarms, were things that might be attributed to equipment failure.

But where were the missing *human* reactions? Why didn't someone try to help her? Nobody was shouting, yelling for help or demanding attention. It was as though she was alone in Freedom.

Alone except for whoever had imprisoned her inside the bunkspace so she would freeze to death.

Lee's mind refused to dwell on who might be out there now, still moving about and apparently impervious to the cold. *Or what?* a devil in her head whispered, screwing up her fear another notch. There was something really frightening about those soft, slithering noises.

'Leave me alone, you fucker!' she suddenly cried, kicking out at the screen.

It slid upwards a few centimetres.

Lee quickly slipped a toe under the door and threw it open with her leg. The air around her flooded out into the module. Tears of frustration and fear were in her eyes as she stared about. 'What the fuck do you—' she started to yell, then stopped.

No one was there.

It was impossible, Lee told herself. She'd *heard* someone moving around. And she would've heard them open a hatch to leave. Her eyes scanned the other bunks. They were empty. There was nowhere to hide. The shower was empty, too. The hatches at both ends were still sealed.

Her training took over and Lee stabbed at the nearest intercom. 'Alex? Lee here. Where are you? What's happening?'

Seerey's voice was relaxed. 'Command Module, Lee. What's up?'

'What's *up?* What just happened to the Climate Control?'

'What? Nothing, as far as I know.' There was a puzzled silence. 'Are you okay?'

Her mind racing, Lee stopped herself saying too much, too quickly. She took a moment to control herself. 'Yeah, I'm okay, but something just happened here.' Lee paused, looking around. The temperature seemed to be climbing back to normal just as fast as it dropped. Beginning to doubt herself already she reached out and touched the nearest metal surface with her fingertips. It was chilled. 'Look,' she continued, 'something weird happened here a minute ago. I'd better come and see you.'

'Sure,' he replied carefully, 'come on over.'

Lee pulled on some boots then waited, taking deep breaths to calm herself. Her hands were trembling. Her gut was fluttering and jumping.

It was no longer cold in the module—she wasn't shivering because of that. It was reaction. Lee had been more scared than she'd realised.

'I tell you, I was nearly frozen in there,' Lee insisted, challenging the sceptical faces of Seerey and Dawkins.

'I believe you,' Seerey said gently. 'I just don't understand it.'

'Assuming it actually *happened*,' Dawkins ventured, 'and Lee didn't dream it or hallucinate, what's the problem, Alex?'

The two men ignored Lee's snort of frustration. 'For any of the Life Support conditions—temperature, atmosphere or anything—to go bad, the whole station would be affected. You'd certainly get a carry-over effect into the other modules. The isolation of the different sections isn't that complete—in fact, they aren't isolated at all, unless we ask for it.'

'Even with the hatchways closed?' asked Dawkins.

'The hatchways only stop *us*. You'd need some pretty serious software commands to shut off the Climate Control to a particular module. Besides, what Lee is describing isn't a shutdown, but a malfunction. If the temperature control unit failed it would take a while before things began to get uncomfortable.' Seerey stopped and thought for a moment. 'You know, the module wouldn't necessarily cool down. Depending on the sun and how much of the exterior was exposed without being shadowed by the rest of Freedom, the air inside might even heat up slowly. The insulation between the bulkheads and the outer skin is very efficient. We couldn't survive without it. But we still have to control the ambient temperature inside.'

'So you're saying the air conditioning must have switched to full-blast cold?' Lee asked uncertainly.

'I'm not sure it's capable of doing that,' Seerey replied.

'So what *do* you think happened?'

Seerey took a deep breath before he answered. 'I'm sorry, but I don't know—and I hate to have to admit that. I'm *supposed* to know. The best we can do is zap all the info Downstairs for them to crunch through their Crays.' He waved a hand. 'Because if the thing happened up here and our stuff ignored it, then we can't rely on a local self-analysis to pick up a bug either.'

'What about the closed hatchway?' Lee pressed him.

'Automatic too, I guess. You know they can do it.'

She gave him a look. 'That's an awful amount of separate systems to go wrong at the same time.'

'Not really,' Seerey said reasonably. 'The modules will start to seal themselves in the event of any serious malfunction.'

'All those malfunctions and not a single alarm?'

Seerey let some of the frustration he was feeling slip through. 'Lee, I just *don't know*, all right?' he snapped. 'I'm not a damned expert in everything.'

'Okay, I'm sorry.' She touched his hand and lowered her voice. 'It rattled me a bit, that's all.'

'I think I know who your mystery person was,' Dawkins offered after a moment, easing the tension. 'You were probably insulated from the cold for a while by your screen. The noises you heard were all the metals contracting with the drop in temperature.'

'You think so?'

'It's not bad,' he smiled.

'Put it all down before you forget,' Seerey told her, 'and we'll send it all down with a Systems Check result. They should come back with something.' He paused, reaching for a nearby clipboard and removing the top pages. 'In the meantime, we have this.' He waved the thin sheaf of papers theatrically.

'Which is?' Lee asked, already guessing.

'Mr Number Five—the man who will return from the dead,' he added cynically.

'So who is he?' she asked. Dawkins echoed her.

'An Australian, would you believe,' Seerey said, surprising them. 'All this time, technology and money—you'd think an American citizen would be the first to benefit.' He shrugged the question away, leafing through the pages. 'By the name of Vasta. European descent, but a few generations ago. Made his money in a variety of ways, not all of them entirely legal, I would say.'

Celia Hereson came into the module at that moment. 'Who's a crook?' she asked, smiling.

'Just in time. Patient Number Five,' Seerey said, motioning her closer. He went on to repeat Vasta's name and details, then went back to the pages. 'It mentions here lots of allegations and charges, which were quashed before they got anywhere near a courthouse. It doesn't go into detail though. A few things were pending when he died, too. A slippery character, it would seem.'

'Hardly deserving a second chance at life?' Dawkins suggested.

'Well, that's not the point. He's supposed to be the first cryogenic patient for whom they've *since* come up with a cure for what killed him. That makes him first cab off the rank. No one chose who'd get to go first. And don't forget, he's already paid for it.'

'Is he married? Will they tell his wife—if she's alive?' Lee asked.

'Yes,' both Seerey and Dawkins answered, and the commander added, 'but I don't know if they'll tell his wife anything just yet.'

Lee turned to Dawkins. 'How did you know he was married?'

'He's the one wearing the gold wedding ring.'

'But it's on his middle finger,' Celia interrupted, sure of herself.

'No, it's not,' he replied, just as confident. 'It's a wedding ring—on his wedding finger. It was there only a few hours ago. I remember wondering whether he might be married to the stiff in container number four. I'm sure that one's a woman.'

Celia was amazed. 'Scott, I was there a few days ago. I distinctly remember the ring was on the middle finger!'

'Wanna go take a look?' Dawkins pointed at the hatchway and smiled his challenge.

'Okay, I do!'

'Uh-uh,' Seerey stopped them. He held out the sheaf of papers. 'At the end of this is a list of stuff they're sending and instructions on what you're expected to do with it. There's a guy waiting in Canaveral right now to go over it with you and Lee. At your earliest convenience.' A heavy accent on the last two words told them Seerey meant immediately. 'So your gold ring, or whatever, can wait until later. Read this, contact Jack Hitchcock and tell him what you're doing and who you want, and get all the info out of this guy you can. Too much won't be enough, if I'm any judge.' Seerey began to move away. 'I've got a quick job I want to do and I'll be back.'

Dawkins and Celia looked at each other, unwilling to let the question go unresolved.

'*Later*,' Seerey repeated sternly, before slipping through the hatchway.

He found Hugh Lyghtson working hard in his laboratory. The scientist was startled by Seerey's arrival.

'Oh. Hi, Alex.'

'Hi, Hugh. How's it going?'

'All right, I suppose.'

'Keeping on top of things?'

'Well, I guess you know now I'm having a few problems, but nothing I can't handle.'

'Good. I didn't think any different, but I thought I'd come over and ask, while no one else was around.'

'No, no problems.' Lyghtson didn't look comfortable.

'Is there anything I can do to help? You know they don't really give me enough stuff to keep me occupied,' Seerey lied. He smiled confidentially, but the effort was lost.

'No—look, it's just a research thing,' Lyghtson said, starting to get agitated. 'I'm finding I need more time for research than I expected. It's slowing everything down.'

Seerey mentally translated that explanation to mean that Lyghtson's employers may have overestimated the man's knowledge in his field—or that Hugh may even have lied to them about his ability in the first place. Seerey understood the other man's program was not that heavy.

'Okay, fine. Just promise me, if everything gets a little too much, don't be scared to yell for help, right? We're a team up here, remember?'

'Sure, sure. I'll call.' Lyghtson didn't look at him, but kept his eyes on a computer monitor.

Seerey later regretted what he said next. It was a reflex action, prompted by the stress he felt from recent events. 'Hugh, you know this company's got to refund any private dollars invested if the customer doesn't think they got their money's worth—or the work wasn't done at all.'

Lyghtson bristled. 'I'm well aware of my responsibilities and the consequences should I fail to meet them.' His voice had a nasty edge.

'All right.' Seerey cursed himself silently. 'I'm just saying the things I'm paid to say. Nothing personal. Don't hold it against me, okay?'

'Yeah, sure. I know what you mean,' Lyghtson answered sullenly.

'Right. Well, I'll see you later,' Seerey said, hating how inadequate it sounded. He pushed himself towards the access tunnel.

After he was gone Hugh Lyghtson put a hard clamp down on his anger. What hurt most was that he had lied, and Seerey probably knew it. He *wasn't* coping, and he should have been asking for help now. Stubborn pride was in the way.

'Damn it,' he muttered fiercely, bringing a clenched fist down onto the bench. 'I'm a fool.'

6

ONCE LAUNCHED, THE REMOTE Lift Vehicle could be controlled by either NASA on the ground or by the crew of Freedom. Usually it was the latter. No astronauts could bring themselves to let Earth-bound desk-jockeys drive several tonnes of supply capsule straight at them when there was the choice of handling the docking themselves.

The RLV, being unmanned and considerably smaller and lighter than most launch vehicles was, of course, cheaper to use. NASA managed a 'milk run' to Freedom on an average of every ten days for a fraction of the cost needed to fly a shuttle.

Seerey docked this one, watched intently by Judith Cianta.

'How fast is it moving towards us?' she asked.

The gleaming, silvery capsule pictured on the camera monitor screen appeared to be still and unchanging.

'A little faster than three feet a minute,' he replied, absorbed in his task.

'That's slow.'

'That's *safe*.'

'How do you steer it so exactly? So it meets our airlock?'

'I don't. I only bring it close, then the computers do the tricky stuff.'

'That was a dumb question, really,' she murmured. 'God forbid, we should do anything around this joint without consulting the computers.

'I can see a difference now. It's slowly getting bigger as it gets closer.'

There was a beep and a message wrote itself across an adjacent computer monitor. Seerey leaned back with a sigh.

'That's it. The computer's got it now.'

They watched until the capsule came so close that the camera lens blacked out. Seerey pushed himself away, heading for the hatch. 'It'll be docked by the time we can get there—coming for a look?'

'Sure, why not?'

At the airlock Seerey first peered at an indicator board on the bulkhead. A row of LEDs glowed a safe green. He undogged the inner door and went into the chamber. Judith came after him, closing the door behind them.

'What a pain in the arse,' she commented good-humouredly. 'Having to close this one before you can unload the capsule.'

Seerey was looking at another, smaller control

panel. 'Not really,' he said, without turning. 'If this outside seal between us and the RLV is corrupted, or the capsule isn't there at all,' he added with a grin, 'we would lose half the atmosphere in Freedom within seconds. It would take that long for the internal hatches to close themselves.'

'What a great thought,' she said, pulling a face. 'Are you sure the capsule's there?'

'Don't worry, all the signs indicate it.' He smiled at her concern as he tapped instructions into a keyboard. Normally the outer door was opened by pushing a single large button—large enough to accommodate the bulky gloves of the spacesuits. However, this would also start a chain of reactions, including bleeding the atmosphere from the airlock chamber. This was to prevent the astronaut from being spat out into space with the escaping air as the door opened. Seerey needed to work through a series of prompt-and-response codes to convince the system that he wanted to open the outer door but still maintain the atmosphere in the chamber.

Finally the hydraulic rams released and the airlock hissed aside. The astronauts suffered slight ear-popping as the air pressure dropped a little, filling the small, airless gap between the airlock and the RLV. Facing them was the exterior of the capsule—a scorched, weather-beaten metal skin. Six bolts were inset in a circle. Seerey retrieved a tool from a nearby bulkhead and, working quickly, removed the round panel. Underneath was a standard style of hatchway, though only eighteen inches in diameter. Behind this was a tubular space filled with padded bags held in a mesh of netting. Seerey pulled them out one by one, handing the first few to Judith. Each was personally addressed to an astronaut, except for the last two, which were marked for Seerey's attention as commander.

'One's the usual junk,' he told her. 'The other must be our special consignment.' Taking out the last package revealed that the rest of the capsule was crammed full of a bulky item. 'And our guest's own spacesuit,' he added, hauling it out. Leaving everything floating close by Seerey reversed the procedure he had used to open the capsule, sealing everything. 'We might as well send it straight back,' he explained. 'Nobody's got any returns.'

They left the outer airlock and Seerey headed for the Command Module. Judith stayed to organise and check the new spacesuit. Seerey found Lee Wynn and Scott Dawkins waiting for him and handed them their personal mail first, holding aloft the extra packages.

'This is next. I'll send off the RLV while you read your stuff.' He moved to a keyboard and punched in commands. The others silently went through their parcels.

Seerey turned back. 'On its way,' he said, satisfied. 'Get anything interesting?'

'A letter from my grandmother,' Lee said. 'She's starting to lose her marbles, poor thing. I'm sure she doesn't really understand where I am.'

'My credit card company's got a computer with the same problem,' Dawkins complained, showing them a letter. 'It keeps sending me a bill. I didn't think I'd need my chequebook up here.' The others laughed.

'And there's this,' Seerey held out the last parcel. 'The wake-up pill for Vasta, I suppose. You two know more about it than I do, now.'

Lee took it. 'Actually, it's a course of injections for his "miracle" cure. We wake him up with a series of software commands. They should be in here, too.'

'How long does it take?'

'It's three weeks just to warm him up,' Dawkins answered. 'Then a few more days to get him on his feet, if he responds.'

'Three weeks.' Seerey frowned. 'That's over our operational limit.'

'Yeah, I know. I was going to tell you, but I haven't had a chance. Sorry.'

Seerey sighed. 'That's okay. We've all been pretty busy. This thing gets worse all the time, doesn't it? I suppose I'd better tell the others. At least I guess they won't mind the overtime.'

'You don't have to.' Dawkins looked guilty. 'You're the only one who doesn't know—apart from Joe King.'

Lee reflected, 'It's amazing how that guy keeps such a low profile in this place. I hardly ever see him.'

'I know what you mean,' Seerey nodded. 'Okay, I'll let him know.' He pointed at the parcel. 'What about this?'

After a pause Dawkins said, 'No time like the present, I suppose.'

'I agree.' Seerey looked at Lee, who nodded too. 'Let me know how it goes, okay?'

Joseph King still believed. He hadn't managed to duplicate the *contact* of before, but he'd succeeded in touching on the edges of a consciousness—the entity who, he was convinced, was a God.

His God.

But the fleeting images he'd seen left him confused and frustrated. Even after he'd been able to recognise some of their content, the question of what they *meant* remained. Nothing made sense.

At first King thought he was being shown a wasteland, a wide open expanse burned almost white by a searing sun. Next time he realised it was no wasteland, but simply a large tract of country in a very hot climate. The whiteness was long, flowing grass dried by the sun. There was rich, red soil, too—something King had never seen. His excited mind, hungry for some sort of startling revelation, overreacted to this image and believed for a brief, heart-stopping moment he was being shown an alien landscape. Another planet. Disappointment flooded over him when he glimpsed tall, bulbous trees familiar to him from films and photographs.

Within the passing, teasing hallucinations King sometimes saw people, too. He felt a conflict between these people, and also a sadness. Oddly, he didn't care. He didn't think they mattered.

His confusion and ignorance remained like a maddening mist across his vision of a glorious future. In the end he could only hope the truth would be revealed to him. He prayed fervently that it would.

Which was why he was trying again.

As Lee and Dawkins took possession of their new instructions, King grasped his grandfather's Bible in his darkened bunkspace and concentrated, reaching out with his mind. He no longer needed to draw with his own blood or write the strange symbols. King was beyond those gates. Now he needed only to hold the leather-bound book, using it to open the subconscious doors and seek out his new mentor.

For King, his God was still a tantalising prize calling out to him from just beyond an impassable barrier.

But not for much longer.

'I don't believe it,' Dawkins was saying. 'I just don't believe it, even though I'm seeing it with my own eyes.' He was looking at Vasta's hand in the inspection panel. The gold ring was on the middle finger. A shiver ran down Dawkins' back and he shook it off irritably. Lee peered around his shoulder.

'It's all those tests you keep doing to yourself. Sticking those electric sensors all over your body—it's starting to affect your eyesight,' she teased him. 'Boy, Celia's going to love this.'

'Well, you could do me a favour and not mention it.'

'You've got a snowball's, pal. Unless you make it worth my while. What's it worth?'

Dawkins rolled his eyes. 'Great. Give me time to think on it, or make me an offer.'

'Okay, you're on.'

They looked at each other, silently agreeing it was time to become serious.

'Right,' he said, taking a breath, 'where do we start?'

'Standard check first. Make sure we're starting

from scratch.' Lee took the clipboard and made the comparisons while Dawkins watched. 'Yeah,' she said, finally. 'Everything's okay, as far as I can see.'

'All right. You want to read this out to me? I'll type it in.'

'Okay.' Lee took a piece of paper from him and began calling out the instructions. 'First, enter in the codeword to access the Revival program. It's "revive", believe it or not,' she added drily.

'Surprise, surprise.' Dawkins entered it in, punching the return button with a flourish. He read the response on the screen. '*Bad Command*. What gives?'

'Capitalise it, like it is here,' she suggested.

He did this, grumbling to himself. 'Ah! Here we go. What's next?'

'Enter the date, time and location—' she stopped and looked over her shoulder.

'What's up?'

'Sorry. I thought I heard someone coming through the tunnel.' She was puzzled.

Dawkins grunted, quickly typed and looked at the computer's next prompt. 'It wants to know who's doing the procedure.' He looked at her, his eyes troubled. 'I'm not sure I want to put my name down on this thing. I reckon it's going to be a fuck-up right from the start. You want the honours?'

'No way,' she shook her head. 'You can keep it. I know, put in Donald Duck. That'll impress the folks back home.'

'Right on,' Dawkins grinned, keying it in. A list of medical histories followed, which Lee read out from the sheet. At one point she stopped and cocked her head to one side.

'Is that it?' he asked her.

'No, there's more, but—' She frowned. 'Did you hear something? Is somebody in the Airlock Module?'

'Don't think so.' He called out, 'Hey! Anybody out there in the Airlock?' After a silence he said, 'You're just getting spooked.'

'Probably,' she admitted. Lee ran her hands down her shoulders. 'Are you getting cold? I'm a bit chilly.'

'A little. It's this place,' Dawkins nodded. 'I'd say it's normally cooler than the rest of Freedom. None of us ever spend more than ten minutes in here to find out.'

'Maybe. So let's get this started and get out, like we normally would.'

'Good idea. What's the rest?'

She read it out and he carefully typed it in. They came to the last command. The screen asked: *Execute Revival?*

'Ready for this?' Dawkins asked.

'Nope, but we've got no damned choice.'

'Right.' He hit the return button.

The result was spectacular—and alarming.

The Cryogenic Module blacked out. Lee let out a shout of panic and Dawkins cursed before the red emergency lighting weakly came alive. With an electric groan, every system in Freedom shut down, flickered ineffectively, then slowly regained partial operation with emergency power. Non-essential systems closed down completely.

'What the hell happened?' Dawkins yelled.

'I don't know, but I don't like it!'

In the distance alarms were sounding all over

Freedom. The intercom was squawking panicked voices. Thinking fast, Dawkins reached out and jammed his thumb on the call switch.

'Alex? It's Scott. We've got the problem here, in cryo.' He released the switch, saying grimly to Lee, 'That'll shut 'em up.'

It did. Seerey's voice overrode everyone, calling, 'Be quiet everybody! Scott? What's going on?'

'The moment we started the Revival program everything went crazy, Alex.'

There was a moment while Seerey absorbed this. Then he snarled, 'Jesus Christ! Well, stop the fucking thing. Something's got to be wrong. The bastard can stay dead a while longer, until we work it out.'

'Okay, you've got it. It doesn't worry me.' Dawkins looked at Lee. 'You heard the man. How do we stop it? Does it say?'

She had to peer at the paper in the dim light. 'No,' she said eventually. 'I can't see it.'

'Oh, well, we'll do it the easy way,' he said, smiling humourlessly. He turned to the computer, which was displaying the corpse's vital statistics. At the back of his mind Dawkins figured that, with the slow thaw-out period, the readings would take several days to alter. *Who cares?* he thought. He quickly typed in *Abort*.

Nothing happened. The program kept running.

'Damn,' he muttered, and entered *Quit*. Again, nothing changed. He got the same result with several other, similar commands.

He couldn't halt the Revival program.

'Jesus,' he said quietly. 'That's not normal. We *must* be able to turn the program off.'

'You're telling me,' Lee answered him. 'You know, I've suddenly got a bad feeling about something.'

He watched her move to another computer and begin entering requests. This keyboard was a terminal of Freedom's main controlling system.

'Oh-oh,' she muttered. 'Looks like I might be right.'

'Yeah? Glad to hear it—but don't keep me in suspense.'

'Hang on a second. One more check.' Deprived of many of its network peripherals, the computer was slower than normal. On the intercom Seerey demanded an update. Dawkins asked him to wait a moment longer. Lee turned back towards him.

'Notice anything about this place?' she asked cryptically.

'What? The lights are out, for Christ's sake!'

'What about the cryogenics systems?'

He gave them a glance. 'They're okay, from the looks of it.'

'According to this,' she pointed at the computer, 'the Closed-Loop Life-Support System—that's *our* life support—' she added unnecessarily, 'is running at about thirty per cent.'

He took a moment to make his own calculations. 'That's a worry,' he said heavily.

'You're damned right that's a worry, but can you see what I'm getting at?'

Dawkins began to understand, but before he could answer Lee spelt it out.

'When all else fails as it seems to have now, the Life Support should get priority number one in power, climate control—everything. That could keep us alive until help arrived, if we didn't use the Lifeboat.' She stabbed her finger at the floor. 'Instead, *this* place is getting priority. The system keeps a bunch of dead people well and truly dead, before it keeps *us* alive.'

'That's ridiculous!'

'I agree. You wait until Alex hears this.'

Dawkins called Seerey to tell him they were coming to the Command Module with important news, adding there didn't seem to be anything more they could do in the Cryogenic Module.

Everything looked strange and unfamiliar in the red lighting as they moved through the station. Lee shuddered as they passed the Airlock.

'It's already colder here, don't you think?'

'It can't be,' Dawkins replied calmly. 'We've only been down a few minutes.'

Lyghtson joined them on the way, following them into the Command Module. Seerey was listening intently to Jack Hitchcock's voice, the video comm-link lost. The shadows of concern on Seerey's face looked darker and deeper in the bad light. Dawkins waited for an opportunity, then explained what they'd learned.

'That's fucking insane,' Seerey commented, then relayed it all to Hitchcock. The controller, after a puzzled silence, admitted he knew nothing about the unusual priorities and promised to check it out.

Seerey looked pensively at the computer keyboard. 'I wonder if we can override that priority?'

'I can try,' Lee offered. 'Let me at it for a few minutes.'

He nodded to her, then looked at Dawkins.

'Scott, with the Life Support running at thirty per cent, can you figure roughly how long we've got before we abandon ship?'

'I can come close.'

Seerey's request was asked lightly, but his words were weighed with a premonition of impending failure. 'Allow a wide margin for error,' he told Dawkins. 'If we have to quit, that's not a problem, I guess. Someone can come back in a shuttle and fix things at their leisure. We should be concentrating on keeping our tails alive—more than anything else.'

'Assuming the Lifeboat works,' Lee said over her shoulder.

'It'll work. They tested two, remember?'

'Yes. Seven years ago.'

The Lifeboat was the Assured Crew Return Vehicle, a glorified re-entry capsule for everyone, which would splash down in the ocean like the space missions of the past.

Celia's voice came through the intercom. 'Alex? Are you there?'

'Here. Where are you?'

'In the galley. I hope you guys are hungry, because the oven is spitting out meals as fast as it can cook 'em.'

Seerey allowed himself a groan. 'Anything else?'

'The waste disposal's operating continually. I think it wants to eat me.' This got a small laugh from Dawkins.

'Shut them right down, Celia,' Seerey ordered.

Judith Cianta came through next. 'My stuff's all going haywire, too,' she called.

At least everyone sounds calm, Seerey thought.

'Okay, shut it all down. Don't bother trying to save any projects. Just turn it all off.'

'Roger.'

Seerey was about to say something to Hugh Lyghtson, but this time Jack Hitchcock stopped him. His voice floated up—it now seemed to Seerey—from the safe confines of Earth. 'I've got some info coming to you in a minute. Can you stay put?'

'Yes, but don't tie me down for long,' Seerey replied crisply, then turned immediately back to Lyghtson. 'Hugh, can you go to the Airlock Module, check all our suits and disable the outer door with the keyboard. We don't want that bastard opening and shutting when we least expect it.'

'All right,' Lyghtson nodded nervously. A flicker of his earlier irritation crossed his face, but he turned away and the commander didn't see it.

Seerey felt a moment of concern as he watched Lyghtson disappear into the darkness of the hatchway, but dismissed it. It was a simple enough job. Any further misgivings were forgotten as Joseph King entered from the opposite hatch. His thin, drawn features looked almost haunted, his white face a picture of distress.

'What's happening?' he asked.

'Everything's gone crazy,' Seerey explained tightly. 'Joe, go back to your section and make sure anything non-essential is turned off. Everything.'

'I've already done that.'

'Well, check it for me.'

'I don't need to check. I know.'

'*Do* it, will you?' Seerey snapped, surprising himself. This was no time to be yelling at anyone, alienating himself from any of the crew. With a flash of guilt he realised he simply wanted to remove King's morbid presence from the Command Module. He wasn't being fair, he knew, but King had left before he could apologise.

Lyghtson moved through the darkened space station, seething. He'd felt Seerey's concern—his *contempt*—as he left the Command Module. His assignment to the Airlock was simple. Lyghtson felt as though he'd been banished from the important centre of things, the Command Module, as if he was someone who couldn't be trusted. He knew he wasn't an astronaut. First and foremost he was a scientist. But he was older than the rest, wasn't he? Didn't that earn him some respect? Some *trust*?

Angry, wishing to justify himself, but not wanting to be found neglecting his duty, Lyghtson headed for the Airlock. As he approached, something about the place struck him as unusual. He realised what it was immediately. The inner door was ajar.

'Hell, well someone *else's* been bloody careless!' he muttered aloud. He put his shoulder to the door to shove it closed.

A voice came from inside and stopped him cold.

'*Hugh?* Is that you?'

Lyghtson felt the hairs rise on the nape of his neck. His skin prickled all over and his breath caught in his throat. It was the voice of a young woman, and despite the years which had passed since he'd last heard her, Lyghtson immediately recognised who it was. Her name was Eilleen Smithey.

And she'd been dead over four years.

Eilleen was his infatuation—an unrequited love which had burned his emotions to uselessness. After years of steady, married life, Eilleen suddenly came into Lyghtson's world with her lithe figure, flaming red hair and sensuous face. He was smitten, cruelly ignoring his wife, pursuing the younger woman and showering her with flowers and gifts.

Eilleen rarely returned the compliments, treating his attentions with amusement and playfully keeping his devotion alive with a touch from her fingers, a wink across a crowded room. Nothing more. Lyghtson's fevered imagination interpreted it all as encouragement. One day, he believed, she would give herself to him.

Then Eilleen Smithey was murdered by another disillusioned lover, a man enraged by her indifference to his feelings. Eilleen had been strangled in her bed. Lyghtson took a long time to recover from his grief. So long, his wife despaired and left him. After Eilleen, he didn't look at another woman. He didn't want anyone else. From the moment of her death, whenever he dreamed or fantasised, the woman in his imagination was always Eilleen Smithey.

'Who—? What's going on?' Lyghtson's senses reeled. More than anything else, it was his heart that suffered from a hammer blow, hearing her voice again. 'Eilleen?' he called weakly, thrusting back reason and hauling the door open more. 'I don't understand . . .' Still stunned by the sound of her voice, Hugh couldn't—wouldn't—begin to analyse what was happening. Before he did anything, he knew he had to try and *look* at her. His infatuation returned like a wave, flooding his mind. 'Eilleen? Is that you?' Lyghtson pulled himself into the Airlock. 'I must be dreaming,' he told himself with a last shred of sanity. What he saw took his breath away. Any thoughts of Freedom, the emergency and danger disappeared.

Eilleen floated in the middle of the Airlock. She was naked, her arms and legs splayed, exposing herself shamelessly. She looked at him with the smouldering expression he had imagined so often.

'Hugh, I've been waiting for you,' she whispered huskily.

Lyghtson tried telling himself this couldn't be real. *None* of it could be real. He should have been fighting it—or trying to understand it with a clinical mind.

She was the only thing he'd ever really wanted. Even now, years later, his sanity seemed a fair price to pay. 'Oh God, Eilleen,' Lyghtson's voice cracked. 'What is this? What's happening?'

'Don't ask. Don't even *care*,' she replied. 'Just come to me.' With one hand she reached down between her legs and touched herself. Her eyes closed and a small moan escaped her lips. 'Now, Hugh. Please, *now*.'

Lyghtson pushed himself further into the Airlock. His gaze locked onto her body. Blood pounded in his ears. His breathing was coming in such short, sharp gasps it made him dizzy.

He didn't notice the inner Airlock door close silently behind him.

Seerey waited impatiently, then asked Lee, 'What do you think?'

She put her hands up in a gesture of frustration. 'I don't know, Alex. It's stupid. The cryogenic systems are like Fort Knox. There're so many passwords and security checks you can't get near anything. None of us have bothered with this shit, ever. Maybe if we had, and seen all this crap, we might have asked a few questions. Too late now, though.'

Seerey patted her shoulder. 'Keep trying.'

'I'm running out of ideas.'

Seconds after she said this, Freedom kicked back into life. The main lighting came on, several computer systems beeped and whirred as power returned and the comm-link sputtered back to life to reveal Hitchcock's anxious face. The three in the Command Module raised a small cheer.

'Well done, Lee,' Seerey smiled, hugely relieved.

'Uh-uh,' she shook her head. 'It wasn't me.'

'So who was it?' Seerey went to the intercom. 'Did somebody press the magic button?'

Celia answered first. 'Nothing to do with me. I was cleaning up here.' It prompted others to reply.

'Nothing here,' Judith called. 'I wasn't trying anything.'

Joseph King answered next, his voice slow and unwilling. 'I haven't changed anything here for several minutes, commander.'

Seerey winced at the formal address, but left it alone. He waited a few moments, then called, 'Hugh? Are you still in the Airlock?' It occurred to him that Lyghtson might have had an idea and gone into the Cryogenic Module to try it. 'Or Cryo? Where are you?'

He was answered by an ominous silence.

'Hugh? Come on, answer me!'

No answer. Seerey didn't wait for a third attempt. In Freedom, you were never far away from an intercom. 'Celia? You're closest. Get to the Airlock Module and check on Hugh. He's supposed to be there.' Seerey's buoyant mood evaporated. He began to move towards the Airlock himself, hearing Celia's acknowledgement from the intercom behind him as he entered the access tunnel.

He found her alone. A row of spacesuits, dangling like hanged men, were all that was in the compartment with her.

'He's not here,' she said, simply.

'Did you look in there?' He jerked his head towards the Cryogenic Module.

'Yes. He's not there either.'

'Then where the hell is he?'

'Alex,' Celia spoke gravely. 'The outer Airlock door is open.'

'What?' Seerey turned and looked at the status board. An angry red light shone brightly. 'Have you tried to close it?'

'It won't close.'

'Christ! This trip's turning into a nightmare.' He tried closing it himself, pressing the commands to operate the outer door. It didn't work. He tried again several more times, saying over his shoulder, 'As if we haven't got enough on our plate right now! I'm worried that Hugh's had some sort of a nervous breakdown—that damned power glitch could have been enough to push him into it. I spoke to him about getting his program up to date and he didn't take it very well. Maybe I should've kept my mouth shut,' he reflected.

Seerey tried opening the door fully, which worked—a second red light confirming it. Another attempt at closing it failed. He went to the intercom. 'Scott? Can you put a camera on the outer Airlock? See if you can find out what's stopping it closing?'

'Okay,' Scott acknowledged quickly.

It was a long thirty seconds before Dawkins came back.

'Alex, you'd better come and see this for yourself.'

Lyghtson's head and one arm hung out in open space, the Airlock door jamming into his armpit and pushing his shoulder against the sealing edge. Because of the intense sunlight flaring off the metal, the camera's lens had dilated, hiding some of the detail.

'My God. How could that have happened?' Seerey whispered, shocked. No one tried to answer him.

'What was he *doing* in there?' Judith asked.

Dawkins stated the obvious. 'The door must've opened while he was in there. It can't have been for very long, or he would've been sucked clean out.'

'What the hell are we going to do?' Judith looked at him.

But it wasn't for Scott Dawkins to decide. Alex Seerey had that responsibility—as he did for everything else, ultimately. Once again they looked to him for the answers. Seeing their expectant faces he felt a moment of tired anger. *Can't they work it out for themselves?* Immediately he quashed this thought, because he knew that none of them deserved it.

Instead he said wearily, 'Go and get him, of course.'

Jack Hitchcock's voice intruded from the comm-link.

'Alex, I know we've got communications back, so things must have improved, but I need an update. We're worried down here.'

Seerey looked at the screen, his eyes filled with sadness and anger. 'The worst possible news, Jack. We've lost another crewmember.'

They could see the incredulity on Hitchcock's face. '*What?* You've got to be kidding!'

Seerey let out a humourless bark of laughter at the trite expression. He explained what had happened without offering any suggestion as to why Lyghtson had gone into the Airlock. Bewildered, Hitchcock needed to be told nearly everything twice.

'This tour's a fucking disaster,' he said.

'Tell me about it,' Seerey replied tersely. He came to a sudden decision. 'Get us out, Jack. Nobody wants to be up here anymore.' He glanced around at the others. No one argued. 'Pull us out,' he repeated.

Hitchcock's face hardened. 'I can't do that, Alex. You're locked in up there.'

'Jack, we've had two deaths. We've had enough. Bring us home.' The anger in Seerey's voice was unmistakable.

'You've started the Cryogenic Revival program. You've got to stay.'

'Fuck the stupid cryogenics. It's a waste of time.'

'Alex, listen to me. I'm talking to you as a friend, not as a professional.' Hitchcock was pleading. 'You've started the revival. No one down here will pull you out until that program is resolved one way or another, understand? Believe me, I know.'

There was a silence.

'Resolved!' Seerey burst out. 'That bloody program will probably kill us, before it gets *resolved*. Did you know that the Cryogenics has priority over everything? While we're gasping for air, that module is still happily ticking over—and there's not a fucking thing we can do about it. I sure as hell don't remember being briefed about *that*.'

'Take it easy, Alex,' Hitchcock said quietly. 'No, I didn't know about that. I'll look into it for you.'

There was a silence. The expression on Hitchcock's face said he was being genuine—he hadn't known about the priority the Cryogenics Module held over the others and the implications worried him, too. Seerey wasn't in the mood to believe anyone, but when he spoke next he knew he was already beaten. Ground Control wasn't going to tell him anything they didn't want him to know.

'Look, ask them to pull us out anyway, okay?' His voice was empty.

'I will, but don't hold any hopes.' The controller was interrupted for a moment, then he turned back. 'We're about to send you something on Lee's experience in the Accommodation Module. It's not much, but it's better than nothing. You never know, there might be a connection with what happened today.' He paused, then added, 'Don't bother with the last suggestion. It's shit. I didn't think we had that sort of stuff programmed into the options.'

'Okay,' Seerey automatically agreed. 'What about today's drama? Any ideas?'

Again, Hitchcock paused before he replied. 'Alex, according to all our relays down here, you didn't *have* any problems.' Behind Seerey the other astronauts let out gasps of surprise. 'The first—the *only*—indication we had of any trouble was losing the visual communications link, which is nothing new. We weren't worried until you started yelling bloody murder.'

'That's impossible,' Seerey snapped. 'We had major power problems here. You *must* have seen them.'

'I'm only telling you what I know, Alex. Which obviously isn't an awful lot.'

'You've got that damned right!'

'Take it easy. Give me a couple of hours, okay? Let me check things out.'

Seerey gave in again. 'All right.' He rubbed a hand across his eyes. 'Send up that other stuff. We'll see if it makes any sense.'

'You've got it. We'll talk soon.'

Hitchcock's image faded. Moments later a readout began printing across one of the computer monitors. Seerey read it as it appeared. The possible causes of Lee's entrapment and the freezing temperatures were all wild and unrealistic. Seerey mentioned this to the others, grunting when the report ended.

'I can see why he thinks the last one's bullshit.'

'Why? What does it say?' Lee asked, not really interested.

He read it aloud, dragging out the words with his contempt. '*Poltergeist activity.*'

Recovering Lyghtson's body wasn't easy. Even with the Airlock Module sealed off, they couldn't open the inner door because of the air pressure. Freedom's atmosphere, laden with oxygen, applied a pressure of around five kilograms per square centimetre against the door, making it difficult for a strong man to heave open—impossible for somebody in a spacesuit.

Dawkins ended up dragging his suit awkwardly through the station to a smaller, secondary airlock, donning the suit then spacewalking the entire length of Freedom back to the main airlock in exactly the sort of untethered EVA that killed Quantey. Once there, he opened the outer door, pushed the corpse inside and followed it in, sealing the door behind him.

Lyghtson's remains were an ugly sight. Those parts of his body which had been exposed to direct sunlight were blistered and burnt a bright red. The rest of his body, which had been shadowed from the sun, was blackened by the intense cold. His lower trunk and legs, trapped inside the Airlock, were frozen stiff.

Celia came up with the idea of encasing him inside his sleeping bag. It wasn't quite long enough, though, and his ruined features poked grotesquely from the open gap at the top, so they pulled John Quantey's bag down over the corpse as well. Seerey sealed them together with electrical tape. Fittingly, they put the body at the far, unused end of the Cryogenic Module.

It hung there, weightless, like a grim offering. One man's life in exchange for the coming resurrection.

7

KINDLING EXPECTED TO BE taken to a military installation, or a secure government institution of some kind. They surprised him by arriving outside a division of the Bureau of Meteorology.

'The Weather Bureau!' Kindling exclaimed.

'Don't call it that,' Michael Lay said, smiling. 'They'll tell you television stations have weather bureaus. *This* is the Department of Meteorology. Big difference.'

'Best satellite-receiving facility for miles around, too,' Smith added from the front seat. Wiley was driving. Lay sat in the back with Kindling.

A token boom gate was raised and a bored security guard, obviously recognising the car's occupants, waved them through with one hand while he stifled a yawn with the other.

'You've been here before?' Kindling asked.

'We had to make sure the equipment was up to scratch, and we've set up tighter security. Nothing to do with that guy falling alseep back there,' Wiley said casually.

'Do they know about it? The extra security, I mean.'

'Oh, they know we've got a few people drifting about, and that there might be one or two they haven't noticed, too.'

'I see.' Kindling looked a bit overwhelmed. 'Is it all necessary?'

'There's a lot of weird people in our world, Mr Kindling,' said Smith. 'It doesn't hurt to keep this sort of project under wraps until we all get more comfortable with the idea.'

Kindling immediately thought that must be a standard answer—but silently admitted that it wasn't a bad one. 'They've treated us real well,' Smith continued. 'There's a separate room for all our stuff and they welcomed the three navy people we brought in like brothers.'

'The navy?'

'Operators for the equipment and familiar with codes, if need be. Don't forget, the military owns a piece of NASA, too.'

'Right.' Kindling nodded as if he understood—which he didn't.

The car pulled into a visitors' car park and they got out. As the others strolled towards the main doors Kindling followed close behind. Inside, the foyer was cool and quiet. A large satellite picture of Australia dominated one wall. Kindling examined it, fascinated, while Michael Lay talked to a receptionist. Soon Lay turned, holding out an identity badge.

'Got a moment, Matthew?'

Kindling was asked to press his finger flat against the card. The receptionist took the card back and scanned the surface with a lightpen, before handing the badge back.

'Fingerprint?' Kindling asked, imitating the others and fixing the card to his chest.

Lay nodded. 'It's not the first line of information, though. If a security guard thinks the identification on your card isn't sufficient, he can request an instant fingerprint test. Don't worry, it never happens.'

As they walked down a grey corridor Kindling wondered why he would worry if they *did* want to test him. Glass windows on either side revealed rooms filled with computers, radar-repeat screens and communications equipment. Wiley led them beyond the glass and through a doorway set into bland white brickwork. Kindling was surprised at the size of the room they entered. It was large, with no windows at all and filled with a perplexing array of electronic devices. Four people were there, three sitting at consoles, while the fourth, a young woman, was standing and watching their work.

'These three men are the operators keeping the link to NASA and Freedom open,' Wiley explained, pointing towards them. 'We have Communications Lieutenant Czowkowski, Communications Lieutenant Bennington and Communications Sub-Lieutenant Hazelhurst.' Wiley smiled as he watched Kindling try to absorb the names. It was a standing joke. 'If you have trouble with all that, just do what we do most of the time—Huey, Dewey and Louie.'

'It doesn't bother us,' Czowkowski, or 'Huey' offered, holding out his hand. Kindling shook it, then moved across to the others. They exchanged greetings and Kindling again recognised the twang of American accents.

'And this charming young lady is Louise Corry,' Wiley continued. 'She prefers to be called Lou, and she's liaison between us and your government.'

'Which means I don't do a damned thing,' Corry explained drily as she shook Kindling's hand. 'They don't tell me a thing or let me know what the hell's going on.' She was olive-skinned and wore her thick black hair past her shoulders. Her dark blue business suit made Kindling feel untidy in his jeans, jacket and worn runners. He thought her sharp good looks suggested a trace of Mediterranean ancestry. As he looked at her, he realised she was also examining him.

'You're one of us,' he blustered, embarrassed.

'Yes. Three Americans is enough,' she said, throwing a meaningful glance over her shoulder.

'Aww, Lou. Give us a break,' Dewey said mournfully, trying to look hurt.

Smith ignored the bantering and wandered over to a computer printout and scanned it. 'What's this?' he asked, frowning.

'They had a bit of excitement up there when they started the new program,' Czowkowski told him grimly. He turned to his computer and began punching information up on the screen. 'Freedom says they lost seventy per cent of their power right across the board. But that's not the worst of it.'

'Seventy per cent!' Wiley said. 'That's damn serious. What are they doing about it?'

'Oh, they're back on line already, but one of the astronauts was in the Airlock when the outer door opened. Seems that some of the things that *were* operating went kind of crazy.'

The visitors looked at him, not fully understanding the implications. Finally Michael Lay asked, 'Is he hurt?'

'He would have been killed almost instantly,' Hazelhurst said flatly. 'It was Lyghtson, the minerals guy.' Younger than the other two operators, Hazelhurst didn't bother disguising his surprise at Lay's ignorance. Czowkowski warned him with a glance.

'Jesus,' Smith murmured. 'That's two people they've lost in one tour. That'll shake them bad.'

Czowkowski nodded. 'The commander up there, Seerey, told Ground Control he wanted out. Reckoned two deaths was enough and they should all be brought back home. But Jack Hitchcock said no. He says the new program has to be resolved one way or another—and nobody is coming home until then.'

'It even means extending their tour-time,' Bennington added. 'And that's not something they usually take lightly.'

Louise Corry was watching Kindling and the expressions of shock and confusion crossing his face. She touched his arm. 'Basically, Mr Kindling, we're just eavesdropping on the communications between Ground Control and Freedom—with their consent,' she explained. 'We can interrupt and make inquiries or requests, as long as they're not too busy. Mostly we just sit here and monitor everything.'

'And go crazy with boredom,' the sub-lieutenant muttered.

It earned him another hard look from his superior. Czowkowski turned to Kindling and shrugged. 'He's right. Right now, there's not a lot happening—well, apart from all the bad stuff today,' he added. 'Later on, when this Vasta guy gets his kick-start and we try to get some sense out of him, I'd say we might be pretty busy.'

Kindling became aware of a low buzzing noise that seemed to reverberate in his skull. A headache starting, perhaps, or just the result of too much information in a short space of time. He certainly felt out of his depth. 'Can someone tell me why the astronaut died?' he asked, aware he was displaying his ignorance.

They looked back at him blankly, and Kindling felt stupid. Corry was first to understand that he was missing some of the facts.

'Lyghtson wasn't wearing his spacesuit, Mr Kindling, even though he was in the Airlock. The crews wear normal clothing most of the time, lightweight overalls. The spacesuits are only worn during take-off and re-entry. So Lyghtson's exposure to open space would have been instantly lethal, before he even had a chance to suffocate.'

'But I thought—' Kindling stopped. He wasn't exactly sure *what* he'd thought.

'He was supposed to disable the Airlock from within the main module. He didn't have to go inside it. No one knows why he did, unless he was simply confused.'

'All right,' Wiley interrupted, cutting off any further explanations, his voice hard and unsympathetic, 'we had another tragedy, but there's nothing we can do about it. It's just a damned shame and that's all there is to it. They know the risks,' he added briskly. 'Right now, I want to know about that power loss. The problem was fixed? Everything's operational?'

'Apparently,' Czowkowski replied. He paused and Kindling wasn't sure whether it was the lieutenant's way of expressing his distaste for Wiley's manner, or whether the operator was uncertain of his next words. 'Funny thing, though. According to Ground Control, Freedom didn't have any problems at all. Nothing serious was relayed down to Earth, yet it was pretty major stuff.' He paused again. 'It's like the crew imagined the whole thing.'

Wiley thought a moment. 'How can that happen? The breakdown in relays, I mean.'

Czowkowski jabbed a thumb over his shoulder at his companions. 'We're supposed to be the communications experts here, but none of us have got it figured. It means a system, then a system backup, and a systems backup *backup* all had to fail. That's pretty long odds.'

'It's like that business in the Accommodation Module,' Bennington explained. 'It happened earlier. One of the 'nauts experienced a big temperature drop in the module, but no alarms triggered. It's weird.'

'They compiled a list of possible causes,' Czowkowski said to Wiley, 'but it's not worth a damn.' Regardless, he brought the document up on his screen, but Wiley took his word for it and ignored the computer.

'What about the Revival program?'

'It's okay. Bennington's system is dedicated to monitoring that. You can check the progress if you like. It's early days, though.'

Wiley nodded and walked to the next console. Czowkowski stood and followed. Kindling took the opportunity to lean forward and read the text on the screen. The moment he started reading, the words blurred before his eyes. The buzzing sound seemed to increase and he turned his face away.

'I know how you feel,' Louise came up behind him. 'Computer screens can bother your eyes sometimes. Would you like a printout instead?' Without waiting for an answer she leaned past him and entered some commands. Her shoulder touched his and Kindling caught a whiff of scent. The contact struck an unfamiliar chord inside him.

'Thank you,' he said awkwardly.

'No problem.' She walked towards a printer, which had begun chattering. After a minute she ripped the paper from the machine and handed it to Kindling. 'It's mostly technical, but according to the guys at Canaveral, there are some pretty wild guesses, too.'

'What happened?'

'One of the women, Lee Wynn, claims the temperature dropped to near freezing in the Accommodation Module in a matter of seconds, stayed that way for a few minutes, then went back to normal just as fast. Nobody else noticed anything—but no one was in the module with her. No alarms were triggered either.'

As she explained, Kindling was trying to make sense of the printout and failing. Only the last, short paragraph made him stop short, his breath caught in his chest.

'You like the last one?' Louise laughed, misunderstanding his reaction. 'Those Crays are so jammed full with information I don't think anyone's familiar with all their programming. They come out with gems like that every now and then. Poltergeists, for Christ's sake—hardly scientific, is it?'

Kindling's head now throbbed, demanding his attention. Louise Corry's voice began to sound distant. He heard himself ask, 'Why is it such an outrageous suggestion?' He immediately regretted it.

She looked puzzled. 'Well, because it doesn't seem *right* to associate that sort of stuff with a modern space station in orbit, I guess. Do you know what I mean? If it was an old building or something I could—Hey! Are you all right?'

Kindling smiled at her weakly. 'A bad headache just hit me out of the blue.' He shook his head and closed his eyes for a moment. 'I don't normally get migraines or anything like that. Have you got some painkillers I could take? Is there a sickbay in this place?'

Bennington overheard him. 'That small door there goes into our own private kitchen. There's a first aid cupboard stocked like a drugstore. You'll find something, for sure.'

'Do you want some help?' Corry asked.

'No, I'll be fine.' Kindling held up his hand. 'I'll find it, thanks.'

He pushed through the door and found himself inside a small, neat kitchen. It was very clean, except for one corner with mugs and traces of coffee and sugar scattered on the benchtop. The first aid cabinet was obvious, a large red cross painted on its front. Kindling quickly found some strong painkillers. He took three and decided to wait a while in the solitude of the kitchen, hoping the pills would act fast.

If anything, the pain behind his eyes began to intensify, making him feel weak and unsteady. A pungent smell in the room didn't help, the aroma flicking at his stomach, and he began to feel nauseous. He realised he had to lie down somewhere—anywhere, he didn't care—until the attack went away. Kindling guessed Louise Corry could take him somewhere, so he made his way back into the control room.

His attention was immediately taken by a newcomer standing behind Hazelhurst's chair. He was an older man whose old-fashioned dress and manner somehow didn't seem to fit into the surroundings. Another striking feature was his thick bristle of silver hair, which stood up like a mane from his scalp. The man stood silently, one hand lying familiarly on the back of Hazelhurst's chair, and Kindling felt a small shock of sympathy when he saw the hand was missing its index finger. The stranger didn't acknowledge Kindling's entrance.

Michael Lay and the two American agents were still discussing the data displayed on Bennington's computer. Corry hovered nearby, but when she saw Kindling she went over to him.

'I was about to come looking for you. Are you okay?'

'Not really. I was wondering if there was somewhere I could lie down for a while?'

'There's a sickbay a few corridors away. I can take you there. It's nothing great, but it's got a bunk you can rest on.'

'I'd appreciate it. Sorry to be such a nuisance.'

'It's all right. You can't help it if you're sick.' Louise looked uncertainly at the men in deep conversation, deciding whether to interrupt and explain where they were going. She left them to it and led Kindling towards the exit.

As he followed her, he suddenly felt better—so suddenly that the absence of pain left him momentarily disorientated. As though a clamp had been snap-released from his skull, the illness swept away.

'Wow,' he muttered, stretching out his hand to support himself on the wall.

Corry quickly stepped back and took hold of his arm. 'What's wrong? Are you going to pass out?'

'No,' Kindling let out a short, embarrassed laugh. 'Actually, I just got better. The headache disappeared—went away just like that.' He blinked and looked around as if to reassure himself. He noticed for the first time that the others were becoming aware of his problems. He also saw that the stranger was gone. Kindling thought he must have walked into the kitchen.

'Are you okay?' Wiley asked.

'I am now,' Kindling said. 'I had a bad headache, but it suddenly went away.'

Wiley nodded curtly and returned to his discussion with Smith and Lay. Bennington was explaining the details on the computer.

'He's full of sympathy,' Louise whispered. She still held his arm and Kindling couldn't stop himself from glancing down at it. She smiled easily and let go. 'I've got some files for you to look at—some easy reading on this cryogenic process. There's also a psychological assessment on how Vasta might behave when he's revived and fully lucid. That's pretty heavy going, though. Do you want to look at them now?'

'It might not be so bad,' he told her. 'I feel okay and I've looked at psychological profiles before—juvenile delinquents going through the church's rehabilitation programs, that sort of thing.'

'That's a help.' Louise took him to a modular desk built against the wall. A computer terminal and two manila folders were the only things on its surface. 'When I give you these I'll have nothing left to make it look like I actually do anything in this place,' she complained. Louise flipped open the first file and began explaining its contents. But Kindling's attention kept sliding towards the kitchen door, waiting for the strange man to reappear. Louise noticed.

'*Now* what's wrong?' she asked, amused.

'I'm sorry—but is there another door to this room?'

'The kitchen door, you mean?'

'No, apart from that one.'

Louise looked around, although she already knew. 'Well, no.' The answer was so obvious she was expecting a hidden meaning.

'Then he must be still in the kitchen. He's been in there a long time, though.'

'Who?'

'The older man who came in while *I* was in the kitchen taking the painkillers. He's dressed in civilian clothes,' Kindling added, in deference to the faded navy dungarees of the three operators.

'I don't know who you mean.'

'The older man—,' Kindling started to insist. 'But he was standing over there behind—' He faltered, unable to remember Hazelhurst's name and unwilling to use his nickname.

'Just call him Louie,' Louise prompted. 'It's easier.'

'Whatever. He was standing behind him, sort of looking at the computer.'

'Sort of?'

'Well, he seemed to be in a bit of a daze, really.'

Corry called out to Hazelhurst, 'Louie, who was that man?'

Hazelhurst had been listening casually and replied over his shoulder as he worked. 'I don't know who you're talking about.'

'This is ridiculous!' Kindling walked over to the operator. He had everyone's attention now. 'He was standing right here.' When nobody said anything he went on, 'He was an older gentleman, wearing sort of *older* person's clothes. He had an amazing head of silver hair.' Kindling waved a hand over his own scalp and remembered something else. 'And he was missing one of his fingers.' He held up his hand, showing them which one.

Their reactions differed. Most regarded Kindling with carefully neutral expressions. Lay looked at him, his eyes narrowed in thought.

Hazelhurst appeared quite upset, his face ashen. 'Hey! That's my father,' he said hoarsely. 'You just described my father.'

'What?'

'You just saw my father. How could you? He's in Michigan.'

Kindling felt pressured by their questioning

eyes. He began to understand that something unusual had just happened—and he didn't like his part in it. Walking over to an empty seat he sat down heavily and stared at his clasped hands in front of him. He was at a loss for words.

'What's going on here?' Smith asked sharply.

'Something damned weird, that's for sure,' Wiley said, glaring accusingly at Kindling.

'You know, I think you should try and contact your father,' Michael Lay suggested quietly to Hazelhurst. 'Can you do that?'

'In Michigan?' The sub-lieutenant looked confused and uncertain. His instincts, too, told him something was wrong.

'Sure. Just call.'

Hazelhurst looked helplessly at the telephone, so Louise went to him. 'Give me the number. I'll put the call through for you. And don't worry, it's probably all a mistake of some kind,' she added calmly.

'The hair? The missing finger? No way, that's my old man all right.' He scribbled a number on a scrap of paper. 'Look, I'll go to the john and be right back.' He stood and hurried out of the room.

'What the hell is this?' Wiley asked, after the door was closed.

'Don't forget, Matthew was feeling ill,' Lay reminded him.

'So he hallucinated a real person he's never met in his life? I don't get it.' Wiley made a disgusted noise. Lay didn't answer him.

They waited for Louise to get through to Michigan, reluctant to return to the job in hand until the mystery was solved. Kindling sat quietly, still staring at his hands.

Finally she said, 'They're putting me through now. It's been engaged for the last few minutes.' At the same time Hazelhurst came back into the room.

Louise identified herself to the person on the other end of the line and asked to speak to Mr Hazelhurst. As she listened her face went pale and she stood very still. She held the handpiece towards the sub-lieutenant. 'It's your brother. You'd better speak to him.' He accepted the telephone gingerly. Louise immediately walked away to a polite distance and the others followed.

She turned to them and said gravely, 'That's Hazelhurst's brother. The phone's been engaged because he's been talking to the General Hospital in a Michigan city. Their father passed away just a short while ago. An unexpected heart attack.'

Automatically they all turned their heads towards Kindling, who hadn't moved. He felt their gaze and looked back at them, his eyes troubled.

Kindling stared down at the scratched top of the linoleum table. He felt as if everyone was looking at him, but knew that was stupid. Around him was the clinking of cutlery, the smell of cooking and strong coffee, and particularly the sickly-sweet tang of a dessert buffet close by.

'Did you actually *see* him?' Louise asked over the rim of her cup.

'What else?' Kindling replied defensively.

'I don't know. I thought maybe you'd *felt* his presence, or something.'

She was unaffected by his sombre mood. They were sitting together in the building's canteen, sandwiches and coffee in front of them. Regular employees bustled around them, occasionally throwing curious looks at the unfamiliar couple. Some of the men wore envious expressions.

'No, I saw him as plainly as I can see you now. But I guess I didn't take much notice. His hair and that missing finger grabbed my attention.' He stopped and took a bite of his sandwich before continuing. 'Now that I know what was happening, I understand why he didn't seem to *fit*. It's hard to describe, but you could see he wasn't really with us.' Kindling made an impatient gesture, dissatisfied with his own words.

'I think I know what you mean,' Louise said, but without conviction. 'Were you scared?'

'Why should I be? I didn't know I was looking at—at some sort of ghost.' Kindling winced and looked around, but no one appeared to have heard him.

'How come *you* could see him, but we couldn't?' she asked, unconcerned that anyone might be listening.

'I don't know.' Kindling looked uncomfortable and poked at his food.

Louise watched him. 'Does that worry you? That you saw him, but nobody else did?' She let her own thoughts flow. 'Do you think you're someone special?'

Like a replay recalled at the press of a mental button, Stewart Andrews' voice dropped with absolute clarity into Kindling's mind. '*It's unfinished business, Matthew.*'

'I'm not special at all,' Kindling said firmly. 'I just don't know what happened.'

'How do you know that? How can you be sure?'

Kindling felt an urge to snap at her, to stop the questions. But she'd shown him nothing except kindness and consideration since he'd arrived, compared to the professional indifference of the others. And her curiosity was understandable.

'I don't know,' he said again, then tried to change the subject. 'What about you? Are you scared?'

'Not really. It doesn't sound like he was a particularly *scary* ghost,' she shrugged.

'Do you believe in them?'

'I sure do now!'

'What about before?' he asked.

'Before today? I *wanted* to, but I'd never seen one or encountered anything like that, so how could I believe in them? I'm a bit like that.' She looked at him, her eyes sparkling, and he could see the excitement rising inside her.

'But you must believe in many things you haven't actually seen,' Kindling pressed her, keeping the conversation away from himself.

'Not ghosts. Nothing like that.'

Kindling made the mistake of taking another bite of his sandwich, giving Louise the chance.

'But now it's different. I'm sitting here having lunch with someone who's actually *seen* a ghost. After what you were saying back there—the way you couldn't believe *we* hadn't seen Hazelhurst's father—' She stopped and gestured, frustrated. 'I mean, short of seeing one myself, how much proof does a person need? We could check, you know,' she added, suddenly changing tack.

'Check what?' He looked at her warily.

'If you were someone special.'

He sighed. 'But I'm not, believe me.'

'I just thought we could go to a library, maybe, and do a bit of research. There's quite a big one down the block.' Her enthusiasm was growing.

'Why? Why are you so interested?'

Louise thought for a second. 'Well, I *am* interested. And besides, I've got nothing better to do.' Now she lowered her voice and leaned closer. 'It'll be weeks before anything serious happens aboard Freedom. It takes that long to thaw the stupid corpse out. Anyway, we might find out something important,' she finished, sitting back again.

'Stupid corpse?' Kindling smiled with genuine amusement for the first time in what seemed a while. 'Don't you think it will work?'

She pulled a face. 'No, and neither do a lot of other people. That won't stop them from trying, though. It's not a good career move to say these things out loud, by the way.'

'I'll take the advice.'

'So? Do we hit the library? What about tomorrow?'

Kindling began to feel he was being rushed into something that wasn't going to do him any good, but he found it hard to refuse her. 'Stubborn, aren't you? Look, I doubt whether the powers that be will let me stray too far while I'm in this neck of the woods.'

'Yes, they will. You're in the same boat as me. During these initial weeks there's nothing really for us to do. Why don't you ask? Here comes Wiley now.'

Wiley was wending his way through the tables, a tray held in front of him. Kindling watched him approach with a certain amount of misgiving. He realised Wiley had other priorities now, and no longer needed to charm Kindling into participating in the program. Still, despite all the reassurances that he was volunteering his time and services for a fee, Kindling couldn't ignore a fear that he'd been drawn into a spider's web—a web spun from the cryogenic program with Wiley the potentially dangerous host at its centre.

With a sigh of relief Wiley sat down at their table before asking, 'Okay if I join you folks?'

'Of course, you're welcome,' Louise replied. 'We're just chatting.'

'There's plenty to chat about. It's sure been a strange day so far.' Wiley lifted off the top of his sandwich and inspected the contents dubiously.

Louise kept her voice casual. 'Evan, about this morning and that business with Hazelhurst's father.'

Kindling was surprised to feel a pang at Louise's familiarity with the American and her use of his first name.

'What about it?' Wiley reconstructed his sandwich and took a cautious bite.

'I'd like to look into it a little bit more. Do some research.'

'If you want. It can't hurt. I guess it's okay with me.'

'Well, there's nothing going to happen around here for a few weeks, right?'

'Probably not.' Wiley was now pulling faces as his tastebuds sent him unpleasant messages.

'In fact, I'd like to take Mr Kindling along

to the library tomorrow. We'll look up a few things.'

Wiley paused and Kindling interjected. 'Please, call me Matthew.'

They both looked at him, and Kindling got a new impression—that he was a stranger in a close, intimate group of people.

'You know, Matthew's being a big help,' Wiley said to Louise. 'We've really thrown him in at the deep end, but he's not complaining.' Kindling shrugged non-committally. He didn't think Wiley was being genuine. 'Anyway, that's no problem,' Wiley was saying. 'Just let us know if you're going to go too far. You've got a pager anyway, haven't you?'

'Always,' Louise said, giving Kindling a look that said, *See? I told you it would be easy.*

'Which brings me to another subject along the same lines,' Wiley announced, sipping his coffee. 'There's a motel a few minutes away called the Gallander. Very nice, apparently. All the mod cons you could ask for. Matthew, we'd like you to stay there.'

'What? Why?' Kindling was caught off-balance. 'What's wrong with my staying at home? I can't afford to live in a motel.' This last was automatic. Kindling had discovered that the remuneration for his services was very good indeed.

'We'll be paying all the bills.'

Kindling felt cornered. Wiley had a way of making suggestions that left little doubt about what the result was going to be. 'Well, okay—but what's the point?'

'Time-zone differences. The way things are operating, we can't guarantee we'll always need you at a civilised hour, or that someone will always be available to come and get you.'

'I have my own car,' Kindling argued.

'Really, Matthew, it's better this way. Think of it as a holiday. Live it up a little. They've got a great restaurant and twenty-four-hour room service. Enjoy it, while Uncle Sam pays the bills.'

'Why do I have the impression I haven't got a choice?' Kindling asked, half-joking.

'Of course you have a choice,' Wiley replied, his voice flat. 'To be honest, I don't see your objection.'

'No, you probably don't,' Kindling sighed. 'Okay, so when do I move in?'

'John will drive you home this afternoon to collect your things.'

8

THE LIBRARY WAS AN old red-brick building. Dull brass plaques commemorating past public figures adorned the outside walls. The early morning chill was winning out over the watery sunshine. Kindling waited on the front steps. He found himself watching the passing traffic anxiously, anticipating his first glimpse of Louise. He jumped, startled, when she walked unannounced up behind him and tapped him on the shoulder.

'Good morning, Matthew.'

'Hello. I didn't see you coming. Did you walk?'

'I parked at the bureau and walked from there. It's easier. Did you walk from the motel?'

'Yeah. It's not far, and it's a nice morning.'

'Is your room okay?'

'Fine, thanks. It's very—*motelish* though.'

She laughed. 'I know what you mean. They're all the same. Well, shall we go in?' Without waiting, she turned and went up the steps. She was wearing jeans and a loose sweater and, as Kindling watched her figure, emotions long buried inside him tried to fight their way to the surface. Louise twisted around unexpectedly, catching his stare.

'Do you think—' she stopped and looked at him, a glint of amusement in her eyes. 'What's wrong? Aren't you coming in?'

'Yes,' Kindling felt himself blushing and tried to mumble an excuse. 'I was just looking at how you're dressed today. It's different.'

She gave him the benefit of the doubt. 'I got smartened up for you yesterday. You were supposed to be an important event. Usually I'm just sitting around twiddling my thumbs. I don't need to wear a suit for that.'

'I wouldn't have thought I rated such treatment.'

'No, I don't think you did either,' she replied. Kindling couldn't tell if she was serious. 'Come on, then. There's no point in standing on the steps all day.'

The library was almost deserted, the cool fluorescent lighting revealing row upon row of books and magazines. Large handwritten signs gave directions to different departments. Two female staff sorted after-hours book returns and glanced up as they entered. Louise was too preoccupied with looking for what she wanted to notice them. Kindling nodded at the women and mouthed a polite 'good morning' as he followed her towards a bank of computers. Each monitor screen flashed an invitation to enter a query.

'Where do we start?' Louise asked, her voice barely above a whisper.

'Why are you asking me? This was your idea.'

'You're going to be a great help, I can see,' she muttered, and sat in front of a keyboard. Louise quickly typed in *Ghosts*.

'My God,' she exclaimed, daunted by the long list of options the screen replied. 'Ancient Ghosts, Society and the Modern Ghost, Ghosts—Fictional,' she read aloud. 'Well, forget the fiction. Let's try this one . . .'

With Kindling supplying minimal assistance they sorted through the various categories of publications. As they progressed Louise wrote down five books she thought would be worth looking at.

'They're all in stock,' Kindling noted, leaning over her shoulder to point at the 'status' bar on the screen. 'Not many people can be interested in this subject, obviously.'

She ignored the subtle jibe. 'I'll bet most of the fiction titles are out. People don't consider that the facts might be more interesting than fiction. 'Here,' she handed him a scrap of paper, 'these two are shelved in the softcover section. Can you find them? I'll get these others from the hardbacks.'

Kindling read the titles dubiously. 'Where will I find you?'

'The cubicles are only designed for one person. We'll have to use one of the tables.' She noticed his expression and edged closer, putting her finger on the paper in his hand. 'Don't look for the titles. Follow the numbers on the shelves and find these catalogue numbers on the books.'

'I know,' he said, piqued. 'I was looking at these titles. *Psychology in Parapsychology*?' He raised his eyebrows.

'Don't worry about that. It's the author I'm more interested in. He's very good.'

'You read this stuff normally?'

'Just go and get the books, will you?' Louise flapped her hands at him in mock exasperation.

The high walls of books with their musty smells closed comfortingly around Kindling as he made his way towards the paperback area. He always liked libraries. Their silence, calm and, most of all, their wealth of information could keep him happy for hours. In the past, when he needed to relax, libraries had often been his retreat.

This time, he realised he wasn't so much at ease. He had a lot of things on his mind—too many to allow him to relax. He moved quickly between the shelves. Usually it would have taken him up to half an hour to cross a room like this, as fascinating titles caught his attention, demanding he stop and leaf through them, examining photographs and scanning the pages.

Kindling stopped in mid-stride and reluctantly admitted to himself that it was Louise Corry that made him hurry. He wanted to find the books she asked for and return to her side. Louise was just that sort of person, he decided, who drew people towards her. No doubt she had a string of admirers all much more interesting than an ex-priest with no future beyond the next four weeks or so. A small voice inside Kindling suggested he was being hard on himself, but he denied this, too.

He kept moving. Such inner conflicts and feelings were new to Kindling, or had been experienced so long ago he couldn't remember how to cope with them. Since leaving the church he'd led a solitary existence, sometimes by choice, but more often because severing his ties with religion also took him away from the limited social life he'd enjoyed. Opportunities never arose for him to meet the opposite sex and relearn the subtle tactics of courtship he'd briefly tried to practise in his youth.

Louise was different. They had been thrown together into a situation removed from any need for the usual social graces. Kindling wasn't so naive as to hope she might be attracted to him—at least, he didn't *think* that was a factor influencing his behaviour. He did, however, recognise a rather immature desire to please her.

When he found them, it was obvious that the books were seldom selected: their protective plastic covers were stuck to the adjacent volumes. Kindling cradled them under his arm and zigzagged through the shelves to the tables. Louise had four books scattered on the polished surface in front of her. One of them was a recent publication with a brightly-coloured cover which she pushed towards Kindling as he sat down opposite her.

'I thought you might like to have a look at this.'

He looked at the cover. On it was a striking photograph of Space Station Freedom poised above a blue, cloud-wreathed Earth. The title explained the book was an illustrated history of space exploration.

'It's only a year or so old,' Corry told him. 'There's quite a long chapter on Freedom with a lot of photographs taken inside the modules. Nothing much has changed, so they'll give you a good idea what it's like up there now. There's none of the Cryogenic Module, of course. Here, I'll show you something,' she gestured towards the book, which Kindling slid towards her. Leaving it upside-down, Louise awkwardly flicked through the pages. 'There, see him?' She tapped a photograph with the end of her pen. 'That's Alex Seerey, the commander on this tour. That picture's about four years old, taken during his first tour, I think.'

Kindling saw a squat, powerful and competent-looking man in his forties, holding a clipboard and staring confidently into the camera lens as he drifted weightlessly in front of a bank of instruments.

'Did you know about this book already?' Kindling looked back down at the photograph and missed her momentary expression of concern.

'Yes, I bought it at a bookstore. I've been involved in this project a bit longer than you, remember.'

'I know.' Kindling looked surprised she'd bothered to explain. Then he had an idea. 'Tell me something.'

'If I can, sure.'

'What's the point of all that stuff?' He jerked his head towards the street, meaning the building down the block.

Louise was confused. 'You mean, the project?'

'No, I know all about the cryogenics, the funding and all that. I'm talking about the set-up at the weather bureau. What's the idea behind all that?'

'So we can monitor what's happening up there.'

'But why *here*? Take me, for instance. Why

don't they just pop me on a plane for Florida? Why have they bothered with all this expense and effort?'

'In Australia? Because Vasta's an Australian. Everything he's ever been involved in was based here.'

Kindling was in two minds whether to persist. It looked as though he wasn't going to get a straight answer. 'Go on,' he tried, not expecting much.

'Okay, let me give you an example. What if Vasta wakes up, but is only semiconscious, right? He starts muttering words, phrases—anything. The scientists are trying to decide whether his head's working properly and Vasta suddenly mumbles, "Bondi". Now, what would *you* think?'

'It's a suburb of Sydney,' Kindling answered promptly.

'All right, but if you were a scientist in Florida whose only interest is freezing dead bodies and bringing them back to life, *then* what would you think?'

Kindling looked at her. Eventually he said, 'God, they're not *that* ignorant about Australia any more, are they?'

'No, of course not. But Vasta *might* come out with the name of his fourth grade mathematics teacher—which again *might* mean that mentally he's regressed to that age. Let's say that teacher's name was Ball, as in B-A-L-L. The people in America might chase around in circles for weeks trying to decipher why Vasta's obsessed with balls after a spell in the afterlife, never realising the true connection. You see, they really need an information base in Australia that can access everywhere. I suppose, if everything was on computer files, NASA could investigate anything, even from the USA via satellite links. But Vasta's too old. Half his life history is on files that will never be transferred to a computer memory. His school records, for instance. We know his old primary school didn't convert to computerised files until two years after he left.' Louise cocked her head to one side. 'Actually, we're talking about my job here. That's what I'll be doing. If NASA need information on something purely Australian, I'm supposed to either find it, or tell them where they can get it. So *that's* why they've gone to all the trouble of having a Ground Control link here.'

'Okay, I'm convinced.' Kindling smiled. 'Now I know why Czowkowski said they might be busy once Vasta's revived. I must admit, it didn't occur to me that Vasta might come out of it only half all right, or half alive. I mean, the very *first* thing I figured was that he'd be some sort of human vegetable,' he winced at the term, hoping she wouldn't be offended. 'But I didn't consider a partial breakdown of any kind. I've been thinking of one extreme or the other.'

'I know what you mean. Read that file I gave you—the first one. It goes through all the possibilities.'

'I will, maybe tonight.'

Louise pointed to the books. 'Now it's back to you and your ghost. Did you find those other books? Good.' She took them and arranged the volumes neatly on the table in front of her.

They spent more than an hour poring over the contents. Kindling acted as her assistant, occasionally photocopying particular pages or looking for other publications recommended in the text. He was impressed by Louise's ability to research so quickly and so thoroughly, unerringly bypassing material likely to be irrelevant.

Other people began to fill the library, but the table where Kindling and Corry worked was a small island of concentration. Kindling wondered what Louise had worked on before her present job.

Louise interrupted his thoughts. 'This is the only ghost you've ever seen, isn't it?' It was more a statement than a question. As she spoke, she didn't raise her head from her notes. Then Louise sensed Kindling faltering before he answered and she looked up.

'No,' he said, hesitating too long.

She searched his face. 'Are you sure?'

Kindling didn't know why he felt Louise shouldn't know about the cemetery or Mr Williams—although the latter wasn't strictly a ghost, anyway. The lie slipped off his tongue instinctively. Then he lied again, covering his hesitation.

'A long time ago, when I was a kid, I thought I saw the ghost of my grandmother leaning over my bed. It was my birthday. I was very young and I guess I was dreaming. Does that count?' It was only a half-lie, really. Kindling's mother claimed she'd gone into his room to make sure he was sleeping and seen the spirit of the old woman herself.

'According to these, you'll never know.' Louise nodded at the books and made another note. She opened her mouth to ask something more, but a shrill beeping stopped her. 'Damn.' She reached to her waist and quickly killed the pager before it annoyed the other library patrons. She read the message displayed on the device. 'Something special's going on at the bureau in an hour,' she told him. 'Wiley says we might like to be there.'

'Is that an order?'

'No. When Mr Wiley gives a directive, he doesn't mince words or bother being polite. Matthew, why don't we leave soon and grab a decent feed at a cafe on the way back. I saw one as I walked here. It looked okay.'

'Sounds good to me.'

'Okay. I'll arrange to take these books out and we'll be off.'

Kindling helped her carry the books across to the checkout desk. There Louise explained she was working on government business nearby and needed the books for research. Seeing the titles, the librarian looked doubtful, but Louise produced a card and flashed it briefly under the woman's gaze. Her expression turned to surprise and she meekly made out a membership form. Kindling wished he could have seen what was on the card. He had a feeling he would be surprised, too. He tried asking.

'How'd you do that?' They walked down the outside steps into warmer sunshine.

'Do what?'

'The last time I joined a library I had to reveal my life's history before they let me take out a book.'

'You mean the card?' Louise gave him a look which told Kindling she knew exactly what he was trying to find out. 'It's my ID for where I usually work. It's nothing special, but handy for things like that.' Her hands full, she jerked her head back towards the library. 'Gets me out of parking tickets, too,' she added with a grin.

They had cappuccinos and sandwiches at the cafe and went back to the bureau. Kindling felt a twinge of disappointment as they passed through the security checks—he would no longer have Louise to himself. In the control room Wiley occupied Hazelhurst's chair. The other two operators were at their normal places. The only other person in the room was a neat, well-dressed man. He wore a close beard and stylish spectacles.

'I thought you'd come,' Wiley said by way of greeting. 'This is Doctor Maine. He's a specialist in radiology.'

'X-rays?' Kindling asked, taking the doctor's offered hand.

Maine nodded, listening as Wiley introduced them both. 'Yes, though today's a new one on me, I'm afraid. I'll do the best I can.'

'No need to worry too much,' Wiley told him. 'You're here for our benefit, really. The real experts will be watching this very closely from Florida—no offence, of course.'

'None taken.' Maine smiled uncertainly.

'What exactly are we doing?' Louise asked, scanning the computers for a clue.

'X-raying our patient,' Wiley explained. 'The astronauts are setting up the equipment now. The results will be relayed straight back to Earth, so we can have a look at them, too. Because I wouldn't know one lung from another we've asked Doctor Maine here to translate for us. It's a bit unofficial, but . . .' He shrugged.

She looked at the doctor. 'What do you expect to see?'

'Everything, I'm told.' Maine gestured at a file

lying on a desk. 'According to this, the preservatives injected into the body were infused with an appropriate level of barium in anticipation of this very exercise.'

'They seem to have thought of everything,' Kindling murmured drily, before he could stop himself.

'What do you expect?' Wiley looked irritated.

'Does the doctor know who we're dealing with?' Louise asked.

Maine answered for himself. 'The name Vasta conjures up some faint memories, but that's about all. The security side of things is no problem for me.' He smiled again. Kindling thought the doctor was amused by all the secrecy.

'We're getting the transmission now, Mr Wiley.'

This was Czowkowski. Everyone apart from Bennington gathered around behind the operator's chair. Czowkowski now had three screens in front of him. One was blank, the other two displayed identical pictures from the inside of one of Freedom's modules. As they watched, two astronauts floated into view, guiding a large piece of equipment between them.

'The black guy's Scott Dawkins,' Louise said for the benefit of Kindling and the doctor. 'The woman is Lee Wynn. They're both doctors too, but I can't recall what fields they specialise in.'

'Lucky they were up there when this came along,' Maine ventured. Kindling thought it a valid comment and was interested to hear Wiley dismiss it.

'With the sort of experimentation that goes on

in Freedom, it's unusual *not* to have a doctor or two in each tour.'

Czowkowski suddenly laughed, gesturing at the screen. 'Did you hear that? Wynn's asking for the instruction booklet.'

'Don't they know what they're doing?' Kindling asked him. Instinctively he avoided asking Wiley, who he thought might be full of abrupt answers.

'Most people didn't think this equipment would *ever* be used. That X-ray machine's been sitting in the corner since the module was fitted out.' Czowkowski shrugged. 'So no, nobody's real sure of what they're doing. They'll cope, though. These people are the best.'

'I assume this X-ray will be taken through the container. They can't remove the body?' Maine asked.

'Not for weeks, and when they do it'll be the big moment,' Czowkowski replied, glancing at Wiley to see if it was all right to speak freely. 'Those containers look like metal, but the tops are actually a very high-grade plastic. Stronger than most metals and lighter, which counts when you need to lift something into orbit.'

'Fascinating,' Maine marvelled. 'How good are these X-rays going to be?'

'Don't know, but we'll soon find out.'

For several minutes they observed the astronauts manoeuvring the machine on top of the coffin-like container. Cables were connected and Dawkins began flicking switches. Chatter flowed freely between Freedom and Ground Control. Jack Hitchcock's voice was clearly recognisable. Occasionally another voice interrupted with additional information.

'That's Seerey,' Louise whispered to Kindling. 'The one I showed you in the book. He'll be in the Command Module keeping communications open.'

'Right.'

'Now we're getting the signal from the X-ray,' Czowkowski told them. The blank screen lit up and displayed *Satellite link—searching*. This disappeared to be replaced by a completely dark blue picture.

'Here we go,' Dawkins called, his voice clear but affected by the electronics. Next to him the machine began to inch along the top of the container. Moments later, dull white images started to move up from the bottom of Czowkowski's screen.

'Head first,' Maine told them, pointing.

Kindling frowned at the picture. 'What's that? How can you tell?'

'His brain, of course.' The doctor seemed to think it was perfectly obvious.

'But—where's his skull?' Looking around, Kindling was glad to see the others shared his confusion.

Maine didn't take his eyes off the screen. 'The machine is set to reveal tissues and organs best. You can see the faint line of the skull, almost like a shadow caused by the transmission. They can do a second pass with a skeletal examination in mind, but basically they're expecting that any degeneration will occur in the vital organs first.'

As the screen displayed more of Vasta's corpse, the images became more recognisable as internal organs. Maine pointed out the important organs, sometimes tracing them with his finger.

'If I didn't know better, I wouldn't believe this

was the body of someone who's been dead for—what? Two years?'

'Close enough,' Wiley nodded.

'Amazing.' The X-ray was now showing the lower abdomen and pelvic area. 'How old was Vasta?'

'Forty-seven when he died.'

The doctor tapped the screen with his fingernail. 'How long ago did he lose the kidney?'

Wiley raised his eyebrows. 'I didn't know he had, but I haven't looked too hard at his medical history. Not my department. I wouldn't understand that sort of stuff, anyway. That's why I asked you along today.'

'Hmm,' Maine's thoughts had already moved on. 'Shouldn't make any difference. See his thigh muscles? There's a large degree of atrophying there, which means it will probably be the same all over his body.'

'What does that mean?' Louise asked.

'It means he certainly won't be able to stand. He'll be very weak in all areas.'

'Well, I guess that's one advantage of reviving him in space,' she commented. 'He won't need a lot of muscle power at first.'

No one noticed that Kindling had stepped back from the group, a puzzled expression on his face. He suddenly had doubts—but his instincts were telling him not to voice them. He remembered, too, Louise's warning at lunch the day before.

The X-ray reached the body's feet, flickered and changed colour, then reversed direction to travel back up the corpse. This time the skeletal structure was clearly visible. Apparently Maine didn't see anything worth mentioning, for he stayed silent. After examining the skull area he turned to Wiley. 'Very interesting exercise, Mr Wiley. There's not much I can tell you, though.'

'What *can* you tell us?'

Maine considered for a moment. 'Well, for all intents and purposes the body appears to be in remarkable condition, considering death occurred two years ago. The X-ray, of course, would only reveal a serious deterioration. Minor degeneration of the tissue won't be obvious without a physical examination. There's the matter of the muscular atrophy, but that's comparable to the sort of condition you might find in, say, an accident victim after a similar period confined to a hospital bed. If the limbs function properly again, there's no reason why the problem can't be addressed and remedied.' He paused. 'What else can I say? I suppose my professional conclusion would be that the decomposition of the body was successfully arrested. Isn't that what you wanted to hear?'

'Yes, I suppose so.' Wiley smiled triumphantly. 'Thank you, Doctor Maine. We appreciate your coming here.' He stood and guided the doctor towards the door. The others said goodbye, then returned to watching the astronauts, who were now deactivating the X-ray machine.

Louise looked at Kindling. 'Well? Now what?'

'I think I'll go back to my motel room and start reading those files. The next time something like this happens, I'd like to know more about what's going on. Besides, they're actually paying me for this, so I'd better do something constructive and earn my wage.'

'I've got a few errands to run.' Louise looked at her watch. 'If anything comes up, I'll give you a call.'

Wiley interrupted. 'It'll take you most of the day to plough through those files. You might as well not come back until tomorrow. Like Louise says, we can always give you a call if something comes up.'

After the initial excitement of being recruited for the program, Kindling now felt more like a spare cog in the system. Until Vasta was revived—*if* they could revive him—the situation wouldn't change. Kindling realised it would be best if he just accepted that. *Take the money and run*, he thought.

Acceptance. That had suddenly become a problem. Kindling's acceptance of the whole program had taken an unexpected blow in the control room—until then he'd thought he didn't particularly care. Something the doctor mentioned bothered Kindling. It completely contradicted one of his personal memories of Vasta. Right now, he intended to check with the official version in the files before he delved into that memory further.

The files were heavy going. Apart from the two Louise Corry gave him, Kindling also had three more supplied by Michael Lay. Determined not to miss a word, Kindling read each of them carefully, sometimes forcing himself to digest passages full of confusing technicalities. He couldn't understand these sections, but at least he could recognise that they didn't contain the information he was looking for.

He drank too much coffee, which left a sour taste on his tongue, and didn't bother about a midday meal. It was nearly six o'clock in the evening when he set aside the last file. Kindling's eyes felt raw from so much reading. When he closed them, his eyelids tingled with soreness.

Despite the fatigue creeping over him, a puzzling anomaly kept his mind turning over the facts—or lack of them, in this case. Kindling lay back on his bed and let his thoughts drift back to a memory that had leapt unbidden into his mind when Maine innocently pointed something out on the X-ray. It wasn't the last time Kindling saw Vasta, but close to it.

Another funeral. Vasta himself would be laid to rest in a different cemetery only a few months later, but of course no one knew about that. Unless the man already had his plans in motion.

Kindling only ever saw Vasta on religious occasions. Sometimes he would join his wife at a normal Sunday service, and he made a point of attending the special ones, like Christmas and Easter. One other time was the funeral Kindling presided over for one of Vasta's closest associates. This man contracted cancer and suffered a series of surgical operations and treatment, only to succumb earlier than expected.

Vasta had been bitter and upset at the loss of his friend. He'd stood next to the open grave, staring at the casket suspended above it as the mourners gathered, and spoke quietly with Kindling.

'Sometimes, Matthew, I can't understand how this world works,' Vasta had whispered, a trace of anger in his voice.

'It's a sad time,' Kindling responded.

'All the medicine and magic money could buy, and still my friend is taken from us when he's only a young man.'

'I'm sure the doctors tried their best. He was very sick.' Kindling felt uncomfortable, not certain whether he should stay properly non-committal or try to agree with Vasta's bitterness.

Vasta took so long to reply that Kindling thought he might not at all. The older man let out a deep sigh. 'I'll have to take your word for that, Matthew. Myself, I haven't been ill since I was a young child. Never been inside a doctor's surgery.' He shook his head. 'Certainly never felt a surgeon's knife. So, I don't know. I have to believe they tried their best.' He nodded at the coffin and fell silent with another sigh. Kindling used the moment to move back to the head of the grave, readying himself to begin the service.

The files seemed to confirm it, although as Wiley said, they rarely touched on medical history. There was no mention of kidney disease and definitely no reference to an operation removing one. Whether the files were concerned with Vasta's past health or not, Kindling figured such an operation would have taken a considerable amount of time away from the man's other activities. Therefore it should have been reflected somewhere in the dossiers.

So what was happening? How could such a man, so much in the authorities' eyes—if not the public's—lose one of his kidneys without someone noticing? The idea was absurd.

But another alternative wasn't quite so ridiculous. Outrageous perhaps, but not beyond the bounds of possibility. A scenario so simple and complete came to Kindling's mind in a rush of inspiration.

The body inside Freedom's container number five wasn't Vasta. In fact, it wasn't even dead.

Kindling could imagine it all. A 'double' for Vasta was installed in Freedom some time before. Now the authorities were going to perform a miraculous revival. The result? More bodies and more funds for a *successful* cryogenic operation. After all, space exploration was a very expensive business and even in these days of reduced defence spending, each government agency had to compete fiercely for budget dollars. Some sort of self-funding would always be welcome. Of course, the whole thing would be kept secret with the 'revived' Vasta put on display for serious customers only.

Another voice inside Kindling rebelled. It was all so fantastic! Governments were held too accountable for them to attempt such a fraud. They would never get away with it—would they?'

He was too tired. Nothing could be quite so simple, after all.

The questions were left hanging in his mind as the phone shrilled, breaking his train of thought. He picked up the handset and said cautiously, 'Hello?'

'Hello? Matthew?'

The caller was female, confusing Kindling for a moment. 'Yes, that's right.'

'It's Louise. Louise Corry.'

'Oh! I'm sorry, I—I was miles away.' He tried to ignore the way his heart quickened.

'Have you been reading those files?'

'All of them. I think my eyes are going to fall out.'

She laughed. 'Welcome to working for the government. You get used to it. Hey, I've been looking at these books we got from the library. I've come up with some very interesting ideas.'

So have I, Kindling thought. 'What about?'

'About you, of course! Do you want to hear them?'

He sighed, but smiled. 'Okay, but don't be surprised if I nod off while you explain.'

'I don't want to tell you over the telephone. I thought I might come over.'

Kindling faltered as his treacherous heart performed a small lurch, then thumped a little harder. 'Sure, why not? Ah, what time?'

He could hear a mischievous tone in her voice as she replied. 'I thought, seeing as the good ol' US of A is picking up the tab there, you might like to take me to the restaurant in the motel.'

'Okay, hang on.' With one hand Kindling scrabbled for a promotional pamphlet and read the restaurant hours. 'How about eight o'clock? It's licensed, too.'

'It's a date. Shall I meet you at your room? Number Twelve, isn't it?'

'Yes.'

'Oh, good. See you then.' The phone clicked in his ear. Kindling held the handpiece in front of him and looked at it with raised eyebrows, as if it might offer him more surprises. He heard a second, very faint click and was instantly swamped by anger. *Don't tell me the damned phone's bugged,* he growled silently. Commonsense quickly told him that it could just as easily be the motel's switchboard cutting the connection.

Kindling paced impatiently about the room as eight o'clock came closer. Finally he heard the crunch of gravel outside and he opened the door. Louise was smiling at him. She wore a figure-hugging dark green dress, with a woollen jacket over the top.

'Hi,' he said, taken aback. 'You—you look great.'

'Thank you. So do you.' She seemed amused by his old-fashioned gallantry. Kindling looked down at his sweater and faded jeans.

'This is all I've got—in various combinations. I don't own a suit or anything.'

'Don't apologise. Honestly, you look fine.' Louise gestured at herself. 'I like getting dressed up—I don't often get the opportunity. But you look great, really. Are you ready?'

'I'll just grab the key.' Kindling slipped quickly inside and snatched the key with its tag, which activated the unit's power through a security device on the wall. He closed the door behind him.

'Shall we do this properly?' Louise held out her arm, expecting him to take it.

'Of course.' He held her arm awkwardly.

They started down the pathway and Kindling suddenly found himself smiling for no real reason—except that Louise seemed to put him at ease about everything. In the restaurant they enjoyed exercising decorum to its limit, selecting good wines and ordering dishes from every course offered. They laughed often, especially when Kindling got the menu confused and Louise had to explain some of the meals.

She began talking about her research during the main course. 'Guess what I think you are,' she asked, stopping her eating to look at him pointedly.

'I don't know. You tell me,' Kindling said, sawing enthusiastically at a rare steak. 'Be nice, though. I have a very fragile ego.'

'*All* men have fragile egos.' Louise tried to keep her face straight, seeing if he took the bait.

'Ah, a feminist,' he countered playfully, holding up his fork. He realised what he was doing and guiltily put it back down.

Louise couldn't help laughing. 'No, I'm not. And besides, you're changing the subject.'

'You started it!' he said, looking suitably aggrieved. She quickly poked her tongue out at him, glancing around the restaurant to see if anyone noticed.

'Do you want to know what you are—or not?'

'Okay,' he surrendered. 'Give it to me straight. Don't pull any punches.'

She mocked him, sighing at his theatrics. 'Well, you're a "focus".'

'A what?'

'A "focus". It's kind of like a medium, but not the same.'

'This is from the ghost stuff you've been reading, right?'

'Right, except some of that "stuff" is pretty good, I think.'

'So what does a focus do?'

'You attract ghosts—well, that's not quite right.' Louise stared down at her plate, considering her words. She didn't notice Kindling blanch and quickly recover. 'A focus is somebody who provides the energy for ghosts to appear. The spirits actually draw power from the focus, like they would a battery.'

He raised his eyebrows. 'Do we have a choice? We focuses, I mean.'

'Apparently not. You just do it.'

'So why aren't ghosts popping up left, right and centre as we talk?' Kindling tried to sound light and a little mocking, but Louise's theory startled him.

'I don't know. I've only skimmed the surface. After I've dug a little deeper I might be able to tell you.'

'Won't Wiley get upset about the amount of time you're spending on something unrelated to the program?'

'Not yet. There's nothing else to do, and I like to keep my mind busy.'

Kindling decided he wanted to end the subject. 'Well, let me know if Frankenstein's monster is suddenly going to appear and ruin our meal, okay?'

'That was a monster, silly. Not a ghost.' She fixed him with a look which, Kindling was beginning to learn, meant an important question was coming next. 'You asked me in the canteen if I believed in ghosts, remember?'

'Sure.'

'What about you? Do you believe in them?'

'I suppose I have to now,' he replied carefully.

'But what about your background in the church? Doesn't that affect you?'

He leaned back and smiled gently. 'I thought

you were leading to something.' Kindling looked at her and tried to decide whether he wanted to explain or not. He realised he did, without really knowing why. He began cautiously, ignoring his meal for the moment.

'My church embraced the idea of teaching the difference between good and bad. How to treat your fellow human beings, and all the other tenets of the Bible. We called ourselves a modern religion because we had one main deviation from the accepted *methods* of Christianity.' Kindling grimaced as he found himself already in too heavy a discussion. He tried to take a short cut. 'We believed in God and all the trimmings that go with Him—but we didn't push *Him*.' Louise watched him expectantly, waiting for him to continue. 'So, basically, we promoted the lessons and teachings of the Bible without suggesting too often that there was somebody up there watching to see if you learnt those lessons. We found people were quite receptive to being *guided* by the Bible, as long as we didn't force upon them a scientifically-unsupported theory of a Greater Being.' Kindling paused, then shrugged and went on. 'It was always a fine line to draw and we attracted a lot of criticism, most of it valid. It's no longer my argument, I'm happy to say. That's one thing I don't miss—continually having to defend our own brand of faith.'

'So why did you leave?'

Kindling knew this question was coming. He wished he had the courage to refuse to answer, but he didn't. Not to Louise, anyway. He didn't want to sound churlish and ruin the evening.

'I discovered there was more to religion and

Christianity than I could accept,' he said simply, hoping his tone would dissuade her from pursuing the subject.

'That sounds like a rather daunting discussion to have over dinner,' she said, reading his thoughts.

'It is a bit.'

They were interrupted by a waiter suggesting another bottle of wine, which they accepted. Kindling thought it might be a good time to try a little digging himself.

'So how do you manage to go out for dinner with strange men?' he asked. 'Don't you have somebody wondering where you are?'

'Not really,' she shrugged, her glass at her lips. 'I've got a few friends. Quite honestly, I'm often too busy to get out much. That's why I talked you into this. I work odd hours.'

'Where do you normally work?'

She looked sly. 'Now that would be telling.' Kindling felt mildly cheated and it must have shown on his face, because she laughed and added, 'Actually, I'm an assistant for a government high-up. She's always attending dinners or guest-speaking at functions. It forces me to have long days, too.' Louise quickly changed the subject. 'Anyway, what about you? I know you're not married, but is there anyone special?'

'Goodness, no!' Kindling was surprised anybody could think such a thing.

'Why so shocked? Is it against your religion?'

Kindling figured she wasn't being serious. 'No, but I guess it might as well have been. While I *was* with the church, it simply wouldn't have worked to have a partner. Sometimes I felt I didn't have a single minute to spare for myself, let alone someone special. And since then, well, I don't get out much, either. That's probably why I'm not doing a very good job of this,' he gestured self-consciously at the restaurant.

'It's okay, you're doing fine,' she told him.

With some of the barriers down the remainder of the dinner passed in pleasant conversation. They swapped stories, neither pressing for more details about the other's personal life, as though there were a tacit agreement that enough was enough. Louise didn't mention ghosts either, sensing Kindling's discomfort about the subject.

For the rest of the evening, Kindling felt wonderfully at ease. The only tension arose when they said their goodbyes. They walked, arm in arm again, back to his motel room. As Kindling inserted the key he felt suddenly awkward, not knowing what he should do or say.

'Would you like to come in for a coffee?' he asked finally. 'I bought some real milk. I can't handle that long-life stuff.'

'No, I'd better not,' said Louise, without her usual self-assuredness. 'We should put in an appearance at the bureau early tomorrow morning.'

'I suppose so. Well, thank you for a lovely night.'

'No, thank *you*. You paid, remember?'

'Uncle Sam, really.' He watched her walk back towards her car.

On impulse she turned and said, 'Hey, why don't we meet for breakfast at that cafe? Say, at seven-thirty? We could plan our day before Mr Wiley has a chance to do it for us. And I'd like to start having something decent to eat at the beginning of the day.'

'Sure, I'd love to.' Kindling felt relieved. The breakfast meeting gave the evening a sort of satisfying conclusion.

He stood at the doorway, waving until her car's tail-lights disappeared down the motel driveway.

Kindling's good mood lasted through breakfast the next day. Then, as he and Louise walked into the bureau Control Room Evan Wiley brought them rudely back to the real world.

'Where the hell have you two been?' he snapped. Wiley looked drawn and fatigued. His tie was loosened untidily around his neck.

'Having breakfast,' Louise replied innocently. 'Why? Is something wrong?'

Instead of answering her, Wiley turned to Kindling. 'How often do you see ghosts, Mr Kindling? All the time? Any time you wish, perhaps?' His tone was strained, almost sneering. The question took Kindling by surprise.

'Why—I don't, of course. I mean, apart from the other day.' Kindling felt helpless, then a spark of anger ignited inside him. 'If you have something to say, I suggest you say it. Is there a rule against Miss Corry and I sharing breakfast?'

Wiley answered with another question. 'Have you got your pager on?' He looked at Louise.

'Yes.' She dug it out of her bag and checked it. Her expression changed to a mixture of guilt and anger at herself. 'No,' she admitted. 'It must have got turned off, rattling around in my bag. I'll make sure I wear it from now on. I'm sorry.'

'Do that,' Wiley said. 'Matthew, would you mind coming over here and looking at something?'

Kindling thought about protesting again. Wiley's manner was still sharp and condescending. He decided to wait a while and see if the American calmed down. 'Okay, what are we looking for?'

'Just watch.' Wiley touched Czowkowski on the shoulder asking, 'Huey, can we ask Freedom for another visual check?'

'I've still got access from the last one,' Czowkowski replied calmly. He managed to glance a greeting at the others.

'Okay, good. Let's start from the top, right through to twenty-two.' Wiley faced Kindling. 'There are twenty-two internal and external cameras throughout Freedom. Huey here is going to take us through each internal one, showing the view the camera's seeing on that screen there,' he pointed. 'I want you to watch carefully and tell me what you see, all right?'

'But I won't recognise any of it,' Kindling protested.

'Then just tell us what you *do* know, okay? Let's roll it, Czowkowski.' Wiley didn't wait for any more objections.

The screen slowly flicked through the different sections of Freedom. After the first three, with Kindling muttering 'I don't know,' and feeling stupid each time, Czowkowski held the picture for a short while, then moved on without waiting for a comment. The sixth camera showed some of the crew.

'Astronauts.' Kindling resented being led like a child in this way.

'How many?' Wiley asked, strangely.

'Two.' Kindling leaned closer to make sure. 'Only two.'

The screen changed. It took nearly five minutes to cover all the cameras, during which Kindling pointed out the other four surviving crewmembers, Lyghtson's body, and recognised the Command Module.

'Nothing else?' Wiley gave him a sharp look. 'Are you sure?'

Kindling snapped, 'I don't know! What the hell am I looking for?'

'Any ghosts?'

'No, of course I didn't see any damned ghost!'

Wiley took a deep breath, looked at the ceiling and let out a long, whistling sigh. 'Well, there's supposed to be one there somewhere,' he announced tiredly. 'As of early this morning. Celia Hereson said she was confronted by a ghostly spirit.'

Kindling and Louise stared at him, stunned by the news. The two operators and Wiley watched them, anticipating their reaction.

'A ghost?' A cold feeling touched the pit of Kindling's stomach. 'The ghost of who?' Somehow he expected it to be one of the dead astronauts.

'Oh, we don't know *who*,' Wiley said. 'That's half the problem.' He looked at Kindling, then Louise. 'Hereson saw it quite clearly. It even spoke to her. But we don't know who it is, because nobody's ever seen her before—'

'Her?' Louise interrupted.

'Yes, *her*.' Wiley let out a snort of disbelief. 'A girl. A little girl about six or seven years old.'

9

TIME FROZE FOR PETER LITTLEWOOD as he stood paralysed with fear, staring into the terrible, grinning face of his dead sister. It might have been only a matter of seconds, a minute at most, but it felt like hours. The longest, most terrifying hours of his young life.

The spell broke and Peter ran headlong from the room, his shoulder crashing painfully into the doorframe as he went. Mocking, girlish laughter filled his mind and seemed to echo down the empty hallway as he fought with the doorknob to his parents' bedroom. His hands were soaked with sweat, and slipped on the simple, old-fashioned brass knob.

'Who's there?' his mother called sleepily, but

he was too absorbed to reply. The door suddenly gave way and he fell into the room.

'Who is it? What's wrong?' Georgina asked, fumbling for her bedside lamp. The soft light showed her face puffed from sleep. Daniel rolled over and squinted painfully at his son.

'Peter? Are you okay?'

Peter stood strangely at the foot of their bed, intense emotions working on his face, his limbs trembling. Having fled into the imagined sanctuary of his parents' room he now fought a childish urge to cry hysterically and bury himself in the bedsheets between his mother and father. The older, maturing youth in him stopped on the edge of breaking down and demanded he stand his ground and hold onto his courage. He knew, somehow, that Ellen's spirit had gone from the next room, fading mockingly with her malicious laughter, but the residue of his fear was strong and filled his mind.

'Peter, for God's sake, what's the matter?' Through sleep-misted eyes, Georgina saw that he was in some sort of trouble. A distant warning note sounded in her mind, like a far-off church bell.

Her own instincts said that something in their lives had just started to go terribly wrong.

'I—I just saw Ellen.' Peter choked on the words. His eyes filled with tears.

Georgina went pale, but Daniel relaxed, believing that his son's crisis wasn't real, but somehow imagined—dreamed, most likely. After Ellen's death there had been a long time when they'd all slept badly and suffered black dreams. He sighed and managed to smile reassuringly.

'Sit down, Pete,' Daniel said gently, patting the

bed with the palm of his hand. 'You've had a bad nightmare. We all had them, remember? Sit down and talk to us for a while. You'll wind down in a minute.' He glanced at his wife, silently saying, *I thought we were all through this stage? Nightmares, now?* He was surprised to see that she had turned quite white and seemed very disturbed, staring at Peter as though with dread. Daniel reached out and touched her arm. 'Come on, love,' he said softly. 'He's just had a bad dream, that's all. You take it easy, too.' For a moment he felt resentful at being wrenched from his comfortable sleep to contend with two overwrought members of his family. He clamped down hard on the thought.

'It wasn't a nightmare, Dad,' Peter insisted flatly, trying to keep the tremor from his voice. 'I was wide awake. It was Ellen's ghost.' His eyes pleaded with them to believe him. It was this, more than anything, that made Daniel and Georgina realise they were dealing with something different this time. Something frightening. Looking at his terrified son, a worm of unease uncoiled in Daniel's stomach.

'Where? Where did you see her?' Georgina asked, her voice troubled.

'In her room.'

Expecting him to say more, they watched Peter lower himself unsteadily to sit at the end of the bed. Instead, he stared unseeingly at the wall. Georgina crawled out from under the sheet and down the length of the mattress, her thin nightdress tangling briefly around her knees. She sat next to him and put an arm around his shoulders.

'What were you doing in there?' Daniel asked

gently, still not wanting to accept any of it.

'I saw the light on—under the door. I was going to the toilet. I thought it might be Rainy again and I wanted to check her out, ask her what the problem was.' He stopped and went on staring at nothing. Georgina realised he was suffering from a mild form of shock and looked with concern at Daniel.

'And?' Daniel prodded.

'I saw her sitting there. She had her back to me, reading one of her books on the floor like she always used to. At first, I thought it *was* Rainy and I asked her what she was doing. Then she turned around and I could see it was *Ellen.*' Peter's voice broke and he took a few shuddering breaths. 'She looked terrible. *Ugly*. It was Ellen, but it *wasn't* Ellen. It's—it's hard to describe. She spoke to me.'

'She spoke?' Georgina gasped, shaken. 'What did she say?' She had to ask, yet she was afraid of the answer.

'She said she was coming back, and asked if I missed her.'

There was a long silence between the three of them. Twice Peter glanced uneasily at the doorway. Georgina followed his gaze and a chill ran down her back. She had no idea how she might react if the ghost of her dead daughter were suddenly to walk into the room. *Looking ugly. Terrible.*

'Peter,' Daniel had to stop and clear his throat. 'Are you sure you didn't dream this? You didn't walk straight from your bedroom into ours?'

Peter's voice was hoarse. 'No, Dad. I saw her. It was real.'

No one wanted to move or say anything. 'I'd better take a look, then,' Daniel decided heavily.

Georgina was startled. 'What? Can't it wait until morning?' Immediately she knew it couldn't.

'No, of course not,' Daniel told her, climbing out of bed.

'Then I'm coming, too,' Georgina announced, standing up. She looked down at Peter. 'Perhaps you'd better stay here.'

'It doesn't matter,' he shrugged tiredly. 'I think she's gone now.'

'How do you know?' asked Daniel, turning from the doorway.

'I don't know. I just *know* she's gone.' Peter got off the bed and tagged reluctantly behind as Daniel, followed closely by Georgina, went out into the hallway.

The door to Ellen's room was slightly ajar, letting a narrow oblong of light spill out onto the hallway floor. Daniel took a deep breath and pushed the door, slowly swinging it wide open.

The bedroom looked empty.

He edged through the entrance, trying to look in every direction at once. It was his little girl's room, the same as it always had been. Daniel, too, had spent many lonely hours in here. He heard Georgina's footsteps just behind him. He walked further into the room and turned to her.

'No one here.'

Georgina didn't know whether she was relieved or oddly disappointed. 'No,' she said quietly.

'I told you,' Peter called from outside the doorway. 'She's gone.'

His parents didn't answer him. 'I think it's colder in here, isn't it?' Daniel asked. 'Much colder than it should be.'

'Well, this room's been shut up.'

'But that wouldn't make it cooler—and look,' he pointed. Georgina noticed it at the same time. One of the books from the shelf lay open on the floor.

'Daniel, could he have imagined it? Dreamed it and sleepwalked in here, perhaps?' she asked desperately.

Peter still stood in the doorway, watching and listening.

'I don't know. Possibly, I suppose.' Daniel felt as if a great weight had settled on his shoulders. Sadly he bent and picked up the book. As he placed it back into the empty space on the shelf he was stunned to see another book pop out of its position and fall to the floor.

'What the—'

The neat lines of books and toys suddenly erupted out of the bookcase. In a blur of movement everything was hurled from the shelves and began to whirl around the centre of the room in a mad maelstrom, bouncing off the walls and ceiling. Georgina screamed and quickly ran out of the room, pushing Peter ahead of her. Daniel yelled, too, cowering away from the hail of missiles. He shouted again as a hard-edged book caught him a blow on the temple and he threw his arms up to protect himself. Through his panic he heard a heavy, threatening, thumping sound.

'Get out! Get out of here!' he yelled, unaware Georgina had already fled to safety. Staggering through the door, he turned to slam it behind him. Despite the danger and his fear, he was shocked to a standstill by the scene in the bedroom.

Ellen's clothes and other possessions were now also flying madly about the room, careering off the walls, floor and ceiling like trapped insects trying to escape. The room was being wrecked. Even the bed was ponderously lifting itself from the floor and falling back with a slow, steady rhythm.

Daniel groaned an oath to cover his emotions—fear, disbelief and utter astonishment. He reached in quickly and pulled the door shut.

No sounds came through the wooden panelling. It was as if everything had stopped the moment the door was shut.

Daniel looked into the frightened eyes of his wife and son. 'What the hell is going on here?' he asked thickly.

Before either of them could reply, Rainy's voice came from the other end of the hallway, making them jump.

'What's happening?' she echoed her father. 'Why's everyone awake? And what was that noise?' She looked small and forlorn in her white nightdress. In the dim light Georgina was suddenly struck by how much she resembled Ellen when she had been that age.

Daniel recovered quickly. 'Grab your blanket and a pillow,' he told Rainy in a manner that brooked no argument. He didn't feel capable of explaining anyway. 'I want you to sleep in our room tonight, with us. You too, Peter,' he turned to his son. 'But drag your mattress in with you. You two can sleep on the floor next to our bed. I don't want you to be alone.'

Rainy took it all calmly. She looked at the three of them huddled together at the other end of the hallway, then she seemed to gaze right through them and into the room beyond.

'That's not Ellen,' she announced unexpectedly, sounding sad and lost. 'She wouldn't do any of that.'

Next morning the Littlewoods slowly gathered in the kitchen. Usually they all bustled around each other like peak hour commuters, readying themselves for the new day between snatches of toast and cups of half-consumed coffee. Instead, they sat around the heavy wooden table, waiting for someone to take the initiative. Earlier that morning the two children had slipped out of their parents' bedroom and back to their own rooms, feeling safer with the first light of dawn. At the table Peter's eyes were gummed through lack of sleep. He blinked as steam from his coffee irritated them. Rainy stayed quiet, unsure what might happen.

Daniel and Georgina joined them, but nothing was said about Ellen or her room. Georgina automatically went about cooking them a big breakfast, taking advantage of the fact that they were all at the table at once. The meal was a subdued affair of muted voices and the scraping of cutlery on plates. Finally Daniel sighed, and the determined way he put his empty cup on the table announced that he was about to say something.

'Peter,' he said quietly. 'I'm sending you out on your own today—well, perhaps. Now that the small dam has a decent level in it, we can afford to bring in the pump on the west bore. It needs a full overhaul and I'd rather do it here, on the workshop bench, than struggle with it out in the open. We've been pushing our luck with that thing for six months now. This rain's a good opportunity to fix it properly. I've got a few things I want to do around here today,' Daniel glanced at Georgina, 'including servicing the generator. If we get our usual run of storms from now on, it'll be working pretty hard for a while. It's something I should have done before now.'

'Okay, Dad.' Peter brightened. He liked going out on his own.

'We need something for the dogs,' Georgina reminded him.

'Right. Well, take the triple-two,' Daniel told him. 'There's ammunition already in the glove box of the truck. Try and make it a 'roo. The donkeys are thin enough.' Donkeys—like kangaroos—were considered a pest because of the amount of feed they consumed. However, they could be relied upon to dig for water in dry creekbeds during droughts, which the cattle wouldn't, although the cattle drank from the holes the donkeys dug. For this reason Daniel opted to keep a small population of the pest on the property.

He turned to Rainy. 'If you want, you can record your lessons and go out with Peter. It's up to you.' Daniel saw the protest forming on his son's face and silenced him with a look.

'I'll be all right,' Rainy decided. 'Anyway, I don't want to go out if Peter's going to be shooting.'

'Are you sure?' Daniel frowned, imagining everyone would be keen to get away from the house for a while.

'Sure, I'm sure.' She gazed back at him.

They split up soon afterwards. Peter collected

the rifle from the gun cupboard, giving the heavier .308 a wistful look, while Georgina made him a snack to take with him. He departed happily, whistling for the two young dogs to keep him company. Rainy went back to her room to read and finish some schoolwork before her first lesson of the day began. Daniel and Georgina found themselves alone in the kitchen.

'So what are *we* going to do?' she asked.

'I think we have to have another look,' he said grimly.

'Yes, I thought so.'

They walked together out of the kitchen, through the living area and into the hallway. Pausing at Rainy's door they listened to her humming the bland music that accompanied the satellite link test pattern. Satisfied, they moved on. The door to Ellen's room looked ominous in the gloom of the hallway. Georgina wished they'd turned on a light. Without any of the other doors open, the passageway was always in darkness, even in the daylight.

They got to the end of the hall. 'You ready for this?' he asked. She nodded and he reached out, grasping the doorknob. With a cry of surprise Daniel jerked his hand back again quickly.

Georgina stayed calm, guessing what had happened—that strange feeling that seemed to come from touching the door. 'Are you all right?'

'Yeah, but that was weird.' He checked his hand. 'It's not like it hurt. It wasn't even painful, really. More like a—a *jolt*,' he finished uncertainly. Daniel put his hand out again, this time tapping the doorknob with his fingers, testing it. 'Nothing there now,' he decided. He took a breath, braced himself, then twisted the knob and pushed the door wide open, as he had the night before.

The room was impeccably neat and tidy.

Everything was where it should be. The bookcase was carefully stacked, segmented as always by Ellen's collection of dolls and favourite toys. The cupboard was closed. The bed was made perfectly, the top blanket tucked in and stretched taut.

'That's impossible,' Daniel whispered, walking slowly into the bedroom. 'You saw it, didn't you? Everything was all over the place, flying around.'

'Of course I remember. How could I forget?' Georgina looked stunned.

'So who tidied it? The kids, this morning? While we were still asleep?'

'No, I'm sure Peter wouldn't come in here. He might never again. And it would take Rainy hours to clean up the mess that was in here. She didn't have enough time.'

Daniel walked around the bed, fingering the blanket and reaching out to touch the shelves. 'What are we dealing with here, George?' he asked, awed.

She watched him. 'I don't know. More important, what are we going to do about it?'

'Christ, how the hell should I know?' He stopped, thinking he should apologise for his insensitivity, but something caught his eye when he looked up. 'Well, I know one thing.' He leaned over the bed, trying not to disturb its perfect neatness, and managed to get his hand on the lightbulb suspended from the ceiling. With a deft twist he took it out. 'There, at least we don't have to worry about the drain on the batteries.' He stood awkwardly, holding the bulb. They'd never taken anything from this room, even something as insignificant as this. Still, Georgina could feel his dilemma.

'We have to do *something*,' she said. 'Or do you think it might just go away? It *came* without warning.'

'It? Or she?' He looked at her sadly. 'Is it Ellen?'

'No,' Georgina almost snapped. 'Our daughter wouldn't do this. She wouldn't come back like this. It's—it's something else,' she stated uncertainly.

Daniel gazed at her, searching her face for something other than stubborn hope. 'I hope so, too,' he said eventually. 'And maybe you're right. It *might* go away. I suggest we keep this door closed, no matter what. Forbid the kids from coming in here—us too. Let's see what happens for a few days. What do you think?'

'What else can we do?'

'Nothing, I suppose. Unless we ask somebody,' he added reluctantly.

'Who?'

Daniel shrugged and sighed, wishing he hadn't said it. 'I don't know. It was just a thought. Forget it.'

They left the room, each of them turning for a last look before closing the door.

That night nobody went to bed until it was late. They sat up as a group watching movies on the satellite television station and quietly keeping each other company. Daniel briefly discussed the situation at their evening meal and was surprised to be convinced by his children that it seemed safe to sleep in their own rooms, although nobody could quite explain why. It was like a *feeling* in the air. Then Rainy made a strange comment.

'She's not strong enough,' she said simply, too absorbed in attacking her meal to see the looks of surprise around her.

Later, Daniel lay in bed, his arms tucked under the pillow behind his head as he stared at the ceiling. Beside him Georgina attempted to read one of her favourite books, but she continually found her eyes sliding over a paragraph without absorbing any of it. She would go back and force herself to read the words, but her heart wasn't in it.

'I can't hear anything,' he said, knowing she understood him.

'No.' Georgina gave up and flipped the book closed. 'Maybe she doesn't come every night, or maybe she's not going to come back at all. You took the light away, remember.'

'I can't see the lack of a lightbulb upsetting a ghost that much,' he said resignedly.

Georgina looked at him, her eyes filled with concern. It was the first time anyone had really used the word *ghost*. Until now it had been *she* or *it*, and even *Ellen*, everyone shying away from that other word which held so many dreadful implications.

Haunting. Evil spirits. Living dead.

Not here, she thought, aware of her own desperation. *Not in our peaceful little home. We've already put up with enough. It wouldn't be fair.*

Daniel sighed and got out of bed. 'Have we

got enough milk to make a hot chocolate? I need something to put me to sleep.'

'Just make up some more milk, so it's chilled in the morning. I won't have one though.'

Daniel nodded and headed for the hallway. He stopped short at the door, his face falling. From where he stood he could see the door to Ellen's room.

'What's wrong?' Georgina asked.

'The light's on again,' he said quietly.

'What? How can it be? Where did you leave the bulb?'

'In the kitchen with the others.' He looked at her, his expression grim. 'Look, don't go in there. Don't even look through the door. I'll check the kitchen.' She nodded dumbly, her face pale.

Daniel went to the stores cupboard first. Because there was no spare protective package for the old bulb from Ellen's room, he'd balanced it carefully on top of the row of replacement light-bulbs. Now it was gone. He stared at the empty spot a long time. *Was she taunting him? Daring him to go back into the bedroom? Why did a fucking ghost need to see in the damn dark, anyway?* He felt a flash of anger. Like Georgina, Daniel was beginning to hate this intrusion into their lives, coming just when they were starting to get over the loss of the real Ellen. *Their* Ellen, not the thing in her bedroom now.

He resolved to stick to his plan. Ignore the room and whoever—whatever—might be in there. Maybe these things thrive on attention. It was possible. *Anything* was possible. And besides, what the hell else could they do?

Daniel mixed himself some milk powder and water, making the brew stronger than usual, as he liked it, then used a saucepan to slowly heat it. It would have been quicker and easier to use the microwave, but he preferred to avoid any unnecessary drain on the solar batteries. The gas stove also gave him extra time to gather his thoughts.

He tried not to look at the crack of light under Ellen's door as he walked back into his own room. Georgina had her eyes closed, the sheet pulled up under her chin, but she stirred as he entered.

'Well? Is it still there?'

'No, the bulb's gone. Somebody must have put it back in—*she* must have.'

Georgina didn't like that. 'How the hell did she do that?' she whispered.

Daniel reached out and caressed her face, massaging the frown on her forehead until it went away and her eyes closed again. 'After what we saw last night, I guess putting a lightbulb back in its socket is no big deal,' he told her gently. 'But don't worry. I don't quite know all of what Rainy was getting at this evening, but I think I understand some of it. If Ellen was going to come beyond her own room, she would've by now. Let's try to ignore things for a few days, as we agreed, and see what happens. I think as long as we don't actually go into the room, we shouldn't upset things too much.'

He saw the muscles in Georgina's face relax as she nodded gratefully, believing him. Daniel turned his head for a moment, hiding his frown and wishing he could believe himself. He was glad Georgina was too tired to see the obvious question.

If she's confined to that room, how did the lightbulb

get from the kitchen cupboard back into the bedroom?

The answer was obvious—and frightening. Ellen's ghost could wander where she wished. And replacing the lightbulb was an act of sheer juvenile malice. A child's game to taunt them.

The ghost of their daughter was having some fun.

The next night was the same. The Littlewoods tried hard to work through their day without dwelling on the strange happenings in Ellen's room. In the evening they stayed together, again watching television with an almost fierce devotion, using it as an excuse to take away any opportunity to talk. As the daylight faded Daniel checked the hallway, seeing the strip of light coming from under the door. He went back to the living room and didn't mention it to anyone.

Then, on the third night, Georgina had a dream.

She'd fallen into an exhausted slumber, the constant tension of the previous nights taking its toll. After lying in bed waiting for sleep to come, it swept over her unexpectedly. Daniel had to stretch over and turn off her bedside lamp before switching off his own and settling down.

In the dream Georgina was walking through the house alone when Ellen's voice called to her from the far end of the homestead. At first, Georgina wasn't surprised—she seemed to expect it. Calling back, she quickly made her way towards the bedrooms.

The next time Ellen called, the sound came from *behind* Georgina. The place she'd just left.

Frowning with annoyance Georgina turned and

retraced her steps. Ellen's cry came again, this time from a spare room filled with junk. Georgina darted to her right, through the door. The room was empty.

Fear began to push aside her frustration.

'*Mum, I'm lost!*'

Now the call came from outside. There was a tear-filled tremor in Ellen's voice. She sounded so distraught Georgina's heart ached.

As Georgina slept, the emotions she was feeling in her dream flickered across her face.

'*No, you're not, honey,*' Georgina shouted, leaving the spare room. '*You're home. Stay where you are. Let me find you.*'

'*But I'm lost! Where am I?*'

'*You're home! Don't move. I'll find you.*' Georgina was rushing through the house now, throwing open doors and frantically checking rooms. Every time she heard her daughter's voice, it seemed to come from a different place.

'*Please, Mum, I'm lost. Help me.*'

'*I'm coming, honey. Just stay put.*'

The house blurred into a confusing maze of passages, doors and strange rooms. Ellen's voice pleaded. Georgina shouted desperately back, urging Ellen to stay still so she could find her.

Georgina squirmed, tangling the sheets and disturbing Daniel, as she saw herself running through the kitchen yet again.

The homestead was like a hall of mirrors, the sheets of glass mixing and distorting the familiar rooms until Georgina was lost in her own home. Suddenly, like the abrupt end to a weird film clip, she stopped at the end of the hallway. In front of her, framed by the eerie, darkened walls of the passageway, the door to Ellen's room beckoned. A glaring line of light spilled from beneath it, blinding her.

She stumbled along the hallway, touching the walls with her fingertips to guide her. Ellen's voice no longer called, but it didn't matter. She was behind the door. Georgina knew.

It opened by itself, swinging aside as she came within reach. The blinding light washed over Georgina, forcing her eyes closed with real pain. Tears quickly came, squeezing out from under her lashes. When she managed to open them again, cracking her lids apart by the fraction, allowing her pupils to contract, she found herself standing at the foot of Ellen's bed. Georgina couldn't recall walking through the door.

Her daughter appeared to stand on the bed, although her weight made no impression on the mattress. She gazed down at her mother, her arms at her sides, her face expressionless. Ellen wore the simple white dress they'd buried her in. The intense light seemed to come from behind her somewhere, so hot now Georgina felt her skin tingle.

'*Ellen*,' she said in her dream. Now tears fell down her cheeks.

In her bed Georgina was sweating profusely. 'Ellen,' she muttered. The word was barely a croak. Daniel didn't stir.

'Mum? What's happening? Where am I?' Ellen's face stayed emotionless, the lips hardly moving. But her voice was filled with a pitiful fear and confusion, which tore at Georgina's soul.

'You're home, love. Home with me.'

'No, I'm not. It's dark in here—and so cold.'

Georgina was choked to silence, a hand of fear and deep sadness clamped across her chest, squeezing the breath from her.

Shockingly, the light behind Ellen began to be smothered by a stronger, forbidding darkness. Georgina tried to cry out a warning, but still her words couldn't come. The blackness grew, blanking out the light. A shadow crept across the walls and ceiling like a horde of black insects. Ellen screamed and twisted around, her image shimmering and flickering.

The shadow fell over her and everything stopped, held in a suspended animation for one long heartbeat.

Ellen's face began to change. At first she was terrified, but her look of horror faded slowly, changing to one of dumb compliance. An evil grin spread across her lips and she turned back to face Georgina. Now the horrible smile leered down at her mother and the little girl's eyes danced and sparkled with madness.

Terrible. Ugly. Peter's words slammed into Georgina's memory.

'No!' She cried out, lunging forward to grab a handful of the white dress and pull Ellen forward, away from the evil Georgina knew lurked in the darkness behind her daughter.

Her reaching fingers sank into Ellen's midriff

as if the child wasn't there—but it was like plunging her hand into boiling water. Georgina screamed with the pain. Worse, her mind cried out at the shriek of delighted laughter coming from Ellen.

Georgina screamed when she awoke, too, sitting bolt upright in the bed. Daniel snapped the light on, almost knocking it over in his haste.

'Jesus! Are you all right? George—?' He broke off as he looked at her properly.

Georgina was soaked with sweat and shaking badly. Her eyes were wide and staring, her mind filled with the nightmare images. His hand trembling, Daniel gently touched her cheek, feeling the heat.

'You're—you're *burnt!*'

She turned her head towards him and he flinched back from her shocked gaze.

'It was the light,' she whispered, her voice cracking. 'So bright. So *hot*.'

'But it was a *dream?*' Daniel asked, stunned.

Wincing with pain, Georgina pulled her right hand from under the sheet. It shook so badly Daniel had to grasp her wrist to steady it while he examined it.

The backs of her fingers were covered with angry, weeping blisters.

Daniel still believed it would be best not to go into Ellen's room. Georgina's nightmare left them confused and very frightened, and it was hard to even begin to decide how to deal with it. But he knew that tempting fate by going into the room wasn't the answer.

Georgina's injuries were real—painfully so. But both were certain she'd never left the bed. Somehow the images in her mind had broken through the barriers separating the real world from the imagined. Georgina had badly burnt her fingers when she tried to grab hold of Ellen's spirit and suffered a mild form of sunburn on her face from the intense white light. Impossibly, she carried these injuries from her nightmare into the waking world.

In the morning she sat at the table while Daniel removed the temporary dressings they had applied during the night. He carefully smeared a disinfectant ointment on the blisters and broken skin, then bandaged them to allow Georgina as much use of her hand as possible. She reluctantly agreed to stay at the house for a few days and give her wounds time to heal, rather than go out onto the property. Besides, Daniel argued, there was no way either of them could leave Rainy in the homestead on her own any more.

Peter and Rainy watched the whole operation with amazement, and waited patiently for an opportunity to pump their mother with questions about how she'd been hurt. Eventually, Georgina gave them a scaled-down version of her dream, explaining she'd seen herself in Ellen's room, confronted by an apparition of Ellen herself. When she tried to reach out to her daughter, to touch her, she was burnt. She didn't mention the ominous and terrifying darkness which had taken over Ellen's ghost. Nor did she tell them of Ellen's dramatic change in demeanour. Georgina couldn't see any point in frightening the children any further. Everyone was scared already. However, a voice of guilt called in the back of her mind.

These kids should be prepared, it said. *They should know everything.*

It had been hard enough explaining her dream to Daniel during the night, with the images fresh in her memory. In the light of day she was bewildered. Had her over-stressed imagination invented some of the details? Was she overreacting?

The last one was easy. All she had to do was glance at her own bandaged fingers. *A bit hard to overreact to something crazy like that*, she thought.

'But it was a *dream*,' Rainy was saying. She pointed to the bandages. Georgina was relieved to notice the younger Littlewoods appeared more fascinated than worried by the phenomenon.

'Yes, I know,' Georgina sighed. 'But we *don't* know. Neither your father nor I can explain it. Maybe I had an—an out-of-body experience,' she added, with a half-hearted flash of inspiration.

Rainy gave her a doubtful look, then surprised everyone by apparently dismissing the whole episode. 'Anyway, I've only got two lessons this morning, and nothing this afternoon. I might go for a ride after lunch.' Rainy had a small minibike she used to get around the expanse of the property. 'I haven't seen any of the dams since it rained.'

'I'd be happier if you stuck around and helped me,' Daniel said in a fatherly tone. Her face fell. 'I'm still trying to get that pump finished, but the workshop and the generator room are a mess. Tools are everywhere. I want someone to help clean up so I can get something finished.'

Rainy accepted this gracefully. At least she could pester Daniel to let her help him, instead of having to sweep the concrete floors or scavenge among the collection of ageing machinery Daniel had been 'fixing' for years, looking for the tools he'd put down somewhere in the past. In her youthful enthusiasm for things mechanical Rainy believed she could probably overhaul the bore pump herself.

'What about you, Peter?' Daniel asked. He could see the teenager wasn't coping as well with their strange circumstances as the rest of them. He looked pale and there were dark rings under his eyes.

He's seen her—for real, Daniel thought sadly. *God knows, she must be a sight.*

'There's still that fence around the dam Mum stuck up last week,' Peter suggested. 'It's got to be done properly. I can do that on my own and be back in time for lunch.' He looked at Georgina.

'Okay, do that,' Daniel agreed. Part of him wondered how he could organise the day like this, totally normally, knowing at the same time that one room of the house was haunted by the malevolent ghost of their daughter. It made everything else seem unreal.

Again, Daniel lingered in the house, waiting for Peter and Rainy to leave so he could talk privately with Georgina.

He gave her a hug and kissed her forehead. 'How're the fingers?'

'Okay.' She pulled away slightly and touched one cheek with her good hand. White spots lingered on the reddened skin before fading away. 'Good thing I already had a tan,' she said trying to make a joke of it. 'That was a pretty amazing light.'

'The whole thing is pretty damn amazing,' he muttered. 'The point is, what are we going to do about it—?' His voice trailed off as he heard himself pointlessly repeating the question they'd been asking each other for days now. The truth was, they hadn't done *anything* about it.

'Oh, Daniel. What *can* we do?'

He took a deep breath. 'There must be somebody who's dealt with this sort of thing before. Someone who'll believe us.'

'Who? Where do we look?'

'God knows,' he shrugged.

'Well, there's an idea. What about the church?'

'What church? I've never been inside one in my life, except for bloody funerals. Have you?'

'I was christened in a church.' Georgina cocked her head to one side and thought about it. 'That's not exactly strong ties, is it?'

'No.' He let go of her and picked his hat up off a chair. 'I'll think about it while I'm working today. Maybe you can try doing the same. Let me know if you come up with any bright ideas.' He smiled, but the smile didn't quite reach his eyes.

Georgina cleaned up after them, picking up the used bandages and wrapping them carefully before putting them in the garbage. There were a few breakfast things, too, which she washed and put away. The operation was made longer and more awkward because she could only use one hand. Georgina didn't mind though. It helped pass the time. Listlessly she tried to pick at some odd jobs, but ended up leafing through a magazine she'd read countless times before. A neighbour regularly flew his light plane into the closest town and often, on the return trip, dropped onto the small landing strip Daniel had carved out of the bush to deliver any supplies the Littlewoods may have ordered, including luxuries like magazines. Usually magazines and books were read and re-read by each member of the family until the pages fell apart.

Georgina finally recognised that although it was only mid-morning she hadn't recovered from last night and felt tired. More than tired—exhausted. But the idea of lying down alone in the bedroom didn't appeal. Georgina hadn't noticed before how much Daniel's presence buoyed her courage.

She was used to falling asleep on the lounge suite in front of the television without too many ill-effects. Georgina decided it would do this time and stretched across the cushions, her feet sticking out over the end armrest. It took only minutes before her eyes closed and she slipped away.

Ellen's voice called again. This time it woke Georgina.

'Mother.'

She sat up quickly, making her head spin. A nearby window was still flooded with morning light. She hadn't been asleep for long. But had she heard someone call? *Ellen?* Memories of her nightmare swept into her mind and Georgina's skin crawled.

'Mother.'

It came again, quite clearly yet somehow different from normal sounds. Numbly, Georgina realised she was the only person who could hear it. And something else. It was Ellen's voice all right, but it had another quality. There was something indefinably *wrong* about it. Georgina couldn't recall Ellen ever calling her 'mother'.

Georgina was usually a positive and confident woman. She made her own decisions and rarely regretted them. But now fear and uncertainty, nurtured by flashes of her dream, made her falter as she tried to decide what to do. One thing was clear. Ellen's ghost was calling to her from the room. Beckoning her. Should she ignore it? Or should she answer it, before the moment vanished? Deliberately she pushed away the thought of how dangerous that might be.

Yelling for help from Daniel was one option, but it meant leaving the house. Georgina took a moment to curse. For years they'd talked about putting a communications system between the homestead and the sheds. It was too far to simply step outside the house and shout. Nothing had been done about it. *Rainy's taking school lessons from three thousand kilometres away*, Georgina thought bitterly, *but I can't talk to Daniel in the damn workshop, only a hundred metres distant*.

Leaving the house, even for a few minutes, meant abandoning Rainy, who was still working in her room, unaware of Ellen's calls.

So send Rainy to get Daniel, idiot! Georgina was getting angry at herself, fretting at her inaction.

That wouldn't work either. Georgina knew this was a *moment*, an opportunity. Any wrong move would snatch that opportunity away. Ellen's ghost was calling *her*, not Daniel. Somehow she knew Ellen wouldn't tolerate any interruptions. Or let Rainy dash off to get her father.

So Georgina could either answer the call, go straight to Ellen's room and confront the spirit—or do nothing.

'Mother.'

The word had a plaintive edge that tugged at Georgina's heart until it hurt. The child's voice was demanding, and its tone insisted it was not to be ignored.

It mocked Georgina too, teasing her.

Is this real? Can you believe it? Why don't you come and see?

Georgina slipped off the couch and stood uncertainly. A shiver ran through her. She knew they needed answers. This thing wasn't just going to go away—and it might get worse. In fact, it *was* getting worse.

She'd kicked off her shoes before falling asleep. Now she padded bare-footed towards the hallway. Georgina realised the spirit knew she was coming. The cries stopped. Her stomach began to churn with fear, her legs trembled and her steps were unsteady. The hallway loomed dark and uninviting. Not so long ago it had been the cool and pleasant centre of the house. As she entered the narrow passageway it felt as if the walls were designed to prevent her turning, changing her mind and fleeing. She passed unthinking beyond Rainy's bedroom. A thin line of light, totally expected now, ran across the bottom of Ellen's door.

Georgina reached out firmly for the brass knob,

not daring to hesitate at any moment in case fear got the better of her. The uncomfortable thrill ran through her arm and struck her heart with its shocking chill. The door opened easily.

Ellen's ghost appeared to sit on the bed this time, her legs straight out in front of her. The pose was unnatural-looking, like a doll's. Her eyes were lifeless. The room was deathly still, as if time had stopped there.

Georgina couldn't breathe. Something told her she mustn't go any closer—certainly she mustn't reach out or try to touch Ellen. An ache in her chest grew at the sight of her daughter, despite the unnaturalness of the spirit's image. Georgina tried to focus on the dead eyes, the impossible posture. *This is not my little girl*, her inner voice insisted harshly. *This is something else.* She found the strength to speak.

'What do you want?' Georgina's voice was hoarse, her body rigid. Terror threatened to burst to the surface.

'*Mother?*' Ellen's lips moved, but the sound came from somewhere else. Everywhere. Just that one word seemed to ask *Where is your love? Your compassion? Aren't you happy to see me?*

'Stop that,' Georgina said, trying to gather in every shred of her anger at this mockery, turning it against her fear. 'Don't bother lying to me. You've never—' she stopped. She was about to say that Ellen had never called her 'mother', and so deny that the spirit was in any way intimate with the real, living Ellen. It might have been a small triumph, but something warned her. *Don't tell her. Don't give away anything.*

The ghost didn't respond, but the room about her flickered with shadows. The blackness of Georgina's nightmare was there somewhere, suppressed, but leaking out at the provocation.

'What do you want?' Georgina asked again. The effort to keep her composure was exhausting. The spirit seemed to wait an eternity, playing on Georgina's tension, before replying.

'*I want to play with Rainy.*'

That nearly broke her. It was so unexpected—yet so typical of a little girl lost and alone. Georgina suddenly wanted to cry.

'You—you *what?*'

'*I want to play with Rainy. I'm lonely.*'

Georgina's response was automatic. 'But that's impossible!' Then she felt foolish. *This whole conversation is impossible,* she thought. *I'm losing control.* She took a breath and fought down her rising hysteria. The moment let her see the spirit's reaction. The dark, menacing flickering swelled out again with disapproval, then reluctantly subsided. Georgina instinctively took a step backwards.

'*Please, Mummy. I only want to play. I'm lonely.*'

Now the voice was pure Ellen Littlewood, but Georgina recognised that the change had come as easily as if she had touched a switch. Nothing was real.

'No, never. I won't allow her in this room.'

'*I want her. I want to play with her. Bring her here.*' Another change. The voice was demanding now.

'I told you, no.' Georgina tried to sound

adamant, but her voice treacherously broke. The shadows grew, skittering around the walls of the room. Georgina took another involuntary step backwards.

'*I will come and take her.*'

This chilled Georgina to the core. It was said with such confidence. Such *certainty*. The blackness was growing, filling the room.

'No! You can't!'

Georgina could feel the pressure in the room building and knew it was time to run. She quickly backed out the door. There was a wail of anguish and anger, and the door slammed closed, shaking the house. Dimly, Georgina imagined it might have cut her in half if she'd stayed in its path. She turned and urgently hurried down the hallway into Rainy's room.

Rainy jumped out of her chair where she'd been reading her computer. 'Mum! What's wrong?'

Georgina bore down on the girl, startling her. 'Don't you *ever* go in that room, do you hear me? *Ever!*' She swept Rainy before her and pushed her from the room, heading out of the house. 'We've got to talk to your father.'

Rainy tried to object, then ducked under her mother's arm and glanced anxiously back along the hallway. She saw the doorway to Ellen's room. Strangely, it seemed to beckon her.

Georgina knew she was acting badly as she led Rainy across the lawn and down the short track to the workshops. But it seemed essential that Daniel back up her order to Rainy not to go into Ellen's room.

More than anything else, it felt right just getting Rainy out of the house.

Or maybe I'm going mad, Georgina thought. *Would anyone blame me?*

'Why do we have to see Dad?' Rainy asked, totally confused.

'We have to discuss Ellen's room together. All three of us,' Georgina replied firmly.

'Can't it wait? What happened?'

'Never mind that.'

Daniel was glad to see them, his face bursting into a smile. 'Hello, hello! Has everybody come to give me a helping hand?' His khaki clothes were streaked with dirt. Both his hands were black. Around them the large shed was cluttered with equipment. The place smelled of the oil and grease which had soaked into the sawdust.

'We have to talk,' Georgina told him grimly.

'What about?'

Rainy put in quickly, 'I think Mum's going crazy.' But Georgina ignored her. Instead she looked at Daniel, imploring him to take her seriously.

'I want you to tell her *not* to go into Ellen's room. Not for any reason.'

Daniel was alarmed. 'Why did you go in there?' he asked Rainy, frowning.

'But I didn't! Mum did!'

'Oh? I don't understand.'

'Just *tell* her please, Dan. You know what she's like. Sometimes Rainy will just ignore anything I tell her.'

Daniel knew this was unfair, but didn't say so. In fact, Rainy had occasionally done this, when she was a lot younger. It hadn't happened for a long time now. Rainy gave her mother a look of annoyance and confusion. She was getting too old to be talked about in this way, as if she wasn't there.

'Rainy, come here for a second,' Daniel asked, sighing patiently. He found a convenient oil drum to sit on and brought his eyes down to meet hers. Rainy stepped closer and stood in front of him. Daniel saw Georgina turn and look worriedly back at the house. He used the opportunity to give Rainy a look that said, *Let's just humour your mother until we find out what's going on, okay?*

'Rainy, I want you to promise you'll never go into Ellen's room on your own—or with Peter, for that matter. Do you understand?'

'Sure!' Rainy burst out, spreading her arms in exasperation. 'I don't want to go in there any more, anyway!'

'That's good. I didn't think you wanted to either, but just in case, don't forget you promised.' Daniel pointed a finger, then went to give her a squeeze, but stopped short. He showed Rainy his greasy hands and smiled an apology.

'Jeez,' Rainy complained. 'Can I go back now?'

'I suppose.' Daniel wiped his hands on his shorts. 'I might come over for a coffee myself in a minute.'

Georgina turned back to them. 'No!' she snapped, startling them. 'I—I'd like Rainy to stay out of the house for a little while. Can she help you here?'

The other two stared at her, puzzled. Daniel touched his daughter gently with one finger.

'Rainy, I don't need any help just yet. Why don't you go for that ride you wanted?'

'Yeah, sure. Thanks, Dad.' Rainy sped away towards the rear of the sheds where her minibike was kept, glad of the excuse to get away.

Without rising from the drum Daniel called out to her as she disappeared. 'Don't go far! And wear your helmet and some shoes. Your old riding boots in the saddle store should do,' he added, in case she went back to the house for her boots. There was a shouted reply.

He faced Georgina. 'What the hell is this all about?' he asked with a trace of exasperation.

Georgina said tightly, 'I went into Ellen's room. I heard her calling me.'

Daniel's face turned white. 'You should have called me first. It could have been very dangerous.'

'But she was calling *me*. I knew there was no—no choice. Either I saw her right then or nothing.'

'You should've ignored it. That's what we agreed to do.'

'That was four days ago, Dan! And I think things are getting worse. It's not working.'

He had no answer to that. Daniel looked down at the dust between his feet, minutely inspecting it as if it might give him some answers. 'So?' he asked eventually. 'What happened?'

Georgina stood still, silhouetted against the sunlight shafting in through the door of the shed. Motes of dust floated about her. 'I spoke to her. She was just sitting on the bed. No bright lights or anything like that.'

'And what did she say?'

'She wants to play with Rainy.'

That brought his head up with a jerk and he looked at her for a long moment. Behind the shed they heard Rainy tinkering with the minibike, getting ready to start it.

'What the hell does *that* mean?'

'I don't know, but it was—frightening. When I refused, she said she would come and *take* her anyway.'

'Take her? Jesus!' Daniel buried his head in his hands for a moment and thought hard. 'She wants Rainy close to her. That's what it is, I'm sure. I don't understand why, though.' Another thought came to him and he sat up suddenly. 'She might not like Rainy getting too far away, either.'

Georgina was lost in speculations of her own. 'What did you say?' she asked.

'I said—'

The minibike burst into life. The machine's muffler had been long since holed and damaged, and the engine emitted a harsh clattering sound, made worse by the surrounding corrugated-iron sheds.

Daniel shouted, 'I said, she might not like Rainy getting too far away, either. I think we'd better stop her, to be safe.'

Georgina watched in alarm as he hurried in the direction Rainy had taken, but the minibike roared and began moving away. Daniel swore as he realised he'd gone the wrong way and turned, retraced his steps and headed for the main front door in the hope of intercepting Rainy as she came out onto the track. He trotted into the sunshine with Georgina close behind, just in time to see Rainy race out from behind the shed.

'Hey! Rainy, hold up a second!' he yelled, waving his arms.

She didn't hear or see him, her back to them.

The minibike kicked up a screen of dust, despite the shallow pools of water left over from the rain. The helmet and riding boots looked ungainly on her small body.

'Damn!' Daniel said. The noise of the minibike started to fade as the distance increased between them. He shaded his eyes with one hand, following her progress. 'I wish we'd stopped her. It's my fault. I didn't think.'

They watched her ride towards the first gate. It was a very old, heavy wooden construction, too awkward even for grown adults to move easily. Daniel had considered chopping it up for firewood for years. He'd already built extra fences and gates further on, creating small holding yards. These pens were seldom used, so the first gate could be left open permanently—as it was now—most of the year.

Shaking his head at his lapse Daniel turned away, but was brought up sharply by Georgina's fingers digging into his shoulder.

'God, Daniel. *Look!*'

He spun around, a rush of sickening fear filling his stomach. He knew by Georgina's cry something bad was happening. He saw Rainy speeding towards the old gate, the minibike going as fast as it could.

The gate was swiftly closing in front of her.

It was timed to perfection, even allowing for Rainy's slow reaction. The parents could see their little girl sit up on the minibike's seat with disbelief before applying the brakes too hard and too late.

Daniel explained later that he was so concerned whether Rainy could safely stop in time that he didn't even consider *why* the gate was closing.

Georgina knew instinctively—perhaps because she'd been closer to the evil thing in their house. When she looked at the swinging gate Georgina saw something glimmer behind the wooden bars, blending in with the golden grass in the background.

Someone small, wearing a white dress, pushed the gate closed with inhuman speed and strength.

Even from a distance, Georgina was struck cold. The ground seemed to tip beneath her feet and she reached out again for Daniel's shoulder. Unthinkingly, he tore away from her, running down the track. Georgina forced herself to stumble dizzily after him.

Rainy's overreaction saved her from serious injury. Instead of skidding into the gate, the bike's front wheel had locked, pitching her forward into the dirt just short of the fenceline. The bike had cartwheeled over her to smash into the wooden barrier at the same time the gate slammed home against the posts. It was all over in an instant.

Rainy lay stunned, listening to the dying motor and the rattle of the fencing as the shockwave shivered through the taut wire. Then, as she burst into tears, Rainy thought she heard a distant, girlish peal of laughter.

Daniel carried Rainy back to the homestead, cradling her in his arms. Under the cover of the girl's sobs Georgina explained what she'd seen. He didn't doubt her, and it made him angry.

They made Rainy sit on the kitchen table while Georgina ran a bowl of hot water. The pungent smell of disinfectant filled the air. Daniel stalked towards the hallway.

'Where are you going?' Georgina asked fearfully, knowing the answer.

'I'm going to *see.*'

'Don't. Please don't—not now.'

'Don't worry,' he said grimly and left before she could protest further.

Daniel walked resolutely through the house, driven by his anger. He mentally brushed aside a moment of doubt as he entered the dark hallway. As he turned the doorknob to Ellen's room his skin crawled, but he pushed his way through, ignoring the tingling sensation in his hand and arm.

Daniel expected almost anything—except nothing.

The room was lit only by the muted sunlight coming through the closed curtains. Everything was neat and tidy. There were no floating toys and books, no blinding lights, no ghostly little girls. The electric bulb wasn't even on.

Surprised, Daniel took a moment to react. 'She's gone!' he said aloud, relief coursing through him as the anger drained away. He almost laughed, letting the good feelings sink in.

'And fucking stay away!' he called, inspired.

He looked around, seeing again all the familiar things, the memories of Ellen untainted by any terrible presence. It was like meeting an old friend. Just then it was easy to imagine that the events of the past few days never happened. Daniel wished it were so and whispered, 'Leave us alone, for God's sake.'

The atmosphere in the room changed. It was

as if someone had thrown a switch, and the air was filled with a sense of foreboding. The feeling grew, building like black anger in the heart of a madman.

The bedroom light came on.

Daniel stood his ground, but his courage was faltering. *She's coming*, he realised. *She's coming back*. Something told him it wasn't just Ellen's ghost returning. Another force was sweeping into the room with her. Bigger than they'd imagined. Infinitely more dangerous. He had a crazy urge to stamp down hard on his fear, face whatever was coming—whatever the cost, if it was going to give him the chance to drive away this threat to his family.

But his nerve broke.

Fear and guilt tortured him as he turned and fled, dragging the door closed behind him. He almost ran to the end of the hallway. Just being on the other side of that door didn't seem enough. He realised he was gasping for breath and stopped. Sweat soaked his shirt. Leaning his shoulder blades against the frame of the hallway entrance, Daniel glared hatefully back at the white line of light coming under Ellen's door.

'Dad?' It was Peter, standing in the living room and looking worried.

He looked down at the youth and was struck by the feeling he'd just let him down in some way. And the rest of the family. *Through cowardice*. 'I—I'm okay, Pete. I just need a moment to catch my breath.' *Don't ask me why*, Daniel thought. *Please, don't ask me why*.

Peter hesitated, as if about to ask, then said, 'There's a call for you on the direct link, in your office.'

This meant the call was 'live'. Many of the communications for Rhianna were stored on the satellite and then sent to the homestead in one brief, energy-saving transmission. This particular call must be important to come through directly. Still, Daniel waved a weary hand.

'Tell them I'll call back soon.'

'It's someone called Matthew Kindling,' Peter explained, thinking the name might change Daniel's mind.

'Whoever—I don't care. Later.'

Peter persisted uneasily. 'Dad, it's about Ellen. He says he wants to talk to somebody about Ellen.'

10

THERE WAS A LONG debate in the Control Room. Wiley naturally played devil's advocate and suggested that Kindling's presence, possibly already responsible for one ghostly visitation, had provoked something similar inside Freedom. The discussion boiled down to whether or not Ground Control in Florida should be informed that their Australian colleagues had had a ghost of their own.

Smith took an opposing view, his voice wooden and unconvincing, saying it had to be sheer coincidence and would only confuse everyone in the US if it was mentioned. With Matthew and the two operators looking on, Louise Corry tried to back him up.

'I agree. How the hell could Matthew cause

a ghost to appear in a space station over five hundred kilometres above Earth? The ghost of someone he never even *knew*.'

'It doesn't seem to matter whether he knew them or not,' Wiley retorted.

'Okay,' she conceded, bobbing her head. 'But Hazelhurst was in this same room. I can understand something happening then—but somewhere else? Somewhere Matthew *isn't*?'

'Hold on a minute.' Kindling held up a hand. 'Let's get something straight. I don't *cause* ghosts, as you people seem to be thinking. I only *see* them—' He stopped, realising he was giving away more than he'd intended. A smug expression came over Wiley's face. Louise looked at him suspiciously, too.

'Really, Matthew?' Wiley raised his eyebrows. 'So, just how many have you seen?'

'Only this one, damn it!' Kindling tried to cover the slip. A flush rose in his cheeks and he was angry at himself. 'Oh, all right—apart from this thing during my childhood,' he admitted, gesturing towards Louise. 'I told Lou about it yesterday. But it was so long ago, no one remembers the details or if it happened at all. Forget it.'

Wiley looked at him a long time. 'Right,' he said finally, obviously unconvinced. Kindling bit back the urge to argue further.

'So, what are NASA going to do?' Louise asked, trying to defuse the situation.

'They're going to trace the ancestry of all the astronauts—especially the dead ones,' Czowkowski answered grimly. 'And they'll check the date for any special significance. They'll be looking for a hoax, too. You never know, some smart-ass in the system might have engineered the whole thing. Programmed a hologram into the computers or something.'

'What about the cryogenics? Could it be one of them?'

'Them too,' he nodded.

Wiley surprised them with an easy change of tack. 'Yes, I think we'll let NASA exhaust a few of those possibilities, see if they come up with anything, before we start telling them about Matthew's little gift.'

Again, Kindling felt the urge to say something more, but stayed silent and ignored the American's infuriatingly condescending manner.

Wiley turned to Louise. 'Are you some sort of ghost expert now, Lou? That's what you were checking out at the library, wasn't it?'

'We took out some books,' she admitted carefully. 'I doubt whether it makes me an expert. What would you like to know?'

'Anything. Anything at all that might throw a bit of light on this shit.'

'Give me time to read more. This is a bit different to what happened the other day. I'll need to dig a bit deeper.'

'Sure.' Before Wiley could say anything more a phone shrilled. He sat down on a corner of the desk and answered it. The others could tell from his side of the conversation that he was talking to Michael Lay and explaining what had occurred aboard Freedom. At one point his eyes flicked to Kindling. 'Yes, he's here,' he said, then listened. 'No, he says he's got no idea. Nothing to do with him.' After a few more terse sentences he broke the connection.

'Guess what, Huey?' Wiley said. 'Mr Lay just confirmed that Hazelhurst's not coming back after the funeral, and he won't be replaced. You and Bennington are *it*—and I want you to keep up a round-the-clock surveillance. No depending on the alarm, either. If things start going crazy on Freedom again, they might not remember to push our button.'

If anything noteworthy occurred in the space station, Ground Control activated an alarm in all the subsidiary control rooms to alert everyone, in case the equipment was unattended. Normally, such events were recorded at Canaveral anyway, but operators like Czowkowski could make their own recordings and finesse the operation as well, concentrating on the particular area concerned rather than absorbing material from all the cameras, which was the automatic procedure.

'Shit, Mr Wiley,' Czowkowski snorted. 'There must be a thousand guys within a day's flight with my rating or better who could take Hazelhurst's place. What gives? Me and Bennington'll have to work our asses into the ground.'

'At a guess,' Smith said soothingly, 'they don't want to bring anyone new into this. Not at this stage of the operation, anyway. We've probably had all our communications access priority ratings downgraded until NASA works out why they've got a damned ghost flying around their space station—meaning, unless we come up with something constructive, we'd better keep our mouths shut and not fuss anyone—about anything,' he added with a meaningful look at Czowkowski. 'The security lid'll be getting screwed on tight all round.

That's why they don't want to give you a third operator.'

'It sucks,' Czowkowski declared, unimpressed by Smith's logic and the subtle threat if he were to look elsewhere for a relief for Hazelhurst. He looked at Louise. 'Lou, would you be able to find us a bunk in this joint? I can't see us getting back to our quarters too often. It might be useful if there's somewhere we can grab forty winks right here.' He swung his chair back towards Bennington. 'Greg, you might want to go back to the motel now and catch some sleep. Start the routine.' Czowkowski didn't bother to keep the mild disgust out of his voice.

Louise waited while Bennington gathered his things. As he walked towards the door he muttered something to Czowkowski, who smiled. She caught the word 'beers' and grinned at the operator as he passed. 'I'll check with the people here,' she told Czowkowski. 'Maybe you could use the sickbay. It's small, but—' she ended with a shrug.

'Don't worry about it, Lou,' Wiley said, standing. 'I'm going to treat myself to a coffee and a sandwich in the canteen, so I'll see the head honcho on my way through, okay? John, you want to join me?' Wiley's tone made it clear that Smith had no choice—and that no one else was welcome.

The two men left, promising to be back within half an hour. Louise waited until she was sure they were gone.

'That is one really strange guy,' she observed, looking at the door.

'What do you expect,' Czowkowski said, relaxing, 'from a couple of spooks?'

'Spooks?' Kindling asked.

'Yeah, spooks. CIA, FBI—the goddamned IRS for all I know. They're all the same.'

Kindling felt a little foolish. 'I suppose I realised they must be something like that, but I didn't give it much thought. Does it mean anything?'

Czowkowski shrugged. 'Not much these days. It's just another government department, except those guys'll look under your bed if you leave your front door unlocked. No big deal, unless you've got something to hide and you do a lousy job of hiding it.'

Kindling thought Wiley could probably be a little more threatening than that. 'I suppose Michael Lay is the Australian equivalent?'

'I guess so,' Czowkowski said briefly. He obviously didn't really feel that Lay and the CIA were in the same league.

Louise perched herself next to the operator's console. 'So come on, Huey. Tell us what happened in Freedom. Where did the ghost appear?'

Czowkowski gave her a wry grin. 'This is pretty crazy stuff, isn't it?'

Watching them, Kindling suddenly felt an outsider again. He kept quiet, wanting to hear the story too.

'More than you bargained for,' Louise smiled back at him. 'And you guys were complaining about being bored.'

'Not any more.' Czowkowski took a breath and puffed out his cheeks. 'Anyway, there's not that much to tell. One of the girls, Celia Hereson, went into the Cryogenic Module on an errand for one of the others—just doing a favour. She says there was nobody else in there when she went in, but while her back was turned she got the feeling she wasn't alone any more. When she turned around she saw a little girl standing between the containers, looking at her.'

'Jesus,' Corry breathed. 'I'll bet that scared the hell out of her. The girl was just standing there?'

'Well, that's weird in itself, see?' Czowkowski gestured, 'There's no gravity up there, remember? Nobody *stands* anywhere.'

'I see what you mean,' Louise murmured, putting a finger to her lips. She raised her eyebrows at Kindling. 'And she spoke?' she went on. 'What did she say?'

'It doesn't make much sense.'

'Okay, but what did she say anyway?'

'She said, "He's wrecking all my books".'

'You're kidding.' Louise threw another glance at Kindling. 'Is that all?'

'That's it.'

'Is Hereson sure that's what she said?'

'Reckons it was as clear as a bell. It just doesn't make much sense.'

'*He's wrecking all my books*,' Louise repeated, thoughtfully. 'I wonder what it means?'

Kindling finally spoke. 'It may not mean anything, you know. At least, nothing that relates to us.' They looked at him, puzzled and interested. 'I mean, imagine this. That little girl's ghost didn't know it materialised inside a space station. She couldn't *see* the astronaut. And she said *what* she said, because she's—well, she's a ghost,' he finished.

Louise gazed at him, weighing his words. He felt uncomfortable under her stare. 'You know a damn sight more about this stuff than you've let on, don't you?' she accused him.

'No, not at all. It's only commonsense. You pick up most of this sort of stuff from the movies,' he added quickly.

'When was the last time you saw a movie? A *ghost* movie?'

'On television, all the time,' he tried, starting to feel cornered. 'I've got nothing better to do, most of the time.'

'Hmm,' she let him off the hook. 'Perhaps. All the same, it's an interesting theory. Better than mine, because I haven't even got one.'

None of the strange events inside Freedom touched on Kindling's own problem—that he suspected a substitution had been made for Vasta's body to give the Cryogenic program its first success. Kindling considered confiding in Louise, but he wasn't sure how she'd react. Conceivably, she might even run straight back to Wiley and repeat everything.

The two of them sat under a tree outside the bureau, eating lunch from a nearby shop. Earlier, Louise had declared that she wanted to get out of the Control Room before Wiley returned, so she took Kindling on a guided tour of the complex. She was on friendly terms with many of the staff and technicians and Kindling guessed she'd been involved with the space program longer than he'd first thought.

He thought about his own involvement. As the days passed Kindling had begun to feel more and more trapped. There was obviously little for him to do during this stage of the operation. He'd read all the files he'd been given. Now he had a choice of hanging around the Control Room waiting for something to happen, or doing exactly the same back at his motel. No one specifically told him not to leave the immediate area, but Wiley's reaction when Louise had accidentally turned off her pager, and the fact that things weren't going as smoothly as expected, made him feel it wouldn't be appreciated if he went wandering off out of contact.

This was awkward, as he had a few things he wanted to do on his own.

'You know that pager of yours?' he asked Louise, who was struggling with a newspaper against the mild breeze.

'Don't worry, it's on,' she said, without looking up.

'No, I was wondering if I could have one, too.'

'Oh?' She lifted her head. 'Why?'

'Because I'm trapped. I can't go anywhere, unless it's here or the motel, so Wiley can find me. Except if I ask someone to go with me.'

'Isn't my company good enough for you?'

'You know that's not the problem.'

'You don't really *have* a problem. All you have to do is tell someone where you're going. Keep in touch.'

'What if I don't want anyone to *know* where I'm going?'

She looked at him carefully. 'Why would you want that, Matthew?'

'Come on, Lou. Give me a break. I've got my own life too, you know.'

'From the conversations we've had, I didn't

think you had much happening in your life right now.'

From anyone else the remark would have been too personal. But Kindling had to admit he'd told Louise more about himself and his present life than anyone, so in a way he had invited such comments. And she was right. There wasn't much in his own life that was worth pursuing.

'So, no pager, huh?' He avoided her probe.

'No, I think it's a good idea, actually. I should be able to arrange it without bothering Wiley.'

Kindling waited a few minutes, watching the traffic roll past beyond the security gate. He hoped she wouldn't make a connection between his next question and the last.

'What about Joanne Vasta? Has anyone told her about all this?'

It didn't work.

'Is that what you want to do? Go and see her?'

'I've thought about it. After all, she was the religious one in the family. She might find the idea of her husband returning from the dead more shocking than he will.' It was a bit thin, Kindling realised, but the best he could come up with.

'Maybe.' Louise suddenly flung out a hand and snatched a loose sheet of newspaper from the air, where it had been picked up by the breeze. 'This is not the place to read newspapers,' she grumbled, then saw Kindling waiting patiently for an answer. 'Vasta's wife doesn't know about the project. As far as she's concerned, he's dead and you buried him. Ultimately, it will be his choice whether or not she's told about this—assuming he survives the revival, of course.'

'I thought at least his wife should know what was going on.'

'No, she knows nothing, and it wouldn't be advisable if you went and saw her. Besides, she's a long way away. Squandering her inheritance in Broome, on the other side of the continent.'

'She sold the house? All the property?'

'Don't be silly.' She laughed without offending him. 'All his property and holdings are controlled by a trust and doing very nicely, thank you.' Louise narrowed her eyes. 'The family house is different, though. That's been left exactly how it was the day he died. Joanne moved out to stay with friends to cope with her grief, and never went back. Somebody collected her personal things and the children's. It must have been strange for her at the time. Now we know it was all part of his plan to return some day.'

'I had no idea. Nothing was said at the funeral—about the house, I mean.'

'Hardly the topic for funerals, I suppose—hey! There go Wiley and Smith. Off somewhere important.' She smiled cheekily. 'Let's get a six-pack of beers and cheer up Huey. I think he needs it.'

'He won't drink on duty, will he?'

'You can bet on it,' Louise winked.

He didn't really know why he was doing it. It was none of his business—at least, nobody could blame him if he turned a blind eye. *Take the money and run*. But something drove him to look for the truth. Perhaps it was an attempt to make up for the last year or so, when he'd ignored the truth of his own personal problems in a search for peace of mind.

In the end, he suspected he didn't know what the hell he was doing, or why. He only hoped Louise Corry was one of the good guys. Maybe that was what he was really trying to find out.

Kindling had to work out where he should look for evidence of a surgical operation. Vasta's house was the obvious place to start. Medical records, hospital bills—anything that would prove Vasta had had a kidney removed at some time late in his adult life. It would be easier to look for evidence that the operation had occurred, rather than to establish consistent good health. And that may have been a lie, too. It was possible that Vasta may not have wanted anyone to know he was ill, and had even lied to Kindling that day at the funeral.

Whatever his reasons, Kindling convinced himself the answers had to be inside the house.

He waited until after midnight. Earlier, Kindling had left a message with the motel's management saying he had a migraine headache and didn't want to be disturbed for any reason. That way, if Wiley wanted him, someone would actually have to come to his room and knock on the door. But it seemed safe to assume that nothing would occur during the night to warrant that. Unless the ghost of the little girl reappeared. Wiley would probably drag him from his deathbed in that case—the American already suspected Matthew was somehow responsible for the phenomenon. It was a risk Kindling decided he would have to take.

He slipped quickly from his room, turning out the lights first, so no one idly watching would notice him leaving. He walked down the motel's driveway and turned right. Kindling wore dark jeans and a navy-blue windcheater, and had a small bag slung over his shoulder. In the bag was a good torch and a few basic tools. The night was already cold and his breath puffed in clouds behind him as he moved.

The city traffic was still heavy, despite the late hour. A continuous line of headlights streamed towards him. Several taxis went by, but Kindling didn't bother hailing them. A cab rank was just up the street. It would have been pointless to go to such lengths to conceal his departure only to drive his own car away.

There was only one cab waiting on the rank. The driver, a thickset man, almost bald, with a wide face, was sitting with his foot jammed in the corner of the door to keep it open, the interior light shining. He squinted at a rumpled sports newspaper.

'You for hire?' Kindling asked, leaning through the window. The driver untidily folded the paper, tossing it next to him.

'Sure, hop in,' he said, jerking his head at the back seat. 'Where to?' Kindling gave him the address and the driver grunted. It was a decent fare.

The taxi darted out into the traffic and the cabbie eyed Kindling in the rear-view mirror. 'Going home?'

'No, going out. Visiting some friends.'

'Must be real night owls,' the driver commented.

He tried to get Kindling in several conversations about sport, but Kindling wasn't sports-minded and couldn't contribute. He didn't want to. He watched the lights of the city slide past.

'What about that poor bastard getting himself killed up in space?' the driver tried.

'Terrible business,' Kindling agreed, hoping he sounded uninformed. 'Two in one trip. They must be feeling pretty bad up there.'

'Two? I thought it was only one.' The cabbie glanced over his shoulder.

'Was it?' Kindling hastily back-tracked. 'I didn't pay too much attention—I've been busy. I suppose one's better than two,' he ended lamely.

Apparently Lyghtson's death had been kept out of the press. It made sense. Too much attention focused on Freedom right now would be unwelcome, to say the least. Especially if the Cryogenic program were revealed on the eve of its first attempt at a revival. Just the existence of such a program would cause a furore. The impending revival would be a sensation, successful or not.

And if my suspicions are correct, Kindling thought, *they won't want the world looking too closely at the new improved Anton Vasta.*

The cabbie gave up trying to draw Kindling into conversation, and they travelled in silence until the taxi pulled up outside Vasta's house.

'Looks like nobody's home,' the driver observed.

Kindling wound down his window and peered into the darkness. It was a quiet street, badly lit. The nearest streetlamp wasn't working. The house occupied a corner block, surrounded by a two-metre-high concrete fence topped with ornamental metalwork. The taxi had stopped adjacent to a pair of wide wrought-iron gates, into which a smaller access gate was cleverly built. Beyond them the two-storey house brooded in the night. There were no lights on anywhere. Not even security lights in the garden. A dog barked nervously in a neighbouring yard at the taxi's arrival.

'There'll be somebody there,' Kindling said, opening his door. The driver answered with a grunt.

Kindling paid the fare. Turning and walking towards the gate he expected the cab to pull away from the curb behind him, but it didn't move.

Go away, Kindling thought, realising the driver probably believed there was no one home and that another substantial fare for the return journey was in the offing. Closer to the wrought-iron entrance Kindling felt panic as he saw a heavy chain and padlock entwined through the metal. He'd expected it to be locked, but he hadn't counted on an ambitious cab-driver waiting around and observing him jumping the wall.

At the last step Kindling said aloud, 'Oh, that's right!' as if he'd just recalled something important. He spun around and headed for the corner. He hoped the cabbie heard him and read the feint correctly—that Kindling was supposed to use another entrance.

Another worry sprang into Kindling's mind as he rounded the bend. What if the cab-driver knew the house? Knew no one had lived in it for over two years? He might use his radio to call the police and wait for them to arrive, making sure Kindling didn't run for it.

A crunch of tyres and the brief glare of headlights on the opposite fence told Kindling his fears were groundless. The taxi was gone. He suddenly felt alone and vulnerable.

The side street was small, running only the distance of Vasta's considerable block of land. The property facing it was likewise a large one. At the end of the street the lights of another house filtered through heavy trees, too far away to concern him.

'No sense in waiting around,' Kindling told himself, screwing up his courage.

He put his hands on top of the wall and hoisted himself up, his feet scrabbling for purchase against the smooth concrete. He balanced precariously on the crown, trying not to stab himself on the ornate ironwork. Looking down into the yard, he saw nothing but an inky blackness. Kindling decided to risk using the torch and awkwardly pulled the bag from his shoulder, fighting to keep his balance and avoid toppling off the wall in either direction. Finally he managed to point the torch downwards and flick on the yellow beam.

The grounds were well kept. Directly below him a narrow garden bed with low rose bushes ran as far as the torchlight could reach. Kindling knew he could jump down and land beyond the roses on the trimmed lawn. He swept the beam away from the wall. The rest of the garden was a maze of hedges and tall shrubs, planted in landscaped islands. Glittering droplets of moisture, the beginnings of the next morning's frost, gleamed on the leaves. The night was very still and getting colder. The growing damp seeped into his windcheater. Kindling couldn't see the house, which was hidden by the dense garden.

The muscles in his leg cramped. He'd been perched on top of the wall too long, postponing the next, irrevocable step.

'I must be crazy,' he said aloud. He jumped and landed sprawling on the wet lawn. His bag caught on one of the wall's ornaments as he fell and jerked painfully around his neck. 'Good start,' he muttered, taking a moment to rub the skin where the strap burned. He realised the dog had stopped barking the instant he touched the ground. It gave him a creepy feeling.

Don't start thinking crazy thoughts now, he told himself. *It's just coincidence. The dog probably got a kick for making a noise, or saw you disappear.*

At least the high wall let him use the torch freely. He shone it around, trying to choose a passage between the clumps of shrubs to take him directly to the house. Nothing looked promising. He mentally flipped a coin, and chose the nearest opening.

The cold, clear night allowed stars to struggle through the ambient light of the surrounding city and cast a faint, silvery wash over the lawn. A thin sliver of moon was climbing into the sky in the east.

It wasn't the same amongst the shrubbery. The taller branches closed over the top of the pathways, blocking out the sky and forming black tunnels. As Kindling picked his way along, using the torch to check his way, he found himself wishing he had another light. The glare of the beam in front served only to throw the surrounding shadows into deeper darkness.

He'd only moved several metres away from the wall when a loud rustling noise made him snap the torch to his right. He caught a fleeting glimpse of two blood-red eyes glaring at him from within the leaves. Kindling's breathing choked and his heart fluttered.

Cats. He tried to reason calmly. *Of course, there'll be hundreds of the bloody things around here. A big garden, an empty house. I should have expected it.* He moved on.

More noises came, startling him every time. The garden began to seem endless and Kindling wondered if he wasn't walking in circles. Some of the branches reached out, thorny leaves tugging at his clothes. He realised that while he must be making progress towards the house, he couldn't make a hasty retreat back to the wall. He'd already made too many twists and turns. He was lost.

Then he heard breathing.

Another rustling sound made him whirl around and shine the torch behind him. Kindling caught his breath again.

But someone else *kept* breathing.

It was a soft, throaty, rattling breath like an asthmatic—or someone dying. Kindling froze, the hairs standing up on the nape of his neck.

It must be an animal. It's got *to be an animal—a sick animal.*

He thought the sound came from his left. He shone the torch into the bushes. There was another flicker of bloody red eyes burning at him from the shadows. The breathing stopped.

This is insane! What the hell am I doing here? Kindling backed away from where the eyes gleamed, convinced it was time to quit—just find his way back to the wall and leave. This simply wasn't worth it.

His faltering, backwards steps carried him beyond the last island of shrubs and into the open. He twisted around and Vasta's house stood before him, glowing a faint white in the weak moonlight.

Kindling felt immediately safer in the open. There was enough light to see all around him. Nothing could creep up on him.

'*Not even a damned cat*,' he told himself shakily.

While one part of his mind called him all sorts of a fool, he decided to press on. The open spaces gave him his confidence back. Kindling had been to Vasta's house once before, at the wake for the same funeral where Vasta mentioned he'd never been to a doctor. Throughout that afternoon Kindling had wandered around the ground level of the building, taking in the expanse and luxury of the house. The kitchen looked too immaculate to cook in. The living area, with its massive billards table and extensive bar, too precious to relax in. Kindling remembered telling Vasta how beautiful everything was—wasn't he afraid of someone breaking in and stealing it all? It had been an inane thing to say, but Kindling had felt awkward and out of his depth since the start of the funeral.

Vasta's reply had been polite. 'No one steals from me, Matthew,' he'd said, a cold smile on his face. 'No one. It's the way of things, understand? Look for yourself,' he gestured around them. 'No alarms, no real security locks. Joanne and I don't even bother locking up when we go out, unless it's for some time. Even then, one of our people is usually here.' By that he meant the permanent gardener or the chef.

So Kindling didn't expect there to be an alarm system. It was possible one had been installed after Vasta's death, but he was gambling it hadn't been done. The house would be locked, certainly, but its isolation was the key. Kindling thought he could break in, even make some noise, and nobody would hear.

His shoes left dark prints on the wet grass. Kindling made his way towards the back of the house where he remembered there were two entrances: one into the kitchen and another into the rear of the adjoining triple garage. There was also a paved area around a fenced swimming pool.

The blank windows seemed to watch him approach and Kindling had to make a conscious effort to shake the idea from his mind. *It's an empty house. It's been empty for over two years. A few mice, a rat or a cat maybe, but nobody else.* No one's watching you.

Kindling felt bolder behind the house. He was safe from anyone observing him through the wrought-iron gates. The air held the acid tang of chlorine from the pool, its undisturbed surface like a mirror. Kindling could keep the torch switched on, another comfort for his rattled nerves. He ran the beam over the kitchen entrance. A screen door, followed by a plain wood-panelled door. Kindling tried the screen, which opened with a small squeak of protest. It wasn't designed for security. He looked closely at the inner door, hoping for hinges he could remove or locks he might dismantle. Kindling wasn't under any illusion he could pick the lock. He'd never tried before, and wasn't about to waste time trying now. He'd come expecting to force a window or something similar. Still, out of sheer habit Kindling grasped the doorknob and gave it an experimental twist.

To his utter astonishment it was unlocked. The door gently opened inwards.

Kindling stood uncertainly outside. It was too easy. A gut feeling told him he was at the entrance to some monster's lair—inside a creature was silently waiting for its victim. He shouldn't go in.

It was probably just the cleaner, Kindling tried to convince himself. *Someone must come regularly and give the place a dusting. Maybe they forgot to lock the door.*

Finally, it was the fact that he'd already come this far—and that the place was unlocked and accessible—that made him keep on. If he gave up and left now Kindling knew that even though he'd be relieved at first, in the light of day he would never forgive himself for the missed opportunity.

He pushed the door open fully and shone the torch through.

The beam reflected off modern chrome fittings, polished benchtops and racks of cooking utensils. The floor was white tiles. Kindling edged cautiously through the door. Adrenalin pounded through him. In the centre of the room he stopped and looked around slowly. There was a microwave, a refrigerator, an empty spice shelf, and pots, pans and coffee mugs hanging from hooks. Everything, in fact, you'd expect to find in a normal kitchen.

'He certainly believed he was coming back,' Kindling said aloud. His voice echoed off the hard surfaces. On an impulse he reached out and ran his finger along one of the benches. There wasn't a speck of dirt. Someone kept the place very clean. He'd have to make sure he left no trace of his visit.

Fingerprints, Kindling suddenly realised. *And I just entered mine into a national security computer system!*

He located the kitchen sink and saw cupboards underneath. He went over and opened one, hoping he was right. He was. The shelves were bare except for a clutch of cleaning detergents, disposable rags, and rubber gloves. Kindling balanced the torch on the sink, the light throwing silvery reflections off the ribbed metal surface, while he pulled the gloves on. He was silently congratulating himself on his fast thinking when the refrigerator kicked into life, frightening him badly. His heart leapt into his mouth in the moment it took to recognise the sound.

Leaving the torch behind Kindling crossed the room and tugged the refrigerator door open. A wash of light spilled out, filling the kitchen. Inside the fridge were four cans of coke held together by a six-pack plastic binder.

'Cleaner,' Kindling muttered. More importantly, the working appliance told him the electricity was connected. He closed the door and went back to the torch. Shining it away from the back door he found the dining room and, beyond that, he thought he recognised the door to the main living area. An archway led to the right. Wherever there were windows, the curtains were tightly drawn.

At the entrance to the dining room he found the kitchen light switch. Kindling paused. He was still at the back of the house and all the curtains were drawn. As an afterthought he glanced at his watch. It was past 1.00 a.m. in a quiet street in a quiet neighbourhood. He decided to risk it.

What the hell, he thought with a shrug. *Wiley will only have to come and bail me out, anyway.* The idea brought a smile to his face.

He flicked the light switch and two fluorescent

tubes stuttered and burst into life. Kindling turned off his torch and stood blinking. The kitchen definitely looked like any normal household kitchen in a luxurious home. With his eyes slowly adjusting to the light Kindling went to the back door and used the bottom of his windcheater to wipe the doorknob. He did the inside of the cupboard handle and, just for good measure, the benchtop where he'd checked for dust. Then he noticed something odd. Two small plastic blocks, snugly fitted together, sat either side of the window seal. A thin electrical cable led from one into the wall.

A magnetic switch for a burglar alarm. Twisting around he examined the edge of the back door. Another switch was positioned at the top of the door frame. The circuit must have been broken by his entry—but nothing had happened. No alarms, no flashing lights. A direct circuit to a local security firm? Kindling stood nervously, ready to run, then he decided, no. House alarms were meant to be a deterrent, not a means of *capturing* criminals.

This one had failed to go off. It was more good luck.

Satisfied, he decided it was time to explore further. Now he could turn on the house lights, except perhaps in the front rooms facing the street, Kindling felt more courageous.

Taking the torch he moved through the archway to the right and came to a narrow room which ran almost the width of the house. Stylish canvas deck-chairs, a plastic outdoor table setting and a table tennis table were scattered around a slate floor. Kindling guessed it was a recreation room for people still wet from the swimming pool. He didn't bother turning on the light. Enough came through the archway from the kitchen. He walked to the row of drapes and flicked one aside, confirming they concealed not windows, but a series of sliding doors which, when pulled wide, would open the entire area to form part of the back patio. Kindling tried to see out through the doors, but the lights in the house made it impenetrably black out there.

Suddenly, level with his own gaze, blood-red eyes filled with hate and menace glared at him from beyond the glass.

Kindling cried out and backed quickly away, stumbling over one of the deckchairs. 'For God's sake! What the hell *is* that thing?' he snarled, hearing the fear in his voice. Reaching back and leaning on the chair he waited, taking deep breaths to calm himself, then he stretched tentatively forward and drew the curtain back again. Nothing. Kindling flicked on the torch. The beam only reflected back into the room from the glass, so he pressed the lens hard against the window.

Beyond the glass he saw that the poles supporting the upper-storey landings all featured latticework with creeping vines and small shelves for potplants. If it had been a cat, as Kindling now desperately wanted to believe, it could easily climb up onto the shelves.

'*Whatever it is, at least I'm in* here *and it's out* there,' Kindling told himself, shaking off the crawling feeling between his shoulder-blades.

A door directly opposite the archway was closed. Kindling guessed where it led, but checked anyway. It opened into the rear of the garage. He was so surprised at what the first few seconds of torchlight showed him, he immediately felt around the doorframe for a light switch and turned it on.

Three parking bays were marked out in the garage. The one nearest the door was empty, a black oil stain the only evidence that a vehicle had once occupied it. *Joanne's car*, Kindling thought. In the middle bay stood a magnificent black Mercedes Benz. The cleaners obviously didn't come in here. The car was covered in a fine coating of dust. All the side windows were heavily tinted, making it impossible to see inside. Kindling cautiously lifted the driver's doorhandle and the door opened with a smooth, efficient click. He bent down and peered inside. A musty smell of leather and stale tobacco drifted out. The interior light glowed feebly, indicating the battery barely held a charge.

'Incredible,' Kindling murmured, gently closing the door.

The object in the third bay confused him for a while. It was a large metal box the size of a small caravan, painted white, with square doors set into one side. Kindling might have recognised it instantly had it been emblazoned with the usual advertising motifs, instead of the blank anonymous paint. When he realised what it was, his mouth went dry.

It was a mobile freezer of the kind seen in service stations and car parks, dispensing bags of crushed ice.

It was the freezer Vasta had killed himself in.

Kindling walked slowly around the rear of the Mercedes, staring. As he neared the front of the garage he could see an access door built into the side of the unit below a large refrigeration motor. A heavy three-phase electrical cord lay untidily on the concrete, falling several metres short of a power point on the nearby wall.

There's no need to look inside, Kindling thought, drawn towards the freezer. *There's nothing in there—certainly nothing I came to find.* He looked at the white metal door. Something made him want to open the access door and see inside. His gut instincts told him to leave it, to walk away.

The moment was broken by the tinkle of cutlery or china coming clearly through the house from the kitchen. Kindling was instantly alarmed, and at the same time relieved that now he had to leave the garage. He couldn't remember closing the kitchen door. The stray cat—or whatever it was—must have found its way inside. He fervently hoped that was all it was.

He hurried back into the house, using the torch to check the enclosed patio for anything creeping through the archway. Seeing nothing, he paused before rushing into the kitchen, listening carefully. Another clinking sound. Kindling slowly put his head around the archway.

An enormous black cat sat on the draining board of the sink, staring at the doorway, as if it was expecting someone. With a huge sigh of relief Kindling obliged by stepping into the kitchen. The cat reacted violently, arching its back and letting out a rattling hiss.

'Easy now, kitty,' Kindling said smoothly.

But there was nothing kitten-like about the animal at all. Apart from its size, which was truly enormous for a cat, it looked ragged and battered. Clumps of filthy stuff clung to its fur and a foul stench filled the room. The cat's eyes glowed feverishly at Kindling. Yellow snot ran from one feline nostril.

'I think you'd better go outside,' Kindling said, pulling a face at the smell. He held his arms wide and circled carefully around, hoping to herd it back towards the door. 'I'm glad I know what you are now,' he added conversationally, moving closer. 'You've been giving me quite a fright.'

With a screech the cat sprang, but instead of dodging away towards the back door and escaping, it leapt directly at Kindling. Ducking away, he let out a shout of surprise and pain as the animal vaulted off his shoulder, managing at the same time to drag one clawed paw across his cheek.

'Damn!' Kindling twisted around to see where it went. The cat flashed across the dining room and disappeared into the doorway leading into the inner living room. Kindling fingered his cheek awkwardly through the rubber glove and discovered he was bleeding. 'Bloody thing can stay in here, for all I care. The cleaner can work out who let it in,' he snapped, shaken.

He knew he should start searching properly before darkness slipped away. Kindling went straight through the dining room and into the living area. He stopped on the threshold and held his breath, shining the torch around.

It was a beautiful room. In its centre a large square of polished timber flooring was sunk nearly a metre below the level of the rest of the room. A single white rug filled most of the square, and a leather lounge suite was arranged around the bare outer edges. On the surrounding raised floor stood the bar and the snooker table complete with a full set of balls ready for a game—two items Kindling remembered from his previous visit—and a gleaming black grand piano, which he didn't.

Kindling let out a slow, appreciative whistle. He'd forgotten the splendour of the place. Playing the torch around the outside of the room he checked the drapes. They were tightly drawn. With a flash of recklessness he wanted to turn on the lights here too. He needed to save time, rather than fumble around with the torch. A switch was nearby and he saw it was fitted with a dimmer control. He turned this down to minimum before pressing the button. The room filled with a very soft light from several standard lamps. He edged the dimmer up a little brighter.

Starting from the outside he began checking the bookshelves for files or metal security boxes, even looking behind paintings for a wall safe—which wouldn't have helped him even if he'd found one, as he wouldn't know how to open it. After several minutes he found nothing. There had to be a study or an office somewhere else. Upstairs, perhaps. He stood, considering his next move and staring at the sunken square. One corner of the rug was flipped up, exposing boards beneath. *Probably the cat*, he thought, *hitting it at speed and losing control*. Automatically he stepped down and bent over to straighten the rug. Something caught his eye.

A cut in the floorboards, across the grain of the pattern.

Frowning, but with a growing sense of discovery, Kindling stepped onto the rug. He grasped the loose corner and pulled, exposing more of the wooden floor. The rug was heavier than he expected, and slipped from his fingers once. A trapdoor, big enough for a person to drop through, was cut neatly into the floorboards. Two brass hinges glimmered in the soft light.

'Well, well. What have we got here?' Kindling got on his hands and knees and looked closer. A single board, part of the trapdoor, had a fingerhole in it. Kindling used this to tug upwards, gently at first but with increasing pressure until he feared the door was somehow locked. His last determined attempt moved the trapdoor slightly, bringing it proud of the rest of the floor. One more aggressive pull and with a squeal of wood the section turned over on the hinges.

'Jackpot,' Kindling murmured, staring down. It was too dark to see anything and he'd left the torch on the piano. He hurried over to get it and returned, shining it through the hole.

Below was a room the same size as the sunken lounge area above. It had a bare concrete floor and walls, except for crude candle-holders fixed crookedly at regular intervals. The concrete next to these was stained black with greasy soot. Half-consumed candles filled the holders. In the centre of the room was a simple wooden table, large enough to seat eight people, but there were no chairs. The surface of the table was covered with ugly stains. In one corner of the floor lay a bundle of cloth.

'My God, what have we got here?' Kindling whispered, knowing in his heart, but wanting to deny it. Steps led down into the room, so steep they were almost a ladder. One-handed because of the torch, he carefully put his feet on the first rung and backed down. Once at the bottom he shone the torch upwards.

The ceiling, the floor of the lounge above, was covered by an artless mural, some of the characters so roughly drawn with thick gobs of paint they were indecipherable. Most of the mural was dominated by a many-pointed star, each point directed at a symbol. Kindling didn't recognise most, but those he did included fertility signs, inverted Christian crosses and others representing the sun and moon. In places the painting continued heedlessly over supporting beams and cross-members.

The mural turned Kindling cold with dread.

Wrenching his eyes away he turned the torch on the table. The stains were dark brown, some of them running over the edge. Kindling knew it was blood. He had no proof—no evidence except what his eyes and instincts told him. Yet he was certain they were bloodstains. Closer inspection of the tabletop showed the surface was scored like a butcher's chopping block. Kindling felt sickened and refused to dwell on what, or who, the blood had come from.

He picked at the pile of material in the corner. It turned out to be hooded cloaks made from a heavy, rough cloth. Probably hessian, Kindling thought. He counted them. There were six in all. At the bottom of the pile lay six pieces of rope, presumably used as sashes to fasten the cloaks.

Kindling sighed in despair and leaned back against the table. What had he found here? What did it mean? What he'd discovered clashed violently with the quiet, self-assured and powerful Anton Vasta he had known. Did Wiley and his associates—for that matter *anyone* in the entire NASA organisation—know the cryogenic program was trying to revive a man who practised satanic rituals and fooled with the occult? Someone who sacrificed living things, animals—maybe even humans. Kindling closed his eyes, suddenly feeling very tired, and rubbed his forehead. *God, not people! Surely not people.* It turned a sick and ugly infatuation into a brutal, murderous obsession. The acts of a madman.

Kindling jerked away from the table, feeling defiled by merely touching it. He came to a quick decision. Wiley and everyone else needed to know about this, regardless of the consequences to himself. He could tell them why he came here in the first place and let them sort out that mess, too. Kindling didn't care. It was all too much for him now, alone.

The trapdoor above him slammed closed.

Kindling looked up, fear sweeping through his body, electrifying every nerve. A round dot of light showed him the fingerhole. A shadow passed across it, then returned and stayed, blocking the hole.

'Who is it? Who's there?' he called. No one answered. Kindling moved quickly, but even as he put his foot on the bottom step he caught a flicker out of the corner of his eye that made him pause. Amazingly, the candle nearest him fluttered with a yellow flame, settling to a perfect teardrop of fire with a hot, blue heart. A tendril of grey smoke drifted upwards.

'Dear God,' Kindling murmured, stunned. One by one he watched the rest of the candles spontaneously burst into flame. He was transfixed by the sight until the last one was lit.

He tried to throw himself up the steps, missing

one and smashing his shin painfully. At the top he punched the trapdoor with the heels of both his hands and it popped upwards, but something heavy on the other side made it drop back again. Before Kindling could try again a voice came up from below.

It was a little girl's voice, pleading and scared.

'*Where are you going?*'

Kindling froze and continued staring at the trapdoor, telling himself not to turn. Not to look.

It was impossible not to look.

He twisted slowly on the step, making sure not to lose his footing, and stared down.

A small girl with fair hair, wearing a white dress, appeared to stand bare-footed on the table. Kindling's exertions had moved the air in the cellar and the candles wavered. The bloodstains under the girl's feet shimmered in the light and seemed to move and flow. She looked up at him with eyes filled with fear and confusion.

'*Don't leave me. I'm lost.*' Her image shivered.

Kindling took a long time to reply. His heart felt it was about to burst from his chest. Sweat soaked his armpits and neck. 'Who are you?' he asked hoarsely.

'*It's cold in here.*'

'Where? Here?' Dimly, Kindling knew she didn't mean the cellar.

But a change came over the spirit, as if a shadow had passed across her face. When she spoke next her voice was different, too. Harsher, with a wicked edge.

'*You can't leave.*'

His panic instantly renewed, Kindling faced the

trapdoor, hitting it again. As before, it fell heavily back into place.

'*You must not leave.*' The voice now cackled like a harridan.

Kindling pressed himself up one more step, so his body hunched below the upper floor. His skin crawled as he waited for something terrible to happen—like a cold, dead hand wrapping itself around his ankle. Placing his hands and one shoulder against the wood he used the strength of his legs to push. The trapdoor lifted significantly and Kindling was elated to see it was only the weight of the rug, lying back over the floor, that was stopping him escaping.

'*Come back, Matthew. I want you.*' The use of his name, and the harsh male voice he recognised all too well, shocked him, but he didn't stop the momentum of his push. Kindling let out a cry of triumph as the rug rolled back and the door opened, leaving him waist-deep in the manhole.

The black cat was waiting. In a flurry of movement it arched its back and lashed out. Kindling threw up an arm to protect his face and the animal's claws tangled in the material of his windcheater. Instead of pulling away the cat attacked his arm, trying to wrap all four legs around it and exposing yellowed fangs as it hissed and snarled. Yelling with pain Kindling grabbed a handful of loose skin on its back with his free hand and tore the cat from his arm. It yowled horribly as he flung it away with his remaining strength.

He hauled himself up from the ladder and had only taken two steps away from the trapdoor, when the room around him turned to chaos. The snooker balls began to fly from the table, spitting out with deadly force in all directions. Books tumbled from the shelves in waves. The piano began to play mad, discordant music and the bottles behind the bar exploded in showers of glass and sticky liquor.

Kindling ducked down desperately, crouched over like a runner in a war zone. A piece of glass cut his eyebrow and one of the snooker balls thudded into his back. He ran for the kitchen.

As he stumbled into the dining room the little girl appeared in the entrance to the kitchen, barring his way.

'*Don't leave. Please stay. I'm lost.*' The young, tortured voice was back.

Kindling grabbed a carved wooden chair from the dining setting and threw it underarm at the image. The girl disappeared an instant before the chair reached her.

In the scant seconds it took for him to cross the kitchen Kindling heard two things. One was the Mercedes, the engine revving to maximum and the tyres screeching in short bursts on the concrete, as though the car was a maddened animal trying to get free.

But the second sound was far worse, and it terrified Kindling. He knew exactly what it meant. It was a loud humming, like a swarm of angry insects.

The sound of Mr Williams' wheelchair, the wheels spinning at incredible speed as it hung in the air.

Kindling tried to close his mind to the sound. He ran out the back door, pushing it so violently it crashed against the wall. Outside, the patio was bathed in brightness. Every light in the house was on. The pool looked red, filled with blood, and a nauseating stench came from it. Something large and black floated there. A body.

The corpse rolled over gently and sat upright, thick red liquid pouring from its head. Father Stewart Andrews, his face rotted and eaten away, his clothes shredded, calmly regarded the horrified Kindling. Andrews waved an arm like a swimmer treading water and he bobbed obscenely in the pool of blood. His voice came clearly.

'*I told you. It's unfinished business, Matthew.*' He sank smoothly below the surface.

Kindling gagged and turned away, fighting the vomit down. He set off at a run around the house, easily seeing his way by the lights now shining from every window. Then he was on the driveway, sprinting for the distant gates. As he moved further from the noises in the house and the tormented screaming of the Mercedes' motor, he began to hear voices whispering at him from the darkness. He couldn't hear what they were saying. He didn't try to listen.

With strength born of fear and pure adrenalin he vaulted to the top of the wall near the gates. As he rolled across the crown and fell awkwardly to the footpath on the other side, one of the ornamental ironworks stabbed him in the leg, ripping his jeans.

He lay sprawled on the footpath for what seemed an eternity, waiting for sounds of pursuit. He forced himself to concentrate on holding onto his sanity.

Slowly, very slowly, he came back from the

brink of madness. In front of him the quiet street slept on, undisturbed.

Kindling walked for several kilometres, making his way out of the suburban streets onto a major road. He needed time to work the trembling out of his body and clear his mind of fear. He tried flagging down a number of taxis, but none stopped. It finally occurred to him he must look quite a sight. Jumping a security chain, he went into a closed service station. There was just enough light for Kindling to use one of the plate glass windows as a mirror. He saw the stiffness in his face wasn't only from his wounds, but blood caking the cut on his temple. It was no wonder the taxis wouldn't stop. Kindling was lucky none of them alerted the police about the blood-covered madman loose in the streets.

He washed his face under a tap, the water shockingly cold and stinging the cuts. Kindling took off his windcheater and T-shirt in case they got wet. The chill in the night air soon had him shivering uncontrollably. He persevered, washing off all the blood he could see in the window glass and drying himself with wads of the paper towelling provided for cleaning windscreens. By the time he finished, the shirt and windcheater felt comparatively warm when he put them on. His leg began to ache badly and Kindling was surprised he hadn't noticed it before. Shock, he supposed. There was nothing he could do about it. It was just lucky the dark cloth of his jeans disguised both the bloodstain and the rip.

Slowly, he was beginning to think properly

again. He moved on, limping markedly now, until he reached a public telephone. Silently he congratulated himself on always buying telephone credit cards, rather than relying on loose change. When the taxi company answered he explained to the operator he'd been in an accident and looked a mess—would the driver not be alarmed?

The cabbie wasn't alarmed, but he looked at his passenger warily as Kindling collapsed in the back seat and closed his eyes, luxuriating in the warmth of the vehicle.

'Been in trouble, mate?'

Kindling reluctantly opened his eyes. 'Yes, an accident. Car accident. Nothing too serious.'

'I'm surprised the police didn't give you a ride home, with you looking like that.'

'No, no police.' He saw the driver's expression become nervous and Kindling fought back the fog of weariness threatening to overwhelm him. 'Ah—I was in my girlfriend's car. But she's already married. I made sure she was all right and the police were on their way, then slipped away. We thought it would be the best thing.' The story sounded bad, but it must have been convincing, because the cab-driver treated him to a stony silence for the rest of the trip. Obviously he was a man who believed in the sanctity of marriage. Kindling was glad. It let him sleep the entire journey, although he was annoyed with himself when he woke up outside the motel units. He'd planned to get out half a block away, so he could return as quietly as he'd left.

He paid the taxi and let himself in, finding the

key in his shoulder bag, which remarkably he still possessed. The torch had been lost somewhere during the final moments at Vasta's house. Inside the motel room a digital clock told him it was 3.00 a.m. Kindling stripped to his underwear, turned the room's heating to maximum and fell on the bed, rolling under the blankets in the last seconds of consciousness.

11

AN INSISTENT TAPPING BROUGHT him awake. Kindling opened his eyes, then quickly shut them again. The light was still on and the glare hurt. The tapping came again.

'Matthew? Come on, open the damn door!' someone hissed outside. It was Louise Corry.

'Lou?' he called groggily. 'Hang on a second.' He tumbled from the bed and groaned as every muscle in his body ached. Then he saw the clock. It was 3.30 a.m. He'd been asleep for only half an hour. 'What the—?' he asked himself. Walking to the door he became aware of his near-nakedness. Fumbling quickly in a drawer he came up with a tracksuit bottom, which he pulled on. He didn't need the top. The room was already sweltering from the heater. Corry rapped on the door again, apparently thinking Kindling had gone back to sleep.

'I'm coming,' he said testily. Unlatching the door he stood back as she bustled in breathing clouds of steam from the cold night air. Corry brought a draft of chill in with her and it awakened Kindling further, bringing up goose bumps on his arms and chest. He hurriedly shut the door.

'Lou, it's bloody three-thirty in the morning. Don't you ever go to sleep or something? I hope you've got a damn good reason for this.' He tried to muster some righteous anger.

She was wearing jeans, a woollen jumper and jacket, with a scarf wrapped tightly around her neck. Louise quickly moved as close as she could to the heater. 'I had to see you,' she explained, then frowned at the heater settings and how hot the room was.

'Why? Couldn't it wait until morning?' He thought he knew the answer. 'Has something happened aboard Freedom?'

'No, nothing there.'

'Then what is it? I can't imagine anything else important enough to drag me out of bed in the middle of the night.' He stared at her, but found it impossible to maintain his anger. 'Well, no doubt you're going to tell me. I suppose you should sit down.' He waved at the only lounge chair, sitting himself on the end of the bed. He couldn't resist lying back and closing his eyes. Sleep hovered dangerously close as he listened to her remove the jacket.

'Matthew, what were you doing at Anton Vasta's house tonight?'

He immediately sat up and looked at her, but too suddenly. The wave of dizziness passed and his eyes focused. 'How do you know where I was?'

'Of course I know,' she replied impatiently. 'What do you expect? I know almost your every move tonight.'

'How? Do you have someone watching me?' Inwardly, he cursed. He should have guessed.

'Most of the time,' she nodded.

'What the hell for?' he demanded, getting angry.

'So you don't do stupid things like you did tonight,' she retorted, then her voice softened. 'Matt, look at yourself.'

His eyes drifted to the mirror. The cuts and scratches on his face were inflamed and looked sore. 'Then why didn't someone come and help?' he asked quietly. He fingered the cuts.

'They weren't allowed to follow you into the house itself, or the grounds. They were waiting outside. It was going to be bad enough if *you* got caught in there. You got into trouble?' she asked unnecessarily, gesturing at his injuries. 'If they'd known you were getting hurt, it might have been different. They said you left the house leaving every light in the place on.'

He let out a bark of laughter, startling her. 'Me? I wish it was! Damn—' His eye filled with tears and unexpectedly he began to shake as reaction set in. She watched him, concerned.

'I've got a small first aid kit in the car. I'll go and get it. Will you put the kettle on? I'd like a strong coffee.'

He nodded, wincing at the blast of cold air from the door as she left, leaving it slightly open. He stood and went to the bathroom, filled the electric jug, returned, and plugged it in next to the television. His eyes fell on one of the small bottles of scotch supplied by the motel and on impulse he broke the seal and poured the contents into a glass. Two cubes of ice went in from the freezer. They tinkled against the side of the tumbler as his hand trembled. Exhaustion and the worst memories from the night were taking over his mind.

'Sit on the bed,' Louise said, closing the door behind her with one foot, her hands full with a soft plastic bag and her own handbag. She watched him limp back to the bed. 'What's wrong with your leg?' She looked closer. 'It looks bad.'

'It's nothing,' he tried.

'Rubbish, Matthew. It's bleeding,' she snapped, pointing. He blinked at her anger and looked down. A red stain was seeping through the tracksuit. 'Take them off,' she ordered. 'Give me a look.'

He began to protest, but gave in under her steely expression. Meekly he sat on the bed and pulled the tracksuit off, grunting as the bloody patch stuck to the wound. Self-conscious, he was glad he still wore his underwear.

'Jesus, Matthew. That's no scratch.' She put her hands on either side of the injury and manipulated the skin gently. He became very aware of her closeness and her hands touching his body. 'We'll start with this one, in case we run out of stuff.'

Louise cleaned the wound as best she could, stopping only to make her coffee. Kindling sipped gratefully on the scotch. She pulled a face as the severity of the wound was revealed. Opting for a large piece of elastoplast over a wad of cotton she asked, 'This will hurt like hell when you take it off, do you mind? I could shave the surrounding skin, if you like.'

'No, just do it.' The disinfectant was stinging.

'Have you had a tetanus shot lately?'

'Three years ago, roughly,' he replied, after some thought.

'Too long. I'll bring you another, tomorrow morning.'

He looked down at the top of her head as she bent to his leg. Her confident manner and calm authority made him whisper, 'Lou, who the hell *are* you?'

'No one special,' she said briefly, then seemed to relent. 'Matthew, I'm not in a position to explain what I do, or who I do it *for*. You'll just have to accept, for the moment, that I have your best interests in mind—and that's because it suits me, too. I can't answer most of your questions. Any of them, probably. You're an intelligent man, so you're likely to ask all the wrong ones.' She smiled. 'Maybe later, when things have slowed down a bit, I can tell you more. I should add you're being a little difficult for me, pulling stunts like tonight.'

'I find that ridiculous,' he said, annoyed. She was treating him like a child. 'And you can't just say, "I can't tell you" and leave it at that.'

She stared up at him and Kindling was surprised by the hard look in her eyes. 'I can, Matthew, and I have. Don't push me. We'll only both get upset.'

He returned her gaze for a moment, then held his hands up in surrender. Any other time he might have persisted, but now he was too tired. 'Okay, I believe you. That doesn't mean I like it.' She didn't answer him.

Louise finished tending his leg and stood back and looked at it, dissatisfied. 'It'll have to do,' she decided, then quickly pulled off her sweater. 'It's damn hot in here—but I guess you're not wearing much.' She stepped close and probed the cut on his eyebrow. Kindling smelled her perfume and felt slightly light-headed. Corry wasn't wearing a bra and her nipples made small points in her T-shirt. He tried not to look, but couldn't stop himself. She moved lower, inspecting the scratches on his cheek.

'What the hell did these?' she asked, frowning. 'It looks like they're infected already. That's damn quick.'

Kindling checked the slashes on his arm where the cat had attacked him. They also appeared reddened and poisoned. 'A cat,' he told her mildly, but when he traced his finger over the scratches a stab of pain ran up to his shoulder. 'A particularly nasty and filthy cat,' he added.

'No such thing,' she murmured, searching the first aid kit. 'As a filthy cat, I mean.'

'This thing was a brute. Biggest cat I've ever seen, and it *was* filthy. Covered in stuff and stinking.'

'And it attacked you?' she asked, suppressing a smile.

Kindling took a long, reflective sip of his drink, thinking about how much he should tell her—not how much he *wanted* to tell her, because he wanted to tell her everything. He desperately needed to talk about his experience in Vasta's house. He gave her a sobering look. 'Lou, I saw the ghost of a little girl in that house tonight. She spoke to me. I think it's the same one.'

This took Louise totally by surprise. She stared at him. 'The same one as what?'

'As the ghost in Freedom. It was a little girl, about seven or eight years old.' As he spoke, Corry's mind clicked too and she realised what he was saying. Stunned, she sat on the bed next to him.

'That's fantastic—but how?'

'That's not all,' Kindling began, a strain entering into his voice. 'There was a room built beneath the house.'

He went on to explain about the ritual cellar with its mural, then stopped and went back to the beginning, telling Louise about the blood-red eyes in the garden, the unlocked doors, the garage and the black cat. He came back to the subject of the cellar and tried to be precise. Corry was fascinated and listened intently. Her coffee went ignored, but Kindling steadily consumed his scotch until the glass was empty. She absently reached out for the bottle and re-filled it for him, not bothering with any ice. Louise looked like she wanted a glass herself, but there was only enough for one more, so she took a sip of Kindling's before handing it back. Absorbed as he was in recounting his night, Kindling noticed and felt a small, youthful thrill at the intimacy.

'And then the ghost appeared?' she asked.

'First, all the candles in the room lit themselves, one by one. It was like an announcement she was coming.' Louise's eyes widened. Kindling stopped uncertainly, then began again. 'That's another thing. Something's been nagging at me since I started walking back here, but I was still too damned scared to even think about it properly. I'm still scared now, but having you here is helping.' He lapsed into a troubled silence.

'I don't understand,' she prompted him gently. He took a deep breath before answering.

'I think the house—the ghost, whatever—knew I was coming. That's why the door was unlocked. I bet *any* door I'd tried would've been unlocked. And the rug being pulled back like that. It was too heavy for the cat to have done it. The security system, too. That's why it didn't go off. Something stopped it—something that can light candles like *that*,' he said wryly, clicking his fingers and shaking his head. 'But that was nothing, compared to when I tried to leave. She said I *couldn't* leave. It put the fear of God into me and I ran for it. The house went crazy. Things flew through the air and hit me. That's how I got this,' he put a finger to the cut on his eyebrow. Louise began gathering the first aid kit together again.

'So, what did she *say*?' Louise asked with a touch of impatience.

'Not much, really. Just that she was scared and alone—and *cold*. Then she seemed to change, she got angry—or mad, insane, I mean. So I tried to run, but I had trouble getting out. She got worse. Angrier or crazier, I don't know. Finally, I made it out.' He glanced up at Louise, who was standing close, cleaning the wound on his head. 'The last time she spoke, it wasn't her voice at all. I swear it was Anton Vasta's.'

That made Louise step back and gaze at him, her eyes searching his. 'That's a pretty crazy thing to say, Matt.'

'I know. I don't understand any of it. By the time I got out of the house, I—' he stopped and took a shaky breath. 'Look, Lou. I just don't know anything any more.'

'Okay,' she began rubbing the back of his neck. 'Take it easy. Tomorrow—' Louise remembered the time and corrected herself '—later today we'll write all this down, before you forget anything.' She didn't want to continue, but knew she must. 'Matthew, just a little more. It's important, in case your mind shuts anything out while you sleep. It can do that, you know, it's like a safety-valve thing. Is there anything else? A brief outline will do, so I can ask you about it later.' Seeing the stress building on his face, she felt cruel pressing him.

'I don't think I'll sleep,' he said quietly.

'Of course you will. As soon as I stop annoying you, you'll probably collapse for about twenty-four hours,' she smiled. 'Except I won't let you do that, either. We'll have to explain all this to Wiley, you know. It's the first thing he'll be told in the morning, if he doesn't know already.' Louise kept her voice light, hoping to ease his tension. She was startled when he suddenly buried his head in his hands.

His voice broke. 'Lou, I heard something tonight that makes everything so damned *impossible*. And it's terrifying for me—as if everything else isn't frightening enough!' He heard the dreadful humming of the wheelchair in his mind again. 'God, I don't understand *anything* any more.'

Louise quickly sat next to him and put her arm around his shoulder. She thought Kindling was going to cry, but he pulled himself under control with a big effort. His glass was empty again and he stared at it ruefully.

'There's no more scotch,' she whispered. 'But there's gin or brandy. I think I'll join you this time.'

He didn't know if she genuinely wanted the liquor, or was simply trying to limit his own intake. She took another glass from the top of the refrigerator and filled them both with gin and ice. Then she crawled onto the centre of the bed and sat with her legs tucked underneath her. Kindling turned around to face her. Despite his inner turmoil, he recognised the intimacy of the moment.

'So, tell me,' she said quietly.

'It's a long story.'

'It's a big drink,' she countered, holding up her glass.

But it wasn't a long story. It only seemed that way because Kindling had kept it bottled up inside himself for so long. And the torment of the recurring nightmares had felt endless.

It took only minutes to recount his visit to the Williams' house, with all the details and its terrifying conclusion. Then he added what he'd heard at Vasta's house—the wheelchair—which connected the two events. When he finished Kindling felt strangely relieved. Apart from Stewart Andrews, he'd never discussed the episode with anyone.

'Matthew, why didn't you tell me about this before?' Louise looked at him over the rim of her glass.

'It's something—personal. It's been as though it was the onset of my own insanity, nothing to do with anyone else. And I've always feared it could get worse, unless I left it alone. I thought I should keep it hidden and not tell anyone.' He smiled wanly. 'Sounds stupid, doesn't it? Well, now I know. It's got worse anyway.' He sounded bitter.

Corry thought for a while. 'So, you're saying your experience of over two years ago has somehow become connected with what's happening now?'

'Somehow. I know what I *heard*. It was unmistakeable. I think I was *meant* to recognise it.'

'It's beyond anything I've had to deal with,' she admitted. 'But Matt, you still haven't told me what you were doing in Vasta's house in the first place.'

He surprised her by laughing. 'Damn, that all seems so insignificant now.' Then he remembered it wasn't, and a guarded expression came over his face.

'You can tell me, you know,' Louise said softly. 'I think you've got some serious doubts and you're holding them in, but we're on the same side here—' She paused and took a deep breath. 'No, there's no *sides* here at all. The American guys tend to create a little tension, I know. But we're all working on the same project with the hope of getting the same result. A successful result. It's just that Wiley and Smith do protect their own interests a little too—enthusiastically,' she finished.

'I've decided I don't like Mr Wiley,' Kindling told her flatly.

'I can understand that. Please, be a little more tolerant of him. It will make life easier for us all.' It sounded like a plea to make her own work go smoothly.

'And what about you?' he asked, more harshly than he intended. 'Is there still someone outside, keeping watch?'

'No, they figured you'd bed down for the night. They don't even know I'm here.'

'How do you *know*?'

'Matt, I do,' she said, sighing with exasperation. 'Look, trust me, okay? Trust me and I promise I'll explain more later, as we go along. Not now. Not tonight.'

Reluctantly he nodded, staying silent. The truth was, he wanted someone to trust and it didn't take much encouragement for him to agree. The silence grew and he realised she was still waiting for him to explain his visit to Vasta's house. Without looking at her he said, 'I don't believe it's Vasta you have up there in Freedom. I don't think it's his body.'

'What?' She was genuinely puzzled.

'The body,' he repeated. 'In the cryogenic section. I don't think it's Vasta's.'

'What on earth makes you say that?'

'Something he told me himself, shortly before he died. It was at the funeral of one of his friends, who'd died of cancer. Vasta told me he'd never been to a doctor in his life—not since he was a child, anyway.'

'So?' Louise shrugged. 'He was a healthy guy.'

'But Doctor Maine pointed out he'd had a kidney removed at some point. It wasn't there in the X-ray.'

'I remember,' she frowned.

'Well? What do you make of that?'

But she changed tack. 'And you went to Vasta's house to find proof he'd never had an operation in his life, right?'

'Something like that,' he muttered, hiding his face in the glass.

'Why, Matt? Why didn't you ask somebody about it?'

He gestured helplessly. 'I don't really know. I guess I've been fooling around for years now, doing nothing. Then this project comes along and gives me something to *do*. Except I end up sitting around waiting—and getting rubbed up the wrong way by Wiley. I suppose the idea of proving something—anything—gave me a new purpose, even if it was a bit negative. I sort of imagined the look on Wiley's face too, when I told him I knew the truth,' he added smiling. 'If I'd thought about it a bit longer, I probably wouldn't have done anything.'

'Or if you'd asked me about it,' she rebuked him mildly.

'Or that,' he agreed. 'Now it looks like I've started something worse.'

Louise shifted on the bed, gingerly shaking a cramp out of her leg. 'Matthew, all I can tell you is that too many people have invested too much time and effort for us to be reviving the wrong guy. That *is* Vasta up there, I promise you. There has to be another explanation.'

'I'd like to hear it,' he persisted, without enthusiasm.

'I agree, there's a few facts we need to check out—especially that missing kidney, even if it's just to find out how something like that was missed by the system.'

She finished her drink and put it on the floor next to the bed. 'Matthew, it's very late, I'm tired and I've had a glass full of gin. It's almost not worth going to bed, but I'd better. Do you mind if I stay with you tonight? I don't think I should drive home.'

The question stunned him, then he realised what she meant. Kindling's room was meant to be a single unit with a double bed, but like most, it also had a second, single bed tucked against the wall. She meant to sleep there. 'Of course I don't mind,' he said, recovering.

'Then can I borrow your toothbrush? In fact, I might have a very quick shower,' she decided. 'If you want to turn the lights out and crash, I'll fumble my way to the bed.'

'Use whatever you want,' he offered. She climbed off the bed and disappeared into the bathroom.

Kindling turned down the heating system and turned off the lights. He crawled under the sheets, but couldn't sleep. In the darkness he lay listening to the water running in the shower. It soon stopped, replaced by smaller splashing sounds. Louise brushing her teeth.

The bathroom door opened and he feigned sleep. Louise must have turned off the light in there too, because the unit stayed dark. His back turned, Kindling waited to hear the squeak of the opposite mattress, but instead he felt a small draft of air as the blanket on his own bed was lifted and a warm body slid in behind his.

'All this talk about ghosts has made me edgy,' she whispered in his ear. 'I didn't think you'd mind.'

Kindling didn't trust himself to speak. She snuggled up against his back, wrapping her arms around his waist. He gave one of her hands a squeeze to let her know he was awake. Her breath was warm on the nape of his neck. Kindling could feel the cloth of her T-shirt against his back and her bare legs touching his. She smelled slightly of soap. He wondered if she could feel the way his heart was beating with impossible strength.

It started with Louise making small, circular motions on his stomach with the tips of her fingers, as if she weren't really aware she was doing it. He responded by running his own fingers up and down her arm. She began kissing him on his neck and shoulders and he almost groaned as he realised what was going to happen. Then she pulled Kindling over onto his back and rolled on top of him.

'I guess I've been thinking about doing this since I first got here,' she whispered, then she sat up and Kindling heard the rustle of clothing as Louise pulled her T-shirt over her head. He reached out with both hands and ran them down her shoulders, past the sides of her breasts, through the curve of her waist and onto her hips. She was completely naked.

He felt shocked and intimidated. It was a long time since he'd been in bed with a woman. The last occasion had been one of only a few fumbling, inexperienced encounters. He felt Louise slide backwards, her skin moving deliciously against his, then her fingers hooked into the waistband of his underpants and drew them off. She lowered herself to lie flat on his body, kissing his neck and shoulders. Kindling tried to touch her properly, but his hands felt clumsy and ignorant. Rubbing instead of caressing, grasping instead of tenderly holding. Louise tried to guide him with whispers, but it made him feel even more immature and useless. He despaired for a moment at his personal history of stupid, pious propriety—unnecessary in his church, but which he'd embraced all the same—that had caused him to refuse sexual offers all those years. Louise snapped his mind back by moving her hand to his groin, touching him. Kindling suddenly panicked that, when they came to couple completely, he wouldn't be able to find her. Louise solved that problem by keeping him on his back and guiding herself down onto him. Instantly out of control he climaxed immediately. As his muscles spasmed it all felt wrong—unfair and shameful. Louise moved with him, murmuring softly, sighing endearments he couldn't hear through his own embarrassment.

Kindling knew it had gone badly, and blamed himself. He was too quick and too inexperienced, offering Louise little and losing control. He felt guilty and inadequate, and didn't know if it would compound his errors to admit to these feelings and apologise. But Louise read his thoughts. She lay on his chest, kissing him gently and caressing his face.

'Don't worry,' she told him, so quietly he could barely hear her above the sound of his own breathing. 'We're both very tired and I expect you haven't done this for a while.' He heard, rather than saw in the dark, the comforting smile in her words. 'It's only natural things don't go quite right. Maybe next time we'll plan it a little better.'

The knowledge there would be a next time was enough to chase away most of Kindling's fears. He hugged her close.

Kindling awoke first to the sound of his breakfast rattling into the servery. He sat up and the movement stirred Louise. She looked blearily at the clock.

'Six-thirty! Less than two hours' sleep.' She flopped back onto the pillow. 'Well, there's only one way to do this, I suppose.' Groaning, she toppled out of bed and went to the bathroom. The brief view of her body stirred Kindling. He quickly got up too and dragged on his tracksuit pants.

He startled the maid with the meals trolley as he burst out the door. She was only a few doors away. 'Good morning!' he called, hurrying towards her. At the same time he noticed her surprise at his bare chest, Kindling realised it was very cold outside. The pavement bit the soles of his feet. 'Sorry to alarm you,' he said, starting to shiver. 'But I was wondering if I could order another breakfast? I have a guest.' He realised what he was saying and his face reddened. 'Ah—she'll pay for staying, of course,' he stammered.

The maid, a pleasant, maternal-looking woman, laughed at his discomfort. 'The price you're paying, Mr Kindling, you can have a football team to stay as far as I'm concerned.' She peeked under the lid of a meal on the trolley. 'Would sausages and eggs do?' She leaned closer and winked. 'One of our regular customers. He won't mind if he gets his breakfast a little bit late.'

'Great, thank you.' Kindling took the offered plate. 'I really appreciate this.'

He carried the meal back to the unit and presented it to Louise as she came out of the bathroom with a towel wrapped around her. She exchanged the towel for Kindling's dressing gown while he found the rest of his tracksuit, then they sat together eating.

Kindling expected there to be some awkwardness between them—though he wasn't sure why. But there was none. They chatted easily about what might happen during the day—which Kindling wasn't looking foward to—and how best to deal with it. At one point Louise put down her knife and fork and grasped Kindling's hands between hers. She forced him to look into her eyes.

'Matt, you realise this has got to stop here.' At his sudden crestfallen expression she quickly reassured him. 'No, you don't understand. I mean, what happened last night and—' she reflected, '—what might happen in the future, that's got to stay between us. Outside of our *very* private moments it's got to be business as usual, okay? I don't want anyone to know there's anything intimate between us. I don't think it would be the best thing to do.'

'Okay,' he agreed, surprised but realising it made sense.

'So, no holding hands or sending little messages—whatever people do, all right? Unless we're absolutely sure we're alone, which will be almost never, considering the stir you're going to cause today.'

'Okay,' he repeated, then looked disappointed.

She gave him a conspiratorial smile. 'Which means I drive to the bureau this morning, but you still have to walk. I don't want to be seen giving you a lift at this time of day.'

'Thanks a bloody lot,' he grumbled. 'After I got you breakfast, too.'

Kindling enjoyed the walk to the weather bureau. The chilly morning was invigorating and as he walked he thought nothing could dampen his high spirits. Entering the Control Room, however, was like stepping into a cloud of disapproval. Bennington was on duty and after a guarded 'good morning' he kept his nose to the computer monitor. Louise waved hello and that was that, setting the scene between the two of them. Wiley, without Smith, didn't even bother with a cordial greeting. His disapproval filled the room with tension. He watched coldly as Kindling walked to the kitchen to make himself a coffee.

'Well, *Mister* Kindling. I'm told we have something to discuss. A midnight foray, it seems.' Wiley's sarcasm cut like a knife.

Kindling stopped in his tracks, aware he was not supposed to know that he'd been discovered. 'How do you know about that?'

'Of course we know about it. It's our *business* to know about it. It wasn't *your* business to go snooping around Vasta's house. Who do you think you are, fucking James Bond?' The American's anger was building. Kindling thought his best defence might be to match it.

'You're having me followed? I should be free to go wherever I want, *when* I want.'

'Nobody's free to jump fences after midnight and go ransacking empty houses,' Wiley said, almost sneering.

'I wasn't ransacking the place. I was looking for something.'

'He was *looking* for something,' Wiley mimicked, addressing the ceiling.

At that moment Smith and Michael Lay came in. They saw the confrontation, but didn't seem surprised. Obviously they were expecting it. Lay nodded curtly to everyone then quietly said to Wiley, 'I asked you to wait, Evan, until we got here.'

Wiley gestured angrily. 'He says he was looking for something.'

'Looking? Looking for what?'

Unexpectedly, Louise came to Kindling's aid. 'Matthew doesn't believe it's Vasta's body we have in Freedom. He thinks it's someone else.'

Wiley raised his eyebrows theatrically. 'Is that so? You've already discussed this?'

'He mentioned it to me yesterday. I didn't know he was going to search the house,' she lied smoothly.

Lay silenced Wiley with a hard glance, then approached Kindling. He spoke patiently. 'Matthew, will you please explain?'

Swallowing his anger, which had changed from contrived to real at the way they were regarding him, Kindling told them about his graveside conversation with Vasta and Doctor Maine's comments on the X-ray.

When he finished, Wiley burst out, 'So you decided all this was just a ruse?' He waved at the Control Room around them. 'None of it's real?'

'I wanted to find out for myself, before I started making any accusations,' Kindling said, getting tired of explaining himself.

'It's worth checking out,' Lay decided calmly.

'Most likely it was removed during the autopsy to check for poisons or disease,' Wiley offered, disgusted anyone thought the matter worth any consideration at all.

Kindling was amazed. It was such an obvious solution, yet he hadn't even considered it. Out of the corner of his eye he saw Louise bite her lip reflectively.

Lay had other ideas. 'There wasn't an autopsy as such. Vasta made arrangements to make sure there wasn't one, citing his cryogenic ambitions—and he needed some pretty influential friends to do that, I might add. He knew there was no point in killing himself the way he did, only to have an autopsy cause a damn sight more damage than any disease. As part of the preserving process any diseased organs should have been removed. Maybe that's what happened.' He turned to Corry. 'Lou, could you map out for us the movements of Vasta's corpse from the moment of death until it was handed over for transportation at the airport?' She nodded and he looked at Wiley. 'And you guys should check the rest of the journey right through to his actual incarceration on Freedom. Somewhere along the line, somebody must have decided he didn't need that kidney any more—unless he lied to Matthew in the first place. I think we should find out.'

Wiley agreed sullenly, not used to accepting orders, or even suggestions, from the Australian. Lay moved to Kindling.

'Matthew, don't do anything like this again, okay?' The threat was subtle, but there was no doubt it was one. 'You might have caused us a hell of a lot more complications than you realise.'

Kindling was stung by the condescending tone and reacted without thinking. 'I might have achieved a hell of a lot more, too. I saw the girl in there.'

Apart from Louise, who gave him a worried glance, the others looked at him blankly.

Lay was the first to ask, 'What girl?'

'Your ghost. The one in Freedom.'

Wiley glared at the monitors and Bennington, who put his hands up in innocence. 'Where did you see her? When?' he demanded.

'In the *house*,' Kindling dismissed the computers with a wave. 'In a cellar below the main lounge. It was like a ritual room. There was a table and candles, and what looked like bloodstains. She appeared in front of me, right there.' Kindling was almost enjoying the moment and the confusion he'd caused, but the memories of the child's spirit and the cellar soured it.

There was a long silence as each of them absorbed Kindling's news. Wiley, thinking furiously, groped behind him for a chair and sat down.

'We know about the room,' Lay admitted slowly. 'And the nasty hobbies that go with it. One of the people who was involved in that—a woman—disappeared. It's possible she ended up on that table herself.'

'Fuck that, Michael! That's ancient history,' Wiley snapped, scowling impatiently at Lay. 'Let him tell us about the girl's ghost.'

Kindling sat down, suddenly drained, and recounted the events of the night before. As he spoke Bennington quietly made some adjustments on his computer and started typing in notes. Kindling didn't mention the sounds from his past—the wheelchair, or Stewart Andrews calling to him from the blood-filled swimming pool.

'It's utterly fantastic,' Lay declared, moving to

sit heavily in a vacant chair. 'So, it appears this girl's spirit is somehow connected to Vasta.'

'Or Matthew,' Wiley suggested, giving Kindling a suspicious glare. Kindling managed to look unimpressed, although at Wiley's suggestion a knot of tension tightened in his gut. Things were bad enough as they were, without everyone believing that he was responsible for it all. His own suspicions were enough to cope with.

'We've been through that argument,' Lay said dismissively, flashing a meaningful glance at the American. 'I assume we haven't had anything unusual occur aboard Freedom since the last sighting? Nobody's reported anything to me.'

'No, of course not. You would have been told,' Smith answered testily. It was the first time he'd spoken. As Kindling had told his story Smith had listened while examining computer printouts and several faxes.

Kindling caught Louise's eye and she broke her own rules, briefly raising her eyebrows as if to say, *The pressure's starting to tell if these guys are beginning to snap at each other.*

'We've got to tell Canaveral,' Wiley decided. 'Right now.'

'And check out the house,' Smith added.

'The first's easy.' Lay turned to Bennington. 'You'd better give Czowkowski a call. Things might get a bit hectic for a while.' The operator nodded and lifted a phone. Lay turned back to the others. 'But if we want to check the house, that's something else. We've only been in there once before—and we went in the same way Matthew did. Legally, that house is locked up tight as Fort Knox and nobody's bothered to do anything about it because we never believed it was worth the effort. Vasta was too slippery a customer to leave a houseful of evidence. Now, two years down the track, to get through the front door with a warrant will be ten times harder and only cause a stir. Vasta's trust people may well tip off the press, and we'd have to explain publicly why we're suddenly interested in Anton Vasta again. And we don't want any attention, right?'

'So, we go in the back door,' Wiley said simply. It was plain this had always been his preferred option. 'We'll take Matthew with us. He knows the way,' he added slyly.

Kindling started nervously. 'I don't know if it's as easy as that.'

'Why? If *you* can do it, it shouldn't be too much trouble for a few trained people like ourselves. Anyway, the doors were unlocked for Christ's sake.'

'That's what I'm trying to tell you,' Kindling persisted, 'I think it was supposed to be easy. Someone *wanted* me to get inside. Now, it might be a different story. Those doors might be locked and the security system working.'

'Are you saying you were expected? You were *meant* to see—see her ghost?' Lay stuttered. The implications of Kindling's words bordered on the unbelievable. 'Why?'

'I don't know. It's something that occurred to me afterwards and I haven't had time to think about it,' Kindling took Louise's cue and found it easier to lie fluently than stumble on with half-truths. 'If I'd thought about it at the time, I probably wouldn't have stuck around to find out,' he finished wryly.

'That's all the more reason to take you along,' Wiley said maliciously, trying to goad Kindling. 'Your ghost can unlock everything again. Hey, we'll ring the doorbell.' He gave a harsh bark of laughter.

Lay tapped the top of the desk thoughtfully. 'We've got a few hours up our sleeve yet. Let's see what we can achieve going through the right channels first.' He ignored Wiley's annoyed look and stood. 'Dewey, turn those notes into a readable report and send it to Jack Hitchcock now. No doubt he'll come straight back to us on a hotline. But this way we'll avoid a lot of knee-jerk reactions and bullshit on the airwaves.' He turned to Kindling. 'Matthew, a lot of people will want to ask you a lot of questions. You'll just have to stay around until we're done. It might take a while.'

'Sure,' Kindling shrugged. 'It'll make a change to be doing something around here.'

'Okay, good. I'll go and see a few people myself and find out what I can.'

Michael Lay left the room. Wiley and Smith huddled together in a corner and left soon afterwards without offering any explanations or farewells. Czowkowski arrived and listened carefully to Bennington's appraisal of the situation and what was expected of them. Kindling had to recite the night's activities again for him—the story was getting shorter with each telling as he got more tired. Louise slipped past and interrupted to say she'd be back in a short while. She disappeared before he had a chance to respond.

Michael Lay was right. Kindling's news caused a boil of activity in Florida. Even though it was short notice, a procession of 'experts' on subjects ranging from psychology to poltergeists confronted Kindling via a one-to-one video communications link. Infuriatingly, they mostly asked the same questions and he began to lose his temper repeating the same answers. Then interest in him started to taper off and eventually Kindling gave up waiting for his next interrogator. He sat on the floor, wedging himself into a corner, and promptly fell asleep. Later someone did ask for him again, but Czowkowski diplomatically replied Kindling was temporarily unavailable. The person faded from the screen and didn't return, the questions remaining unasked.

'Matthew, wake up.'

It was Louise, crouched in front of him and shaking his knee. 'Come on, wake up. We have to see someone.'

He opened his eyes and fought back the fog of sleep. The bright lights of the Control Room hurt and he dimly saw Louise as a black silhouette. His entire body seemed filled with different sorts of pain.

'What?' he groaned.

'We're going for a drive,' she said, helping him to his feet. He winced and gingerly flexed his limbs. Louise moved closer. 'I want to get you out of here before Wiley or Lay return and stop you leaving.' The two operators could easily hear this, but Louise apparently trusted them to be discreet.

'I feel bloody awful.'

'Serves you right for falling asleep on the floor. Why didn't you borrow the guys' cot?'

'I didn't mean to sleep,' he muttered, stretching and trying to work some of the pain away.

'Well, don't worry. We're going to see a doctor.'

Louise moved away and explained to Czowkowski that they were going out for a while. Then she half-dragged Kindling out the door. By the time they reached the car park he began to recover properly.

'Where are we going?'

'Wait until we're on the move.'

She opened the door of a smart, near-new Toyota. Kindling watched as she drove quickly but smoothly through the traffic. He wondered if he should be offering some sort of intimacy, like holding her hand or touching her leg. Louise's serious, professional manner didn't invite it. She began to explain herself.

'We're going to see a Doctor Kempthorne. He was the guy on duty the night Vasta's frozen body was brought into the hospital. He's head of a department now. Doesn't get his hands dirty quite so often.'

'You did well,' Kindling said, impressed. 'And quick. How did you manage that?'

'I got lucky with some calls. The ambulance people had his signature on the receipt for Vasta's body and it was readable. Did you know there was no Death Certificate issued? Vasta had a damned sight more pull than I realised. Anyway, I phoned Kempthorne and told him what we were after, in a roundabout way, and it got very interesting.' She waited for Kindling to ask, so he obliged.

'How?'

'Well, he finally admitted to removing the

kidney. Said he had to, so I told him we had no record of that and I'd have to come and see him. Take a few notes and probably make some copies of his records. I hinted it was a government red-tape thing, like a watchdog on medical practices, and I'd show him ample identification when I got there. That's when it got even funnier.'

Kindling waited while she negotiated a busy intersection.

'He said he had no records of removing the organ. Can you believe it? I sure as hell can't. Even when you're talking about a dead person, you can't go removing bits and pieces and not make some sort of official record of it.'

'I suppose not,' Kindling murmured, not really knowing about these things.

'Anyway, I definitely got the feeling from this doctor that he was unhappy discussing the subject, which is good enough reason to pay him a visit.' She became brisk. 'Now listen, I've got good ID, but you haven't. So I'll just introduce you as my associate and if he complains about your presence, you might have to leave. Otherwise, play it by ear along with me, okay?'

'Okay,' he nodded nervously. Louise surprised him with her businesslike manner.

They were led into a spacious and well-decorated office. The walls and ceiling were painted in light pastel colours and winter sunshine filled the room from generous windows framed by sheer drapes. Low bookshelves, a coffee table and paintings completed the decor. The only indication it was an office was the large desk with two visitors' chairs arranged neatly in front of it. One corner of the desk held a compact computer terminal.

Kindling and Corry sat in the visitors' chairs and waited, but not for long. A tall man, ill-dressed in a wide-shouldered, baggy suit, entered. He wore stylish glasses and walked as if he was self-conscious about his height. At the sight of two people, not one, he did a momentary double-take.

'Ms Corry?' His voice had a deep timbre. 'I expected you alone.'

Louise stood and offered her hand. Kindling did the same, introducing himself quietly. As Kempthorne moved around the desk he motioned them to sit.

'I hope this won't take too long,' he said. 'I'm quite busy.'

'Of course. No, we shan't take long,' Louise assured him with a non-committal smile. She searched in her shoulder bag and produced a plastic identity card. 'If you don't recognise this, or doubt its authenticity, there are several phone numbers on the back you can call now and I guarantee someone will convince you we're okay.'

Kempthorne squinted at the card, raised his eyebrows briefly and handed it back. He looked towards Kindling, expecting something similar, but when Kindling stayed still and silent the doctor seemed more impressed than offended. 'I'll take your word for it.'

'Thank you. We're here to discuss Anton Vasta. You were in charge the night his body was brought in?'

Kempthorne steepled his fingers in front of his

face and looked resolute. 'As we discussed on the telephone, yes.'

'Doctor, you're aware of what happened to his body afterwards, aren't you? In a small way, you were a part of that process.'

'I was—informed—he was going to be preserved in a manner so that he may live again,' Kempthorne said, his tone clipped and precise. 'As against someone who is to be, say, embalmed for the purpose of an extended viewing after death, or someone who has donated their cadaver for medical research. A cryogenic process, if I remember correctly.'

Kindling felt a cold shiver run down his spine at the word 'cadaver'. It sounded grotesque. At the same time he heard a note of disapproval in the doctor's voice.

'What exactly does that mean? That you're expected to preserve the body? What would you normally do?' Louise asked, pulling a notepad from her bag and setting it on her knee. She crossed her legs so Kempthorne couldn't see what she wrote, her pen poised over the blank page. Kempthorne looked concerned for a moment.

'Not much, really. It's very rare we need to touch a corpse. The funeral parlour people are normally the first to physically alter the body. And if a criminal autopsy had to be performed, it would be done by someone employed by the police department or authorised to act on their behalf, not me, and not at this hospital either. So you see, I normally wouldn't have worked on the body.'

'But you removed a kidney. You told me.'

Kempthorne glanced at Kindling, who didn't

respond, not trusting himself to act his part. Kindling didn't realise his continued silence and steadfast expression were disconcerting the doctor.

'At the same time I was told about the intention to preserve the body, I was also asked to examine it and remove anything potentially harmful. Some diseases and infections can spread much more quickly in a corpse, of course.'

'Right,' Louise murmured, scribbling on the pad. Out the corner of his eye Kindling was amazed to see meaningless scrawls and doodles on the pad. 'So, the kidney was diseased?'

'Yes.'

'How did you find out? Did you cut the body open? That doesn't sound like keeping Vasta in one piece for preservation.'

'Blood tests,' Kempthorne said shortly.

'Really?' Louise wrote again. 'Very thorough.' She looked up and sounded almost apologetic. 'I mean, considering the body was only passing through your hands, right?'

Instead of explaining further Kempthorne asked, 'How did you discover the kidney was missing? Why has it taken so long?'

'A routine X-ray of the corpse, just to make sure everything's all right. Someone noticed the organ missing, somebody else noted it didn't gel with our records—one thing led to another and everyone started asking questions.' Louise smiled and shrugged at the ways of the world, but Kempthorne stared at her stonily.

'Why? Are they concerned he might require his kidney at a later date?'

Louise looked surprised. 'Well, that's one point,

of course. But our main concern here is the body arrived for processing in the States in a different condition to that described in his medical records—records we supplied believing them as complete and up-to-date. There's been a breakdown in the system here and we want to make sure it doesn't happen again.' She added, seriously, 'And there's the very real possibility that one day we might have to explain to Mr Vasta where his kidney disappeared. It could be a little embarrassing, if we don't know.'

'Utterly ridiculous,' Kempthorne said, not bothering to hide his disdain.

'You're entitled to that opinion, Doctor Kempthorne. It doesn't concern us,' Louise replied, making more notes. She took her time, almost filling the page. The silence lengthened and Kempthorne became agitated.

'Is that it?' he asked eventually. 'Is that the end of it?'

Louise re-read her notes and looked doubtful. 'I'm not sure, Doctor. At a guess, I'd say someone else will come and see you with a typed statement, ask you to verify it and sign it, too. Probably ask you some more questions—nothing serious. After that,' she paused and tapped the pad with her biro, 'I really don't know. We're not too happy with these people,' she said. 'And this is the first real incident where it looks like they fouled up. It might be worth an inquiry.'

'An *inquiry*?' It was hard to tell if Kempthorne was outraged or merely startled.

Louise tapped the pad again. 'The point is, I don't think they were in a position to authorise your removing *anything*. Not even a fingernail.' Kempthorne didn't respond. 'Actually,' Louise frowned, as if the idea had just occurred to her, 'you might be in rather a bad position.'

'That is preposterous,' Kempthorne snapped, his face white.

'Well, I'll admit it needs some clarification,' Louise mused, pondering her notes and unruffled by his anger.

'*Clarification?*' Kempthorne looked at both of them, his eyes glittering. Then he glanced around his office, as if deciding whether or not his next words were worth the price. Kindling could feel Kempthorne struggling with something inside of himself, and he willed the doctor to break down. Louise, who'd hoped the doctor could be pushed to this, kept tensely quiet.

'Can I offer you some *off-the-record* clarification, Miss Corry?' Kempthorne leaned forward, as if he wanted to push his anger into her face. 'I assure you, it will clarify everything, but you might not like it.'

Louise stared calmly at him, then flipped the notepad closed. 'Okay, we can do that and maybe discuss the consequences later.' She glanced at Kindling for confirmation and he managed a nod.

'I'm so grateful,' Kempthorne said drily, leaning back. His anger was set in the lines on his face and the hard edge in his words. 'Your clarification, Miss Corry, is some fool with more millions than commonsense, who believes he can freeze the very essence that keeps this fantastic machine we call the human body functioning. He believes he can store it God knows where, so he can be revived when the world's pastures are greener. A fool who suicides in favour of a million-to-one chance—more, probably—instead of living his remaining years with dignity.' Kempthorne leaned closer again. 'In the same building as this man's corpse we have a little girl less than eight years old. Both her kidneys are ruined beyond repair, but she still wants to have a shot at living, even though it's impossible. Do you know what these two people have in common?'

Neither of his two listeners answered. Kindling held his breath.

'Blood,' Kempthorne continued with a sudden, defeated sigh. 'An uncommon blood type—not rare, but uncommon enough. In fact, rare in the circumstances.' He folded his hands neatly on the desk in front of him and waited for their reaction. Kempthorne could see they were shocked, but he didn't know it was who he'd mentioned, not what he'd done, that stunned them.

'You mean, you *donated* his kidney?' Louise whispered, all pretence falling away.

Kempthorne slumped and passed a hand across his face. 'It was a very long shot, but we thought it was worth a try.'

'But she died,' Kindling spoke, his voice a dry rasp. The doctor looked at him, surprised at the emotion in Kindling's words.

'Yes, about two days later—but how did you know that?'

'You didn't look as though the story had a happy ending,' Louise said quickly. 'Doctor, do you remember her name?'

'No, forgive me, I don't.' Kempthorne sighed again. 'But it shouldn't be hard to find. I suppose it's necessary?'

'If you give us all the information you've got, I swear you won't hear of this again,' Louise stated firmly.

The doctor stared at her, then turned his gaze briefly to Kindling. Kempthorne looked like a man who realised too late that he'd been bluffed. His anger flickered for a moment, then slowly faded.

It wasn't worth the trouble. Get the matter over and done with.

He was, after all, a busy man.

'I'll pull the file,' he said quietly, reaching for his computer.

Kempthorne entered some data and jotted down a reference number, then excused himself and left the room. Kindling and Louise waited in silence, wrapped in their own thoughts.

Kempthorne returned and dropped a thin manila folder in Corry's lap. 'I extracted the X-rays. They'll mean nothing to you.'

Louise opened the file and flipped through the pages. Most of them were a jumble of technical medical data, but near the end she found a glossy document. It was more a sales brochure than an official report. It was designed, Louise realised, to convince an undecided donor that the girl was a worthy cause—a cause worth donating a kidney for. The article was probably distributed nationwide through major hospitals. In the top corner of the single page a colour photograph showed a cute, fair-haired little girl with a captivating smile.

'Ellen Georgina Littlewood,' Louise read the name aloud and tipped the file slightly, so Kindling could see it better. 'Well?'

A line of sweat formed on his top lip and he

sat very still, staring at the photograph.

'That's her,' he nodded shakily. 'That's the little girl I saw.'

12

CELIA HERESON WAS A dedicated astronaut. It was her job. She doted on Freedom's systems exactly the way NASA wanted her to—it was why she was up there, more than anything else. Celia helped the others, particularly Seerey, but her main responsibility was carrying out tests and experiments on Freedom itself. She evaluated how well the space station performed, made suggestions on how it might be improved, and noted which areas were becoming obsolete or unserviceable. She knew more about Freedom than any of the others, including Seerey.

The rest of the crew were trained in specific areas of the space station, though their skills overlapped as a precaution against illness or—as this tour savagely illustrated—tragedy. It was part of the preparation for their stay in orbit, aside from what they hoped to achieve within their own scientific fields. In theory, each tour included an expert on every system built into Freedom, understudied by someone like Celia Hereson. Unless there was a severe attrition rate among the crew, there should always be somebody well trained in operating and repairing any part of the space station.

To the best of its ability, through its intensive training, NASA tried to prepare their astronauts for every eventuality.

It didn't include the paranormal.

Celia's encounter with Ellen Littlewood's ghost came after a grim announcement from Alex Seerey. The crew of Freedom were eating their meals together now, although this often interfered with their schedules. The deaths of two of their members brought them closer together, and it scared them, too. All except for Joseph King, who still led an extraordinarily solitary existence.

Seerey, Celia Hereson, Judith Cianta and Lee Wynn floated easily about the Command Module as Seerey pointed out a hurricane that had formed off the Florida coast. 'If it moves any closer to Canaveral, it might mess up communications a little, but I doubt it. Even if they do take precautions and shut down some things, they can always relay a landline through Houston.'

'What's it called?' Judith asked, fascinated by the spiral whirl of cloud on the screen.

'Hurricane Ben. It's already a bad one and building up, too. It's a wait-and-see situation at the moment. You never know what the damn things are going to do, they're so unpredictable.'

'Get it while it's hot!' Dawkins interrupted, coming through the access tunnel with five plastic-and-aluminium meal containers stacked between his hands. He read the labels on the lids and gave them out, then pulled five plastic spoons from his top pocket.

'What about Joe?' Seerey asked above the crackle of lids being prised off trays.

'Couldn't see him, but his bunk shield's down, so I guess he's having a sleep.'

'Strange guy,' Judith murmured, echoing the others' thoughts.

'You know,' Seerey said, chewing reflectively. 'When I'm home, I avoid anything even remotely like jelly.' He was referring to their meals. Unless the contents were by nature a moist, cohesive substance, the individual ingredients were held together by an appropriately-flavoured jelly to prevent crumbs or tid-bits getting loose in the atmosphere. Much of the food resembled chunky baby food.

'I quite like this stuff,' Dawkins said amiably. 'Better than my home cooking, that's for sure,' he added with a laugh.

'If Jack Hitchcock knew we were eating in here, he'd have a fit,' Seerey said. 'One morsel of gravy in one of his computer systems and we'd never hear the end of it.'

'One day he'll pop up on the comm-link and catch us,' Lee warned.

'No doubt,' Seerey nodded, but no one moved to turn the system off. He finished his meal, waited until the others had done so too, then sighed. 'I've been avoiding this for a few hours, because I don't like it. I suppose now's as good a time as any, though. I can fill Joe in later.'

His tone made them look up sharply. Dawkins said, 'It doesn't sound like we're going to like it, either.'

'No, probably not,' Seerey said. 'The Revival program is scheduled to run at least another ten days, and after that we're all guessing. Who knows how long it'll last? Though we know *we* can only stay up here for a finite period of time. Regardless, Hugh's body won't last much longer at all,' he finished sombrely.

Everyone looked at him. Dawkins muttered, 'I wondered about that.'

'He'll be decomposing even now,' Seerey went on. 'Apart from the obvious factor of discomfort to those working nearby, there's an enormous health risk. Body bags are not standard equipment in a space station. I suspect they might be after this tour,' he ended drily.

'Jesus, what a fuck-up.' Celia frowned at her empty tray, suddenly feeling slightly nauseous. 'So, what do we do?'

'We have to bury him.'

'Bury him? How?'

'Easy. We take him out through the Airlock and push him towards home. Like John, he'll re-enter on his own and burn up to nothing.'

'Hell, it still doesn't seem right,' Dawkins pulled a face. 'What about his family? What do they say about it?'

'That's not a deciding factor. His wife left him some time ago and doesn't give a damn. It must have been a nasty separation. They had one child, a boy, and he was killed in a plane accident five years ago travelling between the two parents.'

'No wonder the guy didn't smile a lot,' Judith said quietly.

Celia saw Seerey looking expectantly at Dawkins and she spoke up before he could say anything. 'I'll do it,' she offered. 'I'll suit up and take him out. I want another walk this tour, and this might be the last chance. I'll do a seal check while I'm out there, if you like.'

Seerey hesitated, then agreed. 'Okay, but forget the seal check. I don't want any extended EVAs at all. Minimum risks for *everybody* is our motto from now on. Just take him out through the Airlock, over the laddertrack and shove him towards Earth, then get back inside. Use the Umbilical since you haven't got far to go.'

'We lost the seal-tester with John, anyway,' Lee reminded them.

'That's true.' Seerey turned back to Celia. 'So check your suit from top to bottom, then get someone to double-check it. And let Scott give you a once-over too, before you go. Nobody leaves anything to chance, okay?'

'Sure thing, Alex,' she said easily, seeing the new lines of strain at the corners of his eyes for the first time. 'When do you want to do it?'

'As soon as you're ready, let me know. The sooner the better, I suppose.'

'I'll check the suit right now.'

The decision sobered them. Celia offered to dispose of the leftovers on her way to the Airlock and carefully gathered the trays together, making sure she didn't dislodge any scraps of food to drift in the atmosphere. In the galley she fed them into the maw of the disposal unit, closed the lid and flipped the switch. She listened as the sharp, powerful jaws crushed the rubbish and gulped it backwards to be compressed into a waiting bag. Later, when the bag was full, it would be ejected towards deeper space. *A fine statement from mankind, for any aliens that might discover it—a bag full of garbage,* Celia thought.

The Airlock seemed colder than the rest of Freedom, but Celia knew she must be imagining it. The suits were strapped against the bulkhead in pairs—all except Scott Dawkins'. His suit had been mated with John Quantey's. The new, custom-made suit for Vasta had a place of its own on another bulkhead. Celia's suit was behind Hugh Lyghtson's and she felt an odd reluctance to touch his as she extracted her own. For a moment she worried Seerey might want to dress Lyghtson in his suit. She shivered at the thought of doing the job and realised it would be pointless. The corpse was securely trussed up already.

Five minutes later Celia was halfway through her suit check, before she realised her mind wasn't on the job. She mustered her concentration and started again, whispering the name of each action to herself as she performed it. Then the beep of a computer came clearly across the access tunnel from the Cryogenic Module, announcing it had completed a program.

'Damn,' Celia said aloud, torn between investigating the program and completing her suit check, which shouldn't be interrupted. The cryogenics was Dawkins' and Lee Wynn's responsibility, she knew, but the Revival program was still in its infancy and nothing too important could have occurred. It was probably something she could verify for them. She came to a decision and finished her spacesuit inspection, being sure not to rush it, then went to an intercom station.

'It's Celia here,' she called. 'Lee or Scott, are you there?'

Lee's voice answered. 'We're both still in the Command Module. What's up, Celia?'

'I think the cryogenics system just completed something. Do you want to come and check? Or I can do it for you, if you like.'

There was a pause before Lee replied and Celia pictured the two of them conferring. While she waited, Celia chided herself. Why didn't she just poke her head through the tunnel and look first? It was probably nothing worth worrying about at all. With a flash of guilt she realised it didn't need much of an excuse for her *not* to go inside the Cryogenics Module. The place gave her the creeps, especially now with Hugh's body at the far end.

'It's almost certain to be a temperature mark,' Lee came back. 'The program makes a note every time the body temp achieves a rise of a full degree. All we have to do is make sure it's happened at the right time—that he's not heating up too fast or too slow. If you turn to page four on the computer, there's a graph table showing where the temperature's supposed to be and compares it to where it actually is. They should match up. The graph's duplicated in the paperwork on the clipboard, too. If everything's okay, just initial the right place. It's no big deal. Do you mind?'

'Piece of cake,' Celia answered easily, hoping her reluctance didn't show in her voice. 'Next time you guys come back here, can you do a check on my suit?'

'That's a trade.'

Celia took her spacesuit back to the bulkhead, putting it on top of Lyghtson's. With a sigh she pushed herself into the access tunnel towards the Cryogenics Module. Coming out the hatchway into the module the first thing her eyes settled on was the long, wrapped bundle at the other end. Celia wrinkled her nose at what may have been a very faint aroma of rotting meat. 'Jesus, Hugh. I'm sorry, but you're going to have to go,' she told the corpse. Her voice echoed flatly off the surrounding metal. Celia wondered why they hadn't thought of putting the body into the blank access tunnel at the other end of the Cryogenics Module. On this side was a normal hatchway, but a metal seal closed off the other end. The tunnel was a dead end, ready for a new module to be attached. 'Maybe in case he wakes up,' she said, then decided it wasn't very funny. She turned to the computer.

A flashing square highlighted a temperature reading and the time it was reached. Celia pressed a key to turn the page on the screen, then clicked her tongue with annoyance as she discovered the program was different from most. It took nearly a minute of trial and error before she managed to reverse the mistake and find the correct command.

'There you are,' she muttered as the graph table spread itself across the screen. She studied it closely, running her finger along the curved glass to the proper reading.

As she did so, she heard a slight rustling noise behind her.

Her heart leapt into her mouth and Celia whirled around. Her mind refused to put a name to the sound, but her eyes locked on the swathed corpse at the other end of the module. It was unchanged and absolutely still.

'I *hate* this fucking place!' Celia exclaimed through gritted teeth, switching her gaze to the myriad of pipes and electrical conduits running along the ceiling, which were often the cause of unexpected noises. She turned back to the computer, determined to finish the favour and get out. The clipboard floated nearby and she snatched it to her, turning the pages until she came across an identical graph table to the one displayed on the screen. Celia quickly found the relevant reading and grabbed the pen drifting on a piece of string attached to the clipboard. As she scrawled her initials another sound came from behind her.

The sobbing breaths of a crying child.

Celia's whole body crawled with fear. She could feel the hairs on the nape of her neck rise. She knew that when she turned to see who was crying, she was going to be very frightened.

The clipboard hung unheeded in the air as she twisted around. She found herself staring at the figure of a small girl dressed in a simple white dress, who stood on one of the cryogenic containers. The girl's face was stricken, and there were dark rings of fatigue under her eyes. A silvery tear glistened on one cheek. She seemed to look straight through the astronaut.

'Jesus Christ, what the fuck is going on here?' Celia breathed, too shocked to move.

'He's wrecking all my books.'

'What?' It was impossible to tell if she heard the words or if they were dropped directly into her mind. Celia began to recover and reached out slowly for an intercom switch, not taking her eyes off the spirit.

The ghost silently disappeared.

'*Shit!*' The whole thing lasted only seconds. After a moment of shocked incomprehension, emotions flooded through Celia. She didn't know if she was relieved because the ghost was gone, or frustrated that it had disappeared before someone else could witness it. Fear still tingled in her nerves. There was something else, too—not just the sight of the crying child. It was like a latent ugliness threatening to burst out. The feeling was gone now, but Celia felt a lingering uneasiness.

Finally she slapped her hand on the intercom switch. 'Alex? Don't ask questions. Just get your ass to the Cryogenics Module right *now*.'

Dawkins and Lee followed Seerey. The three of them clustered around Celia as she told her story. Her face was pale and her hands still trembled slightly.

'It's this fucking program. This whole project,' Dawkins snapped, stabbing a finger at the computer screen, and surprising them with his vehemence.

'Take it easy, Scott,' Seerey held up a hand. 'That doesn't make any sense at all. You know that.'

'As soon as we started it, things began to go wrong. Hugh was killed, that crazy power blackout—' Dawkins stopped and shook his head, angrily realising his argument was on thin ground. 'Oh, what the hell do I know?'

'Don't forget, John was killed before any of this,' Lee said.

'Yeah? And what do you think killed him? Have you thought about that, since this place turned into a haunted house?' he replied flatly. He made a disgusted noise and passed a hand through his short, wiry hair to calm himself.

Seerey said quietly, 'Let's not allow our imaginations to get carried away here.' But it was too late. Doubt already showed in the others' expressions. 'Scott, take Celia back to your department and give her a full medical.'

Celia bristled. 'There's nothing wrong with me. I didn't imagine the damn thing.'

'I'm not saying you did,' Seerey told her sharply. 'But do you expect me *not* to have you checked out?'

She backed off. 'No, of course not. You're right.' A thought struck her. 'If Scott's going to do that, we might as well carry the thing right through and I'll do the EVA to move Hugh out.'

'No, you shouldn't do that now,' Seerey said, looking at her doubtfully. 'Someone else should do it. You've had a bit of a shock.'

'Shit, Alex!' She started to get angry again, 'Okay, so I've had a fright. But I'm fine. I *want* to do this walk, whatever the reason for it. I might not get another chance and you guys don't care much for EVAs. I *like* them.'

It was stretching the truth. Celia would almost certainly be offered another tour of Freedom, giving her opportunities for other spacewalks. And, like all astronauts, the others also enjoyed the exhilarating experience of 'walking' in space. It was only the long and arduous seal checks that got a unanimous vote of disapproval. Seerey saw the determined expression in Celia's eyes. He appealed silently to the others for help, but Dawkins only shrugged.

'Besides,' Celia added forcefully. 'It's got to be done now.' She paused before saying quietly, 'I think I can smell him.'

Automatically they looked to Dawkins, who had the most medical knowledge of them all. 'Yeah,' he said reluctantly. 'It's likely to be a problem already. It doesn't take long. We should get rid of him now.'

'All right,' Seerey sighed. 'Give Celia her medical check-up and we'll do it now. Did you finish testing your suit?' he asked her.

'Yes,' she nodded.

'Well, Lee and I will double-check it for you while you're with Scott. Then we'll get the damn thing over and done with.'

Celia was naked except for a pair of running shorts. Sensors were taped to her chest, throat and lower back. Dawkins was turned away from her, making adjustments on some equipment and studying the results. She hugged her arms across her breasts.

'This is stupid. I don't need it.'

'We *all* need it.' Dawkins didn't turn around. 'Regular check-ups. You might as well have yours now.'

'I'm fine—well, I'm damn cold.'

'Good. Reaction to the cold gives me a better idea of your condition.'

'There's nothing *wrong* with me.'

'Yeah, I know.' He pushed himself towards her and pulled a stethoscope from a nearby rack. 'You know the ropes.' He listened to her lungs and heart, and fastened a blood pressure testing device to her arm. 'Okay,' he announced. 'You get my seal of approval. Are you going out straightaway?'

'Right now.' She gingerly pulled the taped sensors from her skin and twisted around so Dawkins could get the ones on her back, then tugged a T-shirt back on. 'I'll suit up.'

'I'll be watching your health from the Command Module.'

Only Seerey waited for her as Celia re-entered the Airlock. Lee was back in the Command Module. 'We'll suit you up now,' he explained, 'then I'll bring Hugh out of Cryogenics for you. You take him straight into the Airlock, attach the Umbilical and run through your own tests, but *don't* evacuate the Airlock or open the outer door until I give you the okay from the Command Module. I'll be your controller, so give me a minute or so to get back there.'

'Okay,' she nodded nervously.

'You sure you're all right? Do you want to take a piss or something, before you suit up?'

'I'm fine. I've done all that.'

Seerey sighed. 'All right, that was your last chance. Let's do it.'

Seerey politely turned his back as she donned a one-piece undergarment for the suit. The underwear was highly insulated, like a swimmer's wetsuit, designed to give the wearer a few minutes grace should the spacesuit's temperature control mechanisms start to malfunction. It also had sensors built in to monitor heart-rate, breathing and body temperature.

The spacesuit was in two main pieces joined together by a circular metal seal at the waist. Similar, smaller seals attached the boots, gloves and helmet. Normally, the astronaut would be fully suited up with the Umbilical plugged into its connection in the outer Airlock and a series of tests would then be carried out by the assisting crewmember. Only then would the 'walker' be allowed outside. This time, Seerey didn't want to risk the outer door opening of its own accord the way it had before, killing Lyghtson. Instead, the inner door would be unlocked only long enough for Celia to enter the Airlock, breathing the air contained within the suit until she attached the Umbilical herself. Seerey would run the tests by remote from the Command Module.

Celia lowered herself into the trousers of the spacesuit and pulled her legs up high so Seerey could attach the boots. 'Did NASA have much to say about our ghost?' she asked him.

'It took a while to convince them we're not all going crazy—especially you. But they had no choice, because I wasn't going to back down. Then somebody remembered that business with Lee in the Accommodation Module. Remember? That last suggestion the computers came up with was poltergeists—and we all laughed ourselves stupid.' He paused and motioned for Celia's other foot. 'Well, now I'm not so sure it's funny.'

'What?' She almost laughed with surprise. 'Are you saying this place is haunted?'

He kept his attention on the seal of her boot. 'You're the one who saw the ghost.'

'Yes, but only the once—' She stopped and thought. 'I mean, I've been thinking it was a one-off. A freak. A *haunting* means it's something that's still here somewhere.' Celia couldn't stop herself suddenly looking around. 'How could that happen? Who could it be?'

Seerey raised himself and plucked one of her gloves from the bulkhead. Celia brought the upper section of the suit over her head and arms, mated the sealing ring together and turned it closed. Without prompting she held her hands out. He said, 'The *whys* of it are anybody's guess. At least NASA are trying to find out *who* it is. They're looking at everyone's past, searching for a deceased daughter, sisters—you name it. Using your description as a rough guideline.'

'Right,' she murmured. 'I never thought of anything like this, and I can't think of anyone in my past it might be, either. What about you?'

'No, nobody comes to mind.'

He finished fastening the second glove and asked her to turn around. From another bulkhead he brought a backpack comprising an emergency air supply, spare battery for the communications and life-support systems in case the power through the Umbilical failed, and a side coupling for the Umbilical itself. The backpack was attached with clips on the shoulders of Celia's suit in addition to straps which Seerey fastened for her. After attaching all the leads and hoses, except for those which would go to her helmet, he asked, 'Are you sure you can reach the Umbilical coupling? You'll be able to plug it in?'

She tried reaching around to her side. 'No problem, I'm sure.'

'Okay.'

The last item on her suit was a small remote control fixed to her chest that allowed Celia to adjust the volume of her communications, the temperature settings in her suit, a feed-or-retrieve control for the Umbilical and a large red button which actuated an alarm should she find herself in trouble and incapable of communicating by voice.

'I'll get Hugh first, then we'll do the helmet,' Seerey told her. On his way to the access tunnel he pressed the intercom. 'Scott, we're about four-five minutes away from an exit. Are you all set up?'

'Ready and on stand-by,' Dawkins replied formally.

Celia watched Seerey disappear through the tunnel. From where she waited she couldn't see inside the Cryogenic Module itself. A minute later the bulky form of the sleeping bags began to emerge through the hatchway. They rubbed slightly against the coaming and Celia found herself hoping the bags wouldn't separate and expose the corpse.

Seerey followed the body out. 'You're right. I don't think we could have left this much longer.' He pulled a face. 'Poor bastard.' He manoeuvred the corpse until it was lined up to slide straight into the outer Airlock, then came back. He held her helmet in front of her and paused, looking very serious. 'I wasn't going to say this, but things have been going a little crazy around here, right?'

Celia didn't say anything, but met his gaze expecting a reminder to be careful.

Seerey went on, 'Just remember, for a while we thought John Quantey was talking to somebody out there, shortly before he got out of control.'

She raised her eyebrows. 'You think he saw someone—like a ghost—outside?'

'I think anything's possible at the moment. Keep your wits about you.'

He lowered the helmet and quickly twisted it closed, clipping over the safety catches. Moving around the back he plugged in the cables and hoses, then pushed himself in front of Celia's face. 'Everything okay?' he shouted. Until she attached the Umbilical or activated the emergency supplies, she had no communications. Celia replied by flapping one hand, indicating she was hot, but immediately followed it with a thumbs-up. Seerey slapped her on the shoulder. 'I'll open the inner door, you take him straight through and plug your Umbilical in. I'll be closing the door behind you.' She gave him another thumbs-up.

Moving fast, knowing the suit would soon become suffocating, Seerey only paused briefly at the intercom. 'She's going into the Airlock now, Scott,' he said and continued to the inner door without waiting for an acknowledgement. He checked the green lights on the indicator panel and undogged the door, swinging it as wide as it could go. Seerey looked anxiously at the outer door. *Stay closed. Don't play any stupid games now.*

Celia moved the corpse through the inner door, pushing the bundle from what she hoped was the feet. It felt like it. Seerey pulled the door closed, but at the last moment ignored his own anxieties and held it open a few centimetres, watching to make sure she had no problems plugging in the Umbilical. Celia wasn't aware he was looking on and it wasn't until her hand left the attached coupling and went straight to the temperature control on her chest that Seerey knew she was all right. He locked the door closed and headed for the Command Module.

'Everything all right?' he asked Dawkins a minute later, coming through the access tunnel.

'Close,' Dawkins replied calmly. 'She got pretty hot during the minute or so the Umbilical wasn't there, so the moment she plugged in and got a breath of fresh air her visor fogged up.'

'Damn,' Seerey muttered, putting on a second pair of headsets. 'Celia, is it clearing?' he called.

Her voice came through the speaker for the benefit of Lee and Judith, who watched quietly. As usual, Joseph King was nowhere to be seen.

'It's slowly clearing.'

'Okay.' Seerey looked undecided for a moment. 'We'll go through your suit test while we wait. Can you hear us all right?'

'Clear as a bell.'

Seerey glanced at Dawkins, who was reading from a computer screen. 'She's still a little warm, but that's okay. Same with the heart and breathing. Celia's just a bit excited.'

'Celia, we'll do the suit test.'

'Roger.'

In the Airlock Celia waited for her ears to pop. Through the Umbilical Seerey would pressurise her suit slightly, then wait to see if the pressure dropped, indicating a faulty seal somewhere. After a moment she felt the suit puff out around her and her ears clogged. She tried swallowing, but only one ear cleared, making her feel unbalanced. The misty visor was annoying. A clear patch on one edge was spreading, but only slowly. The wrapped body floated beside her.

Celia thought she saw the fabric of the sleeping bag move.

'Bullshit,' she said aloud, her nerves jumping. She tilted her head and body so the clear part of her visor focused on the corpse.

'Celia, what's wrong?' Seerey's voice came sharply into her helmet.

'Nothing. Just my eyes playing tricks on me,' she replied, convincing herself as she spoke.

'What sort of tricks?' Dawkins asked, alert for unhealthy symptoms.

'It's nothing, like I said. Just the fog on my visor. Can I go now?' There was a muffled discussion, both men covering their microphones.

Seerey answered. 'If you're comfortable, I'd prefer we wait a few minutes for that mask to clear.'

'Okay,' Celia sighed, not happy at all. 'Can I drop the air, at least? The change in temperature might clear my visor.'

'Yes, bleed the chamber, but don't open the door.'

Celia frowned to herself at Seerey's overcautiousness. Of course she wasn't going to open the outer door without asking permission. She knew the routine. Celia pushed herself to the control panel for the outer door and punched in the commands to evacuate the atmosphere from the Airlock. She knew a small valve above her would crack open and she gripped a handhold to prevent being pulled upwards with the escaping air.

She had forgotten about the corpse and was alarmed to see it rising towards the ceiling. Celia reached out with her free hand and, despite the heavy gloves, managed to get a grip on the sleeping bag and pull it back down.

Something inside the cloth moved against her gloved fingers.

'Jesus Christ!' She jerked her hand back. 'He *is* moving!' She backed away from the corpse.

'Say again?' Seerey asked, overriding Dawkins.

Her voice was crackling with panic. 'Hugh's body is *moving*. I thought I saw it before. Now I just felt it with my hand.'

'He's what?' Seerey was incredulous, but Dawkins spoke calmly.

'Celia, be cool, all right? Just stay calm. It happens.'

'What do you mean, it happens?' she snapped back. 'Hugh's dead, for Christ's sake!'

Dawkins kept his voice level. 'Listen to me, Celia. His body will be coming out of rigor mortis about now. There'll be gases trying to escape. Now we've disturbed the body, it's possible the limbs will move as some muscles relax against others that are still stiff, understand?' He forced a laugh out. It sounded hollow and strained. 'A few med students have nearly cut their careers short, the first time something like this happened to them.'

There was a long silence. In the Command Module Seerey and Dawkins looked at each other worriedly.

Seerey called, 'I think we should abort this now,

Celia. Leave him there and come back inside.'

'No, I'm okay,' she answered, sounding steadier. 'Let's get this done. I'm opening the outer door now.'

Seerey opened his mouth to protest, but stopped himself. She was right. If Celia felt capable of doing it, it should be done.

In the Airlock she leaned over and hit the button for the outer door. Without any atmosphere to lose first, it slid aside almost immediately. Harsh sunlight flooded into the Airlock, making her visor darken, but the sudden heat also instantly cleared the remaining condensation inside.

'Thank God for that,' Celia muttered, turning to the corpse. Beyond the Airlock portal deep space beckoned, and it was tempting to shove the body straight out. But the only shred of human compassion in this hasty disposal of Lyghtson's remains was to send him back towards mother Earth. Celia felt an obligation to do that, at least.

In the normal scheme of things, disregarding the zero gravity, the Airlock was considered to be on top of Freedom, facing away from Earth. Most of the modules faced towards the world on whose behalf the experiments and observations were carried out. The Airlock was on the opposite side, where a docking shuttle or RLV wouldn't shadow any of the Earth's surface. Freedom lay on its side in orbit with the structural top and bottom parallel with the station's path around the world. This meant Celia had to manoeuvre Lyghtson's body out of the Airlock and around the bulk of the module until she had a clear view of Earth between the laddertracks.

Before even moving the corpse outside she

noticed the direct sunlight shrivelling and breaking the electrical tape Seerey had used to bind the two sleeping bags together. Celia stopped herself from cursing aloud, knowing it would alarm the listeners in the Command Module. Clamping down an urge to hurry, she carefully pushed the body through the doorway and held it for a moment. Any momentum not arrested would see it drifting away. Then she climbed out herself, standing on a ladder built into the side of the module's outer skin, leading to the laddertrack. Celia used one hand to press the switch paying out more Umbilical. Next, she moved upwards two steps and crouched, reaching down to pull the corpse up behind her.

As she did the cadaver moved again inside its improvised shroud.

'Jesus.' Hereson tried to close her mind to it.

'Tell us what's happening,' Seerey demanded instantly.

'He's moving again. It's grotesque.'

'Hang in there, Celia. You're doing fine.'

The occupants of the Command Module could now watch Celia's progress on an external camera. Seerey turned to Dawkins, clamping his hand over the microphone again.

'That stuff about rigor mortis and the limbs moving—is it true?'

'Sure it is,' Dawkins shrugged. 'I've heard of bodies moving maybe four or five days after death.' He turned back to the camera monitor. 'I gotta admit, I've never heard of them dancing the jitterbug like this guy, though.'

'That's what I thought,' Seerey said, his eyes troubled.

Celia repeated the climb-and-pull procedure four times and on the last reached the laddertrack. With each rung she climbed the magnificent vista of the blue-green Earth below revealed itself, stretching from one impossible horizon to the other.

With the fourth move Lyghtson's hand and wrist fell from between the sleeping bags. It was the hand that had been trapped outside the Airlock when the astronaut died. The skin was blackened and shrunken. Two fingernails hung by strands of skin. Celia groaned at the sight of it. Seerey heard her.

'What's happening, Celia?'

'The bag's coming apart. He's falling out of the damn bag.'

Seerey swore over the system. 'I thought I tied him up pretty good.'

'The tape disintegrated in the sunlight.'

After a pause he said, 'It would. I should have thought of that. It's my fault. Look, push the poor bastard away. Who gives a fuck about sending him home any more? Send him to the moon, for all I care. You're more important.'

'If he stays where he is, I'll be fine. If I see much more of him I might be the first astronaut to puke in my suit,' she replied grimly.

The end was in sight. Determinedly she made her way onto the laddertrack and managed to guide Lyghtson's corpse into position next to her. Looking down, it was a clear path straight through Freedom's superstructure to Earth.

'Good riddance,' Celia muttered, without a trace of guilt. She gripped one end of the bags and found herself holding a foot. Grasping the ladder-track with her other hand to anchor herself, she went to launch the corpse downwards.

At the moment her muscles tensed, the corpse bucked and kicked out like a live thing, thrashing about inside the bags.

Celia screamed and in a reflex action pushed the body away, sending it on its intended course by accident. It tumbled like an acrobat doing somersaults, almost identical to the way John Quantey had fallen to his death. The tumbling motion began to pull the two sleeping bags apart, and they spread out like wings from the corpse. Celia watched, horrified, oblivious to the shouted demands filling her helmet. Still well within sight the upper bag drifted off completely, exposing Lyghtson's head, arms and torso.

Each time he rolled to face Celia he seemed to stare at her. His face was terribly disfigured and bloated by the advancing decomposition—but his eyes were still intact, and they seemed to glare at her with hate and accusation.

Before she managed to tear her eyes away, she swore he began to smile.

Celia finally answered the Command Module. She whispered, 'He's gone. It's all right, he's gone.' She had to repeat herself to be heard above the men's voices. Her body trembled and she knew Dawkins would see the signs of stress on his monitors. For a moment, she couldn't stop shaking.

'For Christ's sake, what happened?' Seerey asked.

'He started kicking and moving around. He was *alive*,' she told them, not quite believing it herself.

Seerey thought it hadn't looked that way on the camera monitor. Rather, the body had seemed to buckle at the waist as Celia pushed. He knew it was no time to argue. 'Can you make it back inside?'

'Yes, I'll be fine,' she replied automatically. A shiver ran down her spine and it snapped some of the shock out of her. 'Yes, I'm coming back now,' she added, stronger.

She took one last look at the corpse, but it was now only a distant, twisting figure. Celia began to make her way off the laddertrack onto the rungs. As the comforting presence of the Earth slipped from view and black, empty space closed in, her mind turned to more frightening, threatening thoughts.

Was she really alone? She remembered Seerey's warning. *We thought John Quantey was talking to someone out there.*

And that terrible, stricken little girl appearing out of nowhere. A ghost. What was stopping her appearing again now, right in front of her?

Her concentration began to slip as she devoted too much energy to looking around anxiously, expecting to see something bad.

'Talk to us, Celia,' Seerey's voice crackled in her helmet. 'You don't look happy. I want to hear your voice.'

'Come on, Celia,' Dawkins added. 'You've got eight feet to go and you're home in the Airlock. Don't let us down.'

'I'm coming, I'm coming.' Their encouragement helped. 'You guys watch my back and I'll make it.'

'Don't worry, we're doing that,' Seerey reassured her. Dawkins raised his eyebrows at her words, but Seerey guessed what was on her mind.

Celia slowly made it inside the Airlock and waited with jangling nerves while the Umbilical retracted. Finally it was in and she quickly closed the outer door. It slid smoothly into place.

'I'm in and the outer door is closed,' she reported, greatly relieved.

'Well done, Celia,' Seerey said. 'We'll get you a medal,' he half-joked.

'Just being safe back inside is enough, thank you. Can someone come and give me a hand?'

'Judith's coming now.'

'You better hurry up, Hereson,' Dawkins called, looking at another monitor screen. 'We've got a good movie just starting on the armed forces network.' The monitor was tuned to a satellite relay of the armed forces network, a station dedicated to sending part of America out to the servicemen and women scattered across the globe. Aside from regular sports and television shows, it often ran the latest movies. At the moment the screen showed a rolling line of credits which included the names of some of the biggest stars of Hollywood.

Celia smiled to herself, imagining the scene. 'I can't wait,' she replied.

At that moment Freedom's systems crashed down in an almost total power failure.

13

JOSEPH KING LAY SUSPENDED above the bunk, his body unconsciously composed like a corpse prepared for viewing—or like one frozen in a cryogenic container. The thin, bony fingers were interlaced across his chest. His eyes were wide open, staring at the blackness around him.

Seeing everything.

King was no longer a schizophrenic. His gentler, more human side was now completely suppressed. The darker side, contemptuous of his fellow astronauts and obsessed by communicating with the being he believed to be a greater God, was totally dominant. He avoided the others, staying mostly in the darkness of his bunkspace, reaching out with his mind. He ate at odd times and consumed very little. He believed his faith would sustain him.

He knew what was happening in the space station around him. He kept the intercom in the Accommodation Module turned up, and listened to the routine messages between the crewmembers, and the crisis calls, too. Through the Module's television monitor he watched Celia Hereson dispose of Lyghtson's remains.

But in addition to these conventional sources of information, King was possessed by a growing awareness of everything about him. It was both telepathic and sensory at the same time. He thought of it as a gift.

When Celia confronted the spirit of Ellen Littlewood, King felt a thrill of almost orgasmic intensity. He realised he was so close to the being he worshipped, he could actually feel it inside Freedom with him. King didn't go searching. That would be interfering where, he knew instinctively, he wasn't welcome. Not yet.

Later, each time Hugh Lyghtson's body quivered and moved to torment Celia, Joseph King smiled at the sheer wickedness of it. He saw his God had a sense of humour. He liked that.

Now he wrapped himself in darkness, the privacy screen closed. As he lay there, his mind filled by the teasing image of Lyghtson tumbling slowly, terribly through space, King suddenly understood there was something he must do. He had a purpose. His devotion was about to be rewarded and he was to be allowed to achieve that purpose.

He had to do it now.

He knew that the incidents plaguing the girl's EVA would upset everyone. Eventually, they would blame the Cryogenic program and perhaps attempt to close it down without consulting their superiors. Shutting off the system would be difficult, almost impossible. But they might try, and in the attempt do irreparable damage. They might even succeed. King's purpose was to protect the Revival program until it was completed. He must go to the Cryogenic Module now and be on guard.

He slid up his bunk's privacy screen and floated into the thoroughfare. King blinked, unaccustomed to the light. At that moment the power systems failed, leaving him in the dim, red emergency lighting, which he preferred.

Leaving Judith Cianta in an access tunnel, groping towards the dull red of the next module.

And leaving Celia Hereson to wait in the darkened Airlock, listening to the panicked voices in the Command Module and wondering if the same thing that killed Hugh Lyghtson was about to kill her, too.

In the Command Module Seerey snarled, 'For fuck's sake, here we go again! What the hell is causing this?'

Dawkins reacted instantly, swinging a computer keyboard towards him. He began typing in requests for data and immediately hissed in annoyance at the much slower speed of the system's responses. 'Lee, can you track down communications? I'll check out the power grid.'

'Okay,' she agreed tightly.

Seerey went to the intercom. 'Judith? Answer me now, no matter where you are.'

Her voice came through a moment later. 'What the hell's going on? I was in an access tunnel. I nearly died of fright.'

'Same as before—meaning we don't know. Now listen, when you get to the Airlock make sure you seal both hatches before you open the inner door for Celia, got it? Seal it tight.'

There was a pause, then she answered, 'I understand.'

I bet you do, Seerey thought grimly. At least this way if the outer Airlock door chose to open at the same critical moment that the *inner* door unsealed, allowing Celia to pass through, only the atmosphere in the Airlock Module would be lost. Judith would probably be badly hurt in the process, possibly even sucked outside with the air. Although Celia might survive quite well, by the time she recovered and closed the inner door again Judith would have suffocated, unless she managed to reach one of the emergency breathing masks that would automatically appear. Otherwise, there was no way Celia could share the oxygen in her suit supply. If it was still working.

'Shit.' Seerey realised the potential danger. He called the Airlock on his headset. 'Celia, are you still with us? Is the Umbilical powered and giving you air?'

'I'm okay.' She sounded scared. 'Has it happened again?'

'Same as before. Jude's still on her way to help.'

'I can sit here, if you like.'

'I don't like it. I want you out of there as quick as you can.'

'Whatever you say.'

Dawkins spoke up. 'Alex, we're down to an average thirty per cent of normal power, just like last time. Everything's slowed, including the data systems, so that figure may not be accurate. My guess is it's correct, though.'

'That's the minimum survival level, isn't it?' Seerey asked. 'Anything less than that thirty per cent and we'd be in serious trouble. It'd be Lifeboat time.'

'Pretty close to it,' Dawkins nodded.

'So put it this way. We're on the brink. If someone was doing this deliberately, they couldn't cut it finer, right?'

In the poor light Dawkins' brow furrowed in dark lines. 'Hell, that's one way of looking at it, Alex. But no one would be doing this deliberately.'

'Maybe not,' Seerey muttered. 'I'm not so sure. Is it a uniform thirty per cent across the board?'

'Yes. Recycling the air's going to be the biggest worry after an hour or so—of course, the cryogenics systems are just dandy, running with no problems at all.'

'We might do something about that,' Seerey said bitterly. 'If we get out of this mess in one piece.' He turned to Lee. 'Any success?'

'Absolutely nothing.' She threw her hands up in despair. 'At least last time we kept voice contact with Canaveral. This time there's nothing. I can't even raise a ham operator anywhere.'

'Now *that* I definitely don't understand,' Dawkins shook his head. 'With all the shit we've got aboard this tub. No communications is scary.'

'The only thing I haven't tried is our S.O.S.,' said Lee.

'We'll wait on that one,' Seerey decided quickly. 'We're not in dire straits yet, and if it got through it'd cause a major reaction on Earth. How long did this shit go on for last time, anyone remember?'

'Less than ten minutes, easily,' Lee offered. 'Maybe even five.'

'Close enough,' Seerey nodded. 'So we'll give it fifteen minutes this time, before we hit the panic button.'

Judith Cianta was used to working in the dark. The experiments she conducted in the module assigned to her included a project to raise edible plants in low light, using mild radiation and infra-red spectrums in place of sunlight. Once she stumbled around in near-darkness for several days as she worked, favouring the low-light schemes.

When the power grid in Freedom cut out Judith was halfway through an access tunnel. The tunnels weren't considered worth lighting separately, and relied on the wash of light reflected from the modules. The sudden change to emergency lighting threw the access tunnel into almost complete darkness, the hatchways round circles of redness at each end.

Still, it wasn't the dark that upset her. It was the electronic groan the space station made when the electricity bled away. Usually the astronauts weren't aware of the ambient noise around them—the quiet throbbing of pumps, the hum of the air conditioning and droning computer systems—but when the power was taken away, the noises died with it. It was not a good sound, that fading groan.

For people as isolated as the crew of Freedom, it was a frightening sound.

'Jesus, what's going on?' Judith murmured uneasily, moving quickly from the tunnel into the galley area. For a moment she was undecided. She knew Celia would be twice as confused, surrounded by emergency lighting and trapped in the bulky spacesuit. Apart from assisting Celia there wasn't much she could do. It was obvious what was wrong—it was the same malfunction as before.

Seerey would expect her to keep going. Celia needed to unsuit in order to contribute to fixing the problem. If things were otherwise, he would let her know.

Seerey chose this moment to ask for her through the intercom.

She was right. She was well aware why he wanted the Airlock sealed before she opened the inner door. Her mind began to mull over the precautions she could take—a lifeline, perhaps, to stop her being dragged outside if the worst happened. Judith realised she would pass through Dawkins' Medical Module, where there were small canisters of reviving oxygen. She might grab one of those, too. It could keep her alive until she or Celia resealed the Airlock and the atmosphere was restored, or at least until she could grab an emergency mask.

Judith suddenly thought she heard someone moving through the access tunnel she'd just left, at the other end of the module. She kept going, entering the Medical Module, and turned herself around to look back the way she'd come.

'Hello?' she called. There was no answer. It was hard to see far in the emergency lighting, but

Judith felt she should at least see *something* of the further module, even if only the red hole of the hatchway. Now the access tunnel was black, as if someone waited in there, hiding. 'Is anybody in there?' she tried again. There was no reply and no movement to be seen. 'Crazy,' she told herself, deciding reluctantly it must be someone just beyond the far access tunnel, too absorbed in something to hear her.

Judith turned back to the Medical Module and looked about for an oxygen canister. She figured Scott would have several in store and always have one to hand. They weren't very big, about the size of an old milk bottle, painted dark green with a large, rubber facemask fitted on top.

Like all the scientific modules this one was a bewildering clutter of instruments and equipment jam-packed together to make the most of the space available. To make matters worse, the emergency lighting washed everything into a variety of red. She couldn't just look for the distinctive, reassuring green of the canister.

Someone started coming through the access tunnel behind her, and she jumped nervously. Turning, Judith saw it was Joseph King and her heart sank a little. The man had gone a bit strange over the last four or five days and he gave her the creeps.

'Hi Joe,' she said easily. 'I thought I heard someone coming up behind me. Didn't you hear me call?'

King pulled himself from the tunnel and Judith was reminded of a long-legged spider emerging from its hole. She shook the thought away. It was being too unkind. King floated in the space near the hatchway and looked at her without replying. His pallid skin appeared fevered in the red light and his eyes were dull black dots. His thin face and hollow cheekbones—accentuated since he stopped eating properly—held dark, haunted shadows.

'Hey Joe, are you okay?' She felt herself edging backwards. King was scaring her. He didn't look good. 'Has Alex sent you to shut down the cryogenics?' she asked, getting more nervous as he didn't answer, just staring with his dead black eyes. 'I say it's a good idea,' she went on, taking comfort in the sound of her own voice. 'Scott's probably right. Nothing seems to have gone properly since we started that Revival project.'

King spoke, his voice as lifeless as his eyes. 'He needs to be protected.'

'Who? Scott?'

'The Revival program mustn't be interrupted.'

Judith was at a loss what to say for a moment. 'Well, maybe not,' she agreed finally, beginning to see King wasn't himself at all.

'It could be the Second Coming.'

Judith let out her breath in a long sigh. *Ah, great. I see what we have here, now*, she thought. 'You know, Joe, you don't look real well, do you mind me saying that? Have you been pushing your work a little too hard lately?' Her eyes slid to the bulkhead and she saw the nearest intercom, over an arm's length away. She went on, 'Probably you just need a good twelve hours' sleep. How about I call Alex and let him know I'm going to put you to bed. We could grab a few tranquillisers from Scott's store here, if you like. Make sure you get a good long nap.' Judith drifted backwards slowly, trying to reach the intercom.

The moment she took her eyes off King to put her finger on the switch he launched himself at her. Judith didn't have time to cry out. King pushed her into the bulkhead, concentrating on putting the flat of his palm against the side of her face and viciously bashing her head against the metal equipment. The first blow knocked her out instantly, but King made sure. He grabbed a handful of hair and twice slammed her forehead into the bulkhead again. Blood sprayed out in a fine mist and hung in the air.

Satisfied, he left her. King headed for the Cryogenic Module, confident no one would stop him.

Judith floated, curled into a defensive ball. The blood in the atmosphere appeared black in the red lighting. More seeped from the wounds on her scalp, drifting away from her skin in fine tendrils like cigarette smoke.

Celia waited impatiently for Judith to arrive. After a few minutes she started the procedure for leaving the Airlock herself. The commands she entered into the control panel reversed the exit system and began filling the chamber with a breathable atmosphere. Still, Celia didn't disconnect the Umbilical. That would be the last thing she did before opening the inner door. It was her precaution against the outer door opening unexpectedly.

In her helmet she could hear Seerey discussing remedies for their power problems with Dawkins and Lee. They sounded too busy to be bothered with the fact that Judith was held up somewhere. And Celia knew Judith was a responsible, competent person. If she was held up, she would have good reason to be.

Celia looked at the inner Airlock door. The locks on it were designed to be manipulated by someone in a spacesuit. In fact, the only reason Judith was coming to give her help was that the astronauts generally returned from an EVA quite weak and exhausted. Celia felt fresh, her spacewalk having been relatively short. The adrenalin from her fear was still pumping through her veins, giving her strength.

What the hell, let me out of here, she decided. *I'm sick of waiting.* She didn't admit that the Airlock scared her, too.

Somehow, it had killed Lyghtson.

She manoeuvred herself in front of the door and undogged it. Even if the chamber depressurised now it wouldn't matter. The air inside the Airlock Module would keep the door closed. Celia took a deep breath for confidence and quickly unplugged the Umbilical. Separated from the remote control it began to retract itself. She grabbed a handhold and firmly pushed the door outwards. There was a moment of resistance—the pressure inside the chamber never quite reached that of the module—then the seal broke and the door opened.

Fearfully expecting to feel a rush of air as the outer door opened behind her, Celia hurried her bulky figure through. She immediately closed the door again, breathing a sigh of relief as she pushed home the last lock.

Like the rest of Freedom, the Airlock Module looked unfamiliar in the emergency lighting. Celia searched around, but there was nobody to be seen.

After hearing Seerey's instructions to Judith through the headset she expected to find the module sealed, but only the hatchcover to the Cryogenics Module was closed and locked into place. Her suit was getting hot and suffocating again without any supply of air coming from the Umbilical.

Celia worked on her gloves first, taking them off and letting them drift in the air next to her. This freed her fingers to tackle the awkward clips on the base of her helmet. Lifting the helmet away she gulped in fresh air. 'That's better,' she said aloud. The air conditioning chilled the beads of sweat that had formed on her face. 'Judith? Anyone here?' Nobody answered. She shrugged to herself. 'Thanks guys,' she said, without rancour. She laboured to remove the rest of the suit, wriggling out of it without disconnecting any of the cables, pushing it against the bulkhead but not storing it properly. She would have to inspect it minutely for damage later.

All the time Celia expected to see Judith arrive through the access tunnel, but nobody came. Frowning, she gave her the benefit of the doubt and didn't call the Command Module yet. She pulled her own clothes closer and stripped off the undergarment. The air felt deliciously cold against her bare skin and she let herself enjoy it for a few brief seconds, then began dressing. Fully clothed, Celia had no more excuses. She went to the intercom.

'Alex? Celia here. I'm back inside and both the Airlock doors are closed tight. I'm on my way to you now.'

'Okay,' his short reply came over the speaker.

'Judith's not here, by the way. Is she still with you?'

There was a puzzled silence. Seerey answered, 'No, she's supposed to be there with you.'

'Well, she's not.'

Seerey called Judith on the intercom, telling her to report in, and waited for a response. When nothing happened he snapped, 'Celia, start making your way back here, searching as you go. She may have had some sort of accident in this shit red lighting. I'll send Lee to do the circuit on the other side of the Command Module.'

'Roger,' Celia replied crisply. She was starting to get a bad feeling.

She looked at the closed access tunnel to the Cryogenic Module and decided it was unlikely Judith was in there—it was especially unlikely that she'd have locked herself in. If anything, it was evidence that Judith had been in the Airlock Module and begun sealing it as Alex ordered, only to be interrupted and drawn away for some reason.

What reason? Celia wondered, looking about uneasily. It would be wrong of her not to have a quick look.

The locks for the hatchways were a single wheel in the centre of the round steel doors. Twirled one way or the other the wheel moved a series of tumblers set around the outside, similar to the door of a security safe. Celia grasped the wheel and hooked her feet into a nearby niche. Any effort like this in zero gravity, unless the person was anchored, usually resulted in the astronaut turning, not the wheel. Celia wasn't expecting any resistance and she was surprised when the lock wouldn't turn.

Setting herself more firmly she tried again. The wheel gave a little, then jammed solid.

'Strange,' she muttered, and vainly gave it one more attempt. The locking mechanisms were a simple design and hardly used enough to cause a failure through metal fatigue or something similar. She stared at the hatch for a moment, trying to figure it out, then she gave up. Whatever it was, it would have to wait. Celia turned and started for the Command Module, taking a cue from Seerey and cursing the inadequate emergency lighting as she went.

When she entered the Medical Module Celia was puzzled and alarmed by the stuff floating in the air. She passed her hand through it and looked at the result. The sticky black liquid clung to her skin. She sniffed it and felt herself go cold as she recognised the smell of blood. Looking up she saw Judith's crouched figure at the far end of the module and swore at herself for not noticing her straightaway. Celia rushed along the length of the module, ignoring the wisps of blood spattering against her as she moved. Reaching Judith she turned her around and involuntarily jerked backwards at the sight of two ugly wounds, one above Judith's scalp line and the other below.

'God, Jude! What happened?'

The injured astronaut wasn't in any condition to reply. Even in the bad light her face was deathly white. Her eyelids fluttered and a small pulse jumped weakly at the base of her neck. Celia tried to brush away some of the blood that was forming into globules and catching in Judith's hair, hiding the injury. It didn't work. Reluctantly, Celia left her a moment to use the intercom.

'Alex, I've found Judith. She's in the Medical Module and she's hurt bad. Head wounds with a lot of blood loss. I need help right now.'

In the Command Module Seerey looked at Dawkins. *What the hell else is going to go wrong on this tour?*

Dawkins said, 'I'd better go.'

'No, Lee can do it. I want you to keep tackling this problem,' he pointed at the computer. 'If we don't find an answer soon, we'll all be in trouble.'

Before Dawkins could reply Lee's voice came through the intercom. 'I'm on my way to Celia.'

'That's what we want,' Seerey acknowledged back. His face dark with worry, he watched Dawkins type queries into the keyboard.

'Damn,' Dawkins swore as another blank reply flashed up on the screen. 'This is too unreal to be true. Where is fucking Joseph King, by the way?' he asked, diverting his anger.

'I don't know, and I don't really care. Between you and me, I'd prefer it if Joe kept out of the way for the moment. He doesn't inspire much confidence.'

In saying this, Seerey was breaking an important rule. In a tightly confined group any mention of discontent with a crewmember could see everyone suddenly taking sides and creating an impossible working environment. But things had been going crazy on this tour and King had made himself unpopular.

'Yeah, I know what you mean,' Dawkins agreed, unsurprised.

Lee gasped as she pulled herself into the Medical Module. Immediately she knew it was blood hanging in the air. 'Christ, is she still alive?'

'Yes, but she's very weak and lost a lot of blood.' Celia had found a compress bandage and was holding it over both wounds, stopping the bleeding. In the red light the scene looked eerie, like a bad dream. 'She's come to, once. Then she slipped back again. I think she's trying now.'

'We should get her out of here. Away from all this stuff flying around.'

'I agree. Do you want to grab some more bandages?'

'Right, give me a moment to close the other hatch. We'd better contain the airborne blood to this module. It's going to be hard enough to clean up as it is.'

The hatch closed, they began guiding Judith towards the Command Module. She started to recover properly as they moved and tried to tell them something, but Lee quietened her gently. The three of them moved awkwardly through the access tunnels, Celia keeping pressure on Judith's bandage. By the time they reached the Command Module Judith had revived enough to move herself a little.

Seerey and Dawkins abandoned their fruitless efforts to restore power when the three women arrived. They gathered around Judith, comforting her while Dawkins took over from Lee and examined her injuries. Someone got Judith a water bottle and she sucked on the straw gratefully.

'Okay Jude, give,' Seerey said, smiling softly. 'What did you do? Try to move too fast?'

She answered weakly, her words taking away his smile. 'It was Joe King. He's gone crazy. He said he was on his way to the Cryogenic Module and must've thought I was going to stop him. I tried to go for the intercom to let you know. Anyway, he attacked me.' She reached up to touch her scalp, but Scott caught her by the wrist.

'King did this?' Seerey was stunned. So were the others.

'He's gone mad, Alex. Said something about having to protect the Revival program, in case you wanted to shut it down.' She remembered something else. 'He said Vasta might be the Second Coming.' Judith tried to raise her eyebrows at the absurdity of this and instantly winced at the pain it caused.

'Take it easy,' Dawkins warned, then looked across at Seerey. 'She may need a transfusion, but I don't think so. You'd be surprised how much blood we can lose before we need that. My biggest problem is I can't see what the hell I'm doing.'

'I know,' Seerey said helplessly.

As if in reply the emergency globes snapped off and the normal lighting began to flicker back to life. All around them systems whined and beeped back into operation. The space station settled back into its normal rhythm. Somebody let out a wry cheer.

'Thank God for that,' Seerey sighed.

'One minute to go,' Lee noted. When Seerey looked at her she explained, 'One minute to go before you were going to activate the S.O.S. We got the power back just in time.'

'But for how long?' Celia asked for all of them. They could see now that she and Lee were spotted all over with blood.

'Don't ask,' Seerey said. 'Scott, there's your light. Do you want to patch up Judy here, or back in the Medical Module?'

'That reminds me,' Celia said quickly, looking down at herself. 'There's blood all through there. We sealed it, but you'd better shut down the air recycling to keep it out of the system. I don't think Scott could work in there. It's going to be a hell of a job to clean it up.'

'You and Lee are a mess, too,' Seerey nodded at them. 'Scott, what do you want to do?'

Dawkins didn't answer. He was staring with a puzzled frown at one of the television monitors.

'Scott?' Seerey repeated, patiently. 'What do you want to do?'

Dawkins stared at him, a strange look on his face. 'That movie's still starting,' he said, confused. 'You know? The one I told Celia about, as she was leaving the Airlock.'

'What?' Seerey twisted around and saw the film's credits rolling up the screen. 'So? This is no time to be watching movies,' he observed mildly. He knew Dawkins didn't really care for the film.

'No, it's nothing,' Dawkins decided flatly, recovering. 'It must be a mistake.' He changed the subject, 'I'm surprised Ground Control aren't screaming at us already.'

After a pause Seerey shrugged, 'You've lost me.' He looked uncertain. The others knew he was torn between pursuing Joseph King and re-establishing communications with Earth. 'Fuck him. Joe can wait—he's sure as hell not going anywhere. When I start to deal with Mr King, I don't want any interruptions,' he added grimly.

Seerey went to the comm-link station and called for a response. A bored duty controller appeared and bid them a good morning.

'I guess it is, now we're back to full operations,' Seerey told him tartly.

The controller blinked, but didn't get excited. 'I'm sorry Freedom, have you had a problem?' He looked almost comical as he peered around the Ground Control facility, as if expecting someone to apologise and confirm Seerey had a complaint.

'Problems?' Seerey tried hard not to lose his temper. 'Are you guys all asleep down there? We lost seventy per cent of our power up here again—for nearly fifteen minutes this time. We were sixty seconds away from activating our emergency S.O.S. What the hell were you doing?'

The controller became formal. 'Freedom, we had no indications of any malfunctions through our systems down here.' The man spoke in a slow southern drawl, mocking Seerey's urgency.

Before Seerey could say anything more Dawkins came over and put a hand on his arm. 'Tell them to get Hitchcock,' he said. 'While they do, I'm going to tell *you* something and you're not going to believe it.' He nodded at the comm-link. 'Get Hitchcock.'

'Believe it?' Seerey muttered, turning back to the screen. 'I can't believe *anything* about this tour anymore.' He raised his voice to the controller. 'Get Jack Hitchcock for me, please.'

'Jack's having a break. He had a long night, last night.'

Seerey became instantly annoyed again. 'I don't care if he's been working for a month solid! Get him, and get him now.'

The controller dared a resigned 'you're-the-boss' look before disappearing from the screen. Shaking his head, Seerey looked at Dawkins. Behind him Lee was at a keyboard, working her way through the commands to stop the climate control in the Medical Module. Celia still comforted Judith, changing the dressing on her head again. The bleeding had nearly stopped. The injured astronaut was apparently asleep, drawing deep slow breaths, her eyes closed.

'That's okay,' Dawkins said, seeing the direction of Seerey's gaze. 'It's just her body shutting down while it works on replenishing the blood. I'll give her a sedative in a minute to keep her out so I can work on the cuts.'

'All right,' Seerey allowed himself a tired groan. 'So what's this new bad news?'

'Remember I said that movie was still starting, when the power grid returned?' He pointed at the screen. 'The film that was going as Celia went outside?'

'Yeah, okay.' Seerey glanced at the television monitor. A famous face looked back at him.

'Well, that movie was starting when Celia came back into the Airlock, right? In fact, I swear the credits were in exactly the same place.'

Seerey looked at him. 'You were right,' he said, after a moment. 'I don't think I *am* going to believe this.'

Dawkins pointed at the movie. 'Unless they had an interruption to their transmission or some weird operator-error, then indications are that the fifteen minutes we just spent trying to save our asses didn't happen.' He said this lightly, as if he knew his theory wasn't right and somebody would immediately explain it away logically. Nobody obliged.

'That's crazy,' Seerey told him.

'You got that right.'

'You're talking about some sort of time-travel, or time *stopping*. That's impossible.'

'I know, but it might explain why Ground Control didn't register any problems.'

In the uneasy quiet that followed they considered the alternatives, refusing to accept Dawkins' idea.

'There's got to be a more logical explanation,' Lee encouraged them. Celia tried first.

'Maybe it's an echo,' she suggested reluctantly. 'We're not picking up the original transmission anymore, but an echo of it. Perhaps it's a relay network in another time zone.'

'Perhaps,' Seerey pulled a face. 'But fifteen minutes is too long for an electronic echo and too short for a time zone difference. No,' he decided, trying to sound confident. 'My money's on a simple breakdown in transmission. They started the movie again, that's all.' He avoided Dawkins' eye as he spoke. 'Of course, we'll run a check. Somebody keep watching that screen for a station identification break.'

'It's the armed forces network,' Dawkins told him. There was another long silence. It was an enigma no one wanted to confront.

Celia changed the subject. 'What are we going to do about Joe?'

'I don't know. Everyone's safety is my first concern, and that means talking to Jack Hitchcock. He's got to pull us out of here now. Things are out of control. I guess Joe's in the Cryogenics Module. Isn't that where Judith said he was heading?'

'The hatch is closed. In fact, it's jammed in some way. He must have done it. He's locked himself in.'

Seerey looked at the bank of camera monitors. At the touch of a switch he could bring up a picture of the cryogenics section and see what King was doing. Instead he took a deep breath to slow himself down and said 'First things first.'.

Dawkins told them he was going to his Medical Module to get what he needed to tend to Judith. As he disappeared into the access tunnel Jack Hitchcock came onto the comm-link screen.

'Alex, you have problems?' he asked shortly. He looked tired and worn-out.

Seerey replied, 'We had another major power blackout, Jack. Your people didn't even notice it happened,' he added, barely concealing his bitterness.

'So I heard. There's a good reason for that. Absolutely nothing showed up on our equipment down here. Not a thing.'

'But that's impossible,' Seerey said, noting to himself that he seemed to be saying that a lot lately.

'That's the way it happened,' Hitchcock snapped back in a rare display of anger. 'Whatever the reason for it, it's got to be up there with you in Freedom.'

We've got one theory, but you're not going to believe it either, Seerey thought. He decided not to relay that piece of information just yet. 'There's something else, Jack. Something bad. One of the crew, Joseph King, seems to have cracked. He attacked Judith Cianta, hurt her badly, and now he's locked himself in the Cryogenics Module. Said something about protecting the program until it was complete and even went a little religious before he assaulted her.'

'How bad is she hurt?' Hitchcock's face had set into hard lines.

'Nothing critical. A couple of bad cuts on her head and she lost a lot of blood, but Scott says she'll be okay.' Seerey paused and considered his next words. 'Still, that's got to be it, Jack. We can't stay up here any longer like this. Our position's untenable. You have to pull us out.'

'Do you think I work twenty-four hour stretches for my health?' Hitchcock asked sharply.

Seerey faltered. 'I don't know what you're talking about.'

'Alex, Hurricane Ben is on its way. We've only got twenty-mile-an-hour winds now, but they're rising. You know as well as I do we need a *minimum* of twelve hours to gather a relief crew and get a shuttle in the air to you. By that time we'll have gale force winds and no one's going to launch diddly-shit in those sorts of conditions. You're on your own for a while, no matter what we all *want* to do.'

Seerey took a moment to absorb this. He heard Celia swear softly behind him. 'We don't want a relief crew,' he tried. 'I want you to get us *out*. You can send another tour up later.'

'The crew's not the delay, Alex. You know what it takes to do a launch.'

'Christ, what a mess.' Seerey ran a hand across his face.

'I'm sorry, Alex. If there was something I could do, I would. Believe me.'

Seerey was tired and frustrated. However, he told himself he was only imagining the false note in Hitchcock's manner, and tried one last time. 'We could always load ourselves into the Lifeboat and pull the pin, Jack. Right now, that doesn't seem like a bad idea.'

'And drop yourselves straight into a hurricane, Alex? We're obligated to leave a recovery vessel out there in case you're *forced* to hit the Lifeboat, but I don't like your chances of being found and recovered in a hurricane.'

'Okay, okay,' Seerey gave in. He punched a fist into his open palm. 'Let us know as soon as a launch is possible, all right? Just get us out of here.'

'The hurricane might stick around for another forty-eight hours yet—more, perhaps.'

'I know how hurricanes work, okay?' Seerey snapped, then got himself back under control. 'I'll get back to you as soon as I've dealt with King.'

Hitchcock had no choice but to agree. 'All right, Alex.'

Seerey angrily flicked off the transmit switch and turned in time to see Dawkins return laden with an armful of medical supplies. Now he, too, was spattered with blood.

'That blood's a real problem, Alex,' he said. 'It's not moving around now, without the Climate Control—it's stuffy as hell in there. But the blood's just hanging in the air and we'll have to get it out, somehow. Every time we move through it, it breaks into smaller droplets. Pretty soon it'll be impossible to capture.'

'I know, but one thing at a time, hey, Scott?'

Dawkins held up a placating hand. 'Sure, I thought I'd mention it, that's all.'

Celia nodded at the comm-link, showing Dawkins who she was talking about. 'It doesn't sound like they're too worried about us.'

'I get the same impression,' Seerey agreed. 'Still, I suppose they've got their reasons.'

He went to a computer and requested data. The screen filled with a map of the southeast of the USA overlaid by a weather map. The whirlpool of Hurricane Ben dominated everything. Seerey consulted some recent forecasts and grunted. 'Well, it's certainly headed their way, allowing for the usual swing north as it gets closer to the coast.'

Celia was holding Judith's arm steady while Dawkins injected a tranquilliser. She frowned across at Seerey. 'They wouldn't lie to us about that, surely? Just to keep us up here?'

'No, I doubt it.' Seerey tried to smile reassuringly. 'I only did that to satisfy myself. They can hardly hide the weather from us, can they?'

Lee grumbled, 'Jack Hitchcock didn't seem too upset about the idea of the hurricane hanging around another forty-eight hours.'

'No, he didn't.'

Seerey focused his attention on the camera monitors. 'I guess it's time we found out what Mr King is up to.'

Lee quietly moved next to him as he operated the camera controls. He selected a camera and executed the command. One of the screens immediately lit up with a picture of the Cryogenics Module. He heard Lee suck in her breath.

'Now *that* is fucking weird,' she said, pointing at the screen.

'It certainly is.' Seerey was dismayed. It appeared their worst fears could be true.

Joseph King lay exactly as he did inside his own bunkspace, stretched out on his back with his hands clasped neatly on his chest. He'd positioned himself directly above Vasta's container, squeezing his thin body between the flat top and the computer station mounted above it. He reminded Seerey of the effigies carved into the lids of ancient tombs.

'Like he said, he's guarding it,' Seerey said.

Dawkins looked over from where he was carefully cutting hair away from Judith's injuries. Beside him, Celia was making sure the cut hair was caught and put in a bag. He squinted at the monitor. 'He looks like some sort of faithful damn dog,' he said.

'Or a corpse himself,' Lee offered.

'That too,' Seerey nodded. 'He can't be asleep, can he?'

'Maybe he's in a trance.'

'Whatever it is, I'm about to wake him up.'

There was one main intercom station in the Command Module. From this the operator could choose which sub-station he contacted, isolating the call from the others. Otherwise, anyone calling from any of the sub-stations distributed abundantly around Freedom was automatically heard everywhere. It was rare for the main station to be used—nobody had anything to hide and usually didn't care who listened. It took Seerey a moment to reacquaint himself with its operation, then, with a final glance at the watching astronauts, he keyed in the Cryogenics Module using a momentary switch, so if he spoke to the others King wouldn't hear.

'Joseph? It's Alex here. We need to talk.'

Lee nudged him. 'Easy, Alex. Who knows what's going through his mind? You should start gently.'

'Okay,' Seerey sighed, adding with a mutter, 'then I'll kill him.' King hadn't moved or spoken. Seerey waited a few more seconds and tried again. 'Joseph, answer me please. We want to help.'

Lee nodded approvingly. Just when it seemed that King wasn't going to answer, his voice came clearly through the intercom. He didn't move, but spoke from where he lay.

'We don't need your help any more. Leave us alone.'

'We?' Celia hissed. 'Us? He's really flipped.'

Seerey waved her to silence and concentrated. 'Who's there with you, Joe?'

'He is with me. He is with us all.'

'Do you mean Vasta?'

There was a slight hesitation. 'Call him what you like. In the end He will judge everyone.'

'Joe, you didn't have to do this. We're all looking after Vasta. You can't do it on your own.'

'He gives me strength.'

Seerey said over his shoulder, 'Sounds like he's got it pretty bad.'

'But who's he really talking about? God?' Lee asked.

'Joseph,' Seerey asked, 'Who is He?'

'He is coming again, and He will judge. Then you will all know Him.'

'Shit, there he goes again with that Second Coming stuff,' Celia murmured.

Dawkins said, 'But does he believe Vasta is God? That *he's* the Second Coming?'

'Somehow he's certainly connecting the two together,' Seerey said, frustrated. Some of his irritation slipped out and he called, 'Joseph, unlock the hatchway now. Let us in. We'll talk this thing over properly, face to face.'

King was unimpressed by his anger. 'No. He doesn't trust you. He only trusts me.'

The astronauts in the Command Module exchanged glances. Seerey asked, 'He *talks* to you?'

'He talks to all of us, but He knows only I choose to listen.'

Seerey made a disgusted noise and flicked his hand at the monitor. 'Great. He's gone crazy. We're getting nowhere fast. Anybody got any suggestions?'

Dawkins was applying the last covering on Judith's scalp. He'd shaved a portion of her hairline away and put two stitches in one of the cuts. Now he was placing a large piece of sticking plaster and cotton over it all. He spoke as he worked.

'Whatever he's got going on inside his head, he seems pretty locked onto it. That doesn't mean he won't lose interest just as fast. We could give him a day. He can't do much harm. See if he comes out of it, or a bit of thirst and hunger might dampen his enthusiasm.'

'Uh-uh,' Lee disagreed, shaking her head. 'We should have seen this coming. He's been acting weird for days, but we've all been avoiding him instead. I'd say it's been building up inside him for a while, so he's not going to snap out of it in a hurry.'

'Well, you're right he can't do any harm,' Seerey

said. 'That's why *I'm* thinking of seeing if he still respects authority—maybe threaten him a little.'

They all looked doubtful, but Dawkins finally said, 'What the hell, give it a go.'

Seerey turned back to the intercom. 'Joseph, are you listening? As the commander of this tour I'm telling you that this situation is unacceptable. I'm ordering you to unlock the hatchway and come out. If you do that now, I promise you we'll discuss your problems fully. If you don't come out, well—' In truth Seerey didn't know what the consequences might be. He waited for a response. King didn't answer. 'Joe, I'm considering shutting down the Cryogenic program anyway. What you're doing won't stop me. I'll simply cut all the power feeds to the module itself and kill off the whole damn thing. I'm prepared to do that.'

Seerey suddenly realised he was, too. Even though interrupting the power supply meant destroying all six of the cryogenic programs in place, not just the Revival project, he would do it. He was sick of the entire program now.

King moved. The watchers in the Command Module held their breath, expecting him to leave the camera's field of focus as he entered the access tunnel. But King slid his body away from the container only so he could address the computer keyboard above it. He began to type in commands.

14

AFTER LEAVING JUDITH, KING went quickly through Freedom to the Cryogenics Module. As he passed through the Airlock Module he watched the inner door for signs that Celia was emerging, but nothing happened. On impulse he reached over and unbuckled one of the retaining straps for the spacesuits. This gave him an inch-wide unbreakable nylon belt.

He entered the access tunnel feet-first, pulling the hatchcover closed behind him. Turning the wheel to 'lock' he ran the strapping through the wheel's spokes and around a handhold inside the tunnel. King was no good with knots and the strap wasn't suited to being tied anyway, but he managed to create an impossible tangle between the two metal fixtures. He tested it, satisfied the wheel couldn't move—at least not enough to unlock the hatchway.

He felt curiously at home in the Cryogenics Module. It was a *welcoming* feeling. He ran his hand lovingly along the top of Vasta's container and read the data on the computer screen, though the medical terminology meant almost nothing to him. He slid into the space above the container and settled himself to wait.

Soon his new awareness began to tell him things. He felt Judith Cianta's pain and growing weakness as her blood filled the air of the Medical Module. King didn't care. He knew Celia Hereson's anxiety as she planned to leave the Airlock unassisted. Later, King could feel the collective fear and concern of the other astronauts gathered in the Command Module. At this, he allowed himself a satisfied smile.

He didn't have to wait long. When, as he'd expected, the commander's voice crackled over the intercom, calling his name, King had already decided he wasn't going to answer Seerey. There was no point. Joseph knew what was required of him. Nothing would alter that.

But the feeling of power and superiority that had filled him since entering the module weakened his resolve. Now he wanted to answer Seerey, not to explain himself, but to show them how right he was, to show them that he was with his God. How wrong they were, not believing.

King and Seerey exchanged words. In the end they didn't want to understand, and even threatened him, as King knew they would. They should have left him alone as he had asked. Now he needed to show them the power of his faith.

Like everyone, Joseph could work his way through the basic menu of any computer program, even if he didn't fully comprehend the software. After Seerey's claim that he would isolate the power to the module, King began keying in commands until he found a 'Help' function with a flashing cursor encouraging him to enter a query.

He typed *Power Down*.

Moments later, for the third time, Freedom's power grid collapsed to minimum operation, dragging the lighting, life support and data systems down with it.

'What's he doing?' Lee asked.

'Fooling with the program, looks like,' Dawkins replied, moving closer. 'He might do the job for you, Alex. That's a complex piece of software. I doubt he knows what he's doing. He'll probably do more harm than good.'

'With luck,' Seerey said.

They watched with only mild interest—until the Command Module went black and the emergency lighting flickered, trying to catch up. The module filled with the cries and curses of the astronauts. Dawkins was loudest.

'Jesus! Did *he* do that?'

'Everyone keep calm,' Seerey called as the red lighting glowed once more. Tense faces looked back at him. 'Take it easy. This time we're not going to run around wasting time. We'll just wait. Something tells me he can't keep this up for long.'

'You think King managed this?' Dawkins repeated.

‘He must have. It makes sense, when you think about it.’ Seerey was annoyed at himself for not considering it before. ‘For the cryogenics to get priority during power failures, the program must have entry to Freedom’s core software controlling the entire space station. King’s obviously accessed the mainframe through the Revival software and done this. The bastard’s checked out the program a bloody sight more than we have.’

‘But he wasn’t around to do this the other two times,’ Lee argued.

‘Maybe it’s automatically programmed into the Revival procedure, though God knows why it should be.’

They thought about this for a minute.

‘What about us losing those fifteen minutes?’ Dawkins asked.

‘We don’t know that we did. We haven’t checked.’ Suddenly, Seerey began to hate their questions. He felt cornered.

‘And the little girl’s ghost, Alex?’ Celia asked, tired and confused. ‘Was she in the software, too?’

‘Christ, I don’t *know*, Celia. Maybe that was a freak and it won’t happen again, like you said. I don’t *know* all the answers,’ he added, failing to keep the frustration from his voice.

They all fell silent. There was nothing to do except look at each other, their faces shadowed with strain in the dim lighting. Finally Dawkins suggested that they would only have to wait less than ten minutes before power was restored. The others tried guessing, too, and finally Seerey suggested it would only be five minutes. He gruffly apologised for his temper.

Seerey was right. Like a robotic animal climbing to its feet after a knockout blow, Freedom's main power grid came back to life in just under five minutes after it failed. Nobody cheered or clapped this time. They were getting used to it. Almost.

They immediately focused on the camera monitor, which had also blacked out with the power. King was back where he'd started, suspended above Vasta's container. Seerey furiously switched the intercom through.

'King, what the fuck do you think you're doing?'

King stayed motionless and silent.

'King, answer me, damn you!'

He didn't respond.

Dawkins put a hand on Seerey's shoulder. 'Don't bother, Alex. You're wasting your time.'

King nearly cried out with delight when Freedom broke down around him. He was *communicating!* He had *asked* and been *answered*. He felt a thrill in every nerve of his body. Moved, he attempted to bow reverently to the container in front of him, spreading his arms wide, but in the zero gravity he only managed an awkward and ungainly ducking motion. He noticed the red lighting was being washed out by a harsh, white glow forming in the air. He turned, words of joy ready on his lips, anticipating a wondrous revelation.

The words turned to a screech of terror and he scrabbled ineffectually away from the thing in front of him.

His grandfather hung in the air of the module. It wasn't the familiar patriarch of King's memories.

The old man's figure emanated a palpable evil. Hate and anger flowed from it. His clothes looked as they always had, creased and stained, but now they hung off his shoulders like rags, not concealing the skeletal, wasted frame. He glared down at his grandson with mad eyes. Words echoed in King's mind.

'Don't fail me. I am torn in two and sometimes I am weak. When I am weak, you must be strong. Don't fail me, or I will eat your soul.'

At the sight of his grandfather King's bowels nearly loosened. Slowly, he recognised that he must pay attention—or pay a terrible penalty. This was a message, and his grandfather's image merely the messenger. He should listen and obey, not cower. Yet the old man's ghost had such a terrifying quality, it needed all of King's perverted courage to reply.

'No, I won't fail you,' he responded in a small voice, then realised he was talking to empty air.

'I think it was a warning,' Celia said as they began to reorganise themselves in the Command Module.

'I agree,' Dawkins nodded. 'He was saying, "Don't fuck with the Cryogenic Module". I don't know *how* he knows what he's doing, but like Alex said, he seems to have studied the Revival software right through.'

'I'm concerned he can do a damn sight more, too,' Seerey fumed. 'Like maybe cut off *our* power, one hundred per cent, and permanently.' They all stopped and looked at him in alarm. 'That's why I want to keep all of us together here. But first, Lee, will you go to the Accommodation Module and look through every inch of Joseph's bunkspace? It's possible he's on some sort of drug which may wear off—I know it's a long shot—' he acknowledged Celia's sceptical look '—but we should check. He may even have snuck through some medication which has reacted—hell, I don't know. Have a look, anyway.' As she nodded and headed for the access tunnel he called, 'And bring Judith's sleeping bag, so we can bundle her up in the corner—and a spare one for any of us.'

Seerey's plan was to restrict all operations to the Command Module, and even have the crew sleep there. That way, if King did decide to throw Freedom into powerless chaos or worse, the remaining astronauts wouldn't waste valuable time finding each other. He expected Ground Control to launch a relief shuttle as soon as the hurricane cleared Florida, and they would go home. The tour was a total disaster, a wipe-out—except for the cryogenics, and Seerey didn't care a damn about that. They'd talked over several ways of dislodging King from the Cryogenic Module, but the suggestions were half-hearted and lacked conviction. Seerey called a temporary halt to the discussion in favour of changing their living arrangements and getting Judith more comfortable.

Lee moved quickly through the space station. She appreciated Seerey's bringing them together now. At first she'd thought it was overreacting, but as she made her way towards the Accommodation Module the space station no longer felt such a friendly place. Before, with eight working astronauts spread the length of Freedom and the certainty you'd run into one of them in almost every module, it had been a close, happy community. Now they had five people—including one injured—grouped at one end of the space station and a madman at the other keeping company with six frozen bodies. All the talk about ghosts didn't help.

Pulling herself into the Accommodation Module Lee suddenly remembered how she had been trapped in her bunkspace and the temperature had plummeted to freezing. *Poltergeists,* the computers on Earth had suggested, and everyone thought it was very funny. Now it was a real possibility. Lee shrugged away a creepy feeling between her shoulder blades.

Each bunkspace had a small cupboard for personal belongings and a single wide drawer for spare clothes. Lee found King's and quickly flipped through the drawer, then searched its furthest corners. There was nothing unusual. She turned to the cupboard.

Most astronauts brought little with them. A couple of favourite novels, their own approved toiletries and maybe some family photographs were usual. Personal compact disc players and a selection of music was common, too. King, however, had almost nothing. A small plastic case held his toothbrush, paste and a stick of deodorant—aerosols were forbidden. The only other item was a thin book on astronomy. Lee leafed through it, wondering why it should take pride of place near his bunk, instead of where he worked. The answer was a short chapter written by King himself.

'At least he's got a normal ego,' she murmured. She crouched down and checked the corners of the cupboard without success. 'I guess he's clean. Poor bastard's just as nutty as a fruitcake,' she said with a shrug. Lee looked at the sleeping bag and recalled Seerey wanting a spare one for the Command Module. She decided King's was as good as anybody's—better, really, because it was the largest and longest available, which would suit everyone. She grabbed the top and tugged it away from the bunk. There was a ripping noise as it separated from the hook-and-loop fastenings holding it to the mattress. Before the last one came loose Lee headed for Judith's bunk, towing the sleeping bag behind her, but as it came free she could still feel a dragging resistance, a weight in the bag that shouldn't have been there.

'Hello,' Lee said, frowning. 'What have we got here?' She thrust her arm up to the shoulder into the bag, searching with her fingers. Sour, male smells wafted out of the bag and she wrinkled her nose. Lee pulled out the Bible.

At first she thought it was the genuine thing. Opening it, she discovered it was upside down—either that or the Christian cross on the cover was inverted, which surely must be a mistake. The book fell open at a page halfway through. Lee wasn't a devout Christian and never read the Bible, so she didn't expect to recognise any of the text. She scanned it without interest for a moment.

Immediately, she understood there was something wrong. She read more, actually reading now, not just letting her eyes pass over the print.

'This is weird,' she decided, searching for an explanation. 'It's like an *anti-Bible.*' She pulled a face. That didn't fit either. Reading more, she tried to pinpoint the essential difference between the words and snatches of Biblical text she could vaguely remember. It was impossible. The individual sentences appeared correct, but an entire page of text absorbed at once left an impression of wickedness. A distortion, like a flawed mirror, the imperfection unseen unless you stepped back to see the entire glass. Lee leafed forward a few chapters and a piece of doubled-over paper drifted out, hanging in the air. She let go of the Bible to open it out. It was the symbols King had drawn, covered in his browning bloodstains. Fingerprints were clear in the smudges. She didn't recognise any of the symbols, but Lee recognised the blood. A feeling of despair filled her, born from a sense of pity for King and how misguided he must have become. Then a new, unexpected thought occurred to her and it scared her.

'My God, Joseph,' she breathed, slowly gathering the book and paper together. 'What the hell have you started?'

'I've never seen anything like this,' Seerey said, opening the Bible and reading odd passages. 'I've never even *heard* of it. It seems okay, but after you've read for a while it leaves something behind, like a bad taste in your mouth. What is it, some kind of witchcraft?'

Dawkins had already seen it. 'Not witchcraft, really, although that's part of it. It's more like the Christian religion seen from the other side. The wrong side, if you like.' He nodded at the book in Seerey's hands. 'I'll say one thing. It's a very cleverly-written piece of literature. It presents the

Devil and all the nasty shit that comes with him as a viable alternative. It's very convincing. A gullible mind could easily fall prey to it.'

'And this bit of paper? The symbols and the bloodstains?' Seerey looked at them again, holding the sheet at arm's length.

'I guess that means Joseph not only read this Bible, but practised some of the things in it,' Dawkins said soberly.

'And what does *that* mean?'

'That Joe's had deep-seated beliefs in this stuff for a long time,' Lee answered, 'and that's not good. There's a written dedication to Joe inside the front flap, like the book was a birthday present, and that's dated nearly twenty years ago, putting Joe in his late teens. That doesn't mean he wasn't *taught* from it even before that. He might have been absorbing this religion his entire life.'

Celia was sucking hot coffee from a bottle. She carefully pinched the straw closed and said, 'So you think he's gone over the edge, pushed somehow by a combination of his religious beliefs and all this bringing-someone-back-from-the-dead business, and now he's beyond help?'

'It's only a guess, and an uneducated one at that, but yes. He's beyond *our* help, at least. The stuff he's fantasising is ingrained too deeply in his psyche.'

'What Lee's saying,' Dawkins said wryly, 'is that King's gone absolutely crazy. The man's a loop. He's a madman in a position to cause us a hell of a lot of trouble if his twisted mind decides to go that way. We cannot afford to fuck around when we're dealing with him. If we try something, he mustn't suspect, in case he overreacts.'

'So why don't we leave him alone?' Celia asked.

'For exactly the same reason. He might at any time decide he doesn't like having *us* around and, say, cut off our fresh air.'

'He wouldn't, would he?' She went pale.

'He might.'

'Jesus.' Celia thought a moment. 'Okay, so why don't we do that to him?' She tried not to sound as though she was suggesting they suffocate King—but that was exactly what she meant.

Seerey had obviously already considered the idea. Without hesitating he replied, 'Because we have to assume he's got overriding software in that Revival program. Once he started running out of breath he'd know what was going on and probably be able to reverse the process. Worse, we might simply put the idea in his head to do the same back to us, and we might not be able to stop *him*.'

In the corner Judith groaned and turned inside her sleeping bag. They watched, expecting her to wake, but she settled back into an uneasy sleep.

'What did Hitchcock have to offer?' Lee asked. Ground Control had been contacted while she searched in the Accommodation Module.

'Nothing,' Seerey said bitterly. 'No suggestions at all, which is bloody strange for him. I don't know what they think they're doing down there, but they sure as hell aren't helping us a lot.'

'Scary, isn't it?' Celia said. 'It's like they still prefer the survival of the Cryogenics program over us.'

At some time over the past few days the same thought had occurred to all of them. Until now no one had been brave enough to voice it. There was an uncomfortable silence.

'You know, we *can* get inside the Cryo Module,' Dawkins began, 'from the other end.'

'From outside?' Lee asked disbelievingly.

'Why not? It's got an access module tacked on the other end already, which means one side of that's the interior hatchway. I'll bet he hasn't jammed that one. All we have to do is take off the blank seal on the outside, crawl through and open the hatch. Presto! You're inside.'

Seerey stared at him, calculating. 'But he'd lose all his atmosphere—come to think of it, you'd be struggling to open the hatch against the pressure.'

'By the time I cracked open the hatch and let the air out, letting me *in*, it'd take about a minute, I figure. King can afford to suffocate for that long. I'll take one of my canisters of oxygen,' Dawkins explained, unwittingly copying Judith's idea. 'Give him a whiff or two to keep him going until I close the inner hatch again. While he's still groggy I'll tie him up somehow.'

'It nearly sounds good,' Seerey said slowly. 'But I can see you're not entirely happy about it. What's the snag?'

Dawkins turned his palms up. 'Of course, the man's going to hear me, soon as I start taking the outer seal off. It won't take him long to work out what's going on. He could just jam that hatchway, too. Leave me with my ass stuck in an access tunnel with nowhere to go.'

'That's another thing,' Seerey grunted, deflated. 'You won't fit through the tunnel fully suited-up.'

'I think I will if I don't wear the backpack.

I can carry it in front of me. The hoses are long enough. I can push it in front of me in the tunnel, too. The other problem of the air pressure isn't so bad. It's only a small hatchway, not like the Airlock door. I'm a strong guy. I'll have to lever it for the first few seconds, that's all.'

Lee shook her head. 'So, everything looks fine, except he'd hear you coming.'

'What about when he's asleep?' Celia asked.

Seerey jerked his thumb at the monitor. 'Who knows when he's asleep? Look at him! He hasn't moved.'

'Could we knock him out somehow? Introduce something into the air?'

'We've got the facility to add anything to the atmosphere we want through the ancillary tank fixtures,' Seerey said. 'Just take off the reserve oxygen tanks and replace them with whatever we're adding. But not without affecting the whole of Freedom—' His voice trailed away as he realised this wasn't quite the case.

'Not necessarily,' Dawkins finished for him, getting excited. 'Cryogenics is at the end of a line! If we turned off the supply to the rest of Freedom, so his module was the *only* one being serviced, we'd be okay.' He spread his arms. 'With only five of us here, and the whole of Freedom as an air reservoir, it'd be hours before we noticed any staleness in the atmosphere.'

'But what have you got to knock him out?' Seerey asked, not letting his hopes get too high.

'Halothane,' Lee and Dawkins answered together. Lee continued, 'There's a whole tank of halothane—it's an anaesthetic for surgery—that's never been used. It's been here since the first days of Freedom, I think. I know it's full.'

All of them were excited now. It wasn't only the plan, but the feeling they weren't helpless anymore. Here was something they could at least *try*.

'Do you know how much to use?' Seerey looked at Dawkins.

'We can dump a lot in first, saturate the atmosphere, then take it easy. Knocking him out's the important thing. It's odourless, so he won't smell it coming. And the beauty is, it'll get flushed out into space when I open the door.'

'Right,' Seerey nodded, checking for any possible flaws in the plan. After a moment he asked, 'Will it work?'

'Damn right it will,' Dawkins nodded eagerly.

Celia said, 'Will Jack Hitchcock let us try it?'

Seerey raised an eyebrow. 'What the hell makes you think I'm going to ask him?'

King wasn't asleep. He was waiting. Waiting to be told what to do next. One thing troubled him—he felt alone. *I am torn in two, and sometimes I am weak,* his grandfather said. This must be one of those times. If King concentrated he could feel the strength of the emotions coming from the Command Module. He judged it was fear. King believed they had every reason to be afraid.

Seerey chose to stay in the Command Module to coordinate the others. He didn't want to use the intercom at all in case King could hear them. Above all else Seerey thought it important that King didn't know they were doing an EVA. It might start a train of thought that led him to disable the far hatchway in the Cryogenics Module.

Dawkins was the one going outside—it was always going to be him from the moment he announced the idea. Once the halothane cylinder was hooked up, Lee and Celia would help him put on his suit and later, if all went well, take King out of the module.

There was a brief moment of panic when the gas fittings on the cylinder didn't match the ancillary connections.

'I don't believe it,' Dawkins said. 'There's got to be an adaptor somewhere. This has been done before, I know. I was controlling from Dallas one tour and the guys up here ran antiseptic through the system to kill off any bacteria.' Searching a little-used toolbox he found the brass adaptor. With sighs of relief all round, the halothane gas was connected.

Dawkins needed to wear a belt of tools. The end seal of the access module was secured by twelve large steel nuts. He took a long spanner to loosen them and a battery-powered drill with the correct socket to wind the nuts off. This would save time and energy. He also had a small lever designed for locating the ends of new laddertracks installed as Freedom expanded. With some experimenting in another access tunnel Seerey and Dawkins deemed it the best available tool for cracking the inside hatch against the air pressure. The longer he held it open, the lower the pressure would get, until he could push the hatch open.

In addition he carried one of the oxygen canisters and a roll of thick binding tape. The tape was renowned for having a thousand uses. Now it had a new one. He was going to use it to tie King's hands and feet.

Seerey was using a second internal camera to monitor their progress in the Airlock. The first was still focused on Joseph King. When Dawkins was ready to leave, Lee and Celia would give their commander a thumbs-up and he would open the ancillary valves. Dawkins would exit the Airlock, make his way the short distance to the end of the next module, and do his best.

'Are we ready?' Dawkins called, everything but his helmet installed. They'd compromised about the backpack life-support unit, fastening it to his back with a single strap. When the time came for him to enter the access tunnel he could release the strap and pull the unit over his head.

'I think so,' Celia replied, running through a checklist in her mind one last time.

'Then put my head on and let's get moving. The battery in this thing's a-wasting.'

With his helmet clipped down Lee gave the signal to the camera in the corner. Moments later, whirring, clicking noises came from the main Closed-Loop Life-Support System behind them as different solenoids opened and shut valves. Gases hissed along the empty lines.

Dawkins moved to the inner Airlock door while Celia swung it wide. No one dwelled on the possibility of the outer door opening. They trusted it only happened during the power grid failures. Still, Celia closed the door with relief after Dawkins moved through.

King felt calm. An inner peace washed over him. For a while he fought it—it threatened his vigilance and he knew he was spiritually alone. The presence guiding him and protecting them both was still missing. He longed for it to return.

The calm took away his strength, sapping the tension from his nerves and easing the ache in his muscles. Perhaps, King thought, as it seemed useless to resist, it was the hand of his God telling him to rest. King was only human, after all.

The outer Airlock door slid aside and Dawkins stared out at a brilliant panorama of stars and a glaring sliver of white moon. He hadn't realised he would be working in their night-time—the sun was hidden behind the Earth. It didn't matter, the ambient light from the night sky was plenty to see by.

He climbed out of the doorway and spread himself across two handholds. These were all over the outer skins of the modules. NASA considered what Dawkins was doing very dangerous. It was similar to the seal-test walk John Quantey had done. Scott wasn't using the Wheelchair or a lifeline either, but Quantey had at least been moving within the web of the laddertracks, giving him room for error. Here, only a single framework extended out above the Airlock door to support an observation camera. On the outer skin of the Airlock Module Dawkins had nothing except open space at his back.

He crabbed his way along the module, taking his time. The basic rules of EVAs still applied—he mustn't overexert himself. He didn't communicate with Seerey in case King accidentally picked up the transmission on the module's monitor. It was strange not to be talking to someone constantly, which was standard practice during EVAs. He felt isolated and exposed.

The access tunnels were small connecting modules like joints in the space station. As Dawkins neared the junction between the Airlock and the Cryogenics Module he saw the access module connecting them was thrown into dark shadows. It made him unexpectedly nervous. He believed, now, that John Quantey had met something out here during his seal-test EVA. Something that frightened him so much he'd panicked and died. Dawkins thought maybe that same something was still out there, waiting for another victim.

He moved into the shadows, his skin crawling, waiting to feel a ghostly hand touch his shoulder or grip his ankle. Then he was climbing the length of the Cryogenic Module. He tried to make better time, uncaring of any noise he made. In any event it was impossible to do this silently. The tiniest sounds reverberated through the hull. He had to trust King was drugged asleep.

There were more eerie shadows at the far end of the vacant access module. Dawkins got into position squarely in front of the blank, round plate which sealed the unused end of the module. The only thing breaking its flat surface was a metal eyelet. The steel nuts gleamed cleanly at him.

First, Dawkins secured a short wire from his waist to the eyelet. This would give him leverage. What he was attempting was nothing new. It was all part of the procedure for adding new modules to Freedom, albeit usually with a little more logistical support. NASA engineers had designed and proved the system years before. It was what Dawkins intended to do *after* he removed the seal that wasn't recommended in the textbooks.

He pulled the long spanner from his toolbelt and fitted it over the first nut. Applying pressure he was relieved to feel the thread crack easily.

Seerey didn't have a camera well-placed to watch Dawkins. All he could see was the astronaut's right arm and leg sometimes drifting out from behind the module. Seerey checked his view of the Airlock Module and just caught Lee making signs at the camera. It took him a moment to understand she could hear noises coming through the hull. Anxiously, he changed his attention to the Cryogenic Module. King hadn't moved. Seerey dared the intercom, selecting the Airlock.

'He has to be out to it,' he reported quietly. 'He's not moving and if *you* can hear Scott, he must be able to.'

'We can definitely hear him clanging around on the hull,' Lee answered.

'I'll try to let you know what's happening.'

At the sound of Seerey's voice in his helmet Dawkins' hopes fell, thinking they'd been discovered.

'The girls can hear you in the Airlock Module, Scott. King hasn't moved, so he must be sleeping tight.'

'Good,' Scott answered, relieved. 'Keep that gas pouring in. Let's not blow it now.'

'Can we hurt him?'

'I don't know.' Seerey could hear the grin in Dawkins' voice. 'I didn't want to tell you that, in case you changed your mind.'

'You shouldn't have worried. I wouldn't have.'

Dawkins worked steadily at the nuts, removing them one by one and leaving them floating nearby. With the last one unscrewed he tried pulling the plate away, but it stuck. Using his improvised lever he broke the seal around the edge. Next time he tried the plate came away effortlessly.

'Going into the access tunnel now,' he called to Seerey.

'Good luck.'

The thick-fingered gloves made it hard for Dawkins to undo the buckle around his waist. Again, he employed the lever, hooking the tip under the webbing. This released, he pulled the backpack gently over his head, being careful not to pinch any pipes or cables.

Dawkins moved slowly into the access tunnel. Another thing they hadn't counted on was that the module, not being an active part of the space station, was totally dark inside. Dawkins had to work by feel—and there wasn't a lot of that in a spacesuit. It wasn't easy manoeuvring himself and the backpack through the narrow passageway. Finally, he felt the unit strike something solid—the hatchway.

Dawkins wriggled himself over the top of his backpack as far as he could, which brought him close to the hatch, but left him cramped. The locking wheel spun smoothly and Dawkins uttered a heartfelt *thank you*. He'd been worried about it more than he cared to admit. He pushed against the hatch, but it didn't budge. That was to be expected. He brought the lever up in front of him and tried to position it where he and Seerey had decided was the best place. The first couple of times he tried, it slipped, but on the third attempt the lever carried the increasing weight Dawkins bore down on it. Satisfied, he eased off a little, took some deep breaths and snapped all his strength against the tool.

He was rewarded by a thin line of light showing around the hatch and he nearly cheered. Dawkins couldn't hear the air escaping or feel it rushing past, although he thought he detected a slight pressure against his facemask. He kept pushing on the lever, even after his muscles began to cramp. He didn't want to relax and let the hatch close again.

Seerey saw King start to move and went to call a warning to Dawkins, but something else he saw stopped him. The clipboard for the cryogenic checks was slowly drifting towards the far end of the module, too. 'You've cracked the seal, Scott,' he called, jubilant.

'Only just.' Dawkins sounded out of breath. 'What can you see?'

'Stuff being drawn down to your end of the module, including King.'

'Okay. Is he still unconscious? No signs of panic?'

'Not a thing.'

Despite the warning, Dawkins was startled when King's body thudded against the hatchway. He'd been about to force the gap wider, get the depressurising over with. He panicked that King was making a frantic attempt to close the hatch, but a lifeless limb flapping beyond the opening calmed him down. Seconds later Dawkins gave a final heave and with the last cushion of resistance broken the hatchway opened, shoving King aside at the same time. Dawkins certainly felt a rush of air flow past his suit and he got another scare as the clipboard, fluttering like a dying bird, smacked against his visor and went on, out into space.

'Going inside,' he said briefly.

'I can see you,' Seerey reminded him.

Dawkins closed the hatchway first, twisting the wheel firmly. It was the only seal against the vacuum of space now. He didn't have the time or inclination to re-strap the backpack behind him and it floated annoyingly in front of his face. Turning back to King he pulled the roll of tape from his belt.

Joseph King looked traumatised. His eyes were wide open and his entire body trembled as it tried hard to draw in air that wasn't there. Already, his lips were turning blue. Dawkins felt no pity at all. Tending Judith Cianta's vicious head wounds had erased any he might have felt. He grabbed one of King's wrists and wound a quantity of tape around it. The weightlessness of both men made it awkward, but Dawkins was grimly determined. Bringing the two wrists behind King's back he finished the job by binding them together. He wound them tight. When he tore the tape apart he left plenty for his gloved fingers to grab. He repeated the process around King's ankles. Only then did he drag King towards one of the breathing masks hanging from their compartments. He figured the pure oxygen in his canister might revive his captive quickly, causing problems.

King didn't look well. Dawkins briefly worried he might have left it too long—he didn't want to kill him. After he clamped the mask on King's face he was relieved to see the thin chest begin to rise and fall with huge lungfuls of air.

Alarms were going off in the Command Module and the face on the comm-link demanded attention. Seerey ignored them all until he was certain Dawkins had everything under control, then dealt with them one at a time. The main alarm was due to the pressure drop in the Cryogenic Module. He keyed in a command to cancel that. The comm-link was Jack Hitchcock.

'What's going on?' he demanded, angry that Seerey had taken his time acknowledging the call.

'We're just removing Joseph from the Cryogenics Module,' Seerey said calmly.

'What? How?'

'From the outside. Scott just EVA'd and let himself in the other end.' Seerey's manner suggested it was something they did every day.

It took a moment for Hitchcock to understand. 'An EVA? Without telling us? What the hell do you think you're doing?'

'I thought you needed your sleep,' Seerey retorted.

'Don't bullshit me,' Hitchcock snapped.

'Well, we've done it and it worked. If you don't like it, bring me home and fire me,' Seerey invited. 'Right now I'm busy.'

Dawkins wasn't concerned about King causing more trouble. The man seemed to have gone into a form of shock, and was barely conscious. Still, Dawkins didn't wait for him to improve. He went to the jammed access tunnel and discovered the tangle of webbing tying the hatch. With no means to cut it Dawkins had to persevere, working his way through the knots until the strap fell away.

'How are we going for atmosphere in here?' he asked Seerey.

'Close to normal,' Seerey replied. 'You can try losing your helmet.'

Dawkins did, and his ears popped slightly. He also found it difficult to breathe, but not too bad. He moved back to King and pulled the mask from his face, breaking the elastic cord holding it. 'Breathe your own damn air,' he told him.

There was a noise from the access tunnel. Dawkins felt the air swirl in the module as someone opened the hatchway and the pressure equalised. Lee poked her head in.

'Scott, you're a fucking genius,' she cried, ignoring King's prone body and coming over quickly to plant a kiss on Dawkins' lips, surprising him.

'Let me do it all again,' he smiled, pleased.

Celia followed and contented herself with ruffling his wiry hair. 'We'll get you a Medal of Honour,' she told him.

'Thanks. Just what I always wanted.'

He rapidly discarded the spacesuit, keeping the undergarment on. 'I'll get dressed later,' he explained. 'Is the Minerals Laboratory ready?'

'No problem,' Celia nodded. They planned to imprison King there, jamming the wheel-locks the same way he'd jammed them in Cryogenics, until the relief shuttle arrived.

For the second time they guided a semi-conscious body through the space station. When they reached the Minerals Laboratory Dawkins told the two women to wait outside. After pulling King in with him he roughly tore the binding tapes away. The skin around King's wrists was creased and bruised.

'Tough,' Dawkins shrugged, and left the module. King waved his arms weakly and groaned. He didn't hear the hatch close. Nearby was his sleeping bag and a bottle of water.

The others gathered in the Command Module. There was an air of triumph. Even Judith, who woke only minutes before and barely understood what had been achieved, smiled at them, sharing their joy.

Seerey said, 'Celia, next report you make out, recommend this ship has at least *one* bottle of booze on board. There are times when nothing else will suffice, and this is one of them.'

'I'll mention it,' she laughed. 'But I don't like your chances.'

They made do with coffee all round. Dawkins recounted every step of his EVA and Seerey told them about his conversation with Jack Hitchcock. King was discussed and it was decided to leave him exactly where he was—leniency of any sort would be a risk. Finally, someone asked the inevitable question.

'So, what are *we* going to do?' said Lee.

'Nothing much different.' Seerey became serious. 'I still don't trust that Revival program which, don't forget, is still running. So I still want to keep us together. Apart from that, Hurricane Ben is getting its teeth into Florida at the moment. They're getting eighty-mile-an-hour winds at Canaveral now. I'd say we've got three or four days to relax and get bored stupid with each other before a shuttle launch is possible.' He shrugged. 'So take it easy. You've all got a few days off.'

He was wrong. It was only six hours before the lives of the remaining crew of Freedom were at risk again.

15

NO MATTER HOW KINDLING sat on the small canvas seat, it created an ache somewhere in his body. Looking across the cabin he saw a kindred spirit in Louise Corry. She caught his eye and smiled sympathetically, but didn't try to speak. The huge noise of the helicopter's blades chopping through the air prevented any attempt at conversation, unless they used the Blackhawk's internal communications system. Louise wasn't wearing a helmet connected to the electronics, but she'd donned a spare helmet for safety's sake. Anything she needed to say she passed through Smith, who'd insisted on wearing the real thing. The American sat next to her and stared moodily out the open door. Kindling watched him for a moment and wondered if Smith was concerned about being sent out on his own. Wiley had stayed behind, claiming there was no point in all of them going.

Below, the gold and red colours of inland Australia raced away beneath the belly of the aircraft. Tinges of green, too, Kindling saw, suggesting the rains had recently come to this part of the country. The pilot was flying lower now, having left the regimented altitudes of the coastal strip. The helicopter tipped slightly and steered a wide berth around some cattle. Kindling reached across, tugged on Louise's sleeve and pointed them out. As they looked the beasts raised their snouts to watch the machine approach. With a rush they were suddenly gone, falling behind the Blackhawk as it roared over the landscape.

Movement inside the cabin attracted Kindling's attention. The helicopter's third crewmember, a corporal whose faded army fatigues suggested long service and experience, was crouched between the two pilots' seats and shouting at the soldiers flying the aircraft, rather than using the intercom. Kindling thought it might be mistrust of the surly Smith, who could listen in. Now the corporal stood and walked easily back towards them, unconcerned by the lurches the aircraft made as it struck thermals close to the ground.

'We're about ten minutes away,' he yelled to Louise. Kindling gave him a grateful look and Louise smiled, but Smith nodded curtly and returned to staring out the doorway. The corporal turned to grin at Kindling. He dug his fingers into a shirt pocket which had the name 'Britten' stencilled above the flap, and pulled out a battered packet of cigarettes. He offered them around without success and put one between his lips. Cupping his hands closely around a disposable lighter he saw Kindling anxiously glance at the canisters of spare aviation fuel stacked at the back of the cabin. 'Don't worry,' he shouted, putting his face close to Kindling's even though they both had intercom. 'They're sealed tight. Fumes can't build up in here.' He grinned again, amused at his passenger's ignorance. Kindling shrugged, not offended.

Britten went casually to the doorway and leaned out into the slipstream, looking back towards the helicopter's rear rotor. The cigarette smoke whipped out of his mouth. Kindling didn't know if it was genuine insouciance or a show of bravado put on for the three civilians. All three soldiers had so far displayed a comforting aura of discipline and competence. They were highly-trained SAS members, confident and quietly sure of themselves. Britten turned his head slightly as the pilot, Castlemaine, spoke over the intercom.

'Geoff, did you disable the Steigers? We don't want any gun-happy stationhands taking one 'roo shooting for a laugh, or something.'

'All three,' Britten replied, not moving from the door.

Kindling felt compelled to speak up. 'There aren't any,' he said. The pilot twisted around to see who was speaking. 'They don't have any stationhands at this time of year. There's just the family.'

'That's what we were told, too,' Castlemaine answered easily. 'But there's no harm in playing it safe.'

The co-pilot, who had introduced himself

simply as 'Bluey', said, 'It must be a bloody lonely place to live, way out here.'

'No neighbours to give you the shits,' Britten suggested.

'Long way to the pub, though.'

'Well, we've got that one covered.'

Britten looked at Kindling and nodded downwards. Incongruous among the military grey, green and brown of the army hardware a bright red icebox was strapped to the floor. The soldiers were treating the trip as a short holiday. Originally, Michael Lay was going to arrange for everyone to fly north on a commercial flight and take an army helicopter from a coastal base for the trip inland. It turned out to be easier to ask the SAS to take them all the way. The defence forces were building up in the north anyway in preparation for a joint exercise with the United States. Kindling and the others didn't object—although they might have had second thoughts if they'd previewed the painful seating arrangements. Just before they'd left, as the rotor blades began to swish slowly, a military van had rushed to the tarmac and Britten, obviously expecting it, had happily taken delivery of the icebox. 'Camping supplies,' he'd told them, winking.

Leaning to look past Smith's legs Kindling noticed a fence with a well-used track beside it flash beneath them, followed quickly by a corrugated-iron roof glowing orange in the late afternoon sunshine. Now the helicopter leaned hard to starboard and flew in a sweeping circle above a cluster of buildings. Kindling picked out the main homestead by the splash of green lawns surrounding it. Britten still stood in the doorway, his only concession to the craft's angle a casual hand gripping the top of the doorframe. Another circuit confirmed the best landing site.

Small figures were walking out from the house, waving and shouting. Three dogs scampered in crazy rings around them. With a swoop the Blackhawk dropped to hover in front of them, the rotors kicking up a storm of leaves, twigs and grit made damp by the recent rain, then the machine touched down gently. Immediately the motor noise changed to a whine as the turbos wound down and the blades began to slow.

Sighing with relief Kindling pulled the helmet off and ran his fingers through his hair. His scalp was sweaty. It still felt as though the aircraft was moving and Britten, seeing the signs, touched him on the elbow.

'Don't be in a hurry to move. You'll still have your sea-legs.'

'Thanks,' Kindling nodded. He watched as Britten jumped to the ground and ran, doubled over, to make sure the waiting Littlewoods didn't stray too close to the rotors. The family seemed a forlorn group, the parents accepting the helicopter's arrival with stoic expressions, as if it heralded a change for the worse. The two children, the boy more a mature teenager than a child, were excited by the impressive machine and eagerly waited to be allowed a closer look.

'No sense in waiting any longer,' Smith declared, gesturing for them to follow. He went to the doorway and affected an exaggerated crouch as he moved out from underneath the blades. Louise went next, throwing a look at Kindling which seemed to echo his own questions about whether the American would be able to cope on his own. Kindling copied Louise's style of merely bowing as he walked, though the moving rotors felt uncomfortably close. Joining the clutch of people he saw Daniel Littlewood's eyes flick away from Britten to the three people approaching. They lingered on Kindling, recognising his face from the audio-visual call. However, Smith purposely blocked Kindling and introduced himself first.

'John Smith,' he said, holding out his hand. Daniel took it, then accepted the others' greetings. If he was surprised by Louise's presence he didn't show it. He introduced his family. Kindling was impressed by the firm handshake Georgina offered and the way she looked him in the eye in a steady, no-nonsense way. Peter and Rainy weren't so self-assured and it occurred to Kindling that they probably had little contact with strangers.

Daniel gestured at the helicopter. 'Things must be bigger than I thought.' He sounded subdued.

After Kindling had established contact with the Littlewoods, explaining he had something very important to discuss about their deceased daughter, he had told them nothing except that he was coming to see them. Daniel wasn't surprised by a helicopter, although the effort to travel out and see them personally was unusual. But a military Blackhawk complete with soldiers certainly wasn't expected.

'Mr Littlewood, we have a lot to talk about,' Kindling said gravely.

'It's Dan—or Daniel, I don't mind. You'd better come inside. The kettle's on and we made an extra big supper, but—' He stopped and looked uncertainly at Britten. The corporal smiled.

'Don't worry about us, Dan. We'll make camp right here next to the 'Hawk, and we've got our own supplies. Can we light a fire?'

'Sure. There's dry wood in the end of that shed over there. Use whatever you need. With this rain we've had, there's no risk of starting a bushfire. How long do you think you'll be staying? We could arrange a big cook-up for tomorrow. We don't often have guests.'

There was a silence and everybody looked at each other. 'We haven't even considered that,' Kindling admitted, annoying Smith by answering first.

'No, I expect not,' Dan said heavily. 'Nobody's quite sure of anything, any more.' He turned and headed for the house, indicating for them to follow. After a few steps he stopped and looked at Peter and Rainy lagging behind. 'Is it okay?' he asked Britten, with a tired smile and a nod at the helicopter.

'Hell, yes,' Britten laughed, then spread his arms to herd the youngsters towards the aircraft. 'Come on, guys. Let me show you the best piece of army hardware this side of the black stump—hey! Isn't that around here someplace?' The adults smiled as the younger Littlewoods abandoned any pretence of being good hosts and accompanying their guests inside, instead eagerly taking up Britten's invitation.

Louise moved closer to Kindling as they approached the homestead. 'Isn't this a fantastic place?' she said. 'It's like an oasis.' He nodded appreciatively.

Inside the cool stonework of the kitchen they seated themselves around the large wooden table. As Georgina busied herself making coffee and tea, Louise took in the contrasts around her. An ornate wood-burning stove, wafting out warmth and the tantalising smells of roast beef, was next to a bench-top where a modern microwave sat digitally displaying the time. A gleaming white refrigerator nestled against the stonework of the inner walls. The wash-basin was a deep ceramic affair—an antique in Louise's world. On the wooden bench surrounding it was a bright plastic draining rack.

Georgina noticed her interest. 'This is the original part of the house, it's about eighty years old,' she explained, smiling. 'The rest was built on over the decades, as it was needed, but Dan's grandfather was a timber man. So this room and the next, which we've turned into a big storeroom because the stone is much cooler, are the only parts made from rocks and mortar. The rest is timber. Our bedroom is the most recent, and that's fifty years old. On the really hot days you can feel the difference in the stonework, though.

'It's magnificent,' Louise said, accepting a coffee.

Georgina nodded and looked wry. 'I know. Some times of the year it's like a paradise. Still, there are days when I wish I had a shopping centre to pop down to.'

Louise glanced at Daniel, expecting him to disagree, but he smiled too and shrugged. Then he became businesslike. 'So, who's going to tell their story first?'

John Smith carefully explained that they were connected with NASA and Space Station Freedom. Daniel blinked in surprise at this revelation, but he stayed quiet and listened. When the tale widened to include the Cryogenic Project, Georgina couldn't stop herself exclaiming, 'I've heard of it, but I'd never have dreamed they were actually going to *try* it. Not in space, that's for sure.'

'Mrs Littlewood, there are a lot of things going on in this world that were only dreams, just a few years ago,' Smith told her. Only Kindling noticed the corner of Louise's mouth twitch at Smith's patronising tone.

'So, what has this got to do with Ellen?' Daniel asked. He looked nervous and Kindling judged their daughter's death was still a very disturbing subject for them. Now he worried that Smith was going to be insensitive.

'Have you heard of a man called Anton Vasta?' Smith asked.

'No,' Daniel decided. Next to him Georgina was frowning at this new, perplexing turn in the conversation.

'Anton Vasta was a very wealthy man who has taken part in the Cryogenic Program.'

This meant nothing to the Littlewoods. They stared impassively back at Smith, who now seemed unsure how to continue. Kindling decided it was time to rescue them from the American's awkward manner.

'John,' he asked before Smith could go on, 'do you mind if I explain the rest? It might be better. After all, I saw her.' Kindling was intent on Smith's reaction, so he missed the alarmed look that passed between the two parents. Smith tried to appear aggrieved at Kindling's interruption, but his relief was obvious. He grunted and nodded, leaning back in his chair. Louise watched them both with professional detachment. Kindling turned to the Littlewoods and spoke gently.

'We know how ill Ellen was—what caused her death. Where our paths cross is that Ellen died after the failure of a last-minute organ donation.' He paused, as if waiting for confirmation from the Littlewoods.

'Yes, yes.' Georgina's voice betrayed her growing impatience. Kindling held up a hand, as if to say he was merely laying out the facts.

'Well, that donated organ was taken from Vasta's body, before he was processed for the cryogenics.' Kindling waited for the words to sink in.

It took a moment for Daniel to reply. 'You mean, the person who donated his kidney to Ellen is still alive? Frozen in space?'

'It's a matter of personal opinion whether he's *alive* or not, but yes, that's where the organ came from and that's where his body is now.'

Georgina wasn't impressed by all the talk of space and scientific theories. 'Mr Kindling, you're dragging up some very painful memories for us,' she said coldly. 'While it's all fascinating about NASA and these frozen bodies, I still can't see why it's worth your coming out to see us, complete with an armed guard.'

'It's not an armed guard. They're the normal crew of the Blackhawk and it was the easiest and quickest way to get us here.'

'So, what was the hurry?'

Louise sensed there was something else happening here that they weren't expecting. The Littlewoods were too tense, too sensitive, even though the subject was one close to their hearts. They didn't look too good, either. Both Daniel and Georgina looked as if they could do with a few extra hours sleep. She heard Kindling draw a deep breath and knew he was about to get to the tricky part.

'Daniel—Georgina, you may find this difficult to accept,' he began, looking at cach of them in turn, 'but I've seen your daughter. A ghost of her, anyway. I saw her in Anton Vasta's house two nights ago.' He waited for a reaction. They only stared at him in disbelief. Kindling decided there was no point in dragging out all the details. It would be best to get it over and done with in one quick hit. 'And there's more,' he went on slowly. 'One of the astronauts, a woman named Celia Hereson, has also seen Ellen's spirit. This time it was up in Freedom, in orbit. It seems the ghost of your little girl is haunting the space station.' He sat back, prepared for a barrage of questions.

Daniel and Georgina looked stunned. In the silence that followed nobody dared move. From outside, thin and distant, they heard Rainy's voice calling for Peter to come and see something she'd discovered on the helicopter. Kindling expected the parents to be outraged or angry—even violent—towards someone who told them such a preposterous story.

Daniel's reply was totally unexpected, and galvanised the visitors.

'She seems to be getting around,' he said.

Peter and Rainy were called in from outside and asked to sit at the table. They looked at the newcomers with troubled eyes. Kindling tried to appear friendly and Louise cheerfully asked them what they thought of the helicopter. They answered reluctantly, throwing glances at Smith who scowled at the delay.

'Peter,' Daniel spoke up. 'They want to hear about Ellen.'

'What about Ellen?'

'They know what's been happening,' he assured him. 'It's important, and they want to know some details.'

Peter nodded and turned instinctively to Kindling, who used the moment to keep the initiative away from Smith.

'What did she look like?' Kindling asked him.

Peter shrugged and earned a stern look from his father, so he tried again, speaking hesitantly. 'She was in her white dress—'

'We buried her in it,' Georgina interrupted.

Daniel corrected, 'We didn't bury her. She was cremated.'

'Are her ashes here?' Kindling asked.

'No—well, yes. I mean, we scattered them across the land. It felt the right thing to do,' Daniel added defensively.

'A lovely thing to do,' Louise murmured, hoping to put them more at ease.

'Go on,' Kindling prompted Peter.

'She was in her white dress, sitting on the floor of her bedroom like she always used to, reading a book. At first, I thought it was Rainy, because Mum said Rainy was—' Peter stopped and waved that away. 'Anyway, she turned to look at me and I saw it was Ellen, not Rainy. I got scared and ran.' Just recalling the night made Peter turn pale.

'Did she say anything?' Kindling asked, sensing there was more.

'She said, "I'm coming back. Did you miss me?" '

'She's coming back,' Louise repeated, awed at the implication.

Georgina picked up her reaction. 'What does that mean?'

Kindling caught a warning in Smith's eyes, but decided to ignore it. Holding back information from these people, he guessed, might only cause them to do the same. It was hard enough already to create an atmosphere of trust in Smith's secretive and official presence.

He explained, simplifying it all, 'Vasta is going to be the first person to be revived. They have a cure for the disease that killed him, so now they're attempting to revive him and bring him back to Earth.'

'Bring him back from the dead?' Daniel said.

'That's the idea.'

Daniel stayed silent as he turned this over in his mind. Louise asked, 'Peter, was she *just* like she used to be, or different? Can you remember?'

'She was different,' he told her, his voice hushed. 'Like, it wasn't Ellen, but somebody else. Somebody—bad, I suppose.'

'Bad? What do you mean, *bad*?'

'I don't know—just someone not very nice.' He shrugged again.

'I know what he means,' Georgina said. She

gave them an account of her dream and her burnt fingers. Then she told them of her real-life meeting with Ellen's ghost, her words stumbling as she tried to convey the sense of menace in the dark shadows growing and flickering in the room, which seemed to control and dominate her daughter's spirit. Georgina was halfway through telling them how the spirit wanted to play with Rainy before she remembered they hadn't told Rainy herself about this. Georgina silently swore and looked to see how Rainy handled the news. She seemed to accept it calmly, only asking, 'Is that why you won't let me in her room?' Watching her, Louise realised that Rainy was handling it all a lot better than the rest of the family. Towards the end of Georgina's story Daniel reached out and took his wife's hand.

There was one more thing to tell the visitors. When Georgina finished Louise ventured that everything happening to them centred around Ellen's old room. It was Daniel's turn to describe strange events—how Rainy had been stopped when she tried to leave the homestead.

'That was yesterday,' he added. 'Just before you called.'

'So you don't think she's confined to her room?' Kindling asked.

'We did before, but not now.'

'Okay.' Kindling puffed out his cheeks and thought. When he realised they were waiting for him to go on, he said, 'Well, this is what *we've* experienced, which isn't anywhere near as detailed or comprehensive as what you've had to put up with, but anyway—'

Kindling's account of his visit to Vasta's house

and the encounter with the ghost of Ellen Littlewood sounded contrived and incomplete—which it was. He didn't want to tell them of the connections between these happenings and the spiritual confrontations of his own past. Despite his resolve not to hide anything, Kindling honestly believed it would confuse things too much and probably didn't really matter as far as the Littlewood family were concerned. Also, he didn't tell them of Vasta's occult activities or the ritual cellar, saying only that he saw Ellen's ghost inside the main room.

He didn't need to alter the facts concerning Ellen's appearance inside Freedom. He knew so little about it himself, as did all the visitors. When Kindling looked at Louise, silently asking if she had anything to add, she shook her head.

'That's about it,' she agreed. 'The ghost appeared, said what she said, and disappeared again before anyone up there had time to react.'

'He's wrecking all my books,' Georgina repeated sadly.

'Now *that* sounds like Ellen,' Rainy declared, surprising them. Kindling gave her a long look.

'Then the only thing left to do is to have a look in the room,' Smith declared, impatient with all these explanations. Louise nodded.

'Not yet,' Daniel said, leaning back in his chair to look through the back door. Outside the world was washed in deep shades of orange and pink. The helicopter was a black silhouette against the setting sun, throwing a long shadow across the ground. A fire glowed brightly near the machine and he saw a figure stride briefly in front of the flames. It made him realise how dim the kitchen had become. 'We may as well wait until nightfall. That's pretty close now.' Daniel stood and turned on the kitchen light. The others blinked in the unexpected glare. 'We can eat first. It smells like it's almost ready.' Georgina nodded.

'Yes, it's probably just right. There's no sense in spoiling a good meal. She's been in there every other night, so I doubt tonight will be any different.'

Kindling and Louise exchanged a glance. Both of them picked up the fatalism in Georgina's words. No one wanted to look in Ellen's room.

But that was what they'd come for.

The three soldiers squatted on their haunches around the fire. All of them were smoking. The fire was large by their standards. Usually they would use low embers, small enough to conceal from even a short distance away, and capable of being extinguished in an instant.

The beers had come out. Because they would most likely be flying the next day, this was breaking the rules, but the three of them had already discussed this—some rules were meant to be broken. Sleeping bags were laid out on the ground near the chopper. They had a tent, but the night was muggy and sleeping outdoors would be better. On the horizon a storm flashed and grumbled faintly. If it rained they'd pile into the Blackhawk—there was plenty of room.

Bluey pitched his cigarette into the flames. 'Anybody got a fucking clue what we're doing here?' He slapped at a mosquito on his arm.

'A bloody expensive taxi, that's all I know,' Castlemaine answered.

Bluey grunted. 'I've had worse jobs.'

'That Yank's a pain in the arse,' Britten said. Castlemaine raised his eyebrow.

'Why? What's he say?'

'Nothing. Just his attitude—a pain in the arse.'

'That Louise is cute,' Bluey said wistfully.

'Yeah?' Castlemaine laughed. 'I reckon she'd have you for dinner and not even fart afterwards. She knows her shit, I reckon.'

'I reckon she knows guns,' Britten said. They looked at him in surprise. 'When I checked the Steigers and went through all the actions, she was watching. But she didn't watch like it was all something new. She looked like she was watching to see if I did it *right*.'

'Bullshit,' Bluey snorted. 'Where the hell would she learn about Steigers, unless she was army?'

'Maybe she is,' Britten shrugged, not willing to take it any further.

'So ask her,' Castlemaine challenged, ending the discussion. 'Let's get some food going. The smells coming from that kitchen are driving me crazy.'

They rose together and headed for the helicopter. Castlemaine fumbled for a work light inside the cabin. Britten located a backpack full of rations he'd pulled from stores before they left and took out some tins, reading the labels as he went.

'Braised steak and onions, spaghetti bolognaise, camp pie. Mix 'em all together and it might be edible. There's peaches in rice cream for dessert.'

'I can smell their roast dinner,' Bluey grumbled.

'Tough shit. You can have roast every night back in the barracks, but I bet you don't.'

'That's not the same,' he said. As Castlemaine went to flick the light off Bluey jabbed his thumb at the spare fuel. 'Refuel first thing in the morning?'

'Yeah. I didn't want to do it now, in case we spill some. I hate stinking of av-gas and having to climb into a sleeping bag. I did it once—never again. Nearly gassed myself and didn't get a wink of sleep.'

They laughed. Britten asked him to leave the light on for a moment while he found some cooking gear and a can opener. Before they returned to the camp fire, Bluey grabbed another three beers from the icebox.

16

DANIEL CHANGED THE SUBJECT over supper. Louise asked him where they got their power from, and that prompted a detailed explanation of how the homestead had evolved over the last twenty years, from using just a normal generator, which couldn't cope with the increasing demands on its services, to the system of solar cells and storage batteries used now. He went on to describe the satellite communications, and the education program Peter and Rainy were involved in. Kindling listened, fascinated, and glad, too, to get away from the daunting topic of their real reason for being there. John Smith wasn't quite so at ease. He hurried through his meal and sullenly watched everyone else, willing them to finish.

When everybody's plates were empty Georgina served coffee again, another frustrating delay for Smith. Louise kept an eye on him, half-expecting the American to take things into his own hands and go searching through the house for Ellen's room. With difficulty, it seemed, he resisted the urge. Finally Daniel put his cup down.

'She'll be there by now,' he announced. They all went quiet. He looked at the two children. 'You two stay right here.'

Neither appeared to have any wish to do otherwise, but Georgina said, 'I'll stay with them. The hall will be crowded enough.'

'Okay.' Daniel was relieved. He was going to suggest she did anyway.

'Be careful.'

'Don't worry.' He stood and Kindling, Louise and Smith did the same. 'Follow me.'

He took them through the living area to the end of the hallway. Daniel stopped and pointed down the dark corridor. 'See?'

They peered down the hallway and saw the line of light under Ellen's door.

'Is that it?' Smith asked, suddenly hushed.

'She turns the light on.'

'Why?' The American looked sceptical.

'I don't know. Do you think this is all a damn hoax? I even took the bulb out one day, and she still managed it.'

'So, what now?' Louise asked quickly to prevent an argument.

'Go and open the door. Take a look.' Daniel sounded more in control than he felt. In fact, remembering the feeling of approaching menace last time he went into the room, he was badly scared now.

'Okay,' Smith agreed and entered the hallway. Kindling was next and was startled to see Smith reach behind him and pull out a pistol from under his shirt.

'What the hell do you think you're doing with that?'

'Protection,' Smith answered shortly.

'Don't be bloody stupid. How in God's name are you going to shoot a ghost? Put it away, in case you shoot one of us instead.'

Smith seemed about to refuse, then scowled at Kindling and agreed. Kindling heard Louise mutter something behind him. Bringing up the rear, Daniel called out, 'When you open the door you'll feel something like an electric shock through the doorknob. It doesn't hurt, it just surprises you.' Smith paused for a second, then went on.

When Smith touched the doorknob he let out a small yelp and drew back his hand. Daniel called again, telling him that was it—the shock didn't occur twice. Smith grunted, annoyed, and Kindling thought he was going to pull the pistol out again, but the agent suddenly snatched at the door and opened it with a quick, deft movement. He kicked it all the way open. Light flooded out into the hallway. Smith leaned cautiously through the doorframe and looked around. Behind him, the others held their breath.

'Nothing here,' he announced, easing the tension and walking into the room. Kindling followed and stopped just inside the room. As Louise went to move forward Daniel put his lips near her ear.

'That's what *he* thinks.' She turned around, surprised, and he nodded for her to go in.

Ellen's room looked immaculately tidy. The bed was made, the books and toys neatly arranged on the shelves as they should be. None of this looked unusual to the three newcomers—they hadn't seen the chaos that had reigned when the loose objects had whirled through the air. Daniel pointed out the bookshelf to Louise.

'They're the books she meant when she said somebody was wrecking them. The first indication we had of anything happening in here was when some of Ellen's favourite books were left on the floor with pages ripped out. At first, we thought it was Rainy. We had a bad time with her, after Ellen died. Peter, too.' Daniel smiled sadly. 'Well, everyone, really. It was very hard to accept. That's one of the reasons we never changed this room.'

'I understand,' she said gently, then sighed. 'Well, the light was on, but we don't have our ghost. Looks like she saw us coming.'

'Skipped out,' Smith said with a trace of smugness.

'Saw the Marines coming?' Louise asked drily, but the sarcasm was lost on him. Smith bent down and examined the books closely.

'That doesn't mean she won't be back—and soon,' Daniel warned.

'That's right,' Louise agreed. 'What do you think, Matt? Any ideas?' Kindling didn't answer. He stood motionless just inside the doorway. 'Matt, are you okay?'

They all turned to look at him. His face was deathly pale and his eyes were wide. His hands made two tight, white-knuckled fists, which he held rigidly at his sides. The muscles in his arms trembled. He looked to be in shock.

Kindling was experiencing something similar to when he had visited Vasta's gravesite—something that now seemed so long ago. The real world inside Ellen's bedroom was pushed back, replaced by a spirit world filled with auras and impressions of lives long since passed on, and others still present. Most of the furniture glowed with energy, traces of the love and grief bestowed upon them after the real object of those emotions, Ellen Littlewood, had become unreachable. And the spirit of the girl lived in the room, too. Not a ghost as such, but a feeling. A *feeling* of Ellen Littlewood. At the moment it was untainted, but Kindling knew bad things had occurred in this room. It frightened him.

'Matt, what the hell is wrong with you?' Louise tugged at his arm.

'What is this shit?' Smith's tone suggested Kindling was behaving like a troublesome child.

'It's not shit, it's real,' Louise snapped. 'Matt, come out of it. What's wrong?'

The single lightbulb popped, throwing the room into impenetrable darkness.

'Fuck it,' Smith snarled. 'Now the damn bulb's gone.'

'No, it's not,' Daniel said, not caring if the others heard the fear in his voice. 'She's coming back. We should get out now.' As if to prove him correct the light came on again, brighter this time. But dark shadows began to flicker around the walls. 'Get out. Now,' he repeated. 'This is not good.' He began to back out of the room then stopped and came forward to take one of Kindling's arms. 'Help me take him out,' he said to Louise. She nodded, alarmed at the growing, menacing shapes moving around the walls.

'This is bullshit,' Smith snarled, torn between glaring at them and keeping an eye on the flickering, creeping blackness.

'Suit yourself,' Dan said, now in the hallway with Kindling. 'We're going.'

Louise added, 'Matthew's having some sort of attack. We've got to help him first.' Her voice faded as she went down the hallway.

'Ah, fuck it!' Smith cried. 'I thought this is what we came to see, damn you!' But he backed out of the room, too. He was just as scared as the others and wasn't prepared to face anything unknown on his own. He was glad they'd backed out first—he wouldn't have lasted much longer. Smith reached to close the door after him and it swung shut on its own, forcing him to jump backwards. It slammed into the frame with enough force to shake the house.

'Sure is peaceful out here,' Britten decided, staring into the flames. He reached forward and pulled a glowing twig from the embers to light another cigarette.

'Boring as hell,' Bluey told him, watching the twig leaving red swirls of light in the air as Britten moved it.

'You're just saying that to give me the shits,' Britten said, smiling.

'Nah, it's boring.' Bluey put his hand out,

gesturing for the twig for his own cigarette.

'Why don't you go inside? See what's going on?'

Castlemaine spoke from the other side of the fire. 'I'm sure they'll invite us in, when their business is over and done with.' It was a subtle order to stay put.

'Business,' Bluey muttered. 'We brought them all this way so they could have a bloody country roast dinner, from the looks of it.'

'So? Maybe they'll ask you over after dessert,' Castlemaine said. 'Why don't you get another beer and shut up?' he added.

'Get me one, too, while you're there,' Britten told him.

'Now I'm a bloody waitress,' Bluey snarled, but got up and walked towards the Blackhawk. The laughter of his crewmates followed him.

After staring into the fire Bluey didn't have much night vision left. It didn't matter because the dark bulk of the helicopter reflected the licking flames of the fire. It had been a long day—a long flight—and he was tired. The first few beers were taking their toll, too. Bluey didn't bother with the interior light for the cabin. He knew exactly where everything was. Climbing through the door he barked his shin and cursed, bending to rub the sore spot. Shuffling to the black shape of the icebox he used his free hand to flip open the lid and take out three beers, putting one of them inside a utility pocket on his fatigue trousers. As he closed the lid, he caught something moving out of the corner of his eye.

'Hey,' he said quietly, expecting one of the kids

had crept back outside to play in the Blackhawk. 'Someone there?' The interior wasn't that big, crammed with equipment and the spare fuel. But somebody small would be able to hide in the shadows. 'Come on, don't muck around in here. It's not a place to play.' No one answered and Bluey, annoyed now, reached out and flicked on the light. The cabin filled with the soft, battery-driven fluorescent. Bluey saw immediately he was alone.

'I must be going fucking crazy,' he told himself, surprised. On impulse he pulled his battle jacket off a hook and put it on, noticing how cold it was away from the fire. He turned the light off again and left the Blackhawk, shaking his head. As he walked Bluey heard an upraised voice coming from the household and he recognised the twang of Smith's American accent, although he couldn't understand the words. He heard a door slam. 'Maybe not such a pleasant meal,' he grunted.

They retreated back to the kitchen. Kindling was rubbing his hands over his face. Louise made him sit in a chair.

'What happened, Matthew? What did you see?'

He looked up at her and needed a moment for his eyes to focus. 'It's hard to describe,' he admitted slowly. 'I don't know if it's some sort of fit I have, or an attack of some kind. I know I can't consciously switch it on when I want. But it's like I can see another *dimension*—a spiritual dimension. I can see auras and even ghosts, if there's any there.'

'Did you see Ellen?' Smith asked quickly.

'No, but she's left an imprint that I can see

on everything in that room. And you have, too,' he added, looking at Daniel. 'The strength of your emotions every time you go in there creates an imprint of its own—' He stopped and shook his head. 'I really don't know. This is something that's happened to me only once before. I don't understand what I'm seeing, myself.'

'What was happening at the end there?' Louise asked. 'Those shadows that Georgina told us about. They're damn frightening.'

'They came back?' Georgina asked fearfully. Daniel nodded at her.

'That was Ellen coming back,' Kindling said quietly, knowing the Littlewoods would find this upsetting. 'But I don't think it's the ghost of your little girl. Something's changed—corrupted, in some way.' He screwed up his face, struggling for the right words. 'By Vasta's spirit, I think. Or someone else,' he added, glancing at Louise, who gave a small nod. She knew he was referring to his own past.

Daniel sighed and rubbed at the corners of his eyes. 'What in God's name can we do about it? Will it ever go away? We can't just board the room up for eternity—besides, we know she can project herself beyond the house anyway.'

'What if *we* just left?' Peter asked. Seeing his parents' alarmed expressions he added, 'I mean, not for ever. What if there wasn't a reason for Ellen to be here, because the house was empty?'

'I don't think she's here for our benefit,' Daniel said, giving it some serious thought. 'And how long would we go for? Who knows what havoc she might wreak while we're gone?'

'She can wait *forever* for us to come back,' Georgina said, despair creeping into her voice.

'She might try to stop us leaving, too,' Daniel reminded them. 'Remember what she did to Rainy when she started riding out the gate.'

'This is getting us nowhere,' Smith declared suddenly. He began pacing the kitchen, looking towards the living area as if he were trying to make up his mind. 'This is a crazy situation to be thrown into, but the solution can't be that hard, for Christ's sake. We should try going back in there. Confront this damn thing and find out what the hell it wants. Maybe it's something simple.'

'Ask if it wants to do a *deal*?' Louise was amazed at the way Smith's mind worked. 'Somehow, I don't think that's the answer.' Her words were laced with sarcasm.

Smith scowled at her. 'Got any better ideas?'

'I might, if you shut up and let me think.' The two tried to stare each other down. A long, uncomfortable silence followed, broken by a low, menacing rumble that rattled the windows.

'Storm coming,' Georgina said quietly, breaking the tension.

Louise turned away from Smith and looked at Daniel. 'Dan, are you saying you've all been virtual prisoners in your own home? How have you been running the property?'

Daniel frowned at her. 'Well, no. You're right. Peter and I have been going out just as we normally do.' He thought some more. 'Even Georgina went out one day, but that was before all this really started happening.'

'It'd just begun,' Georgina told them, remembering the book being ripped while she was out, and how she'd blamed Rainy.

'So it seems only Rainy isn't allowed to leave,' Louise said slowly, mulling over the idea as she spoke. She looked at the young girl. 'What do you think, Rainy? Do you think you'd feel threatened if you tried to leave?' Louise felt she was following a hunch, a spark of intuition.

'Maybe,' Rainy said easily.

She knows, Louise thought. *Perhaps she doesn't realise it with any certainty, but inside she knows she's* not *threatened by Ellen's ghost—except if she tries to leave. That's why Rainy's not as scared as the rest of them. It's why she's not losing any sleep, and I'll bet she's not bothered about being in the house on her own, either.*

'When you were all out on the property, was Rainy at home alone?' Louise asked.

'We didn't know there was any danger,' Georgina said quickly. 'She's been capable of looking after herself for a few years now—and she needs to stay and do her lessons.'

'I'm not accusing you of anything,' Louise assured her. 'But I've got an idea.' She clicked her fingers as she concentrated, staring at Kindling for inspiration. 'Remember all that reading I did about you? I ended up telling you I thought you might be a "focus" for ghosts—someone who supplies the energy for spirits to appear?' Kindling nodded, but Louise had to explain the theory to the others, adding, 'The thing was, often in poltergeist cases the focus was a young child. In fact, many classic instances of haunting and poltergeist activity ended when a certain child moved away or simply matured.'

'Do you think all this might stop if Rainy was to go away—for a little while?' Daniel added, seeing a look of shock on his daughter's face.

'It might, if she really is supplying some form of energy for Ellen's ghost to appear here.'

'What about up in Freedom?' Smith asked. 'Don't forget, that's what we're here for in the first place.'

Louise bit back her anger at his selfishness. 'It's possible if we fix the problems down here, it might carry through to Freedom.' Privately, she wasn't sure it would be so easy, but she was more interested in keeping Smith quiet.

Kindling seemed to have recovered, the colour was back in his face and he'd nearly stopped shaking. 'It might be as simple as loading Rainy onto the chopper and taking her on a holiday to the city for a while.'

'It's got to be worth a try. We could do it first thing in the morning, and some of us could stay behind and check the results.'

Daniel reached out and pulled Rainy close. 'What do you think, love? Would you mind having a few days away, see if things improve? I'm sure they'd look after you very well. It'd be fun.' On impulse he added, 'Your mother could go with you.' He looked at Louise and saw her nod.

Rainy replied with the same casual manner, apparently unmoved by the events going on around her. 'Sure,' she shrugged. 'Why not?'

The storm climbed quickly over the horizon and bore down on the property. Impressed with the jagged lightning and rolls of thunder the soldiers fell silent. Finally Britten asked, 'Should we sleep in one of the sheds? Might be a bit more comfortable than the chopper.'

Castlemaine replied, 'One of us—me, I suppose—should stay with the machine. You guys can sleep in the sheds if you want.'

'What a guy,' Bluey murmured. 'What a leader.'

'Get fucked, Bluey.'

A breeze picked up around them, disturbing the pre-storm stillness. Overhead the anvil of cloud began to blot out the stars, like a vast aircraft hovering over the property.

'Damn,' Castlemaine said, nodding at the fire. 'That breeze puts us upwind of the chopper—and it's full to the gills with spare bloody fuel.' As if to emphasise his words a flurry of wind stirred the fire and a shower of sparks lifted into the air, drifting away towards the aircraft. 'We'd better put it out.'

'Might get ready for bedding down, then,' Bluey decided, standing. Castlemaine and Britten did the same. A noise came from the helicopter and they all stopped, looking at each other.

'What would that be?' Castlemaine said, more curious than alarmed.

'Buggered if I know,' Bluey said and began striding towards the Blackhawk calling over his shoulder, 'I thought I saw one of the kids playing in there earlier on, but I didn't catch 'em. I'll catch the little bastards this time.'

'Take it easy on them,' Castlemaine said. 'They don't get a lot of visitors out here, remember. They're only kids.' The fire forgotten for the moment, they watched Bluey's figure disappear into the darkness, heading towards the barely discernible bulk of the helicopter.

Bluey realised whoever was in the Blackhawk probably knew he was coming. The gathering wind would have carried their voices from the camp fire easily. He decided that if he didn't find anybody, he'd yell into the darkness, warning them not to come back. That would be his duty done.

As he got closer, alarms started ringing in his mind. The clink of metal on metal and a pungent aroma made him hurry. 'Bullshit,' he said aloud. It was the smell of aviation fuel—and if he could smell it against the breeze there must be plenty of it lying around. Then he heard a gurgling noise and his heart went cold. A flash of lightning suddenly illuminated the scene with a dreadful clarity. In the doorway of the Blackhawk two of the fuel canisters lay on their sides, the black holes of their open lids plainly visible. From one of them a stream of liquid poured out. The pool surrounding the aircraft was already huge and he judged much more must have soaked into the ground. Bluey instantly changed his priorities, and whirled around to warn the others to kill the fire and be bloody careful about it. Before the words formed on his lips something large fell into the flames of the camp fire and a huge cloud of sparks leapt high into the air between the silhouetted figures of Castlemaine and Britten. The glittering redness cascaded down towards Bluey and he knew that most of it, aided by an untimely gust of wind, would reach the Blackhawk.

'*Get the fuck down!*' he screamed, throwing himself into a dead run towards the others. He wrapped one arm around his face as he passed through the flying shower of cinders and allowed himself half a dozen more steps before hurling himself flat on the ground.

Castlemaine noticed nothing, but Britten swore he saw the spectral figure of a small girl dressed in white toss a piece of timber, which should have been too large for her to lift, into the fire between them. He opened his mouth to exclaim as he backed away from the fountain of sparks, then he heard Bluey's scream. Both men reacted instantly as they were trained to do—and did what they were told.

The Blackhawk exploded in a fantastic ball of orange flame. A searing wave of concussive heat washed over the soldiers. The sound of the blast was deafening. After a few seconds falling debris dropped to the ground around them, one piece hitting the dirt close to Castlemaine and forcing him to risk a look up. Incredibly, the helicopter had disappeared. Only a glowing frame comprising the landing skids and some of the flooring remained. The blast had been so intense that most of the flammable material was consumed in the instant of detonation. Only a few pieces of burning wreckage lay scattered around them. Shocked, Castlemaine saw one of the flaming pieces moving.

'Jesus! Bluey!' He leapt to his feet and sprinted the short distance to the prone figure. Castlemaine heard the thud of Britten's boots close behind him. They dropped to the ground next to Bluey. Straightaway Castlemaine saw that the soldier wasn't badly hurt. In fact, he was intentionally rolling and twisting onto his back in an attempt to smother the flames on his jacket. 'Let me take it off!' Castlemaine yelled and with Britten's help quickly fought down his thrashing and flipped him onto his stomach, then savagely ripped the jacket down and away from his back. Bluey let out a stifled half-scream as one of the cuffs caught on his wrist and the combined strength of his crewmates dislocated his shoulder.

With a string of oaths Castlemaine tossed the burning clothing away. The flaming cloth fluttered prettily through the air.

The blast blew in all the windows of the living area, showering the room with lethal shards of glass. It was fortunate everybody was in the kitchen at the time. Screaming and yelling they fell to the floor, instinctively seeking protection. Daniel was the first to recover and discovered he had pinned Rainy beneath him. He scrambled to his feet and picked her up. The little girl's face was white with shock, but she seemed unhurt. Daniel thrust Rainy into Georgina's arms as his wife stood and stared in utter confusion, then he ran outside.

The scene awaiting him was like a battleground. Burning wreckage was scattered far and wide. The yard was garishly lit by the flames and lightning clawed down from the sky, accompanied by rolling booms of thunder. As Daniel stood, transfixed by the scene, large drops of rain began to plop onto his face. The scorched remains of the helicopter told their own story. Then he noticed the three men struggling inside the circle of smouldering debris and he rushed to join them.

'Anyone badly hurt?' he cried, dropping to the ground next to them.

Castlemaine looked up. 'No, only Bluey here. Got himself a bit burnt and hurt his shoulder.'

'Tore me fucking arm out of its socket,' Bluey grunted from the ground. In the dim light of the nearby flames his face was sheened with sweat.

'Ungrateful bastard,' Castlemaine told him, then turned back to Daniel. 'Can you get one of the other guys to give us a hand? Four of us should be able to lift him safely inside.'

'I've got a stretcher,' Daniel offered, surprising them.

Castlemaine looked up at the sky, feeling the drops of rain on his face and judging. 'Yeah, it might be better in the long run. This rain's not going to get serious for a few minutes yet.' He let his control slip a moment. 'Jesus, what the hell went wrong?'

At that moment Georgina, Peter, Kindling and Smith all emerged from the house. Daniel shouted at them from where he crouched. 'George! We need the stretcher from the shed. Peter, don't worry about all these fires, check the rest of the house. Make sure the place isn't going to bloody burn down somewhere.' Peter didn't react for a moment, his body framed by the light from the kitchen doorway. Daniel recognised the bulkier figure of Kindling take the boy by the arm. The two of them headed off at a trot, doing a circuit of the house. Georgina disappeared into the kitchen and emerged with Louise. The beam of a flashlight wavered and jumped in the direction of the sheds. Left alone, Smith came quickly to the men on the ground.

'What the fuck happened?' His voice was jerky and betrayed his shock.

'The chopper blew up,' Britten snapped back angrily. 'What do you think happened?'

'Someone was pouring the fuel out,' Bluey breathed weakly. The adrenalin in his system was fading, leaving behind the pain of his shoulder and the burns.

'*What?*' Castlemaine and Daniel exclaimed together.

'Someone took the tops off the spare av-gas and spilled it out on the ground. That's what we heard. I thought it was one of the kids. Whoever it was, they must have gone up with the chopper.'

'It wasn't the kids,' Daniel said numbly, understanding now. He knew exactly who it was. Castlemaine and Britten looked stunned and he gestured hopelessly. 'There's nothing you could have done to stop it. I know. Believe me for now and I'll explain when we get back inside.'

'That sounds crazy,' Castlemaine said.

'That's because it is. My whole world's going crazy right now.'

The rain slowly increased. Daniel was beginning to wonder whether it was worth waiting for Georgina to return with the stretcher when he saw the wavering beam of the torch coming from the sheds. A minute later Georgina and Louise were next to them, quickly spreading the aluminium poles apart.

'What's he done?' Georgina asked briskly.

Castlemaine answered, 'A few burns, nothing too serious from what we can see. But we dislocated his shoulder when we took his jacket off.'

'Did you put it back in?'

'No, we'll wait until we get inside in the light.'

A shrill scream cut through the night, coming from inside the house. Daniel jerked his head up and stared at Georgina. 'Where the hell is Rainy?' he demanded harshly.

'I told her to clear the kitchen table and get the first aid kit out.'

In a moment of terrible indecision Daniel looked down at the injured shoulder, but Castlemaine reached across and roughly pushed him away. 'Go, for Christ's sake! He'll be all right. Go and find Rainy.'

Daniel set off at a run towards the house. Half-way there Matthew Kindling appeared from the other direction and rushed through the kitchen door ahead of him. Seconds later Peter arrived and as Daniel ran he called, 'No, Peter! You stay outside. Go and help the soldiers.' Peter only had time to dodge aside as his father reached the house and flung the screen door open.

The kitchen was empty. Daniel knew where they would be. His feet crunched on the broken glass as he ran into the living area and turned to enter the hallway. There he stopped, momentarily paralysed by what he saw. The door to Ellen's room was open and a brilliant light spilled from it. Matthew Kindling was silhouetted in the door-frame, his feet apart and his body set solidly, as if he were trying to resist some force. Daniel broke his trance and walked into the hallway until he stood just behind Kindling. He looked into the room beyond.

The spirit of Ellen Littlewood stood above the bed, much as she'd appeared to her mother. Rainy stood next to it, looking up at the image with a mixture of amazement and fear. Tears ran down her cheeks. The face of the ghost was terrible. It was still a young girl's face, but ruined by greed and evil. The eyes danced with a gleeful malevolence and they turned from Rainy to Kindling and back again. Kindling was speaking in calm, measured tones.

'Rainy, leave the room.'

The ghost's voice was a harsh, guttural bark. It sounded so alien coming from the little girl's image. '*Leave her. She's come to play.*' The creeping shadows flickered around the walls of the bedroom.

'Rainy, walk away and leave the room. Now.' Kindling seemed so calm, but Daniel could see the tension in the back of his neck and in the way he held his body.

'*Leave her. She's mine. She must not leave.*'

'Rainy! You heard me! Come away now. Get out of the room.'

The girl responded by edging slightly away from the bedside, but she couldn't take her eyes off the glowing spirit.

'*You're a fool, Kindling. One day, you and I will talk. One day soon. And there won't be any little boy fucking priest to stop me. I already have* his *soul.*' The image chuckled with a delight that chilled Kindling. It deeply saddened him, too. He'd guessed that Stewart Andrews had died fighting *his* personal demon, but had never confirmed it. Now he knew.

'Rainy, get out of the room now.' Kindling was afraid that his command over the child wouldn't be enough. Suddenly the sound of her father's voice just behind him startled and relieved him.

'Rainy, you heard him! Get out now. Do as you're told, for God's sake!'

The shadows in the room seemed to flutter with anger at Daniel's words. Rainy reacted, dragging herself towards the door exactly like the child she was, torn between obeying two masters. The bedroom door started to swing closed with unnatural speed, but Kindling was ready for it. He caught the edge of the door and threw his weight against it. His muscles trembled with the effort. When Rainy came close enough Daniel ducked under Kindling's body and grabbed her, hauling his daughter out past Kindling and into the hallway. A cry filled the room, part laughter and part howl of anger. Kindling threw an agonised look over his shoulder to see if they were clear, then toppled backwards out of the room, falling against Daniel and Rainy. The door crashed closed in front of him.

The three of them lay together in a heap on the hallway floor. Rainy was crying uncontrollably and Daniel gathered her into a hug. In the light reflected from the harsh white line coming under the door he blinked tears at Kindling.

'Thank you,' he said hoarsely.

'I nearly failed,' Kindling muttered, puzzling Daniel. 'Again.'

17

THE STORM STOPPED THEM from communicating with Wiley until several hours later. He listened to the story of the destroyed helicopter with a wooden face. Kindling didn't explain everything—the network wasn't secure in any way. Wiley had to read between the lines for himself. After some consultation with others on a different system Wiley returned to tell them two relief Blackhawks would be leaving within the next three to four hours, meaning they wouldn't reach Rhianna until early afternoon the next day. Kindling and the rest would have to look after themselves for that long.

'Friendly sort of guy,' Daniel ventured wryly after the transmission ended.

'Not known for his humour,' Louise told him.

With Kindling and Smith they returned to the kitchen.

Georgina recruited Castlemaine and Britten to help clean up the broken glass in the living area. Luckily during the storm the damaged windows were in the lee of the house, so only a little rain came in. Peter half-heartedly assisted the soldiers. Everyone bustled around Rainy, who fell asleep on one of the lounge suites. A mattress was brought out from Peter's bed and Bluey lay on it, his face still showing pain despite the near-overdose of mild painkillers Georgina had given him. Castlemaine had succeeded in replacing the shoulder joint after careful guidance by the Flying Doctor service over the radio, but the remedy proved as painful as the injury. While everyone cleaned up or made endless hot drinks, the conversation ebbed and flowed on the subject of Ellen's haunting. The situation seemed hopeless and this was reflected in Georgina's dull, mechanical manner as she moved about the house. Peter was the same, but Daniel in contrast was preoccupied and constantly frowning in thought. Some things had to be explained to the soldiers, not the least of which was exactly who had destroyed their aircraft. They listened with amazement and didn't dispute anything, although Castlemaine allowed himself one angry remark.

'You could've warned us. We'd have been on alert and maybe prevented it.'

'We had no idea she was capable of anything like this,' Kindling replied. Castlemaine didn't persist.

Eventually they all settled in the living area. Extra chairs were brought in from the kitchen, and blankets were spread on the floor as bedding for the soldiers. Daniel dimmed the lights for anyone who wanted to sleep, but only the children succumbed while the adults talked. Kindling longed to huddle up to Louise, but stuck to the rules in the face of Smith's imposing presence. The American sat backwards on a kitchen chair, leaning his arms on the backrest and chain-smoking. He watched everyone through half-closed eyes and spoke little, as if he was a guard and the others his captives. Mostly they ignored him. Georgina would normally have complained about his smoking, especially as Castlemaine and Britten assumed from his actions that it must be okay and lit up, too. Now it seemed such a trivial thing. Kindling contented himself with sitting on the floor next to Louise as close as decorum allowed.

It was during a thoughtful silence that Daniel nodded at Rainy. 'It's incredible,' he said quietly, 'that somehow she might be providing the energy for all this to happen.'

'I don't think it's only her,' Kindling said, surprising Louise who was listening closely. 'I think Ellen's room is just as important a reason for her spirit's existence. After all, your family has been keeping Ellen alive in one way by preserving that room. I can see a sort of power being drawn from the strength of your emotions. I guess I even saw it when we first went in there tonight.'

'What do you think would happen if we destroyed what's in the room? Would it make a difference?'

'It might,' Kindling nodded reluctantly. 'But we come back to the problem of how to do it. Ellen's ghost could probably stop us somehow. After tonight, I wouldn't like to try and estimate exactly what she's capable of.'

'Unless we somehow took Rainy away first and denied her this energy we keep talking about.'

'Maybe, but that's fraught with the same risks.'

'We've got two Blackhawks coming, and this time we'll know what to expect,' Castlemaine said.

'It's still a risk—perhaps not even a justifiable risk,' Daniel told him. 'Besides, I have a better idea.' Everyone stirred with interest and he went on, 'I don't reckon anything could stop us walking out of here. Just walking—Rainy and I.' There was a silence. Georgina reached out and stroked Rainy's face. The girl didn't wake or move. Daniel explained further, 'With nothing mechanical to interfere with, nothing inflammable to blow up, just our own two feet and a backpack of supplies, I don't think she could stop us.'

'I see what you mean,' Louise said slowly. 'But what do you hope to achieve? You could only stay out there for a few hours, maybe a day at the most. It's not the same as whisking her away to the city for a few weeks.'

'That's what I've been thinking about. I couldn't see anything concrete coming out of it either, until Matthew mentioned her room could also be important. What if I got her away long enough for you to destroy her room? Without Rainy, she might not be strong enough to stop you. Without the room, she might not be able to stay around with *only* Rainy.'

After a moment Smith said, 'I think it's a very good idea.' No one wanted to be heard supporting him, but their silence spoke agreement.

'What would we do with the room?' Georgina asked, distressed at the prospect of it being dismantled, despite the reasons.

'We can't do anything about the room itself, obviously,' Kindling said. 'But if we take absolutely everything out and destroy it, there's a good chance it would have some effect.'

'Destroy it? Couldn't we store it all somewhere? In one of the sheds?'

'No,' Kindling told her firmly, saddened as he saw how much the idea hurt her.

'Burn it,' Castlemaine suggested drily. 'Your ghost seems to understand that.'

They all slept fitfully in the living room. Britten was the first to stir, shaking Castlemaine awake and disturbing the others. 'Getting light outside,' he said. 'You want to do it?'

Georgina opened her eyes and whispered, 'It'll be too dark to see anything for ten minutes yet. I'll make you both some fresh coffee.' She eased Rainy's head from her lap and stood, stretching, before going into the kitchen. Britten shrugged at Castlemaine and followed.

Kindling awoke on the floor and found himself with his arms around Louise. With a guilty start he pulled away and looked for Smith. He was nowhere to be seen. Louise sat up and blinked at the room around them. On impulse, seeing it was safe, she leaned close and quickly kissed Kindling.

'Could be an interesting day,' she murmured, her voice thick with sleep. She got up and went to investigate the noises coming from the kitchen, leaving Kindling to wonder about her once again. Her ability to cope and adjust amazed him. He decided he needed a breath of fresh air and walked straight through the kitchen and outside, smiling and nodding at Georgina as he went.

The approaching dawn was only a slash of pink across the eastern sky. A red spark showed someone smoking nearby and Kindling recognised the tall, thin figure of Smith. He realised he could hardly ignore the man and after allowing himself a moment of irritation went over.

'Get some sleep?' Kindling asked.

'No,' Smith replied, his voice gruff with fatigue. 'I kept waiting for some damn thing to come floating through the walls.'

'I know what you mean,' Kindling agreed, trying to be kind in spite of his feelings. It never occurred to him during the night that Ellen's ghost might come into the main house.

'You seem pretty friendly with Louise Corry.'

The remark took Kindling by surprise. 'Just one of those things—comforting each other in a crisis,' he said awkwardly.

Smith flicked away his cigarette and it glowed in a red arc before extinguishing itself with a hiss in a puddle. 'Can't say I blame you.' He turned and went back inside.

Within ten minutes the horizon had brightened enough for them to see what they were doing outside. The two soldiers stopped and forlornly inspected the wreckage of their Blackhawk on their way to the shed where the dry wood was stored. Pieces of charred metal and melted aluminium were scattered over a wide area. They picked through some of it, recognising various parts of the aircraft.

'Jesus Christ, somebody's going to be upset,' Britten observed glumly.

'Yeah.' Castlemaine looked wry. 'You wait until I fill out my report. "Aircraft destroyed by malicious ghost". That'll be the end of my career.'

They went to the sheds and began carrying out loads of dry wood, piling it up on a patch of yard free of puddles. It took several trips each. They were building a big bonfire.

Inside Daniel accompanied Rainy into her room as she got dressed, then made sure she went back into the kitchen while he got himself ready in the main bedroom. Equipped with a rucksack each, tough clothing and good boots, Daniel calculated they would have no problems surviving the day. He briefly considered taking a rifle, but remembered Kindling's words to Smith. And after all, it wasn't much different to what they normally did every working day—except they weren't taking a vehicle. He went back to the kitchen where Georgina was packing them enough food for the day and preparing a solid breakfast as well. Peter had gone outside to help with the bonfire. Apart from Rainy, nobody else was in the room.

Daniel hugged his wife, then held her at arm's length, looking into her eyes. 'Burn everything, George. Don't be tempted to keep anything. There's no point in destroying *any* of it, if we don't do the whole lot.'

Her eyes flicked downwards for a moment and Daniel guessed she had been thinking of perhaps keeping something small. 'Okay,' she nodded.

Georgina had arranged to feed the others afterwards, so she, Daniel and Rainy ate together undisturbed. Daniel checked the packing of their rucksacks once more before shrugging his on. 'Ready for this?' he asked Rainy, holding out her rucksack.

'Sure,' she agreed.

Outside the bonfire was well ablaze. It was almost smokeless. A haze of heat drifted up to the clearing sky. Everyone stood around it, watching it burn. Even Bluey was on his feet, claiming the pain in his shoulder had settled down overnight. Daniel jammed his hat on, made sure Rainy did the same and he turned to Castlemaine.

'We're going to walk directly north, following the fenceline. Peter knows it well. I reckon by midday, if nothing else happens, we'll reach the middle dam. There's plenty of trees and water there, so we can make ourselves comfortable. Then we'll just wait for you to come and get us at the end of the day.' He didn't mention what the rest of them would be doing while he was gone. It had been discussed over and over again during the night.

Castlemaine nodded. 'If you hear the choppers coming and they seem to be driving a line over the top of you, step out and wave. They'll probably drop down and pick you up. I doubt they'll be coming in from the north, though,' he added.

'Whatever, we'll just wait for someone.' Daniel turned and he and Rainy exchanged hugs and kisses with Georgina. Then he waved at Peter. 'Don't let them burn the house down, Pete.' His son waved awkwardly back.

There was nothing more to say. Daniel headed

across the yard for the north fenceline with Rainy close at his side. He didn't turn around again. Those left behind heard Rainy's bright chatter in the early morning air, and watched until the two were small figures in the distance.

They had been walking for only five minutes with Rainy keeping up a continuous monologue about one of her school lessons when there was a soft popping noise and Ellen's spirit appeared in front of them, blocking their way. Daniel stopped and immediately swept Rainy under his arm. She let out a squeal of alarm.

He stared at the image, hardly believing his own eyes. It was his first little girl, with every vestige of the fresh-faced innocence he remembered, before illness had begun to age her prematurely. At the sight of her Daniel's heart cried out with a grief so intense he'd forgotten how much it could hurt. The white dress reminded him of the agony they'd suffered over the simple decision of what she would wear in death.

'Don't leave me. Please don't leave me.'

'Ellen,' Rainy said in a small voice and tried to walk forward.

'No!' Daniel reached forward and grabbed a handful of her shirt, snatching her back. 'No, don't take any notice. Walk around her. Don't look.' With a tremendous effort Daniel averted his eyes and forced Rainy to leave the wheelruts and make a wide berth around the spirit. No sooner had they regained the track than Ellen materialised in front of them again.

'I want to come back. Please don't leave me.'

'Walk around her again,' Daniel ordered.

'But it's Ellen.'

'It's *not* Ellen, Rainy. It's a trick. It's something else.'

'It's Ellen. You can *see* it's Ellen.'

'Walk *around* her, Rainy.'

This time the ghost stayed behind, calling after them in a pitiful voice that brought tears to Daniel's eyes. *'Please don't leave me, Daddy. Don't leave me alone out here.'*

'Dan wanted us to wait an hour,' Castlemaine reminded them. 'But this wood's burning at a very fast rate. We might run out of supplies by then.'

'What do you want to do?' Kindling asked.

Castlemaine sighed, putting off the decision for a second. 'I suppose we'll wait until they're out of sight, then we can start.'

'Something's happening,' Peter announced. He'd driven the flat-bed truck from the other side of the house and was using it as a platform to watch the distant figures through a pair of old binoculars.

'What?' Castlemaine jumped up next to him and took the binoculars. There was a pause while he focused them, then he let out an oath. 'There's somebody else with them,' he said, awed.

'Who?' Georgina called, knowing the answer.

'Someone small—like a child,' he added meaningfully. 'She's wearing white, that's all I can tell you.'

'Then that's her,' Georgina said, a lump coming into her throat.

Castlemaine startled her by tossing the binoculars back at Peter and calling, 'Let's do it now! Let's hope she can't be in two places at once.'

As they'd planned, Castlemaine and Britten ran towards the kitchen door to go into Ellen's room and start passing the contents out through the window to the others waiting outside. Kindling unexpectedly stopped them with an anxious shout.

'No! Go *in* through the window, too. Don't use the door—especially don't touch the doorknob.'

Still running, Castlemaine twisted around to throw a querying look at Britten, but did as Kindling said and swerved away to go straight to the window. He clawed at the woodwork and yelled, 'It's locked.' He didn't wait, but stooped and picked up a stone from the surrounding garden and smashed the window. He reached through the shards and unlocked the catch. Swinging the windows wide Castlemaine neatly vaulted through, with Britten close behind. Within moments items were being handed out to Louise, Smith and Bluey, the latter struggling with one hand.

As he moved to help, Kindling explained to Georgina gently, 'I think that shock you feel when you open the door—I don't know how it works, but in some way it must warn Ellen somebody's entering the room. It's an alarm.' He was trying to keep an eye on Georgina, seeing her distress as more and more of her daughter's belongings were thrown onto the fire. 'I don't think you should do any of this,' he told her, feeling totally unable to comfort her. 'But I'd better help. Every second might count.' He backed away as Georgina nodded, not taking her eyes from the fire.

Daniel tried counting his steps to keep his mind off the ghost's pleading voice. Rainy was crying now and dragging her feet in the dirt. Daniel grasped her hand and forced her to walk at his pace. As he counted to fifty, the girlish voice became more distant. He almost cried out in despair when Ellen's form appeared again to bar their way. This time her image seemed vague and uncertain, flickering as if it lacked strength.

'*Please don't leave me, Daddy. I'm scared to be alone.*'

Daniel didn't answer, but suddenly reached down and scooped Rainy up, cradling her on his hip. He staggered for a moment—she was almost too big to be carried this way—but he kept going. He took another wide circle off the track.

'*Please don't go.*'

Daniel believed if he didn't answer, didn't actually talk to the thing that looked and sounded so much like his own little girl, he could keep going.

'*Now* he'll *take me.*' This was followed by a wail of dismay so heart-wrenching Daniel couldn't prevent himself stopping and looking back at the spectral child, his vision blurred with tears.

'*Who? Who will take you?*' he whispered, choking on the words.

Like the last flames of a dying fire her image glimmered briefly against the sunlight and faded.

Georgina couldn't take her eyes off the fire. The books were burning with fierce intensity, the pages quickly curling and disappearing in a lick of the hungry flames. The dolls were worse, blackening and shrivelling into tortured shapes. The stench of melting plastic was sickening.

A crashing, tearing noise came from the house. Castlemaine was using the axe to smash the furniture into pieces small enough to pass through the window. The shattered sections were hurriedly fed into the flames. A shouted debate was resolved when the mattress, doubled over, was squeezed through the opening. Louise, helped by Smith, was careful to lay it around the edge of the bonfire in case it smothered the lot. The broken wooden bedframe, decades old, came next, then there was more shouting. Georgina couldn't imagine what might be left, then the blunt bulk of rolled-up carpeting emerged. The soldiers' efficiency was frightening in itself and she suddenly wondered if they might start ripping up the floorboards, but just then Castlemaine and Britten climbed out agilely and crossed to the fire and began fussing over a few things not burning properly.

Georgina felt the tears streaming down her face. An arm crept around her waist, startling her, and she looked down to see Peter. She put her own arm across his shoulders and hugged him.

The others gathered around the bonfire and surveyed their handiwork.

'Did you see anything? Feel anything?' Kindling called above the flames to Castlemaine.

'Nothing. Not a thing.'

Kindling turned to ask Peter if he could still see his father through the binoculars, but stopped when he saw the teenager comforting his mother. Instead, Kindling moved closer to Louise and held her as they both stared into the fire. She didn't resist.

'Maybe we've done it,' he said.

Before she could reply the answer came out of the fire. In an explosion of sparks a figure rose out of the embers and up into the flames. With cries of horror everyone fell back, though most of them barely had time to register what they saw. Only Kindling, fighting down his terror, recognised who it was—and heard his words.

With his skin peeling back from the heat, the fat beneath bubbling and the flesh crisping away exposing raw sinew and yellowed bones, Stewart Andrews' ravaged face stared with seared, empty sockets at Kindling.

'He tells me to thank you for releasing him.'

18

JOSEPH KING WAS TRYING to rise to the surface of a deep pool. The water around him was grey and still, smothering and endless. He reached out his hands, but couldn't break free. When his knuckles struck the edge of something solid, breaking the skin and bringing a stinging pain, it gave him a focus. The pain was real, a familiar sensation. It followed that the swimming feeling was familiar, too. Weightlessness. He was in space, he remembered, in orbit. Space Station Freedom. King forced his mind to properly interpret the things around him and began to see the instruments and scientific apparatus of the Minerals Laboratory. The blurred grey of his vision sharpened to show meters, dials and switches, racks of labelled samples and the ubiquitous computer workstation.

A nervous shock physically jolted his body as King recognised he was no longer in the Cryogenic Module. A wave of fear and guilt swept over him. He'd failed. God alone—his *own* God—knew what price he would pay now. A nervous crawling began in his stomach.

I will eat your soul.

King couldn't recall anything since falling asleep above Vasta's cryogenic container. The module had been secure, he was sure. Somehow, the others had tricked him into letting them in and captured him. What had they done to him? King felt sick. His head buzzed with the beginnings of a migraine. Every muscle in his body ached as if he'd driven himself through a severe exercise workout. King hadn't bothered to go beyond the rudimentary first aid all the astronauts learnt. He didn't recognise the symptoms of oxygen starvation.

Alex Seerey's voice slapped at him through the intercom. 'Joseph, can you hear me?' There wasn't a trace of sympathy or compassion. King wanted to ignore the call, but betrayed his newly-regained consciousness when he let his eyes stray to the small camera mounted in a corner of the module. Still, he didn't move to the intercom to reply.

'I can see you can,' Seerey continued. 'Joseph, you realise we cannot trust you at liberty within Freedom any more. I've taken the step of locking you in that module, and that's where you'll stay until a relief shuttle reaches us, probably within the next four or five days. I don't know what will happen to you when we return to Earth—perhaps less than you deserve.' This was said with bitterness and King needed a moment to understand what Seerey was referring to. With difficulty he recollected attacking Judith Cianta. No regrets came with the memory. It had been necessary. She would have tried to stop him.

And things were much worse now, because they *had* stopped him. A dreadful fate awaited King long before he set foot back on Earth again—unless he somehow redeemed himself. Seerey's words meant nothing.

The commander was saying, 'We'll bring you regular meals and fresh drinks. At the same time we'll escort you to the toilet, if need be. I won't let you communicate with anyone on Earth. That can wait until you get there. Have you anything to say?' In response King pointedly turned his back on the lens. Seerey gave him the benefit of one last opportunity. 'Joseph, have you anything you want to say?' Another silence. Seerey snapped, 'Okay, do it your way.' The intercom clicked off.

Seerey turned to the others. 'It doesn't look like I got through to him. Let's make sure nobody goes in there with him alone. He could be capable of anything.'

'Five days is a long time to keep him locked up,' Lee pondered.

'I know. We'll have to escort him to the toilet and take him meals, but we'll always do it in pairs, right? If he starts getting violent again, hit him—and hit him *hard*. We can't afford to have a madman running around the space station again.'

'If it wasn't for that damn hurricane, we could

have a shuttle up here in twenty-four hours. I'd let him starve for that long,' Dawkins said.

'Don't keep reminding me,' Seerey looked grim. 'That five-day estimate is pretty conservative, though. It might be much sooner.'

'Let's hope so. I guess the worst he can do is trash the Minerals Laboratory. If we keep it sealed, the only person he can hurt is himself. That'd serve the stupid bastard right.'

Celia surprised them by saying, 'Come on, guys. Don't forget he's probably a very sick man. It's not his fault.'

'Yeah?' Dawkins' expression didn't soften. 'Celia, I don't care. All I know is, in his present condition, he's a dangerous man. A liability that could cost us our lives. Don't *you* forget where we are—a long way from home. We can't give him an inch, in case he takes a fucking mile. Like Alex says, we can't afford to have a madman loose in Freedom again. Getting him out of the Cryogenics Module like that was the only trick we had up our sleeve. Setting him free could be a very bad situation.' He slowly emphasised the last three words.

Celia felt anger building up inside her as Dawkins spoke. She felt he was suggesting that because she was a woman she would be more likely to feel sympathy for King and be drawn into giving the man a chance to slip free. But when Dawkins touched her arm, she looked into his eyes and saw fear and anxiety, not condescension.

'I just don't think we're out of the woods yet, Celia,' he added quietly. 'I won't be happy until we're all back safe on Earth. This tour's been jinxed in a big way.'

She bit back her anger and smiled softly at him. 'Jinxed? I wish it were that simple.'

It was impossible for them to just sit waiting in the Command Module for the relief shuttle to arrive. So Celia gave them work. Much of her assigned program, concerned with testing and evaluating the systems aboard Freedom, was run from the Command Module anyway, so at her suggestion the astronauts split into two teams and began working. Seerey was content as long as everyone was together. Celia, Seerey and Judith combined on one side with Lee and Dawkins on the other. Soon they were absorbed in their tasks and things had almost returned to normal. It was several hours before Seerey suddenly announced he was hungry.

'Two of us should go to the galley and bring back meals for all of us,' he suggested.

'I guess that means we should take something in to Joseph,' Lee said.

'Now's as good a time as any.'

They turned to check the camera monitor and Seerey swore as they saw the blank screen.

'How's he done that?' Dawkins grumbled.

'Could be anything,' Seerey told him. 'A cloth over the lens—a piece of tape. He may even have cut through the cable. There's bound to be a few tools in there that would slice through it.'

'Do you think he's up to something?'

'What the hell can he do?'

Dawkins thought about it and eventually shrugged. 'Not much, I guess.'

King could only wait. He knew the time would come soon when he must answer for his actions. Sometimes his mind grappled with the anomaly of his fear of his God's return. Why should he be afraid of such an exalted moment? Wasn't God a benevolent, understanding and forgiving person? Towards His servants, at least?

The answer was no, King realised. Not now. Not since he'd failed. Beyond that, he dared not question further. The possibilities were too frightening.

One of his first lucid actions was to fold a piece of paper over the spying camera lens. The confrontation was coming and King believed he might be pleading for his life—and a second chance to serve his master. Any interference from the people in the Command Module could be disastrous. They'd caused enough trouble. Disabling the camera was the only thing King could do to keep them ignorant. He was powerless to stop them coming into the Minerals Laboratory. He could refuse food and drink, but King knew Seerey's idea of being humanitarian would include delivering supplies of both regardless.

These thoughts, along with new ideas and a recurring fear of what the next few hours might bring, moved constantly through King's mind as he waited. The process was interrupted suddenly when he felt a sharp decrease in the module's air temperature. He knew someone was coming and he began to tremble with dread and excitement. The brilliant white light started to form in midair and King unconsciously backed away. With the atmosphere plummeting to near-freezing, and amid blinding shafts of light, a recognisable figure appeared suspended before King. Again, it was his grandfather. King let out a mindless wail of emotion as the voice snarled inside his head.

'*You are a fool. You have failed me.*'

His grandfather's figure was imbued with a new strength, a greater sense of power. The inherent evil was heightened to a terrifying degree. Cowering, yet enraptured by the spirit's presence, King tried to get on his knees, but the weightlessness prevented it. He fawned pathetically in front of the ghost and babbled desperately.

'Forgive me! They tricked me into letting them in—I don't know how. Believe me. I won't fail you again.'

Without warning King's mind filled with a series of images. He was being dragged, screaming, to be burnt alive. Bound, surrounded by a jeering mob, he could feel the searing pain of the flames and the splintered texture of the wooden stake against his bare back. The stench of roasting flesh and singed hair gagged him. The worst scene was of his own body, rotting and imprisoned beneath heavy soil. Fat, white worms burrowed through his skin and decaying muscle, twisting their way between his bones. King could actually *feel* the insatiable larvae eating their way into his corpse.

He opened his mouth to scream, but the breath locked in his throat. King clamped his hands against the sides of his head, trying to force out the mental pictures. Just as he became aware of a black wall—of death or insanity, he didn't know—rushing towards him, the torturing scenes disappeared. King gasped for breath and went limp, weak with relief.

'That will be your fate, if you fail me again. Now go, and do as I say.'

'Go?' King asked, tears springing to his eyes as he understood he *would* fail again, at the very outset of his second chance. 'I can't go! I'm locked in here.'

'Have faith or perish in your ignorance.'

The spirit vanished before King could ask more. He curled himself up into a ball and started to sob with fear and frustration at the hopelessness of his situation. He understood what his new task was, but it was impossible while he was still incarcerated in the module. Images of his torture returned to taunt him, and remind him of the fate awaiting him when his God discovered he'd failed Him again.

King didn't know how long he stayed like this. A sound brought his head up. His vision misted by tears, he looked along the length of the module. The wheel-lock on the far hatchway was slowly turning.

Because it needed only two of them, and because Lee and Dawkins already considered themselves a team, it was they who volunteered to get the meals and offer food to their captive at the same time. Before they left Seerey tried to get a response from King over the intercom, calling that a meal was on its way. There was no reply.

'Be damn careful,' Seerey told them. 'Maybe I'd better come along, too.'

'No, don't.' Dawkins held up a hand. 'If there is any trouble, it's going to be easier for only two of us to get back through the access tunnel, instead of three.'

'True,' Seerey nodded. He was about to suggest he take Lee's place, but knew he would only offend her and end up backing down anyway, so he satisfied himself by repeating, 'Okay—well, just be careful, right?'

'You can watch us almost the whole way,' Dawkins reminded him, pointing at the camera monitors.

'I will be.'

Dawkins led the way. To reach the Galley the two of them needed to do a long circuit through most of Freedom's modules to avoid passing through the Minerals Laboratory where King was held. In fact, his improvised prison cell adjoined the Galley, which in turn connected to the Accommodation Module. This meant King only needed access to three modules in a row, minimising the amount of movement his bodily functions might require within the space station. Lee and Dawkins tested the air in the Medical Module as they went in. It had been the only exercise beyond the Command Module Seerey had allowed, cleaning the atmosphere in there of Judith's blood. They'd put absorbent paper over the air conditioning intakes, and switched the system back to 'Full', first closing the hatchways to isolate the area, then frequently replaced the paper filters until it seemed clear all the droplets were removed. In the end, it had been easier than they'd imagined.

'Do you need anything from here on the way back?' Lee asked him.

'No,' he replied over his shoulder, then changed

his mind. 'Maybe some more dressings for Judy's head. Do you think anyone will have trouble sleeping? I could grab some sedatives.'

'The only trouble with sleeping *I'll* have will be getting too much,' Lee said ruefully. 'It's not going to be easy, keeping us all occupied for five days or so.'

'I agree, but I think Alex is right. We should stay together all the time, even if it does get a bit tedious.'

They moved past the hatchway leading to the Airlock Module and, beyond that, the Cryogenics. Lee couldn't stop a shiver running down her back as she glanced through the opening, thinking of the gleaming containers.

'Should we check the Revival program?' she asked without enthusiasm. She was glad of Dawkins' reply.

'I couldn't give a damn if it's stopped.'

They went quickly through the Accommodation Module and into the Galley.

'Home sweet home,' Dawkins read the sign a previous occupant had pasted above the meals dispenser. 'What culinary delights do we all want, and what shall we feed the condemned man?' A menu was displayed next to the control panel. Lee looked over his shoulder, making her choice. Dawkins hummed aloud as he read. Both of them were startled when Seerey's voice crackled urgently from a nearby intercom station.

'Lee! Scott! Look behind you!'

They twisted around, alarmed by his tone, then froze at the sight in front of them.

On the camera monitor in the Command

Module, Seerey could see the entire Galley—and something was happening behind the two astronauts' backs.

'Jesus Christ,' Dawkins whispered. Lee was speechless.

Ellen Littlewood's ghost drifted in midair. A glowing white aura surrounded her figure. Her face was solemn and intent as she stared back at them.

'It must be what—who—Celia saw,' Lee breathed, not daring to move. The three of them remained motionless for long seconds, then the astronauts flinched as the spirit turned, gliding away from them towards the hatchway. Lee realised what was happening as the ghost laid her small white hands on the wheel-lock.

'No!' Lee cried out, leaning forward. At the same time Dawkins put a restraining hand on her arm.

'Lee, don't go close!'

The spirit spun the wheel and turned back towards them. Lee gasped as she saw the change come over the little girl's face. The youth and innocence disappeared to be replaced by haunting dark shadows and a terrifying, evil smile. The ghost said nothing, did nothing, except move towards them, yet in a flash of insight Dawkins understood he'd never been so threatened in his life. Next to him Lee was backing away, but in a vague sort of way, as if she wasn't sure how to act.

'Get the fuck out of here,' Dawkins snapped at her, grabbing the fabric of her shirt and thrusting her towards the opposite hatchway. Lee shook her head, coming out of a trance, and pushed herself away from the advancing ghost. Dawkins followed so closely she kicked him once in the face, but he didn't cry out. 'You first,' he ordered unnecessarily as she reached the access tunnel first. They scrambled through and Dawkins didn't even try to slam the end hatchway closed. He knew it would be pointless. Dimly he heard Seerey's voice shouting at them from the intercom, but the words didn't penetrate his shock to make sense.

Pausing at the far end of the Accommodation Module they watched as Ellen's ghost emerged from the access tunnel after them. As they turned to make for the next module another voice came from behind them.

'*Leave me alone.*'

It was a guttural, horrible voice, alien to the little girl's body.

'What's it doing, trying to catch us?' Lee cried, panting with the effort to move quickly.

'God knows—just keep going,' Dawkins replied, throwing an anxious glance over his shoulder. The spirit still followed, without seeming to gain on them. They went through Judith Cianta's Earth Science Module and turned to pass the Airlock Module entrance, going into the Utilities Module, a little used section housing the water supply, batteries and other low-maintenance equipment.

'Don't go in the Airlock, for Christ's sake,' Dawkins shouted.

'Are you fucking kidding?' she yelled back. 'It's a dead end!'

They paused again before leaving Utilities. The ghost floated easily into the far end, but as Dawkins was about to urge Lee to keep going he realised the spirit had stopped, hovering just beyond the access tunnel.

'Now what?' Dawkins grated.

Lee was halfway into their own tunnel. 'Maybe it's tired and needs a fucking rest,' she said with an edge of panic.

They heard Seerey again and recognised he'd been repeating himself, trying to alert them to something.

'She's let King out of the Minerals Laboratory! He's following her,' he was calling over the intercom.

'So *that's* it,' Lee whispered, staring at Dawkins with an awed expression. At that moment he saw movement behind the spirit.

'Look!' he cried, pointing.

Joseph King moved into the access tunnel beyond the ghostly child and slipped left, into the Airlock Module. He didn't look at the ghost or the two astronauts.

'Joe!' Lee called, but he didn't turn back. They saw his figure blot out the light as it filled the access tunnel, then move out of sight.

'He's going back to Cryogenics,' Dawkins said, appalled.

'And we won't get him out this time,' Lee added quietly.

Ellen Littlewood's ghost vanished.

King entered the Cryogenics Module and allowed himself a small laugh of triumph. Immediately he twisted around and re-entered the access tunnel. The piece of strapping he'd used last time to tie up the hatchway was still attached at one end. He used it again, taking more care with the knot this time. Returning inside, his eyes went straight to the opposite hatch—presumably a dead end keeping out the open space beyond an unused Access Module. Something told him that the wheel-lock there had been moved, and with a rush of understanding King knew how they'd captured him. It explained his sickened condition, too. He must have come close to asphyxiating, he realised. With a grim smile he moved the length of the module and studied the wheel. There were several points he could similarly tie it to, but he had no strap. Without hesitation he removed his shirt and used that.

Satisfied, he went to the computer keyboard controlling Vasta's container and started typing instructions.

Lee and Dawkins pulled themselves into the Command Module. Seerey looked at their white faces and couldn't stop himself glancing beyond them into the access tunnel.

'It's okay,' Dawkins said, his voice drained of emotion. 'She disappeared as soon as King was safely past us.'

'That was the goddamned strangest thing I've ever seen,' Seerey said hoarsely, shaking his head slowly. Before he could say more, Celia called urgently.

'He's gone to the computer!'

'Shit, here we go again,' Seerey said, moving closer to the camera monitor. They all watched anxiously, expecting the power to be cut at any moment. 'What the—?' Seerey muttered as King, apparently satisfied, pushed himself away from the keyboard.

'What do you think he's done?' Celia asked.

'God knows,' Seerey replied. 'Isn't there some way we can tap into that software and at least *look* at what he's doing, even if we can't stop it?'

Celia chewed her lip and thought hard. 'Probably, but I'd need some time to work it out.'

'Damn.' Seerey looked grim, then grunted a short laugh. 'Well, I guess there's no harm in asking the bastard.' No one offered him any hope of success as he went to the intercom and flipped the switch. Calling clearly he said, 'Joseph, it's Alex Seerey. For God's sake, what are you trying to do?' He looked around at the others and added, 'Why don't you let us help you?'

They watched the camera monitor, expecting King to ignore them again. Instead, he reached out for an intercom switch and replied, peering at them through the lens as he spoke.

'Prepare yourselves. As He did before, He will rise from the dead again. In three days.' He turned away from the camera.

'*Three days?*' Seerey repeated, stunned. His eyes went to a nearby computer screen and everyone followed his gaze. The screen displayed the map of Florida overlaid by weather patterns. The gigantic swirl of Hurricane Ben consumed the coastline and the small red dot signifying Cape Canaveral. No help would be coming from there in time. Vasta's resurrection would have a small, exclusive audience.

19

FOR THE FIRST TIME in weeks the dream returned to rack Kindling. He wasn't prepared for it. It hadn't taken long, even after so many disturbed, fearful nights, to forget how painful those nightmares had been. He'd begun to take restful, satisfying sleep for granted.

Once again he was standing on the doorstep of the Williams' house. As the familiar images slammed into his mind Kindling groaned and rolled over. Beside him, Louise automatically compensated for the lack of room. The nightmare scene developed as the door opened, but instead of revealing a concerned Mrs Williams it was Louise, dressed in her prim business suit, beckoning them to enter. Kindling saw himself walk past and as before heard Stewart Andrews' footsteps behind him. But this time Kindling turned to see who followed and was confronted by the grinning, rotting visage of a walking corpse. The dream wouldn't let Kindling scream or run. He merely turned and continued into the hallway past Louise.

'*First door on the left. Just go on in. Don't mind anything he says.*' Apparently unmoved by the frightful apparition that followed him, Louise's sweet voice echoed in Kindling's mind. He made his way through the hallway into the darkened room, which was the same as before. The drawn curtains and flickering television, the electronic images sending splinters of light off the gleaming chrome of a wheelchair standing near the fireplace. When the body occupying the chair lifted its head to stare at Kindling, it wasn't Mr Williams. It was Anton Vasta. An enormous black cat lay untidily in his lap.

'*You are a fool, Kindling,*' Vasta mouthed, the spittle on his chin glistening in the reflected light. '*Did you really believe we would never meet again? I've waited for you. You will be my prize.*' Startling Kindling, the animal on Vasta's lap suddenly sprang to its feet and faced him, arching its back and hissing with bared fangs and glaring eyes. Automatically Kindling took a step backwards and felt himself bump into Stewart Andrews. Revolted he twisted around. The decaying corpse tried to smile at him sympathetically, but the result was a ghastly death's head of splitting skin and blackened teeth.

'*I tried to warn you, Matthew. It's unfinished business.*'

Vasta was convulsing, his chest heaving, soft

gurgling noises coming from his throat. Suddenly he vomited onto the cat's back, the bile dripping down off the matted fur of the animal's haunches to stain Vasta's legs. He smiled as the last dregs dripped in long strings from his slack lips.

'*Oh Allen*,' Louise cried, moving forward to pick up the roll of paper towelling.

'*No!*' Kindling heard himself cry, watching her as she neared Vasta, knowing she would be struck down. '*Stay away! Don't go near him!*' He tried to lunge forward to pull her back, but something held him where he stood. He fought against it, but it was useless.

'Matthew! Wake up, for Christ's sake. You're having a nightmare.'

Kindling opened his eyes, pushing back the images, concentrating on what he could see in the dim motel room. Louise knelt next to him, making a tent of the bedclothes which allowed the cooler air of the room to chill the sweat on his chest.

He forced himself awake. 'Damn, that scared the hell out of me,' he muttered, slowly pulling himself into a sitting position. He rubbed his eyes with both hands.

'You scared the hell out of me, too,' Louise told him. 'You kept yelling my name.'

He nodded wearily. 'It was the same nightmare I've had for years—I told you about it, remember?'

'About your visit to that house?'

'Yes, but this time the people in it were different. You were in it—and Vasta.' When she looked puzzled, he gave her the details.

'Sometimes it happens,' she said when he finished. 'People and things you've associated with recently usually populate our dreams.'

'Perhaps,' he said quietly, thinking there was more to it than that. 'But it was still the same dream.' She looked at him for a long time and he could see she wanted to help him, say the right things to make him feel better, but it was so hard to find the right words. He reached out and put the backs of his fingers against her cheek, then let his hand trail over her neck and shoulder to trace a line down the skin of her back. He could see her smile at him in the darkness.

'Are you cold?' she asked softly.

'No.'

'Do you want to try and sleep again, or do you want to talk a while?'

'Let's talk.'

'What about?'

Kindling paused, gathering his thoughts. 'Why are those astronauts still up there? Why didn't they pull them out at the first sign of trouble?' He heard Louise draw in her breath quickly and he thought she was annoyed that he wanted to discuss their work.

'There's a hurricane lashing Florida. Hurricane Ben. They can't launch a shuttle to go and get them.'

'But that's now. They could've called the whole thing off days ago. They could have launched a shuttle before the hurricane even formed.'

There was a long moment of silence and Kindling guessed that Louise was deciding how much she wanted to tell him. Finally she said, 'I'll simplify it for you, Matt. The legalities of it all, at least, okay?' He nodded, but before she went on Louise settled herself more comfortably, sitting on the bed and swinging her legs over his body and forming a bridge across his stomach. They arranged the blankets so both of them were warm. 'Do you know how much it cost Vasta to be a part of the Cryogenic program? To buy his way in?'

'Fifty million, Wiley told me.'

She nodded. 'But that's only a fraction of what Vasta's worth. He had interests in the USA—all over the world—making him worth a hell of a lot more. Of course, not a lot of it's what you'd call legal earnings. It's "dirty money", most of it.'

'I was surprised he even had the fifty million,' Kindling admitted.

'He was very good at keeping a low profile. And he was very, *very* good at hiding his money. Several governments, including Australia, would have made serious efforts to get it from him in the courts, if they'd ever had a concrete idea where to look. Vasta would make a new fortune for himself every week, and it would simply disappear—melt into his corporate structure and be diluted by legitimate businesses. Somewhere further down the line he'd syphon it off again and tuck it away.' She gave Kindling a meaningful look. 'In fact, only one thing caused enough havoc, enough movement within his personal finances, to reveal where Vasta had had his money invested—in places nobody thought of looking before.'

'His death.'

'You got it. Except guess what?' She didn't wait for him to answer. 'Now all that money's tied up in a deceased estate, which is exactly what he'd known would happen. The authorities still can't get their hands on it. So what's the next step?'

Kindling could see the scenario emerging and spoke slowly, not quite believing his own words. 'Bring him back to life.'

'Congratulations. You get a prize.' Louise leaned close and gave him a kiss.

Kindling was bewildered. 'But what's the point of it? He's back to where he started, isn't he?'

'No, because everyone knows where all the money is now. It's like getting a whole new set of clues to a mystery. Vasta was in such a hurry to kill himself before the disease took hold and did too much damage, he either accepted the risk or plain overlooked how his death would cause such a ripple through his finances.'

'So this whole thing's about money?' Kindling didn't know whether to be amazed or outraged. 'Those astronauts are taking unnecessary risks with their lives because somebody wants to recover a bit of stolen money?'

'A *lot* of stolen money,' she reminded him. 'And yes, that's originally why they pressed ahead with the project, despite the deaths of two crewmembers. If they'd known what they were getting into, I don't think it'd be the same. Things got out of control before anyone realised.'

'And that's why Wiley didn't like me snooping around Vasta's house? In case I found out about it?'

Louise hesitated. 'No, he was worried you'd find out Vasta didn't have to die.'

This stunned Kindling even more. 'What? What do you mean?'

'Part of the process of applying for the Cryogenic program is detailing exactly what threatens your life. If things had gone normally for Vasta, he would have been told a cure for his disease already existed in an experimental form. He could have bought his way into that program instead—at a much cheaper price, I might add—and got the same treatment he's about to receive now. Without killing himself, obviously.'

'You mean that information was deliberately withheld from him, in the hope he would suicide and reveal his financial secrets?'

'Basically, yes.' She shrugged. 'I told you I was simplifying it—there're a lot of things like psychological profiles, informers within his organisation, those sort of things, which made the entire operation more feasible. And I have to admit, it worked.'

Kindling gently pushed her legs from his body and got off the bed. He went to the refrigerator and made himself a scotch and coke, looking at Louise as he did so. She said, 'Yes, please.' He made a second drink and returned. When he came back she looked into his eyes.

'Matthew, I've told you all this because I decided you should know. You're more involved than anyone thought you'd become. You should also realise that no one you've met—not even Wiley or Michael Lay—are remotely close to the decision-makers in this program. We're all just soldiers in the field. And you've read the files on Vasta. You know some of things he did to earn that money—terrible things—and that information still only scratches the surface, we think. So when it came to the Cryogenic program he was almost perfect.

The authorities had something to gain if it all worked. But if it failed and Vasta died in the true sense of the word, nobody would care, either. Except for a few nutty scientists perhaps, who would scratch their heads over what went wrong.'

Kindling sipped his scotch and realised it wasn't the morality of allowing a man to die unnecessarily that shocked him—though admitting this to himself caused a moment of guilty self-examination—it was the complex machinations of governments, criminals and science that seemed, above all else, to be bringing his own personal dilemma to a climax. After taking a long pull on his drink he said as much to Louise.

'Yes, I suppose that's one way of looking at it.'

'But what happens now? Nobody seems to be doing anything.'

'That's because of the hurricane, I guess. And there's still another twenty-four hours before Vasta is supposed to revive.'

'Do you think he will?'

'No chance,' she shook her head firmly. 'Czowkowski explained it's far too quick. Vasta's body won't stand the sudden transformation and will probably turn to mush—his words, by the way,' she added with a smile.

'So, that's that. The end.'

She nodded. 'It seems safe to assume that Ellen Littlewood's ghost at the property and in the space station, and some of the other funny happenings aboard Freedom, were all driven by whatever tiny spark of life we created by commencing the Revival program. Now Joseph King's gone crazy, and in his madness he's going to kill that spark when he destroys Vasta's remains. He must—there's no other logical conclusion. Nothing else can happen, as far as I can see.' She paused and seemed about to say more, perhaps something concerning the two of them, because she suddenly lay down and held Kindling tightly. But all she added was, 'I guess that will be the end of it.'

They made love again. Kindling's confidence was growing and he touched her with more familiarity, exploring her body, searching for the things she enjoyed, while keeping his own distance in case he got too excited, too soon. He believed her groans were of genuine pleasure, not contrived to massage his ego, and thought she had a small orgasm. He didn't dare ask. And he felt all right about his own quick climax, knowing he was still only a novice in these things and she understood. Afterwards they lay in the dark hugging each other close. Neither of them went to sleep. Finally Kindling asked, 'What about us, Lou? When this is over?'

She moved and kissed him on the cheek. 'I like this, Matt. The two of us together, I mean. But we have to do one day at a time. I can't make any promises, okay?' She bit her lip at his hurt silence, but didn't change her mind and say anything more. They were worlds apart, two people thrown together in a crisis. Without the crisis, who knew what it would be like? It wasn't something Louise wanted to think about right now.

20

LEE AND CELIA TRIED for two solid hours to break into the Revival software from the Command Module and see what King had actually done. Working among the labyrinth of computer programs running Freedom, each avenue they investigated eventually came to the same dead end: a message stating *file access denied, program is already running.* It was as if the student had become the master. The astronauts couldn't control one of their own computers—albeit from a remote position in another module. Lee wondered aloud if the Revival program could be interrupted even from the main computer in the Cryogenic Module. King may have initiated a part of the program which couldn't be stopped unless power was denied to the whole system.

Despite his earlier threats Seerey wasn't prepared to try that. King appeared to be too powerful with the Revival software at his fingertips.

Although she announced several times that she'd given up completely, over the two days following King's escape Lee occasionally wandered back to a computer terminal and attempted once more to force her way into the rogue software. Sometimes she was prompted by a suggestion from the others, or someone on Earth would appear on the comm-link with an idea. The communications lines with Earth stayed open almost continuously, Ground Control's previous vague unhelpfulness gone. It seemed tacitly accepted that nothing could be salvaged from the tour—least of all the cryogenics. Vasta's rushed revival was unanimously doomed to failure. The astronauts noted their controller's renewed concern but refrained from saying anything directly to Canaveral in case it frayed tempers down there.

Seerey dreaded explaining to Jack Hitchcock how King had escaped. The whole thing just sounded too fantastic. The total lack of reaction from Ground Control during the event made him assume that the girl's spirit hadn't shown up on their equipment, even though she'd come up so clearly on the Command Module's own cameras. Via a guarded enquiry over the comm-link Seerey discovered that one of the controllers actually saw Lee and Dawkins fleeing through the space station, but without any sound he'd assumed from their manner and violent actions that they were heatedly arguing.

However, Seerey was pre-empted by Hitchcock's information from Australia about the connection between Vasta and the ghost of the young girl—Ellen Littlewood. Celia did some rapid chronological figuring and realised that the drama that had unfolded on a remote station in the outback coincided with their capture of Joseph King from the Cryogenics Module.

'It's like she wasn't here to help him,' she said. Her words brought concern all around—it obviously wasn't the case now. If Jack Hitchcock was alarmed that the supernatural activity on Freedom seemed unaffected by the events at Rhianna Station, he was careful not to show it. At the same time everyone tried to convince each other that their problems would be over in less than twenty-four hours when the three days were up and Vasta would be freed from all the artificial life-support, in theory, to re-enter life. In reality they believed he would be dead, and any spiritual presence the Revival program appeared to have created would be extinguished with him. His body tissues would be ruined by the rapid thawing and thus unfit for reinstating into the Cryogenic program, even if the authorities wished to. Someone suggested any supernatural activities would diminish as that moment neared. Seerey fervently hoped so.

Meanwhile, Hurricane Ben slowed and sat off the Florida coastline, reluctant to move west and batter itself to death inland. Instead it pounded the beaches and mangrove swamps of Canaveral with monstrous waves and screaming winds. Launch technicians sat at their blank computers and idly debated how much damage was being wrought upon the launchtower and the tethered shuttle which waited to bring the beleaguered astronauts on Freedom home. The shuttle crew were at the lowest state of readiness, expecting several more days of bad weather to hold up their mission.

Scott Dawkins was briefed through the comm-link on the exact procedures for the last hours of Vasta's revival. After referring to notes and diagrams faxed up to Freedom, he gave the others the main facts.

'Right now is when things really start to happen,' he said. 'And it all occurs inside the container. In the last twelve hours the preservatives are replaced by a correct amount of his blood-type. Then, when his body temperature is exactly right, electrodes on his head and body kick-start his heart and encourage brain activity. If it works, the lid comes off and he gets out, says, "Thanks guys" and that's that.'

'What do they think *will* happen?' Celia asked.

'Nothing. I suppose Joe will eventually take the lid off anyway to have a look and find himself worshipping a piece of dead meat.'

'Yeah, and *then* what will he do?' Judith asked bitterly, fingering the bandage on her head.

'Go crazy, I guess. But everyone seems pretty confident that once the Revival software runs its course, everything will return to normal. He won't have that overriding control we've suffered until now. We still won't be able to get him out of there, but it becomes a different problem altogether.'

'Let him stay in there and rot with the damn body,' Seerey grumbled. 'We'll go home in the shuttle without even telling him we're going.'

'The relief crew might have something to say

about that,' Dawkins laughed. It was a strange sound, rarely heard over the last few days.

The time neared for the completion of the Revival program. None of the astronauts could concentrate enough to try any constructive tasks, so they talked idly to pass the hours and kept one eye on the camera monitor showing King serenely resting above Vasta's container. Another worry was the white, spiralling chaos of Hurricane Ben on the computer screen like the petals of a ghostly rose. The pattern was imposed resolutely over the map of the Florida coastline and represented an insurmountable barrier to the astronauts' return.

'How long now?' Lee asked.

'We didn't make an exact note of the time when Joseph told us what he'd done,' Dawkins replied. 'But I make it about three hours.'

'We should all try to get some rest,' Seerey said. 'God knows what Joseph will do when he realises things haven't worked out. We might end up chasing him around the damned space station with a sedative.'

'I can't wait,' Dawkins said. 'Except I might chase him with an axe.'

'I'll be glad when that Revival program's finished and we can move around a bit better,' Lee said.

'Getting back to normal will be a help,' Seerey agreed.

There was no fanfare. No flashing lights or expectant drumroll. The Revival program announced its completion with a single beep and wrote the words *Program Complete* across the screen. However, the beep resounded in King's mind like the klaxon of a diving submarine. His time had come. He was going to meet his maker.

He pushed himself away from the container and looked at it with wonder. The computer screen told him nothing more than the final message. Inside, still imprisoned in darkness, but hearing a taped recording triggered by the computer urging calm and patience, his Lord incarnate waited to be set free. King became anxious when he realised he hadn't prepared himself for removing the lid. The twelve countersunk bolts spaced around the edge of the container required a special tool to undo them. He panicked when it occurred to him it might have been sucked out into space when the end hatchway was opened—he could picture the whole incident now and believed he was lucky to be alive. But the logical place for the tool was with the uninhabited containers and this is where he found it, clamped securely to the bulkhead.

Returning to Vasta's container he reverently began to undo the bolts. He was like a child removing the wrapping from a long-awaited present. With each bolt his excitement grew. Finally, the last one was free. King gripped the edge of the lid and lifted. With a wet, sucking sound a plastic seal broke and there was a slight hiss as the different air pressures equalised. An extra, tantalising moment had to pass while King awkwardly manoeuvred the long lid out of the way.

Anton Vasta lay naked on his back on a thin mattress of white rubber. His head was cradled on a thick, soft pillow. The most striking thing about him was his skin. It was almost translucent and revealed the feathery network of veins and capillaries across his entire body. The skin didn't look healthy. It was badly wrinkled and prunish, as if the body had been immersed in water for too long. The lack of body hair heightened the effect. Only a faint blue shadow showed on his head, like a skull cap, and a similar shading spread around his groin.

King could see the electrodes attached to his scalp, chest and lower abdomen. Thin wires curled beneath the small of his back indicated where others were taped close to his kidneys and lower spine. Two thick plastic tubes ran into his body connecting to major arteries, one in his wrist and the other deep in his upper thigh. Minute traces of the liquid they'd held suggested one was for the preservative fluid, while the other replaced this with real blood. Vasta looked undoubtedly dead, but more so at his body's extremities. The fingertips and toes were white and lifeless, the skin puckered. The nails, without the darker preserving fluid to colour them, were transparent. The shrivelled penis was an impotent, useless appendage.

Just as he began to fear the worst, a violent tremor racked the body. King cried out in alarm and backed away. Another attack followed and the convulsion lifted Vasta from the mattress. A third made his legs and arms thrash about within the confines of the container, hitting the edges hard. As he watched King let out incoherent moans of both fear and exaltation. Then the corpse became still again, bouncing gently against the container walls as it settled. When no further convulsions occurred for over a minute King dared to move back closer to see.

Vasta's mouth hung slackly open and his chest arose and fell in a ragged, uncertain rhythm.

'Dear God,' King uttered, his breath taken away by the moment. Then he added fervently, '*My* God.'

Vasta's eyes flickered open and focused on him. Two terrible eyes. The entire corneas had turned black, like a reptile's. The effect was so startling King cried out again, this time only with fear, before bringing himself under control. He'd jerked violently, making himself drift slightly. The eyes watched him with a sly malevolence, sliding to follow his movement while Vasta's head remained still.

One hand groped and curled over the lip of the container. The muscles were weak and quivered with the effort. Vasta's body tensed as he tried to pull himself upright, but the unfamiliar weightlessness made him slip uncontrollably within the container. His eyes widened, registering surprise and fear, and he began twitching all over. It wasn't the convulsions of before, but the start of an alarmed flailing. It grew to wild threshing which catapulted him from the container, his arms and legs windmilling without coordination to smash against the computer terminal and other equipment. Vasta made his first sound, a low agonised moan like a tortured animal. The electrodes ripped off one by one, followed by the intravenous tubes. Fine droplets of blood began to spray out from his arm to hang in the air. His groin began to smear with redness, too.

'No! Stop! You'll hurt yourself.' King found

his courage and tried to grab one of the thrashing limbs. He didn't see the metamorphosis occurring—with every frenzied movement Vasta grew stronger, an unnatural power filling his body. King was taken totally by surprise when Vasta suddenly directed his contortions to grab King's forearms in each of his white, sickened hands. The strength was incredible. King felt he was being held in two vice-grips. He stared into the black eyes and a wave of fetid breath washed over his face.

'Donald?' Vasta whispered. The question was barely recognisable as human speech. The tormented vocal chords that produced it had a harsh, raw sound.

King couldn't reply. He stared back and willed his brain to answer, but nothing came. The pressure on his forearms increased until he began to squeal with the pain. There were two distinct, brittle snaps as his bones broke. Shock and agony cut off King's scream. He hung limply in front of Vasta, his mouth gaping as he gazed into the other's face, unseeing now as his mind closed down.

Vasta pushed him away, then drifted grotesquely in the centre of the module, his ruined skin and nakedness an appalling sight. His newborn sensations struggled with the unexpected weightlessness and unfamiliar surroundings.

The astronauts in the Command Module watched the whole thing, their own horror mounting as the scene played out silently on the camera monitor. Only Seerey moved, punching in commands to relay the picture to Ground Control. A burst of voices came from the comm-link, but everyone ignored them. As the lid pulled away from the container and Vasta's body came into view several of the crew gasped.

'That is one dead sucker,' Dawkins announced gravely.

'God, it looks like he came close, though,' Lee said, leaning forward to try to see more detail. 'He certainly looks preserved, if a little ragged around the edges.'

'What's Joe going to do now?'

'He looks like he's found the Holy Grail,' Seerey said. 'The truth should dawn on him in a moment.'

Instead, the convulsions started to rattle through Vasta's body and they witnessed the awful resurrection. When it was over Seerey looked around at their shocked faces and said quietly, 'I think, somehow, we'd better find a way of locking ourselves in here. I don't know about dead anymore,' his eyes flicked to Dawkins. 'But I'd say he's one mean, dangerous sucker.'

'We should try to talk to him. Communicate in some way,' Celia suggested.

'There's the intercom,' Seerey looked doubtfully at the device. 'I suppose we can try.' He suddenly shot an annoyed look at the comm-link, which squawked a fresh barrage of demands for attention. 'Shut them up, someone. I'll see if I can get a response from this freak.'

As Dawkins spoke quietly to an angry Jack Hitchcock, Seerey moved to the intercom. At the last moment he asked, 'What's his damn name again?'

'Vasta,' Lee replied, puzzled, then saw what he meant. 'Anton,' she added. 'Anton Vasta.'

'Jesus,' Seerey muttered. 'What do I call him? Tony? Tone, for Christ's sake?' Without waiting for an answer he flicked the intercom switch and took a deep breath. 'Anton? Can you understand me? This is an intercom speaker on the bulkhead behind you.' He paused and watched the camera monitor for a response. Vasta didn't move. Seerey went on, speaking slowly. 'If you go over to it, you'll find a red switch which will let you answer me. Press it and talk towards the speaker—' Seerey's voice trailed away as he saw his words were having no effect on Vasta.

'Keep going,' Celia urged. 'Don't forget, he's been dead nearly two years! He's not going to catch onto anything too quickly for a while.'

Seerey grunted, uncomfortable with the task, but tried again. 'You took part in a Cryogenic program to preserve your remains, and you have been revived after being dead nearly two years.' In the brief pause that followed Dawkins muttered if *that* didn't make Vasta at least blink, nothing would. 'You are in Space Station Freedom, in orbit around Earth,' Seerey went on relentlessly, though his voice became mechanical as Vasta still didn't acknowledge him.

'Perhaps he's deaf,' Celia suggested. 'It's possible he hasn't come out of the Revival process complete. Look at him. He's barely holding together.'

Before Seerey could reply Lee cried, 'Look!' and pointed at the screen. Vasta had raised his head and was staring directly into the camera lens. 'What the hell's wrong with his eyes?' she asked, after a moment.

Dawkins examined the picture more closely. 'Either they've completely dilated, or they've turned black.'

'It looks weird,' Lee decided, repulsed by the sight. A shiver ran down her back before she could stop it. 'It's unnatural.'

'And I don't think he's feeling very friendly,' Celia murmured, suffering the same reaction to the black, pitiless eyes.

Hours of debate followed among the astronauts, and in countless discussions with Ground Control, who insisted on parading a line of administrators and top-ranking officials in front of the comm-link, none of whom contributed anything worthwhile. During this time Seerey insisted none of the crew leave the Command Module. Seerey repeated he didn't like the look of Vasta one little bit, especially the way he broke King's arms with so little effort and no apparent concern. Everyone agreed they didn't want Vasta coming into their module. Equally undesirable was the prospect of bumping into him in some other part of Freedom. At least not before they had a better idea of what they were dealing with.

The astronauts had a scare when Vasta suddenly began to move only minutes after bringing himself back into the living world. With careful, searching movements he pulled himself down the length of the Cryogenics Module until he disappeared out of sight beneath the field of the lens.

'He's coming out!' Lee cried. No one knew what to do or say. Dawkins found himself casting about for some sort of weapon, but it was pointless. There was nothing. An air of helplessness filled the module with everyone silently pleading for someone to come up with a solution. Before anything else could happen Vasta wandered back into view, heading in the opposite direction. There were audible sighs of relief in the Command Module.

He started to move regularly, going from one end of the module to the other, dodging around the inert King as if he wasn't there at all. Each time he came close to the camera Vasta would leave the screen for several seconds, then return. The watchers in the Command Module got used to it after a while, then Celia realised what he was doing.

'He's teaching himself to *move*,' she decided, marvelling that the creature—she couldn't bring herself to think of Vasta as a real human being—had some sort of logical and creative thought processes.

'That's damn interesting,' Lee murmured, watching the screen intently. 'And look at that scar on his back. It must be new—I think I can see the stitches still in it.' Within the folds of flabby, dead-white skin it was difficult to tell.

'It's scary, too,' Celia added. 'I don't like him being able to move around like this.' She took comfort from the system Dawkins had devised, using tools scavenged from the adjacent Space Engineering Module, to jam the hatches locked. Engineering had been John Quantey's department, the module unattended since his death.

'Don't worry,' Dawkins said, seeing her look. 'He may be strong, but he ain't no superman.'

Decisions were finally made—predictably, in Seerey's opinion. The word from Earth was that the astronauts do nothing about their new 'crew-member'. Vasta was in a controlled and enclosed environment, probably the best place for him to stay until the specialists being assembled arrived in the shuttle to return him to Earth. The surviving astronauts aboard Freedom were to leave the reborn Vasta alone.

The instructions came from a severe-looking Jack Hitchcock. Seerey asked him what they should do if Vasta got loose in the rest of Freedom. Hitchcock rejected the possibility, then gave him some almost nonsensical suggestions anyway. The controller quickly signed off, denying Seerey the opportunity for any more questions.

'That's crazy.' Seerey shook his head. 'It's like they've gone back to the bullshit of not giving a flying fuck about us—did you notice no one's even mentioned poor bloody Joseph King? What's he supposed to do, stay in there until he dies of shock?'

'Sounds like it,' Celia agreed sombrely. 'The only good thing is they'll want to get that freak back to Earth as quick as possible, which means we'll get home soon, too.'

Lee laughed. 'Yeah, and I'll bet we'll have to be fast, so we don't accidentally get left behind. We should tell them to make sure there's enough room on the shuttle for all of us.' She became serious as she finished, realising it wasn't such a silly notion.

Judith pulled a face. 'We'll have to ride down in the shuttle compartment with that thing?'

'Jack said there's a crew of specialists coming up to take care of our patient,' Seerey told her. 'I imagine they'll sedate him somehow.'

Dawkins was checking his improvised locks. He called over his shoulder, 'Judging by the way he fixed up Joe, I reckon those guys might need more than just a sedative.'

'And they have to get him out of the module first,' Lee reminded them. 'Has anyone thought about that?'

Celia pensively watched Vasta continue his progress up and down the Cryogenics Module. 'My guess is they figure he'll let himself out before we have to worry about breaking down the door.'

Soon afterwards everything was quiet. Ground Control left them alone, having enough information to analyse. Judith decided to take advantage of the lull.

'Alex,' she said, tugging his sleeve as he worked at a computer station, wearily updating his reports. 'I need to go to the toilet. Either of you guys feel like volunteering to ride shotgun?' The toilet was alongside the shower in the Accommodation Module.

'Sure, I'll do it myself,' he said, glad of the excuse to stop. I've been bustin' for a leak for a while, but I keep putting it off. We can grab some more food and maybe some coffees from the Galley on the way back,' he added, looking about to see if Lee, Celia and Dawkins agreed. They were having a huddled discussion about NASA policy. All three nodded gratefully.

Dawkins went to the hatchway and dismantled his locking mechanism. Celia and Alex took a last look at the camera monitor. Vasta was still moving mechanically up and down the module like some dreadful automaton.

'He's not going anywhere,' Seerey decided.

Dawkins let them out. They would travel down the left arm of Freedom. There was no real logic to calling it the 'left' side any more than the other arm was the 'right'. It was a piece of terminology of forgotten origin unique to Freedom. It did mean Seerey and Judith would have the shortest route to the Accommodation Module and they wouldn't have to move past the Airlock—something all of them unconsciously avoided now, since the outer Airlock door apparently malfunctioned. It hadn't yet occurred to anyone, in the light of the recent events in the space station, to form a new theory about Lyghtson's death. In truth, they hadn't had the time. And now it was ancient history.

The two astronauts came first to the Astronomy Module. Freedom always had telescopes and other equipment looking out at the stars, a facility included in the initial plans for the space station as soon as the Hubble Telescope satellite fell short of expectations. Joseph King, however, was the first astronaut exclusive to the field to go into orbit. On impulse Seerey stopped and quickly leafed through a hand-written journal he recognised as a daily tool of King's. Immediately, he saw from the dates that King hadn't been attending to his work for some time before he attacked Judith. Seerey felt a surge of guilt. It was something he should have noticed—*could* have noticed—and perhaps have avoided the mess they were in now. Without saying anything he pushed the journal away.

Next was the Minerals Laboratory, with its reminders of Hugh Lyghtson. They stopped briefly to repair the internal camera, then moved into the Galley. Seerey considered getting the meal preparations underway but decided his bladder, and probably Judith's too, was getting more important. They continued into the Accommodation Module.

With gentlemanly deference Seerey motioned Judith to use the toilet first. While he waited an idea came to him and he searched his bunkspace, finding the two novels he always brought with him into space that he never tired of reading. They could fill some of the empty hours in the Command Module, perhaps for the other crewmembers, too. Seerey was looking through the books, reading pages at random and fondly remembering favourite passages when Judith emerged from the toilet.

'I just remembered I had these,' he told her, offering the books so she could hold them for him. 'Somebody might like to read them.' He went into the cubicle, leaving her with the novels.

The books appealed to Judith, but they gave her another idea. She was feeling much better now, the throbbing from her injuries was only weak and easily controlled by mild painkillers. Despite the work Celia offered from her program in the Command Module, time still weighed heavily. It would be good, Judith thought, to quickly grab some of her books and papers from the Earth Science Module nextdoor and do some of her own work back in the Command Module.

She let her eyes drift to the access tunnel and the idea firmed in her mind. Leaving the novels to float freely she pushed her way hastily past the bunks and into the tunnel, hurrying in case Seerey came out and stopped her.

Inside her own familiar territory Judith quickly tucked some reference manuals under one arm and located a clipboard with sheaves of notes attached to it. The top paper reminded her she needed to print out the latest data and she powered up the workstation. Judith clicked her tongue impatiently, listening to the whir of the hard disk building to speed and the clicks and buzzes as the program initiated itself. Finally she began scrolling through the electronic pages, looking for a particular file.

At the very moment Judith found the figures she needed, a noise came from behind her. She turned, thinking of excuses to give Seerey about why she'd strayed away.

Vasta floated an arm's length away, the black eyes staring into hers. Seen up close his damaged body was an obscenity. The ugly, dead white skin hung in wrinkles. Judith screamed.

'Donald?' he asked her in a silky whisper.

She couldn't stop her eyes sliding down his monstrous figure. Horror threatened to choke her as she saw Vasta's limp penis begin to swell and rise.

'Come closer,' he croaked, reaching slowly out. The eyes remained black, empty holes, but something resembling a leer formed on the bloodless lips.

21

AFTER SEEREY AND JUDITH disappeared from the Command Module Dawkins closed the hatchway again and, as an experiment, reconstructed his locking mechanism. It took him less than twenty seconds. Shrugging, he took it off and reopened the hatch in anticipation of the returning astronauts, laden with food and drinks.

He returned to Celia and Lee, picked up the thread of their discussion and began arguing earnestly. Some minutes later they were interrupted by Jack Hitchcock on the comm-link. Pulling a tired face at the two women Dawkins answered. Hitchcock wanted Seerey.

'He's not here,' Dawkins told him. 'He's gone to the crapper, as a matter of fact.' He enjoyed the irreverence over the communications network and the frown of disapproval on Hitchcock's face. But nothing was the same any more.

'I need a decision about the relief crew. What's needed to effect any repairs to damage caused by this current tour?'

Dawkins smelled a rat. 'What exactly does that mean?'

'It's really a question for Alex.'

'Well, Alex will discuss it with us anyway,' Dawkins said reasonably. 'So why don't you tell us now? Alex won't mind.'

Hitchcock paused. 'It might be best if one or two of you stayed up there with the relief crew, just until we're certain everything's been brought back into line. Another shuttle will fly up about a week later, so it's no big thing. Maybe you guys want to draw straws, see who stays and who goes.'

This was said too casually. Dawkins turned to Lee and Celia and whispered, 'What the hell is he trying to pull?' He turned back to the comm-link.

A cat-and-mouse conversation followed with Dawkins asking all the questions and Hitchcock trying his hardest not to answer them. It soon became apparent, especially to the two women listening, that Hitchcock simply wanted to reduce the number of relief personnel so the team of specialists looking after Vasta could be enlarged. Near the end of the discussion Celia interrupted Dawkins.

'Scott, I'm worried.' The tone of her voice made him curtly silence Hitchcock and turn to her.

'Why? What's up?'

She nodded at the camera monitor. 'I don't

think I've seen Vasta on the screen for over a minute, at least.'

'Shit!' He went to the controls and after an instant of indecision altered the view to the Airlock Module. It was empty. He was about to change monitors again when Lee exclaimed, 'Christ, look! The access tunnel.'

The camera in the Airlock was set at the same angle as the others, so the access tunnel immediately below it wasn't visible. But what had been obscured in the previous frame of the Cryogenic Module was now the most distant object in the view of the Airlock. The dark hole of the hatchway to the Cryogenics Module clearly boasted a crescent of white light, shining like a quartered new moon.

'Goddamn it, the bastard's out!' Dawkins reprogrammed the camera view to the next module, Utilities. He fumbled the controls in his haste. The screen showed another deserted area. Likewise the Medical Module and the last before the Command Module itself, Engineering. 'Hell, he must have gone the other way towards the Accommodation Module.' He was angry at himself—it was the first direction he should have checked. Seerey and Judith were down there. Too late, another thought came to him. 'Tell Alex,' he snarled over his shoulder. 'Use the intercom and just yell that Vasta's loose somewhere—' The words died in his throat as a picture of the Earth Science Module flicked onto the camera monitor. It showed Judith Cianta face to face with the naked, threatening figure. Behind Dawkins, Lee stifled a scream.

Vasta's movements were slow and uncoordinated. As he reached out, there was enough time for Judith to snap out of her frozen terror. She ducked desperately beneath his hands and pushed herself away from the bulkhead, heading for the access tunnel. Loath to turn her back, but with no choice she scrambled inside. Halfway through, trying to watch her feet in case one of those horrid white hands grasped her ankle, someone gripped her collar and hauled her roughly into the Accommodation Module. Before she could scream again Judith found herself staring into the panicked face of Seerey.

'What the fuck's going on?' he yelled at her.

'He's in there,' she sobbed, indicating the next module. Seerey didn't have to ask who she was talking about. He looked past her shoulder and saw the white circle of the access tunnel darken as someone entered at the other end.

'Let's get the hell out of here.'

Judith didn't need any more urging. They fled out of the Accommodation Module into the Galley. Coming out of the access tunnel Seerey risked a moment to turn and peer back after them. A cumbersome form, the white skin reflecting ghoulishly in the artificial light, followed them between the bunkspaces.

'Keep going,' Seerey told her. By the time they emerged into the Minerals Laboratory he judged they were moving fast enough to risk a brief stop at the intercom. Vasta was obviously still having trouble getting around at any great speed in the zero gravity. 'Scott,' Seerey called, praying there was nothing seriously wrong in the Command Module. He couldn't imagine why they hadn't seen

Vasta leave the Cryogenic Module and called a warning. 'For Christ's sake, open the hatchway. We're coming through in a big hurry.' He left the intercom in time to see Judith's feet disappear into the next tunnel. He was relieved to hear Dawkins' terse acknowledgement behind him.

They burst into the Command Module. Judith was shaking and Seerey let out a string of curses. Dawkins quickly slammed the hatch closed and installed the lock. He blurted out what had happened.

'Jesus, Alex. Hitchcock called with a whole shit-load of lies and we all took our eyes off the screen for too long. We saw what was happening just as Judith got away. It's all my fault. Christ, I'm sorry.'

'You'd be a damn sight sorrier if Judith hadn't got away,' Seerey snapped, trying to get his breath back. But he couldn't maintain his anger. Nobody up here was a fool. With brittle professionalism he accepted that sometimes things combined to beat the best of them. 'Shit, that was close.' He shook his head.

Lee took over the internal cameras while Celia hugged Judith. She announced, 'He's getting closer.' They watched Vasta's figure drift through the modules, moving out of sight each time he went into access tunnels, until he finally disappeared into the last connecting the Astronomy Module to their Command Module. Anxiously they turned their attention to the circular metal of the wheel-lock.

A shuffling, tapping noise filtered through the metal. Barely discernible, there came a grunt. Slowly the wheel-lock tried to turn. One of the metal spokes wedged hard against Dawkins' jury-rigged locking system. For a moment the whole assembly trembled as strong pressure was applied and the lock shifted a fraction before holding fast. Dawkins sucked in his breath, the only person to understand the power needed to have any effect on his handiwork. Another grunt, louder this time, came from the other side. Then nothing. Finally Lee said, 'He's going.'

They switched their eyes to the camera screen and saw Vasta retreating the way he'd come.

'So, he's looking for somebody, but that somebody isn't here.' Seerey mused. 'He could've picked a better place to look than a damn space station in orbit.'

'*Donald*,' Lee repeated the name. Judith had explained all she could about her brief encounter. Seerey tried again to provoke a response from Vasta using the name. It hadn't worked.

'How the hell does he come out of the deep-freeze with a name like that on his mind?' A distant memory nagged Lee, but she couldn't pin it down.

Back on Earth experts in human behaviour were analysing the facts and watching the available tapes of Vasta's movements. The final scene was still being enacted for them—Vasta returned to the Cryogenic Module like an animal returning to its lair and resumed his relentless motion up and down the centre passageway, brushing heedlessly by the still comatose Joseph King with each pass. All the information was also sent to an agent NASA had in Australia, where Vasta's past was being searched for anyone by the name of Donald who might have a significant place in the man's subconscious. The theory was that perhaps Donald was someone who had considerable influence over Vasta, someone who could provide more clues about what might be going on in Vasta's mind. Memories, loves—even hatreds. Anything to improve the level of communication between the astronauts and their problem newcomer.

The experts replied first, sending a detailed report of their conclusions. The wording and hurried accumulation of disparate opinions made the document nearly indecipherable to the astronauts. A doctor in psychology was put in front of the comm-link to explain it all in simple terms. They silently listened to the man's analysis of the report. Only Seerey occasionally asked for more clarification. Towards the end of the interview some of the Freedom crew were beginning to get restless.

Finally Seerey thanked the doctor and closed down the intercom. 'Did he tell us something we don't already know?' he asked with a sigh.

'I don't think so,' Dawkins answered. 'If he did, I didn't hear it—or I didn't understand it, anyway.'

'So, what have we got?'

Dawkins ticked points off on his fingers. 'A psychotic obsessed with getting something—in this case *somebody*—he can't get. The guy has no regard for human rights or maybe even for human life. The rejuvenation seems to have mutated his body in some way and given him freakish strength. And he appears to have been reduced to the most basic instincts.' Dawkins glanced at Judith as he said this. She merely shrugged.

'At least now I understand what was happening. They're saying Vasta hasn't returned as some maniac rapist, but he recognised me as a female and felt a basic urge to mate, something stemming from right back in the caveman era.' She shrugged again. 'Okay, I'll buy that. Maybe it means if we put a plate of food in front of him, he'll instinctively feed. The same with water. Self-preservation will insist he drink, given the opportunity.'

'That's an interesting thought,' Dawkins said. 'It might give us a way of sedating the bastard. Lace a meal of some sort and leave it out there for him to find. He might jam it down his throat without a second's thought and all our worries would be over.'

'Sounds easy,' Seerey said. 'Except it means somebody has to go to the Galley and get some food, and also go to the Medical Module for a large handful of sleeping tablets or whatever, then go out *again* to bait the trap. What's the chances of running into our friend before all that's achieved?'

'We can just watch from here,' Lee told him, uncomfortable because it was exactly what they had failed to do last time. 'And scream bloody murder over the intercom if he leaves Cryogenics.'

'Maybe,' Seerey nodded. 'It's worth some thought. We'd have to plan it properly, of course.'

Dawkins gestured at the behavioural report floating discarded in the air next to Seerey. 'Apart from all that, we still don't know who the hell "Donald" is, right?' Nobody noticed Lee screw up her eyes for a moment in concentration. Still the niggling memory wouldn't come to the front of her mind.

It was NASA's people in Australia who unwittingly provided the answer. Seerey was told a woman called Louise Corry would tell him what they'd achieved so far in their search for the mysterious Donald. At the appointed time a striking girl appeared on the comm-link and introduced herself.

Corry said, 'You'll appreciate we're working with a very large database here. Vasta came into contact with a lot of people, especially during his last years alive.' Seerey expected her to make excuses for a lack of success, but instead she went on, 'Predictably, we've already come up with four Donalds and that's without really trying. We've managed to check out three of them pretty thoroughly, while the fourth is proving a little hard to track down. Of the three, it's my opinion they didn't have any marked effect on Vasta. Not enough to trigger the sort of subconscious trauma NASA is talking about.' She made them smile adding, 'Of course, who the hell knows? Donald could be his favourite football star, who might be damned important to *him*. And he was a man with a lot of secrets, remember. The most insignificant acquaintance could actually be his most important associate.'

'I appreciate what you're trying to say,' Seerey told her.

'I wish we could do more. But like I said, going by NASA's guidelines, we haven't come up with anyone worth mentioning, while we have a fourth who may amount to something.'

'Could you contact us as soon as you know, either way?'

'Sure. And maybe if your patient says or does anything that might help, could you contact us directly?'

'I'd be glad to. Will you be there all the time?'

Corry looked uncertain and he saw her glance around. 'No, but the best person to speak to here is Czowkowski. He'll pass everything on.'

Seerey drew a writing pad close, 'Czowkowski,' he murmured, pulling a face.

'Just ask for Huey.' Corry smiled, understanding.

'Huey Czowkowski?' Seerey let out a grunt of amusement.

'Actually, there used to be three operators—Huey, Duey and Louie. Then—'

The rest of Corry's explanation was drowned out by Lee Wynn. She punched Dawkins on the shoulder. 'Jesus, Scott! We're a pair of idiots! *We* know who Donald is! It's Donald Duck. Remember what we entered when the computer wanted to know who was initiating the program?'

Dawkins rolled his eyes and groaned at his own stupidity. 'Hell, yes. What took us so long to catch on?'

Seerey kept himself calm and told Corry, 'Excuse us a moment.' He turned back to Dawkins and Lee and listened to their explanation, then returned to the comm-link and thanked Corry sincerely, saying he thought they'd solved the mystery. She faded from the screen.

They chewed it over and decided it had to be the only explanation. 'Well, that's great,' Seerey announced, his voice heavy with sarcasm. 'Now that we know exactly who Vasta wants and where he got the name from, I think I can safely say we have nothing to offer him.'

'Unless they fax us up some comics,' Dawkins suggested glumly. No one laughed.

'He's moving again,' Lee called. She was keeping watch on the camera monitor. The lights of the module had been dimmed and the others were attempting to rest. Immediately Seerey shook himself awake and moved behind her. The blue-white light from the screen enhanced the sleep lines around his eyes. Lee, Dawkins and Judith joined him around the screen.

Still ignoring the stricken Joseph King, who had balled himself into a foetal position and floated motionlessly at the end of the module, Vasta left the Cryogenics Module and emerged into the Airlock. Lee tracked his progress with the cameras. There he slowed, apparently taking in his surroundings. He went to the row of spacesuits, fingered the cloth and touched the metal fittings. The way he handled things and looked at objects in a hesitant, myopic manner suggested a new puppy sniffing around its mother for a teat, its eyesight not fully developed. There the analogy stopped. The soft, warm, appealing body of a pup was a grotesque contrast with Vasta's sickened, naked figure.

'Shit, I wish the inner Airlock door was open,' Celia said grimly. 'I reckon I could override the Airlock software from here and open the outer door. Suck the bastard straight out into space.' She saw Seerey was troubled by her words and the conflict of interests.

He said softly, 'Don't forget, you guys, we're the only ones who'd like to get rid of this freak.

NASA would love to get him back home. Be careful what you say.'

'It'd be an accident, Alex. Like the one that killed Hugh.'

He didn't answer. Vasta made the question irrelevant by leaving the Airlock. During the moments he was obscured in the access tunnel Seerey muttered, 'Which way will he go?'

He reappeared in the Earth Science Module and slowly made his way down the length of the section, feeling, touching and seeing in his confused way. Judith gritted her teeth as he fumbled with her equipment and experiments, although most of her plants were dying and beyond saving. The astronauts couldn't tell if the way Vasta clumsily gripped the small stems, ripping them from their beds, was intentional.

Leaving the shredded plants and clouds of damp soil suspended in the air, he moved on through the next access tunnel to the Accommodation Module. Vasta seemed to find little of interest here, hardly pausing on his way through. At the other end he had a choice of direction, left towards the Galley and, ultimately, the Command Module, or right, which would take him directly into the dead end of the Assured Crew Return Vehicle—the Lifeboat.

The Lifeboat was a completely self-contained spacecraft, preprogrammed to splash down in the Pacific, where a U.S. Naval destroyer stayed on patrol all year round in case of just such an emergency. NASA expected the term 'assured' to be taken literally. It didn't require any controlling by the crew, allowing for the extreme possibility of any survivors being incapable of concentrated effort. Once inside, all they needed to do was punch a large red button the size of a saucer, and the automatic systems took over. The Lifeboat's door would slam hydraulically closed and sealed, then propulsion jets would fire, sending it on the journey home. Similar equipment would instantly cap the open wound of the deserted access tunnel, maintaining the integrity of Freedom's atmosphere—NASA wasn't about to let their multi-billion-dollar investment be jeopardised by a bunch of panicked astronauts. In complexity and cost the Lifeboat rivalled only the Command Module.

In anticipation, Lee activated the camera in the Galley and waited expectantly for Vasta's white body to slide in through the access tunnel. When nothing happened after thirty seconds she changed the settings and displayed the interior of the Lifeboat. This was a smaller, cramped view, but enough to show Vasta fumbling around inside the craft like a blind man.

'Bullshit,' Seerey breathed, hardly daring to believe their luck. '*Do* it! Do it for us.' Everyone silently agreed. For Vasta to eject himself to Earth and make himself somebody else's problem would be just fine by them, even at the cost of the Lifeboat.

No one dared to speak as they watched Vasta spend long minutes inspecting the instruments and safety couches. When he stared intently at the red launch button and traced his fingers over the outline of its roundness Dawkins blurted, 'He's going to do it!' But Vasta moved on, circling the craft until he returned to the access tunnel.

While everyone else bemoaned how close it had

been, Lee changed the camera back to the Galley and waited to see Vasta. But again, he didn't appear and, frowning, she tried the Accommodation Module just in time to see a pair of bare white feet disappear into the far access tunnel. 'He's going back,' she said.

Vasta moved with a sense of purpose, ignoring his surroundings now to travel directly back to the Cryogenics Module. When the camera showed him pulling into his home territory—as everyone was beginning to think of it—Seerey sighed, expressing the relief they all felt. 'Well, he didn't hit the panic button, but at least he's gone home to roost—'

His words died as they watched Vasta go straight to Joseph King, take hold of him above one elbow and begin towing him towards the access tunnel. The silent cameras registered the agony on King's face as he snapped out of the protection of his coma and screamed, his injured limbs pulled uncaringly. Judith Cianta remembered how she'd thought King had resembled a spider when he climbed out of the access tunnel just before he attacked her. The image was equally appropriate now. As Vasta hauled King along, cruelly forcing his captive's broken arms into the narrower confines of the access tunnel, he resembled a spider dragging his prey into the centre of its web.

'Oh God,' someone muttered. 'What's going on?'

They could only watch as Vasta continued to drag King through the space station behind him like a piece of baggage on a string, ignoring the man's suffering as his broken arms collided against the walls of the tunnels. At the same time they noted King only protested against his pain—as far as the astronauts in the Command Module could see, he wasn't physically fighting against his treatment. His open mouth suggested he was imploring his new-found master for mercy, not release.

Back through the Earth Science Module, stirring the swirls of drifting dirt and leaves, down between the bunks of the Accommodation Module. The cameras caught every detail of King's entreaties. Tears filled his eyes, his face contorted in grimaces of agony whenever his broken limbs smashed against something.

And into the Lifeboat.

'He's taking King with him?' Celia asked. It seemed so improbable.

When Vasta turned and left King alone in the Lifeboat only Seerey realised what was going to happen. He suddenly lunged at the intercom and cried, 'Joe! No, don't do it! You have no idea what you're doing.' But it was too late. Even without the threat of encountering Vasta lurking in the modules between them, no one could have moved through Freedom fast enough to stop King.

As she stared at Vasta's retreating figure, Celia realised what was going to happen. 'For Christ's sake, he doesn't want to leave.'

Joseph King threw one last, despairing look towards the access tunnel, then slowly lifted his broken arms to the launch button. Sobbing, he leaned on the red disc, but even that small weight was enough to send flames of pain shooting down his limbs. With a cry of misery and agony he jerked away. After the waves of nausea faded, his face set into an expression of resolve and he rolled slowly over. Lashing out with a foot he kicked the button.

The lights in the Command Module flickered for a moment. At the same moment the camera picture of King vanished, severed with all the other electrics in the Lifeboat Module. There was a distant thud as the hatches of all the intervening modules automatically slammed closed at the small drop in air pressure, which the capping system for the departing Lifeboat was marginally too slow to prevent. For the people in the Command Module, these were the only indications that a launch had occurred at the other end of the space station. The Lifeboat was gone.

Shock and dismay filled the Command Module. Now they were stranded, the last resort of abandoning Freedom in the Lifeboat taken from them. That it was a deliberate act by Vasta there was no doubt in anyone's mind. Dawkins voiced their concern. 'Just how smart is that freak getting?'

'Is he getting smarter?' Celia looked worried.

'We'd better find him first.' Seerey nodded at the monitor, which was still blanked out by the missing Lifeboat camera.

Lee quickly punched in commands and brought up the Galley area in case Vasta was making his way towards the Command Module again. She was rewarded by a blurred, grey picture without any recognisable shapes. 'What's wrong with this?' She turned to Seerey. 'I hope the Lifeboat leaving hasn't taken out the camera system.'

No one had to say what a blow to their security and sense of well-being this would be—to be rendered blind to Vasta's movements. 'Try the next one,' Seerey asked her, staying calm, but his breath hissed out between his teeth when the screen revealed a similar picture for the Minerals Lab. Lee keyed in the next module, Astronomy. They were almost startled as a clear picture of the section lit up the monitor. Vasta was moving towards the camera.

'Check your lock again,' Seerey said to Dawkins. 'Looks like he's coming back for a second try.' As Dawkins pushed himself towards the hatchway Lee's small cry of alarm made him stop and look back.

His dead, black eyes looming close, Vasta was reaching for the camera. Unconsciously the watchers in the Command Module backed away from the screen. The picture went dark as a hand closed over the lens, then came a blur of indistinct movement. The darkness dissolved to be replaced by the same greyness of the other cameras.

'He's twisting them around on their mounts,' Dawkins said, awed. 'Turning them to face the wall.' It wasn't the act, but the reasoning behind it which amazed them. Vasta had answered Celia's question—he was getting smarter.

Vasta didn't try forcing the Command Module hatchway again. Lee activated the Accommodation Module camera and they waited fatalistically for him to appear. However, the camera was mounted at the same end of the module where Vasta would emerge, so they only caught a glimpse of his figure before there was a repeat performance and the unit was rendered useless. Lee leap-frogged ahead of him. In the 'right' side of Freedom the lenses again offered a view of Vasta traversing the length of the module to disable the cameras. This was the first time he had entered this part of the space station and he took his time, examining his surroundings as he went, but always finishing by twisting the camera on its mount. The need to reopen all the hatchways, which had automatically closed when the Lifeboat was launched, slowed his progress. He came all the way to Engineering and the astronauts expected him to try forcing the opposite hatchway, something he hadn't attempted before, but nothing happened.

'That's even worse,' Dawkins observed grimly. 'It means he's capable of logical assumption—that if one end of the Command Module is locked, the other must be, too. So it's not worth the effort.'

The last camera to be disabled was in the Cryogenics Module. Vasta floated teasingly in the middle of the frame, staring at the astronauts through the lens, before finishing his task. Celia wondered aloud if he *was* taunting them.

'I hope not,' Lee replied, gravely. 'It would mean his mental processes are developing in leaps and bounds.'

22

CONFINED TO THE COMMAND Module and electronically blind to the rest of Freedom, the astronauts' sense of isolation increased keenly. It didn't help matters when Seerey insisted on a summary of their situation—though they recognised it was necessary. The situation looked bleak.

Communications with Earth were uninterrupted, which was good, but everyone accepted there may be only scant help from that quarter. Bringing Vasta back to Earth alive would be their major concern, even perhaps to the detriment of the surviving astronauts. The same communications also showed a clear picture of Hurricane Ben still poised over Florida, ruining any chances of a shuttle launch.

No one could see any benefit in attempting a direct confrontation with Vasta. His obvious strength and developing cunning made it an unreasonable risk. They were virtual prisoners in the Command Module, which posed several serious dilemmas.

They had to assume Vasta would wander about the different sections of Freedom at will—why else would he have gone to the trouble of disabling all the cameras? Unless they took the risk of running into him, the astronauts had no access to the Accommodation Module. Their body wastes couldn't be dealt with in their present environment, the Command Module.

The other bodily function, sustenance, presented identical problems. All food and water was stored in the Galley. No emergency supplies were held in the Command Module. Again, someone would need to run the gauntlet of going to the Galley and bringing back supplies. At least, being only one module back from Accommodation and thus third from the Command Module, this represented slightly better odds of success.

All the facts were sent to Ground Control for their input. None of the Freedom crew expected anything to come of that, so there was surprise all around when one of the younger technicians came up with a simple idea, which had real possibilities.

'Reverse the wiring in the intercom master,' he told them through the comm-link. 'If you can get inside the console and get yourselves a soldering iron, I can probably guide you through a few quick changes.'

'A soldering iron?' Celia asked incredulously.

'What the hell does he think this is, a hardware store?'

'Actually, I know of two,' Dawkins said. 'There's one next door in Engineering—a little heavy for this sort of work, but it'll do. There's a better one in the tools in the Airlock, but that's a bit risky.' Celia's expression turned hopeful.

'But what will that achieve?' Seerey asked the technician doubtfully.

'You can make the entire system live—like, leave it on continuously. You can *listen* to where your friend is. What's more, if you key in a separate station like you normally could, the reverse will apply. You'll turn that station off, because it's already on with the rest of the system, understand? It'd be awkward, but by a process of elimination you could pinpoint down to the exact module where he is—as long as he's making a noise. Just keeping turning on the different substations—which means you'll be actually turning them off—and as long as you can still hear the guy, you've got the wrong place. Like, if you turn a station off and the guy's noises cut out, you know you've found the right module—do you see what I mean?'

Seerey was already nodding before the technician had finished. 'You are a fucking genius.'

Their excitement dimmed a little when they realised somebody would have to make a trip into the Engineering Module nextdoor.

'Jesus, he might be waiting just outside,' Judith said.

'Thanks. Just what I wanted to hear.' In saying this, Dawkins was volunteering to make the attempt.

'Do you know where the soldering iron is?' Seerey asked him.

'I know where it was a few days ago, long after—' He broke off awkwardly. *Long after John was killed.* 'You know, if he isn't waiting for me in there, what's to stop me installing one of my makeshift locks on the next hatch? Give us some more room.'

'No,' Seerey said slowly, thinking about it. 'I'd feel uncomfortable not being able to actually watch the lock and know he's not tampering with it. Unless someone stayed in there all the time, which I don't like either. I want us to keep together. If you made an extra one, that'd be different.'

'No,' Lee exclaimed. 'We should save it, because if we *knew* Vasta was in his Cryogenics Module, we could sneak up and put the lock between Accommodation and Judy's Earth Science! That would give us access to the whole left side *and* the Galley and Accommodation Modules. It would solve all our problems.'

'I should try it, anyway,' Dawkins said gruffly.

Seerey shook his head. 'Let's see if we can jigger this intercom system first. It might take a lot of the risk out of things. Sending you out into Engineering is risky enough, right now.'

Opening the hatchway was a tense moment. Dawkins eased the hatch aside, preparing to slam it again, expecting a white, naked arm to come snaking through at any moment. Then, crawling out of the access tunnel at the other end he waited for an attack from the hidden corners next to the hatchway. Again, it didn't happen.

Seerey watched through the access tunnel, looking to see if the opposite hatchway darkened with Vasta's figure. Encouraged, Dawkins grabbed the soldering iron and some small pliers, then stuffed several screwdrivers into his pockets which he knew they'd need to open the intercom console. No one yelled a warning, so he looked about for anything else they might find useful, especially anything that might make the hatch-locks more secure. He managed to gather a few more things in his arms when Seerey called urgently.

'I think he's coming! Get out of there!'

Dawkins didn't wait. He fled, worming his way through the access tunnel back into the Command Module, trying not to lose any of his haul in the process. He didn't look backwards, but Seerey hesitated a moment before shutting the hatch. Long enough to see two arms and a bald head begin to emerge from the far tunnel.

'How does he *know*?' Dawkins asked, catching his breath between words. 'How does that bastard know we're outside?' No one could answer him.

Doctoring the intercom console was a long and involved procedure, made more difficult by the chain of instructions coming up from Ground Control and relayed by Celia to Seerey and Dawkins, who worked with more hope than expertise among the jungle of wiring. It worked though, and Seerey let out a whoop as the speaker crackled into life when the last wire touched its terminal. Immediately they heard a sound—a voice—and stopped to listen. Judith didn't need to say, 'That's him.'

'Quick, solder it,' Seerey told Dawkins, who held the soldering iron. The job finished, they concentrated on the voice. It was Vasta, and his monologue revealed a new and disturbing side of him.

'I am he, but this body is forlorn and weak, like his spirit.'

A pause, filled with stertorous, laboured breathing.

'And I am she, but she is mine now. She suffers within us and that is well. Her screaming strengthens me.'

More agonised breathing, as if the act of speaking required a huge effort.

'This foul body needs strength. That fool apostle erred and he will pay, when his time comes. I need strength. I need Donald. They must give me Donald.'

In the Command Module the astronauts stared at each other.

'What's he saying?' Judith asked.

Celia explained, 'He's saying Donald is responsible for his condition—Donald and Joseph King. And he thinks Donald can make him better. That's where we come in. He thinks one of *us* must be Donald—' She stopped as Vasta spoke again. This time he mentioned a new name. One nobody recognised.

'They must give me Donald, or give me Kindling. I want Matthew Kindling.'

Vasta forced their hand. The astronauts' plan to lock off the access tunnel between the Accommodation and the Earth Science modules depended on ensuring Vasta would leave the Cryogenic Module to investigate something on the right side of Freedom while somebody crept up the left to seal the access tunnel. It was crucial he went the correct way.

The intercom system was left on. Vasta's mutterings, while strange, intriguing, and of course frightening, became monotonous to listen to. Sometimes he lapsed into an incomprehensible language no one could understand, but when he was lucid it was always the same. The theme never changed. He hated the body he now possessed and wanted Donald. The name Kindling arose now and again, but when Seerey queried Ground Control about the name his request was acknowledged, processed—and not answered, until a rather bland explanation eventually came from Louise Corry. He watched the controlled expression on her face as she spoke, and Seerey suddenly realised that other things had been happening on Earth. Things they should have been told about. He tried to think of a way to ask her without causing a furore. He thought she might tell him, if she could.

Then the power died in the Command Module.

It was different this time. It wasn't like the sudden blackouts of before. The different systems dropped out gradually. After the initial shock of the module converting to emergency lighting—normal lighting was power consuming and always one of the first electrical facilities to fail—Celia hastened to stop the others' confused and frightened cursing.

'Look,' she said, pointing at the various systems still operating. As they watched the equipment closed the systems down one by one, as Freedom's software decided just how much the reduced power supply could handle. 'It's the load-shed on the Closed-Loop Life-Support System, not the Revival program.'

'Oh, you're kidding!' Seerey burst out. 'Right now, on top of this shit, we've got a normal hardware failure?'

Without answering Celia moved quickly to the intercom master and keyed in commands. Nobody had noticed anything unusual in Vasta's muttering voice, but then again they hadn't been paying close attention. Celia killed the intercom and looked pointedly at the others as Vasta's voice vanished. Then she keyed in only the Airlock Module, where the Life Support System operated. The growling monologue returned.

'He's there,' she said. 'He's done it. He's overloaded the damn Cloop system. We're running on batteries right now.'

'How the hell did he do that?' Seerey said, exasperated.

'Easy,' she replied. 'Just press every button in sight until the system says "I don't understand" and closes down.'

Only Dawkins didn't grasp the significance of what had happened. In the overlapping style of NASA's training it was one of the few areas he wasn't familiar with. He looked around at their grave faces. 'How long does it take to reset it?' he asked, glancing at the computer station.

'Uh-uh,' Celia shook her head. 'As long as it takes to press the big green button on the side of the Cloop plant.'

'In the Airlock Module? You have to do it manually?' He was appalled.

'You got it.'

Lee was manipulating the controls of the intercom. She announced, 'I think he's on the move again. He sounds stronger in the—' She fell silent and concentrated on her adjustments. Vasta's voice came through clearly again. 'That's Accommodation,' she said, then a minute later, 'Now he's in the Galley. Do you think he might be coming all the way here?' She looked anxiously at the others.

A groaning, electronic sound came from the intercom. It took a moment for someone—Dawkins—to recognise it. 'That's the meal dispenser,' he said, frowning.

Seerey glanced at the emergency lighting around them. 'How come that's still operating?'

Celia replied, 'Feeding us is an essential service. It'd be one of the last things to be cut off.'

'So what's he doing? Preparing a banquet?'

'Who knows?'

Seerey informed Ground Control of the latest problem. The voice of the duty controller—they were reduced to audio communications only—almost sounded bored at yet another cry for help from Freedom. Angrily, Seerey returned to the intercom. 'They don't give a damn.' He noticed the meal dispenser was still operating. 'What the hell? How much can the bastard eat?'

Lee looked worried. 'It consumes a lot of power. Scott thinks he might be using it to wear down the batteries. Force us out of here.'

Seerey's anger disappeared instantly. Dawkins agreed with a nod.

'Yeah, he's getting smarter.'

Ten minutes later they were still arguing with Judith Cianta. The Closed-Loop Life-Support System was her speciality outside her own field. 'I tell you, not only can I reset it,' she repeated strongly, 'but I can program the thing to supply a standard replenishment cycle without it needing to respond to demand. Once it's locked into that mode, I doubt if our friendly freak could overload it again. He'd have to know those codes, too. And we can do it *now*, while he's fooling around in the Galley. It's perfect.'

'I'm sure I could remember how to do it,' Seerey said, repeating himself.

'I keep *telling* you, I can't remember enough to explain it to you. I need to see the prompt-and-response program on the control panel to jog my memory.'

'You could guide me over the intercom.'

'Alex, please don't argue anymore. I can do it. It will be quicker and simpler.'

Seerey scowled and tried to think of objections. Instead, Dawkins suggested his own plan.

'Alex, why don't you go with her?'

'Sure, I can try to look after her,' he accepted reluctantly. 'It's not as good as me doing it on my own.'

'So, once you kick the Cloop back into life, what's going to happen? Vasta's going to come chasing back after you, right?'

'Yes, and that's what worries—'

Dawkins cut him off. 'But you'll still have three or four minutes to get out of there. Plenty of time. Enough time, in fact, for you to bring back that auxiliary air cylinder we disconnected, too. Just in case.'

'What's on your mind, Scott?'

Dawkins looked sly. 'So, why don't I sneak up to the Galley and wait until our freak takes off after you, then follow him and lock him out of the Accommodation Module? That way we know where he is, and where he's heading.' He smiled. 'The bastard can chase us around in circles for a change.'

'That could work,' Lee offered enthusiastically. Seerey frowned.

'Come on, Alex,' Judith insisted. 'Lee's right. It *will* work. We can get on top of this situation, keep that freak alive and ourselves safe. But we have to do it now, before he gets bored with the meal dispenser.'

Seerey looked undecided, so Dawkins pressed him. 'Either that, or we try to lock him out without really knowing where he is. The longer we wait, the more systems Freedom will drop out to conserve power. The intercom will go soon. Then we'll be finished. We'll have to attempt resetting the Cloop system without having a clue where he is. He might pick us off one by one.' Still Seerey didn't reply. Dawkins gestured at the blank comm-link. 'The hurricane's still there, Alex. No one's coming to save us in a hurry. We'll run out of power and air before they get a shuttle off the pad.'

Seerey suddenly put up his hands in defeat. 'Okay, okay. We'll do it your way. I'll go with Judith and you try and lock him out. We can go without food and water for a few days, but I'm damned if we can go without a fucking toilet.'

Seerey and Judith left first, aware that even if they didn't achieve their object, they might still draw Vasta into a short pursuit allowing Dawkins to close off half of Freedom behind him. Lee sat at the intercom master and deftly controlled the settings, blanking out sections of the space station to concentrate on the areas where the astronauts would be. In the Galley the meal dispenser still noisily spat out meals. She guessed supplies of those must run out soon.

Seerey led the way with Judith following close behind. Once again the interior of Freedom looked strange and alien in the dim red emergency lighting. Lee would call a warning over the intercom if she thought there was even a hint of danger, but still Seerey felt extremely nervous. His eyes flicked into the corners of the modules as soon as they came into view. Behind him he could hear Judith's quick breathing. The first three modules were almost friendly territory, but as they approached the junction which led to the Earth Science Module and the Airlock, Seerey felt they were crossing into Vasta's territory. His apprehension grew, but he managed to turn and give Judith a reassuring grin.

Moving through the access tunnel into the Airlock he glanced left into the Earth Science section. It was hard to see far and much of it was hidden from this angle, but it looked empty. Then they were in the Airlock itself, and past the point where they could be cut off if they didn't move fast enough.

Judith pushed past him and went straight to the complex jumble of cylinders and pipes that was the Closed-Loop Life-Support System—the 'Cloop'. A control panel glowed with red lights. She had to put her face right up to the LED display in the dim light, but grunted her satisfaction and began tapping in commands. Meanwhile Seerey detached the auxiliary air tank and held it at the ready to take out with him.

'How's it going?' he asked her nervously.

'Nearly.'

More commands went in, then she lifted herself to another, less complicated control above the first. 'Ready?' she looked down at him. He nodded back. Judith pressed the green button and the Cloop system moaned into life. Moments later the normal lighting flickered back. Equipment all around them clicked and whirred into operation.

'Let's get the hell out of here,' he snapped.

They went quickly to the access tunnel, Seerey pushing the air tank in front of him. At the hatchway he lined the cylinder up and gently propelled it through the tunnel, then pulled himself after it to catch the tank, before it collided with something. He was in the Utilities Module now, feeling safer already, and he turned back to check Judith was right behind him. To Seerey's alarm she had stopped at the far end of the access tunnel.

'Come on, Jude!' he called. 'What's wrong?'

'The inner Airlock door,' she shouted back, her voice thinned by the tunnel. 'Remember Celia wanted it open so she could try overriding the Airlock software? I'm going to do it. It won't take a moment.' Without giving him a chance to argue she turned around.

Seerey went to the lip of the hatchway and watched, his heart thudding in his chest. He wanted her out of there. Judith quickly undogged the inner door and swung it wide open. There was no way of clipping it in place, so she looked around for some means of jamming it there.

'Forget it,' he yelled. 'That's good enough.' He was glad to see her nod and push herself towards the exit.

Something large and white came into Seerey's vision from his left, entering the access tunnel from the Earth Science Module. Instinctively he jerked away backwards. As Vasta's figure filled the tunnel, cutting the two astronauts off from each other, Dawkins' frantic voice burst out of the intercom. Over that Seerey heard Judith scream.

Dawkins crept carefully into the Astronomy Module, the ingredients for one of his improvised locks in one hand. Like Seerey, he tried to see into the furthest corners of the gloom, watching for any sign that he wasn't alone. His skin crawled as he traversed the access tunnel into the Minerals Laboratory. He intended to stay here until the power restored itself. Through the next hatchway he should be able to see Vasta leave the Galley to return to the Airlock. Dawkins tried to disregard the gnawing anxiety about the way Vasta seemed to sense their presence outside the Command Module. The astronaut was banking on his being too absorbed in the meal dispenser.

There was no sign of movement through the hatchway, and finally Dawkins crept up to the tunnel and peered through. It was a strange sight. Dozens of meals, their silver aluminium trays glinting in the red light, hung suspended in the air like a toy universe or an invasion of miniature flying saucers. The meal dispenser ground on, slowly spitting out more food. But nothing else moved.

'Where are you, you freak?' Dawkins whispered. He strained his ears, listening for sounds of muttering or breathing, but heard neither. He sensed trouble—big trouble and an impending tragedy—and overcame his fear enough to push himself into the access tunnel, but like an animal hiding in its burrow he stopped short of going out the other end. He waited for an arm to dart inside and drag him through. Dawkins listened again, but apart from the meal dispenser he heard nothing. With a burst of bravado he launched himself through the hatchway, expecting to be snared into a strong grasp and ready to fight furiously, madly.

He was alone in the module. Sucking in huge, relieved gasps of air Dawkins looked around. He pushed aside the food trays that drifted around him like bothersome insects. But the Galley held no darkened corners. He was definitely by himself. His thoughts were interrupted as the power flickered back to life in the module, making Dawkins jump nervously. The Life Support was restored. Half the equipment kicked into operation with the restored electricity and he quickly moved around the module, shutting it down again. As he finished, he let out a quiet cheer to himself, but the noise died on his lips as it suddenly dawned on him. What was he doing wasting time and fooling around like this? If Vasta wasn't here in the Galley, where the hell was he?

'Christ, Alex and Judith!' He rushed to the meal dispenser and looked at the controls. Vasta had programmed in countless meals to be produced while he wasn't there. Cursing himself again for getting his priorities wrong Dawkins went to the intercom, depressed the switch and yelled into it. Then he realised he was probably turning the unit off instead, so he shouted out, 'Alex! Look out! He's not in the Galley anymore.'

As he called, Dawkins heard a scream followed by confused shouting. His instincts told him to run, to get back to the Command Module. But his courage and commonsense said this might be the only chance they had of confining Vasta to one half of Freedom. The sounds he heard didn't necessarily mean the other two weren't escaping, exactly as planned. God knew, he'd probably scream too, if he was face to face with Vasta.

Against all his better judgement Dawkins headed further into the space station.

Vasta ignored Seerey and turned into the Airlock, moving towards Judith. She tried to back away and saw herself heading for the Cryogenics Module, a very bad option. Then she realised the Airlock chamber was at her back and she moved into it, desperately hauling the door closed with her.

But Vasta caught the spokes of the dogging mechanism and pulled the door out of her hands. Sobbing, she edged into the chamber with Vasta following. Seerey was shouting, but she couldn't understand him, her mind filled with terror. The outer door pressed against her shoulder blades and there was nowhere to hide.

Vasta brought his face close to hers. The dead eyes bored into hers, his rancid breath washed over her cheeks. One hand groped her waist, her breasts, squeezing them painfully, then slid down to grip her crotch. The other hand, the fingers slick and cold, closed around her neck with massive strength. Judith started screaming and tried with all her might to twist away.

Intentionally or not, the grip at her throat snapped Judith's neck like a dry stick, cutting off her last sounds.

At that moment Seerey appeared at the Airlock doorway. He held the spare cylinder above his shoulder—he'd dragged it back in with him, the only weapon he could think of. He let out a howl of anguish as he understood the scene before him. Judith hung limply in Vasta's grasp like prey in a bird's talons. The angle of her head and the empty, staring eyes told him she was dead. He'd been too slow. Vasta didn't bother with Seerey, instead bending over his captive, drool drifting from his open mouth as he fumbled with her clothing.

With an animal snarl Seerey thrust the cylinder at Vasta's head. The bottom edge caught him at the back of his skull and there was a gentle cracking sound like an eggshell. Clear fluid, mixed with blood, oozed from the wound. Pieces of skin and tiny skull fragments stuck to the base of the cylinder.

Vasta grunted at the impact, then straightened and pushed the tank away. He twisted his head to look at Seerey. His eyes were glazed and tendrils of dribble interlaced over his face. A cloud of blood was forming at the base of his skull. '*You will be next.*' The guttural voice bubbled with phlegm.

Seerey fled from the Airlock, fear numbing his mind while his limbs automatically took him away from the horror in the Airlock. Vasta didn't pursue him, though he was probably capable of catching him now, with his greater strength and improved agility. But there were other things on his mind as he ripped at Judith Cianta's clothing.

All Dawkins saw as he came to the end of the Accommodation Module was Seerey's legs and feet disappearing through the distant access tunnel. Dawkins waited, and when Judith didn't appear as well he assumed she must be in front of Seerey. He allowed himself a small cheer as he backed away and slammed the hatchway closed. He made doubly sure his locking device was secure and decided a second wouldn't hurt either. He might do that when he returned.

'Let's hear it for the good guys,' he said happily to himself. He'd pick something up from the Galley on his way through for a little celebration back in the Command Module.

When Vasta finished with her, he revelled in his triumph. He'd taken her life, her essence and even her knowledge, drawing it from her like water from a well. Only the woman's spirit had slipped through his fingers, his focus destroyed at that vital moment by the man's attack. The loss made him angry, but his ire was tempered with the knowledge that other opportunities would come. And there were other women, too.

Vasta left Judith's broken body in the Airlock and closed the inner door. Then he went to the Closed-Loop Life-Support System and slowly, meticulously, reversed the procedure Judith had given her life to initiate.

The system overloaded and Freedom yet again went onto emergency power.

Vasta waited. They would have to come out again.

23

'MY GUESS WOULD BE around eighteen hours,' Czowkowski offered. His chair squeaked as he leaned back and put his hands above his head. He reviewed his calculations. 'Maybe twenty at the most.'

'That's all the air they've got to breathe?' Louise was amazed. 'Half the space station and only four of them now?'

'No, that's about all the time they've got before the lack of *good* atmosphere forces them to act. After that they'll be getting headaches, feeling lethargic, and that'll be the end. No one'll want to try and save themselves. They might actually live for twice that long, I suppose, but they'll be just lying around feeling like shit.'

'Any news on a shuttle launch?'

'Twenty-four hours before they even look at it.' Czowkowski didn't need to tell the others what this meant.

Kindling stood in a corner, sipping mechanically on a cup of coffee. Apart from Bennington, who was too overtired to sleep, they were alone in the Control Room. The events of the last few days weighed heavily on Kindling. He felt responsible somehow, in a way he couldn't explain. He wanted desperately to talk to Louise again, to get her opinion and advice. Now Czowkowski's tragic forecast made him feel even worse, and he moved closer.

'Isn't there anything we can do?' he asked.

The operator twisted in his seat to look at him. 'They can only help themselves, unless we can get some people up there.'

'They just tried that, and it got somebody killed,' Kindling said bitterly. 'There must be something we can do,' he muttered. After a moment he put his coffee cup down and excusing himself, left the room.

Kindling went outside and sat under the tree where he and Louise had earlier whiled away the empty hours. Beyond the perimeter fence traffic still flowed unceasingly, the vehicles' occupants unaware that time and a hurricane called Ben had condemned four astronauts to their deaths, either by asphyxiation or at the hands of a monstrous, scientific miscalculation. Kindling acutely wished he, too, could be ignorant. Go back in time to when he knew nothing about astronauts, cryogenics, or Space Station Freedom.

He'd hoped getting out into the open air, away from the sterile confines of the Control Room, would help him relax. But his melancholy deepened. Kindling realised that even miraculously going back in time wouldn't save him from this crisis. It would only come again in a different guise. All the signs were there for him to see.

'I am he, but this body is forlorn and weak, like his spirit.'

Did anyone else notice when Vasta began to speak of himself in the third person? And the harsh, guttural voice. Kindling had heard that ruined, throaty rasp before—in the Williams' front room two years ago. And in his dreams ever since.

'And I am she, but she is mine now. Her screaming strengthens me.'

The young girl's spirit was a part of him, too. She was an innocent bystander, caught up in events through a criminal, if well-meaning, act by a principled doctor. The surgeon had no idea what torment he'd inflicted on Ellen Littlewood. Kindling could only be thankful her parents now believed it was all over.

'They must give me Donald, or give me Kindling. I want Matthew Kindling.'

The others in the Control Room knew who Vasta meant. Kindling had been standing right there with them. But only Kindling realised it wasn't Vasta asking for him. It was somebody—*something*—else calling his name through the walking corpse. Perhaps Louise Corry understood. She'd been quick to tell the astronauts that Kindling had provided religious guidance for Vasta during his life, glossing over the facts as if they were of little importance. Still, NASA was actually considering taking Kindling up on the relief shuttle, a notion that terrified him. It had been done before, apparently. Senators, Congressmen, all sorts of influential civilians who might put in a kind word for NASA's funding had been given the ultimate joyride. It wasn't the spaceflight that worried Kindling. It was the thought of confronting his nemesis in a totally alien, hostile environment. Things were going to be bad enough as it was.

He accepted it was a confrontation that had to come.

'Penny for your thoughts.' It was Louise, walking across the grass towards him.

'Hello, stranger,' he waved.

She sat next to him and offered a drink from a can of coke she carried. He took it and as he sipped, she said, 'It's been a couple of hectic days.'

'I thought I might have seen you last night.'

'I had a lot of phone calls to make. Long calls, too. By the time I'd finished and had a shower, I just fell into bed. I was going to give you a call, but it was late. I figured you'd be asleep already.' She took the drink back and saw the despondent look in his eyes. 'Hey, I still have a life beyond all this, you know.'

'I know. I'm sorry.'

'My, we are cheerful. There's still hope left up there. It's the only way we should be thinking. That's how I want to look at it.'

He made a frustrated gesture, then grasped her hands in his. 'Lou, if we come out of all this in one piece, can we go away together for a while? Say, two weeks, just you and me. Are you allowed to do that? We could go anywhere. I'm rich—by my normal standards, anyway. I'll pay.' He stared into her eyes, then suddenly dropped his gaze, embarrassed by his outburst. 'Look, it—ah, probably sounds a bit stupid. It only occurred to me just now.'

'No, not at all,' she said quietly. Louise looked at him for a long time, making her decision. 'I could do that,' she said carefully, adding with a quirky smile, 'And I'd pay my own way, thank you very much.' Her expression turned serious. 'But there'd be no strings attached, Matt. Just two weeks of fun somewhere, without any pressure from either of us.'

'I won't bring any strings, if you don't bring any reservations,' he countered, looking up. 'An open mind, that's all.'

'Okay, it's a deal. Where are we going to go?' Louise admitted to herself that she liked the idea.

'Who cares? We'll think of somewhere.' He leaned forward and kissed her quickly on the forehead. 'Thank you,' he said simply.

She was glad he didn't gush any rash promises. In fact, he slumped down again and looked moodily at the ground between his feet. 'Thanks a lot,' she nudged him. 'Now you've just twisted my arm into something, you don't seem particularly overjoyed I accepted.'

'It's not that. It's something else. This situation is getting very bad, and very personal for me. I'm beginning to feel responsible, too, though I know that doesn't make much sense.'

'I know what you mean.' She paused, 'Why does Vasta want you?'

'It's not Vasta.'

Louise sighed. 'I thought you were going to tell me that.'

He flicked his fingers at the sky. 'Oh, Vasta's in there somewhere. Suppressed in some way, I think. And poor Ellen Littlewood. But the main entity driving that corpse around is the same thing I met in Allen Williams that day. Remember? The cripple in the wheelchair. The start of all my problems.' He rubbed his face tiredly.

'How could I forget?' she murmured. 'What a story.'

His manner changed, and he became thoughtful, forcing the despondency back. Louise listened, fascinated. 'I've been trying to work it out. I think we've been the victims of an amazing coincidence. This—demon, for want of a better, a *correct* word—has been waiting for his chance at me. God knows why, I certainly don't. But Vasta dabbled in the occult, and so did Joseph King, and between the two of them I think they opened a door. And he came in, using Vasta as an easy ticket. But you know what?' He stared at her, his eyes glittering with inspiration. 'I think he made a mistake. I don't think he expected to be where he is—in fact I don't think he *knows* where he is. In orbit. In space.' He pointed a finger at his own chest. 'I'll bet he thinks I'm in the Command Module with the others—except he doesn't think of it as a Command Module. He thinks it's another strange room in a strange place.'

Louise looked doubtful. 'How can you say that? The sort of—of *being* we're talking about? Surely it must know everything.'

'Perhaps not,' Kindling sighed, staring into the distance. 'Perhaps it's like us in some way—it can only know what it experiences or learns itself. It might be hundreds or thousands of years old. Who knows? It may be an immortal being of some kind. Still, it can't know of certain things until Mankind manages to create them—and this demon could well be behind the times a little. I mean, why *should* it know about things like cellular phones or fibre optics? Or space stations,' he added, pointedly.

She finished her drink and looked at the aluminium can in her hand. Slowly she crushed it between her fingers. 'So, what the hell can we do about it? Anything?'

'We've already been doing the wrong thing.'

'Wrong? What do you mean?'

'We could draw the thing back down here, out of Vasta's body,' Kindling said, the theory forming as he spoke. 'But we've closed the best avenues we've had for doing that, like Ellen Littlewood's room. There was a real contact there between the world down here and the entity in Freedom, but we've destroyed that bridge along with the room.'

'I think I know what you mean,' Louise said slowly. 'So, what about his house?'

'It's not the same. That's full of all *his* preparations. Ellen's room was a place of worship for Dan and Georgina, created by them. I could *see* the intensity of emotion filling the place. It was a shrine in honour of their daughter.'

'Which we burnt to the ground,' she nodded grimly. 'But all the same, you think it might be possible to bring this demon out of Vasta's body down to Earth? Like an exorcism?'

He shook his head. 'Not an exorcism. They are very complex and strict rituals and I wouldn't have the first clue how to perform one. But if there was some way we could make contact with Vasta, we might be able to make him an offer he can't refuse. At least tempt him.'

'Like—with what?' Louise looked at him suspiciously, knowing the answer and not liking it one bit.

'Me, of course.'

Louise finally agreed they should talk it over with somebody else. Michael Lay was the obvious choice. They avoided the abrasive Wiley and his assistant. Kindling was surprised at the ease with which Louise contacted Lay, and how readily he agreed to meeting them somewhere the Americans wouldn't accidentally stumble across them. It wasn't that there was anything secretive in what they wanted to discuss. Only that the theory was so improbable, even preposterous, to someone used to dealing with normal, everyday values, they both decided it was best to deal with one person at a time.

In the end Michael Lay wasn't sceptical at all, but he quickly pinpointed possible weaknesses. 'Are you talking about a seance? An exorcism down here?' he asked, tapping the table in front of him with a fork. They'd met in a rowdy tavern for lunch. The tables around them were filled with shouting students and workers from a nearby plant. Kindling was concerned that among so many people they might be overheard. Lay smiled and reassured him that everyone was struggling to hear themselves, let alone somebody at the next table. Kindling realised that, as usual, Lay knew exactly what he was doing.

'I don't even know what we can do,' he admitted to Lay. 'But it can't be an exorcism.' He went on to explain again, finishing with, 'I've only got this basic theory that the spirit inside Vasta might be drawn back to Earth, if it thinks it's worth it.'

'And you say *you* are worth it. It wants you that badly?'

'I can't understand its motivation, but yes. It's beyond my experience. The last time I came face to face with this thing, I ran away. But it's been haunting me ever since. The only man I knew who could explain it further is dead. Father Stewart Andrews. I believe he was killed getting rid of this demon from a crippled old man called Allen Williams. That's where I saw it, too, but I ran. I ran from the church as well. Apparently it hasn't done me any good.' Kindling closed his eyes and pinched the bridge of his nose. 'There seems to be some sort of personal vendetta against me.'

Lay looked at them both long and hard, unconsciously pursing his lips as he weighed up the facts. 'What do you think will happen to Vasta, if this works?'

'I don't think he's even alive. Once this spirit leaves, the corpse will simply collapse. The crew will be free to reset their life support again and wait indefinitely for the relief shuttle.'

There was a pause while a harassed waitress came and took their orders. Lay paid and as he concentrated on pulling money from his wallet

Louise gave Kindling a reassuring glance. Then Lay went on, thoughtfully, 'That's obviously what we and NASA would like. Christ, if they lost the entire crew it'd be impossible to cover up. But they couldn't tell the truth, either. NASA would have to concoct some plausible story—a gas leak or something, I suppose. Whatever, it'll cause a sensation.' He stopped to light a cigarette and squinted at them through the smoke. 'What I'm saying is NASA will probably grasp at this straw, though I'm damned if I know how we can explain it to them. One thing I don't understand. What's to stop this thing going back and—what's the term?—repossessing?—Vasta's body?'

'I think he only managed it in the first place because of Vasta's occult worship, and because his body was in a state of suspended animation. And King fooling around with the same stuff would have helped. If this works Vasta will be truly dead, and King's gone.'

Louise was listening patiently, but now she interrupted, frowning. 'Do you mean it will come to Earth hoping to possess you?'

'That, or kill me. Or both, I imagine. I really don't know.' At her alarmed look he broke their rules and reached across and took her hand. 'Lou, it's going to happen anyway,' he insisted. 'If not this time, then the next, or if I avoid it again, the time after that. One day I'll have to face this thing. I should do it now, while I'm still young and strong. And I have the incentive to help those people in the space station. It doesn't *have* to go his way. I must be able to fight it off somehow.'

'Using a religion you rejected,' she said flatly.

'You said it killed Stewart Andrews, and he knew more about it than you do.'

'He also told me I was different. I have a special ability—you've seen part of that. I can see things others don't. It might make a difference.'

Louise pulled her hand away and looked out the window. A trace of anger crossed her face. 'It sounds like a stupid sacrifice to me. I didn't realise this is what you meant to do.'

Michael Lay watched them both impassively, drawing on his cigarette. 'But Matthew, you don't know how to do any of this. You admitted that.' Kindling shrugged and nodded, more concerned with Louise's anger for the moment. 'And you said that property in the middle of nowhere is no good, because you burned the girl's room?'

'Everything in it,' Kindling replied. 'Otherwise I might have been able to just step inside it and he'd know. It was like one end of a bridge, with Freedom at the other end.'

'Fascinating,' Lay murmured, lost in thought. 'Vasta's house—no?' He reiterated some of their previous suggestions. Kindling shook his head. 'What about the cellar there? Have you thought about that? You saw the girl's ghost there.'

'The cellar's all I was thinking of, but I'm sure it's different. I didn't *see* the sort of things I saw when I walked into Ellen Littlewood's room. We could try something there, I suppose. But it's a place devoted to rites and rituals I know even less about. We'd be groping in the dark.'

Lay looked sly. 'But there are people who *do* know about Vasta's rituals. He had half a dozen disciples who joined him in that cellar. Perhaps they can give us a clue.'

Louise spoke, a little reluctantly. 'We can find out. I've still got those files. They've been pulled for weeks and I was looking at them just the other day for any reference to a Donald.'

'There you go, it's like it was meant to be,' Lay said with just the smallest hint of a smile. 'Let's look at them again.'

Back in the Control Room Wiley and Smith eyed the three of them suspiciously as they entered. It was obvious they'd been out somewhere together and it wasn't in the Americans' nature to view something like that favourably. Lay ignored their looks and announced, 'Make yourselves comfortable, gentlemen. We have something to discuss.'

But before he said any more he asked Czowkowski for a situation update. The operator reported the surviving crew of Freedom had extended their breathable atmosphere by simply opening the other hatchway into the Engineering Module once they were certain, by listening to the intercom, that Vasta was still in the cryogenics section. They were also trying various methods of manually circulating the air, but it was questionable whether the extra energy expended to do this, and the amount of extra oxygen it consumed, made the effort viable.

Lay did most of the talking, only occasionally referring to Kindling or Louise if some point needed clarifying. The agents greeted his words with mounting disbelief.

Wiley looked openly contemptuous. Finally, he

burst out, 'There's a lot of shit here you should have told us weeks ago, Matthew.'

'You're pretty good at keeping a secret,' Kindling shot back. 'What would you have done?'

'It doesn't matter,' Lay snapped, stopping an argument. 'What's more important is what we're going to do now.'

'And what's that?' Wiley asked. 'Brew up some bat's wings and frog's legs in Vasta's living room? Fax Freedom a ouija board?'

'If that's what it takes, that's what we'll do,' Lay glared at him, daring Wiley to take it further. The American backed down under Lay's steady gaze. 'Now, Lou's got some files here on people who used to join Vasta down in that cellar. The idea is we go through them and see if we can decide whether any of them might give us a clue on how that cellar worked—with bat's wings or frog's legs, if necessary.' When Wiley didn't comment Lay let his eyes move to Louise. 'Lou, could you get those files, please?'

Louise went to her desk and pulled six manila folders from a drawer and gave them to Lay. He in turn handed one to each of them except Czowkowski, keeping two for himself. He pointedly put one on the benchtop beside him.

'To speed this up, everybody read their file and form their own impressions. Then swap with somebody without discussing it, and do it again.'

There was a rustle of paper as everyone opened the files. Wiley dared a heavy sigh and gave Smith a resigned look, but didn't speak. Lay let it go. Silence followed as they read. There were a few moments of impatience as some finished their files faster than others and had to wait for somebody to exchange with. Kindling couldn't help feeling he was back at school. It didn't help when Czowkowski rolled his eyes at him theatrically. Louise closed her second file and announced she was going to get a pot of coffee while the others finished reading. By the time she returned, carrying a tray laden with the pot, mugs, milk and sugar, everyone had come to the end of their files.

'Well?' Lay began. 'Any suggestions?'

Wiley's voice was harsh with derision. 'It's a bunch of bored housewives and suck-holing executives hoping to stay in favour by playing the boss's silly games.'

'Some of those silly games might have involved the ritual sacrifice of real people,' Lay reminded him thinly.

'So? It was still playing games. And you've got absolutely no proof of that, anyway,' Wiley added, trying to score points.

Lay turned away from him in disgust, and looked at Louise for a more considered evaluation. She looked apologetic.

'I have to agree, Michael. None of these people amounted to anything within Vasta's organisation, which is probably why he invited them to join in this stuff. He didn't want to risk being laughed at by more important associates. And none of them appear to have taken the occult any further than that cellar. Not like Vasta, who really wanted to cheat his disease. There's no one here who might have taken over as a leader since his death. These activities finished when he died.' She gestured at the stack of files now sitting beside him. 'If you want one person out of those who might help, I say take your pick. Maybe take the most successful one, business-wise. But they're all leading normal lives now—almost as they did before. And my guess is they won't want to remember much about the times they killed chickens or puppies in Vasta's cellar, or whatever they used to do. *Especially* if they went overboard sometime and sliced up a human being.'

Kindling was confused and hurt by the way everyone calmly discussed the possibility of murders taking place and the way such subjects didn't appear to touch them emotionally. He had to clear his throat before asking, 'What about the last one?' He nodded at the final, unread file. It was much thicker than the others. Lay picked it up and flourished it.

'This young lady would be our best bet, but unfortunately she disappeared shortly before Vasta's death. In fact, she's the strongest candidate for having ended up on that wooden table,' Lay said sadly. Kindling was sure he regretted her unavailability, not her death. 'She was younger than the others and single. In and out of foster homes, youth detention centres. She narrowly missed going inside properly on a dealing charge when she was nineteen. They gaoled her for twenty-four hours and released her on parole. That's why we have so much more information about her. We also know she was quite heavily into the occult, in an adolescent sort of way. She wore the T-shirts, got a "devil" tattoo and fooled with midnight seances in cemeteries.' Lay stopped to refer to the file. 'In the last year she joined two witches' covens, but dismissed them as a collection of Mr Wiley's bored housewives. The second group wasn't quite so boring—that's where she got nearly a quarter of a kilo of cocaine. Beats the *Midday Show*, I guess.' He went on, 'Anyway, she met up with Vasta and joined his group. Two months later she didn't meet a parole deadline. In fact, she never met another one. It was only because of her association with Vasta that we looked a little harder, but not a trace came up. If we'd had due cause the garden around his house would've been searched, because that's where she is, I'll bet, fertilising the roses. Either that, or she got her witch act together and flew away on her damn broom.' Lay tried to snap the file shut, but the pages bulged and flapped. 'None of which helps us at all. She's gone.'

Louise gestured helplessly for all of them. 'So, where does that leave us?'

There was a silence and Lay looked heavily at Kindling. 'Back to the house, I suppose. It's the only shot we've got—and I know it's not a very good one.'

Wiley laughed cruelly, knowing Lay would hate what he was going to say. 'Which is exactly what I wanted us to do about seven damn days ago.' He looked around at them, his expression both mocking and triumphant.

24

IT WAS NEARLY DUSK by the time they had organised torches, tools and transport out to Vasta's house. For Kindling the place didn't seem so threatening in the twilight, although dark shadows gathered and quickly grew around the shrubs and gardens. It helped having other people with him, too.

They parked at the front gate. Lay went to the boot of their vehicle and took out a pair of large bolt cutters. The chain around the main gates fell to the ground in a cascade of chinking metal.

'Whatever happens, we're going to be in trouble with his lawyers,' he explained, shrugging. Kindling looked nervously around for outraged neighbours, but no one raised any alarm. He figured the big plain white cars, with their distinctive government plates would go unchallenged.

As they walked up the winding driveway the sun sank behind the high garden walls. The night insects started their chorus of calls and the air temperature immediately chilled by several degrees. In front of them the darkened house looked forbidding. The black squares of the windows were like the hollow eyes of a sick man, and seemed to watch the five people approach. Their feet crunched on the gravel driveway. Michael Lay led the way with Louise and Kindling beside him. The two Americans followed close behind. Wiley muttered comments to Smith, still crowing that Lay considered this too legally hazardous to do only a week or so before, but was now prepared to justify the break and enter chasing a vague hunch. Kindling couldn't tell if Lay heard or not.

'Where did you get in?' Lay asked him suddenly.

'The back door. It was open.'

Lay grunted. 'I doubt we'll be that lucky this time.'

Kindling went to the lead, and took them around the side of the house where he'd run for his life. As they came to the open brick-paved patio he saw the swimming pool fence and on impulse went over to it. The water was in deep shadow, so Kindling shone his torch. In the late dusk the beam threw only a weak orange light, but it was enough to reveal that it *was* water, brackish and ill-tended—not blood. No body floated there, either.

'What are you looking for?' Lay asked, waiting.

'Nothing. Just a thought.' Kindling glanced at Louise and she nodded. To distract any more questions Kindling went straight to the kitchen door. 'It was this one—' he began, flipping open the screen door and experimentally twisting the handle. Once again, to his surprise, the door fell back under his pressure revealing the black interior of the house.

'Well, well,' Lay murmured, raising his eyebrows. 'Somebody didn't learn their lesson.'

'Or they're expecting us,' Kindling said, suddenly feeling numb. The security alarm hadn't triggered either. He hadn't anticipated anything to come of this visit. His gut feeling was that, despite the cellar, the house didn't possess the same qualities as Ellen Littlewood's room. There was no 'bridge' here to his demon's consciousness. It was just a bad place.

Now, he wasn't so sure.

Shaking off the shiver running down his spine Kindling moved quickly inside and snapped on the light. The fluorescent flickered, then burst into life.

As he came through the door Wiley started to complain, 'Hey—' But he stopped and looked at the torch in his hand with disgust. 'Why the hell did we bring these things?'

'To look in the garden, if we have to,' Lay told him absently. He was intently examining the room.

'Kitchen,' Kindling muttered unnecessarily, then moved to the two doors in the corner. He pointed through the archway. 'This is an extension of the patio. The glass doors open out to make it a sort of covered outdoor area. There's a door at the end which goes straight into the garage.' He nodded at the other entrance. 'This goes through to the dining room and the main living room.' In the dining room Kindling noticed the chair he'd thrown at Ellen Littlewood's spirit was neatly back in its place. Without waiting for the others he walked through to the living room, paused a moment while he remembered where the light switch was, then turned it on.

The whole room was neatly restored back to its former splendour. Only the shelves above the bar were bare—the exploded bottles had not been replaced. The rug in the centre of the room lay flat, hiding the trapdoor.

'Nice place,' Wiley said, pushing past. 'Someone's cleaned up, huh?' He looked doubtfully at Kindling. He turned to Lay. 'Did anyone report Matthew's little visit? According to him there should have been a real mess left behind.'

'No, nobody called the police. Nothing I've been told about, anyway.' Lay stepped away from the doorframe to let Smith and Louise pass inside. They all watched Kindling go down into the sunken area and pull back the rug, revealing the trapdoor.

'There it is,' he called.

In the silence that followed Wiley decided, 'Not very original, but a neat job.'

Kindling used the fingerhole to haul the trap upwards. This time it came more easily. 'You'll need the torches,' he said, indicating the dark hole. 'Unless you want to light the candles.' He waited for another smart comment from Wiley, but the American was silent. Lay came over, briefly flashed his torch into the cellar and climbed down the ladder. Louise followed him, then Wiley. Smith contented himself with lying flat on the floor and putting his head through the trap. Kindling, having seen it before and also aware of the restricted space down there, stayed where he was. From below he heard the echoing exclamations of the others as they discovered the mural above them and the pile of cloaks. While he waited he looked around nervously for the cat to appear, worried it might attack him again. At the moment, his nervous system could do well without it.

They spent some time inspecting the cellar, finally emerging and comparing their impressions. Wiley and Smith disappeared in the direction of the main hallway. Louise and Lay gathered around Kindling and looked at him expectantly.

'Well?' Lay asked. 'What do you think?'

Kindling stared back at him, confused. 'What do I think? You *know* what I think—'

Lay cut him off. 'You know what I mean. What do you *feel*? Anything? This whole thing was your idea, remember.'

Kindling was about to protest. It had been more of a general consensus to try the house again, but he saw Louise's warning look. Instead, he tried to relax and take in the room around him. After a moment he shrugged, 'There's nothing here. Not like I experienced back on the property. There's something missing.'

'What if you go down into the cellar on your own? Maybe we could close the door after you. We'd keep watch.'

Kindling eyed the hole in the floor reluctantly. He didn't like that idea at all. Louise came to his rescue.

'Michael, I know what he means. Even I could pick a certain feeling in that girl's room. Something that's just not here now.'

Lay stared at her, trying to decide if she was genuine or just trying to avoid incarcerating Kindling in the cellar. 'Right,' he said slowly. At that moment muffled, bumping sounds came from above them. Lay cast his eyes up and frowned. 'That's Wiley, checking out the upstairs. There isn't any damn need, it's all history up there. I don't think they can help themselves,' he added, shaking his head. He turned back to Kindling. 'Well, Matthew, the ball appears to be—'

Kindling held his finger to his lips, watching the doorway. Lay and Louise followed his gaze. Slinking through the door was the black cat. Kindling was again surprised at the animal's size, even though he'd seen it before.

'Jesus, I thought you said it was a *cat*,' Lay whispered.

'It *is* a damn cat,' Kindling hissed back. 'It's just so big.'

The cat watched them as it stalked with feline grace around the perimeter of the room. When the light caught its eyes, they glowed like red hot coals. Lay edged slowly towards the doorway, cutting off the animal's retreat. The cat arched its back and hissed angrily as he came closer, but Lay managed to snick the door closed. The three of them automatically tried to herd the cat into a corner. Seeing the threat it sprang up onto the piano and confronted them, arching its back and exposing the yellowed fangs.

'What an ugly cat,' Louise said.

'It looks diseased,' Lay observed. They kept their voices low, not wanting to alarm it any further.

'What are we trying to do here?' Kindling asked.

'Catch the bloody thing, I suppose. Maybe we can lock it in a cupboard or something. I don't want it attacking us the way it attacked Matthew.'

They closed in. The cat became more skittish as they approached. Lay was setting himself to lunge at the animal when Wiley walked back into the room from the front hallway.

'You guys might be interested to see what we've—'

The cat let out a screeching yowl and leapt away between Lay and Kindling. Cursing, Lay made a desperate grab for it, but missed. The cat scampered with agility off some furniture, headed for the closed door before realising there was no escape there, then bolted for Wiley and the freedom beyond. Kindling had to admire the American's reflexes. Wiley took in the situation, saw the animal coming and flung out one hand to grasp a handful of fur on its back. Spitting fury the cat twisted around and lashed out frantically with its claws. Wiley yelped with pain and his face turned dark. His other hand closed around the cat's neck and Lay, without knowing why, quickly yelled, 'Don't kill it!'

Snarling curses Wiley managed to transfer his hand to the loose skin on the back of the animal's neck, then extricated the other hand, scratched and bleeding, from the cat's grappling forepaws. Hanging from its scruff the animal still impotently hissed and clawed at the air around it for a few moments, then slowly settled to glare at them and utter low growls.

'Shit, what the hell is this?' Wiley cried. They could see he was struggling to hold its weight off the floor.

'This is the cat,' Lay told him, keeping his voice calm. 'Impressive, isn't it?'

'It stinks like hell and it nearly tore my fucking arm off.' Wiley gave the animal a shake and it wailed angrily. 'We'd do it a favour by putting a bullet through it right now.'

'Like hell,' Lay said. 'I want to take it back. Forensics might scrape something interesting off its fur.'

Wiley snorted. 'For Christ's sake, now you're getting really hopeful! Take it back? How? In your damn lap?'

Lay thought a moment. 'In the boot of the car.'

'Well, you can put the bastard in and take it out again,' Wiley laughed without humour and looked down at the cat. Then he looked up. 'I've got something to show you, upstairs. It's important.'

Lay paused, making up his mind. 'Okay.'

Everyone was suddenly undecided except Wiley, who strode over to the trapdoor and dropped the cat through. He quickly closed the trap. 'Somebody else can pick him up again,' he said, rubbing at the scratches on his arm. Lay looked angry, but Wiley ignored him. 'Wait,' he said, going back out to the kitchen. They heard the click of the light switch and he reappeared, turning off the lights in the living room, too.

'Is this necessary?' Lay asked icily.

'Yes. You'll see.'

They all switched on their torches and followed Wiley out of the room into the hallway and up the stairs. In the darkness the house closed in around them. Kindling wasn't particularly interested in what Wiley had found, but didn't want to be left alone. They followed his wavering torch beam into the main bedroom, where Smith waited.

'What happened?' he asked them as soon as they walked in. His face was white and nervous in the reflected torchlight.

'Playing county fucking dogcatcher,' Wiley replied drily. He played his light over the bed and furniture. The bedclothes were rumpled. Items of clothing were strewn about the floor. The dressing table was untidy.

'Somebody's living here?' Lay asked, stating the obvious. 'Is this the only room disturbed?'

Wiley nodded. 'Except for the bathroom. That's being used.'

'Who could it be?' Lay said to himself.

'After the way we stormed in here and turned all the lights on, we'll never find out,' Wiley said contemptuously. 'They'll be hiding outside somewhere, waiting for us to go away. Or they've just made a run for it anyway.'

'Maybe,' Lay muttered, unwilling to concede their mistake. He searched the room while Wiley and Smith looked on. He took his time and their sly amusement eventually turned to impatience. Louise slipped to the bathroom and searched that, followed by Kindling, then came back to the bedroom. 'Okay, okay,' Lay was sighing, 'We fucked up. But there's still a chance whoever it is hasn't tumbled to us. Let's tread quietly and keep our eyes open.' He ignored Wiley's small snort. 'We might as well get out of here. Matthew says there's no point hanging around. He can't pick up anything.' Kindling heard the note of frustration in Lay's voice.

Kindling found himself leading the way downstairs. Everyone walked softly now and tried to keep their torches shining strictly at the floor in front of them. At the base of the staircase Kindling turned to enter the living room and suddenly halted, drawing in his breath sharply. The others jostled against him, but immediately saw what had stopped him.

The edges of the trapdoor glowed with a brilliant, cold blue. Shafts of light escaped past the imperfect seal and speared up to the ceiling. The light fluctuated a moment, grew to a new, higher intensity, then started to fade.

Following Lay's example they all killed their torches and tried to press themselves back into shadows. Kindling felt exposed and vulnerable, still at the front of the group. When the light faded altogether it left everyone completely blind. There was a shuffling noise—the sound of the trapdoor lid being pushed up—followed by the sound of breathing.

A torch suddenly flicked on next to Kindling's face, startling him. The beam captured a young woman dressed in torn jeans, T-shirt and a heavy jacket, as she lowered the trap closed. Her face was a picture of pale fear as she blinked into the torchlight.

'Fuck,' she said, her voice jumping. 'You went upstairs! I thought you bastards had gone.'

There was the click of a weapon being cocked and Lay said clearly, 'You were mistaken. Don't move an inch, understand?'

25

THEY TURNED THE LIGHTS back on. The girl stood unmoving, blinking owlishly at them. Lay gestured with his pistol and she edged away from the trapdoor and sat on the nearest lounge chair. Everyone gathered around her, staring. But they didn't get too close, regarding her in much the same way as the cat. Her hair was dark and long, clean but unkempt. Her wrists, poking from the ends of the jacket, were thin and pale like her face. Her eyes were red-rimmed and sore, a slightly feverish daze within them. She wore white basketball shoes crisscrossed with garish coloured stripes. Kindling recognised some of the signs from his days helping streetkids through the church. This girl was using a lot of drugs. She probably preferred them to a good, square meal.

'Let's start with a name,' Lay said.

'Okay, who are you?' she replied.

'And don't get smart,' Lay snapped.

'Piss off the gun, then. I'm not going anywhere.'

Lay reluctantly agreed, tucking it slowly back under his jacket. 'My guess is Michelle Weldon, right?'

She hesitated. 'If you already knew, why'd you ask?'

Lay glanced at the others and said, 'File number six, remember? Would you believe it, this is our missing girl.' He turned back to her. 'What are you doing here?'

'I live here. This is my place.'

'This house belongs to Anton Vasta.'

'He's dead. He gave it to me.'

'I don't fucking get it,' Wiley suddenly muttered angrily. They watched as he went to the trapdoor, carefully opened it and shone his torch down. 'Where's the cat?' he asked, staring at her.

She pulled a face at Lay. 'Is he for real?' He said nothing. 'I *am* the fucking cat, you jerk,' she told Wiley.

'That's crap.'

'Suit yourself,' she shrugged.

Lay crouched down on his haunches in front of her, bringing his face level with hers. He stared into her eyes a long time. The girl tried to return the stare, but eventually turned her head away and squirmed in the seat.

'We're very impressed,' he said quietly. 'It's not often you get to meet a real, live witch. That's what you are, isn't it? Is that what you call yourself?' She didn't answer. The others were amazed at Lay's calm acceptance.

'How'd you know I was here?'

'We didn't. You're a bonus. Matthew here thought he might be able to talk to somebody. In this house.' He gestured at Kindling and she turned her eyes to him. Kindling could see they were a brilliant green.

She searched his face for a long moment. 'Boy, do you have problems,' she said.

Kindling flinched. 'What's that supposed to mean?'

'I can see them. They're all around you, like a bad smell.' She turned back to Lay, recognising him as the one in authority and dismissing Kindling.

Lay steepled his fingers in front of his face. 'You know, I think you might be able to help us,' he said gently.

'I don't want to help anybody.'

Wiley spoke up harshly, 'Stick your pistol back in her ear and ask again. I'll bet she changes her mind.'

'Who *is* that arsehole?'

Lay ignored her question, though a frown crossed his face at Wiley's outburst. He waited and let the tension fade. 'So, Vasta left you the house, did he?'

'Just before he died.' She tilted her face defiantly upwards.

'But he's not dead. I think you know that.'

'Yes, he is.' She looked uncomfortable, made a quick judgement and added, 'Well, okay. So he got himself frozen, in case they could bring him back. But that's as good as dead, isn't it?'

'Do you know where his body is? Where they

put him?' As Lay spoke, the others slowly found seats and settled to listen.

'In a freezer some place, I suppose. I wouldn't know.'

'Didn't he tell you?'

The house itself, every stick of furniture, seemed to be listening.

'No. I don't reckon he knew himself, exactly.'

At this Kindling raised his eyebrows and Louise nodded back at him slightly.

'Well, I'll tell you,' Lay said, speaking slowly and clearly. 'He's in space. In orbit. They're keeping his body in a space station.'

She stared at him, wide-eyed, then surprised them by bursting into a childish peal of delighted laughter. 'Shit! Well, he's going to get a shock when he steps out the fucking door, isn't he?'

Lay laughed with her a moment, waiting for her to quieten, then told her, 'He's already had that shock, actually.'

Her smile disappeared. 'What do you mean? They've done it? They've brought him back to life already?'

Lay let the silence drag on, and she began to fidget uneasily. 'Not quite.' He suddenly scratched his neck with one finger, as if he wasn't sure how to go on. Watching, Kindling was sure it was a carefully practised act. 'It didn't work very well—bringing him back, I mean. He's not very healthy, or happy, for that matter.'

He had her rapt attention now, the wonder and curiosity on her face betraying her youth. 'Why? What happened?'

'Matthew, would you mind explaining the next

bit? You're much better at this subject than I am.'

Kindling was caught by surprise. He blinked and gathered his thoughts. The girl watched him expectantly. He stammered, 'Ah, he seems to have been possessed by something bad—like a bad spirit. A demon, I suppose you'd call it. It's not good, whatever it is.' He lapsed into silence, feeling his description was inadequate.

The girl's pale face managed to turn even whiter as the blood drained away and she visibly tried to shrink back into her seat. 'That *is* bad,' she said, obviously frightened. 'You don't want to fuck around with those sorts of things. They're bad, bad news. I don't know what you guys are thinking I can do. I can't help no one.'

'We want to bring him down here to Earth,' Lay explained.

'Give him a fucking parachute.'

Out of the corner of his eye he saw Wiley and Smith both getting restless and he feared they might try another pointless threat. 'We can't do that. We wish it was that easy. No, we only want to bring his spirit down, not his body. In fact, we *can't* bring his body down. There's been some problems.'

There was another long silence while she digested this. Around them the big house ticked and creaked, settling to the colder night air. She looked again at Kindling. 'Why doesn't he do it? He can do it. He nearly brought this fucking place down around my ears last time. Must've whistled up every fucking poltergeist in the damn neighbourhood.'

Kindling was about to tell her it wasn't poltergeists that were causing all the problems, but the one spirit they needed to deal with now. He realised at the last moment this might scare her off, and they needed her. Instead he said lamely, 'I don't know how. I really don't.'

She looked disbelieving. 'Anyway, I don't think I want any part of this. It sounds like really bad shit, if you ask me.' The way her eyes darted nervously, unwilling to meet his stare, told Lay she knew a lot more about what they were talking about than she was prepared to reveal.

A whisper of dismay went through those watching. Kindling appeared to take it the worst. However, Lay shrugged and spread his hands. 'If you can't help us, then I guess we can't help you stay in this place, either.'

She laughed, but her eyes skittered nervously. 'Don't lay that shit on me. It's mine. He gave it to me.'

'Don't count on it.'

'It's *mine!*' Her voice cracked a little.

Lay spread his hands. 'Look, Michelle. I can believe Vasta asked you to look after the place until he came back, or something like that. He may even have *given* it to you. But let me tell you, I've spent the last two years trying to squeeze even the smallest piece of property out of his estate to repay criminal costs and I've failed. Everything he owns, everything he's associated with, is tied up in the tightest legal red tape you could imagine. I know, because I reckon I've read every damn document there is, and there's hundreds of them. Vasta was a very smart man and he now has very smart lawyers working for him.' He paused. 'But you know what? On not one single document did I see the name "Michelle Weldon". In fact, you're a missing person. You sure as hell don't have a legal leg to stand on regarding this place. You're a legal nothing.'

Her face turned stonily stubborn as he spoke. 'But you can never stop me coming here,' she announced. Startling them, a shimmering blue aura began to form around her figure. From within it her expression turned to a smug, yet sad, smile. Wiley shouted, but Lay smoothly pulled his pistol from its holster and cocked it, aiming at her head. The fluttering light burst into an intense glare, a blinding incandescence that made everyone look away from its hot core. It flared briefly, then began to fade. Through the dancing blotches left on their retinas by the explosion of light, they could see the cat now occupied the spot where the girl had sat. The animal was tensed to flee. Lay still had his gun levelled. He didn't know if Michelle would understand him in her feline form.

'Don't,' he said quietly. 'Remember, no one's going to accuse me of anything if I shoot a damn cat. And I will, because I'm not in the mood to fuck around here. We don't have the time.' His words were flat and undeniable. No one doubted he would shoot.

The animal seemed to glare hatefully at him, then incredibly the change reversed itself with the same stunning display of blue-white light. The aura slowly faded and Michelle returned, looking sulky.

As if nothing had happened she suddenly exclaimed, 'Well, fuck! You just told me I haven't got a hope of having this place myself, no matter what he told me. Why should I do anything?' Surprising them, tears came into her eyes. Kindling found himself feeling sorry for her. He doubted

Lay had any intention of letting her stay in the house, under any circumstances.

Everyone was quiet, including Lay, who managed to keep his composure and patiently wait for her to listen again. He, too, behaved as if the amazing transformation had never taken place, and said calmly, 'Because, Michelle, if you can do this for us, Vasta will be properly, legally dead. Some powerful people will be very grateful and all the legal rules will change. Then, I might be able to do something for you.'

She stared at him. 'He'll be dead? Totally?' She couldn't stop a fleeting look of hope—and greed—transforming her expression. They watched as she thought hard, unaware how her face betrayed her feelings. Finally she looked very wary and nervous. 'Hey, if I do it, I'll tell you something right now,' she pointed a finger at Lay, determined. '*If* I do it, and it gets bad at all, I'm going to be out of there, got it?'

'Got it,' Lay sensed triumph.

'And I get the house?'

'I'll try my best,' Lay replied, guarded.

Wiley announced loudly, 'I don't think I believe I'm even here. This isn't happening.' No one took any notice.

But the girl still had a capacity for surprising them, for she suddenly slumped in the chair and said despairingly, 'I still don't honestly think I can do it. You've got to have the right place, and this isn't it. It never has been,' she dismissed the trap-door in the floor. 'I don't know where for Chrissake's you'd try it. It has to be just right.'

Michael Lay allowed himself a weary sigh and

passed his hands across his face. He looked defeated. Then Kindling spoke up behind him.

'I know,' he said, his voice strained, as if the words tortured him. 'I've just remembered a place I think will work.'

26

MICHELLE—OR 'MITCH', AS she insisted on being called—wanted to make preparations so they could be ready by midnight. Wiley asked her if there was a real significance in the timing, or if she was just being melodramatic. She merely glared contemptuously and refused to answer.

She made them help her duplicate the cellar's mural on a large white bedsheet. They used coloured pens and some paints they found in the garage. It took some time to do. Mitch had never taken much notice of what was on the ceiling and needed to make a rough sketch on paper first, then transfer the design onto the bedsheet. Luckily, the original wasn't a piece of art, either. It was the correct symbols in their rightful place that mattered, Mitch claimed, not the quality of the drawing.

Kindling tried to help, but increasingly found his mind wandering, trying to imagine what would happen when they tried to call the demon out of Vasta's body. The details of Stewart Andrews' death came back to him sharply now. His naked body had been found behind the Williams' back fence in a narrow laneway. Andrews had looked like the victim of a torture chamber, his whole body battered and bruised. The autopsy claimed some of the injuries had been caused by someone wielding a thin, blunt instrument. The heavy poker from the Williams' fireplace lay in the grass nearby. But the puzzled coroner also insisted many of Andrews' wounds appeared to be self-inflicted.

What sort of mental torment would cause a man like Stewart Andrews to deliberately hurt himself? He would have gone in there with some idea of what was going to happen. He would have had an opportunity to prepare himself, but still he died. In a terrible way.

Kindling didn't know what might occur tonight, but he knew he should be very frightened.

'Are you ready?' It was Mitch, looking at him with knowing eyes. She alone had any real idea of what they were in for.

He sighed and shook his head. 'No, but it doesn't make any difference.'

'You're a fucking loon, do you know that? This thing's going to eat you alive.'

Kindling was stung. 'Maybe,' he said angrily.

'Yeah, maybe,' she mimicked. 'Anyway, how're we getting there?'

'The cars are out the front.'

They all trooped out into the cold night. The skies above were clear and a half-moon glowed brightly. Mitch looked up at it as they walked down the driveway.

'Good,' she announced. 'Plenty to see by.' Then, when they were gathered around the cars debating who was going to ride in which, she took them all in with a surprised glance. 'Are you all coming?'

After a confused silence Michael Lay replied, 'Of course.'

She muttered, 'You're all fucking loons,' and let herself into the front seat of a car. She promptly pulled a plastic coin bag full of green leaf from her jacket pocket and began rolling a joint of marijuana. Lay, getting into the driver's seat, opened his mouth to scold her, but she stopped him with a look.

'Don't bitch, okay? This stuff helps me relax. It's going to make a difference. In fact, we all should have some,' she added with a laugh, knowing no one would take up her offer.

To explain his choice of venue Kindling needed to tell them about his visit to the cemetery the morning after he first met Wiley, Smith and Michael Lay. How a hand came out of the grave and grasped his, a hand undoubtedly Anton Vasta's. Kindling recognised the ring, he told them.

'Heavy shit,' was Mitch's only comment.

'But it's not Vasta's corpse in there,' Louise argued, puzzled.

'Ellen Littlewood's corpse wasn't in her room, either,' Kindling replied. 'It's the representation of them, and the emotions directed towards their memory. I imagine even Vasta's grave would have seen some mourning, if only briefly. He had a wife and daughters, remember.'

'I wonder how they coped with his occult worship,' Louise mused.

Mitch answered from the front seat, 'They didn't know. It was always their treat, to go away and stay with her relatives anywhere in the country. He just paid for the tickets and off they went, thinking Anton was the nicest guy in the world. It never occurred to the dumb bitch he wanted her out of the house for a few days.'

Kindling felt a tightening in his gut as the car's headlights swept across the low wall of the cemetery, picking out the taller headstones rising above it. He squeezed Louise's hand harder. Lay killed the motor and in the sudden silence they listened to the ticking metal contracting. No one said anything. Moments later Wiley and Smith pulled up next to them with a crunch of gravel.

'Let's do it.' Mitch opened her door. A cold blast of air swept away the warm fug created by the car's heater. They all got out and grouped around the front of the cars. Their breath steamed. Wiley blew into his cupped hands to warm them.

'Where to?' Lay asked Kindling.

He looked around and saw the gates, getting his bearings. 'I'll find it, but we have to jump the wall. The gates will be locked.'

'You lead the way.'

They carried the torches but nobody turned them on. Lay didn't want any residents nearby to get alarmed by a procession of lights moving through the graveyard. They didn't need them, anyway. The moon highlighted the stonework of the graves, making it easier to walk between them. The group went in single file, picking their way behind Kindling as he wound his way through the headstones. Some of the taller monoliths seemed to moodily watch them pass.

'Why couldn't we do this in daylight?' Wiley asked nervously, his voice clear in the night.

'I hate an audience,' Mitch replied drily. They'd missed her midnight deadline, but she hadn't mentioned it.

Kindling stopped next to a plain white grave. 'Here it is.' The others clustered around and read the simple inscription.

Mitch got them to spread out on either side of the grave, making sure Kindling was next to her at the foot. She flicked the bedsheet out and it floated gracefully down to cover most of the tiny, white pebbles filling the stone border.

'I don't believe I'm doing this,' Wiley muttered.

'You wait until the party starts,' Mitch told him. Then she became very serious, her pale face solemn and commanding their attention.

'I'll explain what's going to happen. Then any of you who don't want to take part must leave—and I mean leave. You can't hide behind a grave somewhere and watch. I'm warning you, you might meet somebody you don't want to know.' She took a breath. 'I'm going to try to call Anton's soul onto our circle here, even though he now lives again, because I don't know the correct name for the one we really need. I'm hoping the demon will hear us too, and dispossess Anton to come here, seeking

Matthew. As I call, don't be frightened by what you see happen to me. I won't be concerned with any of you. What we want, and what I expect, will be Matthew's demon to respond and come, instead of Anton's soul, which will want to stay with his living body.' Her voice dropped lower, chilling them more than the cold night ever could. 'This is a bad spirit we're calling. It feeds on what the church calls a person's soul. It captures them, gathers them like a prize and takes them away to a place we could never touch, feel or see. It's his place, and he does with them what he wishes. He is never kind or gentle. He is always evil and greedy. He delights in the things good people detest. He creates hate and anger.' She paused, looking to see if anyone was losing their nerve. No one dared to speak or move. Only Kindling looked up into the sky at the sparkling stars. He briefly wondered if any of them were Freedom, reflecting the moon.

'He can possess one living, human body at a time, but he doesn't possess that soul *while* they live. He will try to torment that person until they die in some way, normally by their own mad actions. Only then can he take their soul for himself. In that moment of death, as their soul releases, he swoops like a bird on a worm. Realise that he is not a god. He can't take a life where he pleases.' She looked at them all. Her eyes glittered in the darkness. 'Now listen closely, because this is the most important thing to us. If I succeed in calling him down to us, this spirit will be without a connection. He will have no soul in his possession and he will have left Anton's body without taking *his*—something they rarely do. He cannot exist among us in this way for long. It's the world's way. He needs his work to anchor him among us, or he'll be drawn back to his place. When he appears here, he'll attack us, but mostly, we know, he'll go for Matthew. The spirit will show you things that may be the truth, but he will show you lies, too. He'll try to make you feel small, unworthy, unimportant or desolate. He will attack your honesty, your self-esteem and try to show you as he thinks you really are, and if it becomes bad and you succumb to what he shows you, he can take you, simple as that. Try to remember you are strong, healthy and happy. You don't despair like the crippled, the sick or the lonely, which is who he usually preys on.'

Now, for the first time Mitch properly mentioned Kindling's part in the scheme. 'Matthew, he knows you are special. You could be a threat to him, much more than your friend Stewart Andrews. This is why he wants to take you now, before you understand how good you could be.'

'What do you mean?' Kindling asked, his voice a mere croak.

She seemed about to explain, then said, 'No, enough talking. Later, if there's a chance. Let's start. Does anybody want to go? Only Matthew's important, believe me.'

Still nobody moved.

'Okay, here we go. Keep quiet, all of you. Don't, for fuck's sake, interrupt me.'

She closed her eyes, took a deep breath, and stretched one hand over the mural. After a long moment her hand began to grope at the air, moving to hover above the different symbols and Mitch began to mumble to herself.

'Where should I go? Where am I strong? Over here? No. Over here? No, not there. Ah! Here is stronger, but it's wrong. Here is stronger too, and I can use this. I can call them around me.'

More fascinated than frightened, they watched. Kindling thought he heard a snort of disgust from Wiley. Mitch's clutching hand began to repeatedly snatch handfuls of air towards her. The white sheet began to shimmer and a white, smoking tendril of light arose from one of the symbols, wrapped itself around her arm and flowed up her body. Kindling was amazed to see Mitch appear to grow. She looked taller, wider. He thought it was her *presence* swelling, growing about them, embodied in an aura spreading around her like a pair of huge black wings. Her voice was getting louder.

'Come here to me. Come here—no, not you. You have no place here. Yes, you—closer, closer. Help your sister. I have work to do and I need your help. Closer, closer. No! You must leave. You will break our circle.'

The white light writhed and twisted over her figure like an electrical charge. Mitch hadn't physically altered, but they all perceived her as enormous now, dominant. Her grasping hand still feverishly pulled the light in to her.

Kindling nearly cried out when he suddenly saw an old, bent woman standing on a nearby grave. She watched them, unblinking. Then a man appeared beside her—her husband, Kindling knew. A baby began wailing. He twisted his head and on a small, tragic gravesite saw a young infant rolling on its back, crying. Another figure, a man, the victim of some terrible accident, sat on the ground next to a simple white cross. His naked body was pieced together like a bad jigsaw puzzle with some of the pieces missing.

Mitch was calling spirits and the gravesites around them were responding. Many of the ghostly figures were elderly. Some were younger, but ravaged by disease or injury. There were cries, muted speech. A bray of maniacal laughter echoed around the cemetery. Everyone standing beside Vasta's grave turned their heads this way and that, trying to look in all directions at once, now with fear written on their faces. Kindling saw the same reaction on Louise and he deeply, painfully, regretted bringing her into this. A memory came to him and he let his eyes drift to a point on the far side of the cemetery. There, once again, was the strange tableau of the soldier grappling with another man. The scene had that extra, misplaced quality.

Mitch shocked them by calling loudly, 'Anton, this is for you! This is for you, do you hear me? This is for *you!*' She fell silent, expectantly looking at the headstone in front of her. When nothing happened her eyes slid to Kindling's before she called, 'Kindling is here. Matthew Kindling is down here.'

A freezing wind blew between them for an instant, then stopped abruptly. Suddenly another light, a brilliant pinpoint, began to grow above the headstone. It got bigger, brighter, until they had to shade their eyes. Michael Lay, who was closest to it, stumbled away backwards.

'He's coming,' Mitch breathed.

The light exploded outwards with a sound that

was deafening—and yet silent. They fell back from the gravesite. All except Mitch and Kindling, who stood their ground as if they were facing into the teeth of a gale. An incredible shining figure hovered above the headstone. The face was beautiful and terrifying, but distorted by hate and greed. The thin, wasted body emanated immense power. The light it burned was intense, yet reflected off nothing around it. Behind the body was a hint of something—wings, a cape or a lashing tail—it was impossible to tell. A voice came into their minds, a guttural, horrid sound.

'*I come to take what is mine. I have been waiting long enough.*'

27

ALL AROUND KINDLING THE ethereal beings dragged from their graves began to moan and shriek at the presence of one so feared. He felt their despair so keenly it was like a knife in his heart, and it sapped his courage. He wanted to fall to the ground and bury his face in his hands, beg for it all to end, no matter what the cost. Not only could Kindling see into the spirit world, but now he could feel the torment of those who belonged to it. It was a devastating experience and he vaguely realised it was being multiplied and thrust at him by the demon, like a barrage of screamed abuse. Still, despite understanding the threat, his resolve wavered, looking for any release. Dragging willpower up from the depths of his soul, Kindling tried forcing his mind closed to the rage of the demon and the terror of the tortured ghosts around him. He tried turning to the living people who were with him for help, searching to add their strength to his own.

But when he finally managed a tenuous focus on the five human beings sprawled around the gravesite, he perceived that they preferred him to be dead, too. He heard the demon howl with delight.

Michael Lay saw the moonlit headstones and glowing, ghostly figures fade back, overlaid by a scene from twenty years ago. He was in a small, run-down house in the outer suburbs of the city. He was a junior in his job, studying at night to help his chances of promotion and spending long hours watching his betters, learning from them. And when he had the chance he earned extra money serving summonses. These people, a meek and helpless middle-aged couple, hadn't paid their rent for months. But instead of serving them a summons Lay was overseeing their eviction. He stood in the musty lounge room and watched as their furniture was carried out and tossed into the street. The couple stood looking at him with pitiful, tortured eyes.

'It's not my fault you didn't pay the rent,' Lay told them. They didn't answer. They just kept staring at him with their pain. Angry, Lay gathered a gob of phlegm in his mouth and suddenly spat on the man.

I didn't! I didn't spit on him. But a whispering voice insisted he had.

'Stop looking at me like that! I'm just doing my job.'

The man took out a handkerchief and carefully cleaned the spittle from his coat. The action was condemnatory, as if to say, 'This is what we expect from people like you'. Lay's mind snapped and he stepped close, pushing the man to the floor. Then he was kicking him—kicking him hard wherever he could land his boot. The man screamed with pain several times, lapsed into agonised grunts, then accepted the last blows silently. Satisfied, wiping his brow and breathing hard, Lay walked outside for some fresh air.

I didn't attack him. I didn't kick him. I just locked them out of their own home and left them. 'But you *wanted* to hurt him, cripple him,' the voice replied. Feathery fingers touched his shoulder.

Lay's superior was outside, a commission cheque in his hand and a congratulating smile on his face. It was Matthew Kindling.

'Well done,' Kindling said, holding out the cheque.

Lay suddenly wanted to kill him. The voice agreed it would be a good idea.

'I can't love you. I can't live with you.'

The graveyard had vanished to become a small one-bedroom flat near the city's oldest university. Louise Corry was explaining the facts to a man slightly younger than her own nineteen years. She saw the pain her words caused in her first lover's eyes. His devotion was fanatical. He bought her endless presents he couldn't afford and called every day, driving her crazy sometimes. She was trying to get somewhere in her career and foolish boys calling at all hours did nothing for her reputation. She'd only gone home with him the once, knowing the mystery of sex seemed essential to her maturity. Louise hadn't enjoyed it. And he had become besotted.

Now he started crying. Big tears ran down his cheeks and his chest heaved with sobs, unmanning him.

'Don't cry,' she told him desperately, hating his tears. She had to get away. 'Look, I'll go down the street and get some wine. Let's talk this over properly and end it right, okay? Just don't cry.'

He didn't reply and she fled in despair, calling that she would return. Minutes later, fighting with her conscience about going back at all, Louise found the apartment door locked in her face. A bottle of wine under her arm, she hammered on the wooden panelling. There was no answer.

'Are you locked out? I can let you in.' It was the building's caretaker, Matthew Kindling, a big friendly smile on his face and a bundle of keys in his hand.

'Please,' she tried to smile back normally. 'I've lost the key he gave me, and I think he's fast asleep.'

No one let me in. I just turned around and left. I didn't know! Freezing ghostly lips brushed against her ear and hissed that she was lying.

The door swung open and she passed inside, leaving Kindling to move on down the hallway. She went into the kitchen to open the wine and there was Robert, hanging from an exposed beam, his face turning blue as he kicked out violently.

I never got inside. God knows I had no idea that's what he'd do. 'No,' the lips said, sighing a chill breath down her neck. 'You knew exactly what he'd do. You even wanted it.'

Louise calmly put the wine on the table and saw the solution to her problem. Judging her moment she grasped his ankles and held them together, then leaned all her weight downwards, hoping the knot around the beam wouldn't slip.

She would never have done it, otherwise. The caretaker should never have let her back inside. He'd turned her into a murderer.

Smith was sick of his wife doing nothing. He could see her now. It was as if the cemetery had been magically transformed into their New York apartment. He worked his butt off all day and sometimes late into the night, only to come home to a filthy house and a frozen dinner. It was her illness, she always said. There was only so much she could do. It made her weak.

She always tried hard. It was me, too stupid to see the good and only seeing the dirt. 'You thought she was a lazy bitch,' someone slyly suggested to him. It seemed to come from the very air beside him.

One night, exhausted from work, he returned to find her asleep in front of the television. Nothing had been done. It was the first time he hit her.

Just the once, dear God. Just the once I lost control. She was sick—she died a year later. The voice hissed, 'It felt good, that backhand across her dumb, pleading face, didn't it?'

The next night she assured him a meal was on its way. Her voice was slurred, the drugs ruining her body. She was always tired, tired, tired. A litany he grew to hate. Smith searched the kitchen. There was no meal anywhere. Not in the fridge, the oven or the microwave. She was lying.

I took her to hospital, when I realised. It was reaction to her drugs, something she ate, for God's sake. None of this ever happened.

He went back to the living room and shouted at her, refused to listen to her confused explanation. Then he was hitting her, and hitting her again. He hated how useless she'd become. His balled fists thumping into her skin felt good. Finally, she slumped to the floor unconscious, and that's when the doorbell rang. It was a delivery man, a grinning Matthew Kindling, holding out a pizza.

'Your wife ordered this.'

Smith's rage still flowed through his veins, and now he wanted to haul this grinning fool through the door and bludgeon him to death, too.

Wiley was back in Vietnam. He was the only one of them not confused by the sudden transformation of his surroundings, because to him it was a change for the better. The horror of the graveyard slipped away to be replaced by familiar scenes, comfortable places. They were good times, back then. Especially for a man who knew where his duty and responsibilities lay. He was there, a raw recruit suddenly requisitioned by the CIA to help them burn records in the last days of the American embassy. As a security guard he'd shown interest. Someone noted it.

Through the walls of the building he could hear

people screaming. Locals trying to gain asylum in the grounds. The whock-whock of helicopter rotors beat on the roof. Everyone was being evacuated to an aircraft-carrier offshore. It was a frightening time, but Wiley was young enough to find it exciting. They were torching files, microfilm—any material evidence. Then the head of internal security, smiling, told him of the three items still in the cellar. Would he take care of them?

Wiley knew it was a test. A career crisis. Copying the smile, he'd said yes.

The noises faded as he descended deeper into the concrete bowels of the building. A place of damp walls, secret rooms and metal bars. And there were the three 'items': three shabby Viet Cong regulars. They were always grinning these days. Their side was winning. Wiley would stop their smiles.

From somewhere—perhaps from the marble of the headstone itself—a voice murmured that it would like to be a part of this. It looked like fun.

'Come and join in!' Wiley called aloud, laughing. Far from putting the prisoners at ease, his laughter made them tremble. Wiley had a weird, not unpleasant feeling, as if he was putting on a coat already warmed by somebody else's body. The coat seemed to fit *inside* him, as well.

Lifting his rifle, noting the shock and fear on their faces, he shot each of the prisoners in the head. Wiley felt uncertain whether he was actually pulling the trigger. But he didn't care. It still felt good—a feeling of power. Strange, when in fact they were being forced to flee this stinking city.

The last one needed two bullets—he'd tried to dodge away within the narrow confines of the cell and Wiley made a mess of it. Still, the most important thing was no one would know who'd done it—apart from those who appreciated his efforts.

As he turned to run back upstairs, suddenly worried about being left behind, he saw a staring face at the end of the corridor. Somebody who'd seen everything and would tell the wrong people. Matthew Kindling.

There was only one solution to that.

Kindling's own impressions were no longer clear. His life, filled with failure and misery, distorted by exaggeration and lies, passed before his eyes.

Stewart Andrews whispered derisively in his ear, the fetid, rotten breath gagging him. Ellen Littlewood cried in agony at his feet, begging him to let her go. Anton Vasta touched his shoulder and softly offered vast sums of money, if Kindling would only open his mind and set himself free. A presence, an indefinable entity, pushed at the limits of his mind and tried to invade his consciousness like an insect trying to burrow under his skin.

Kindling fought back the images, finding a strength he never knew he possessed, concentrating on the good things in his life. He could suddenly understand why a man might maim himself to take his mind away from this kind of torment. Then, like a light in a tunnel, he discovered that thinking about Louise Corry, about her kindness towards him, her beauty, pushed the frightful scenes back. He tried to call her name and thought he heard her whisper it back. He opened his eyes. The light coming from above the headstone blinded him and

Kindling held his hand up to shield his eyes.

The spirits in the graveyard were screeching with renewed suffering at the open sky. The baby's screams cut the air. Mitch was curled in a ball on the ground, sobbing.

Wiley, his legs spread in a classic gunman's pose and his face twisted with fear, levelled a pistol at Kindling's head.

Kindling could barely see beyond the confusion in his own mind. But it was clear Wiley was no longer himself. His burning eyes, the hunched and racked body, all spoke of the same captive existence Kindling last saw in Allen Williams' crippled form in the wheelchair. The man had been taken over.

At that moment the light above the headstone vanished. Wiley didn't change his stance and Kindling was suddenly filled with rage. He'd deliberately put his life—more than his life—at risk to help others. He expected to battle with his wits and his willpower against the worst opponent. But the demon wasn't confronting him directly. Instead, it had chosen to manipulate the emotions and hatreds of others against him. Despite all the supposed demonic power at its disposal, it was using a bullet.

Possessed, Wiley was going to kill Kindling for him, releasing the greater prize which the demon would snatch into his keeping.

Enraged, Kindling instinctively threw himself at the agent, who fired at the same instant. The bullet took Kindling in his left armpit, tearing away the muscle and sinew there. But he didn't feel any pain, and concentrated on his good hand which was closing in a clawing grip over Wiley's face. As they struggled they crashed to the ground and Wiley squeezed off another shot. This time Kindling felt a crushing shock to his lower abdomen. Blood spilled from his gut to soak his groin and he immediately felt weaker. Knowing he might have only seconds to live he savagely twisted himself around and sank his knee squarely on Wiley's throat. The gun fired again, but Kindling didn't feel a new wound—though he dimly realised he was probably beyond recognising more pain.

His eyes misted and blurred everything but the very centre of his vision. In this was Wiley's contorted face. His features began to change, becoming alternately the demon's terrifying visage, Stewart Andrews' tormented face and Ellen Littlewood's stolen innocence. Kindling hardly registered the changes, concentrating on applying his weight against the flesh of Wiley's throat. He thought he felt cold fingers plucking at his back and shoulders. An angry, sibilant hiss shrieked inside his head. Finally the graveyard began to spin around him and Kindling toppled forward to land face-down in the white pebbles of Vasta's grave.

The ghosts hovering above their tombs fell silent, and their images faded like smothered flames. Darkness swept like a blanket across the cemetery. For a long moment nobody dared move.

Slowly Mitch straightened up. Her eyes, wet with tears, took in the two men sprawled across the grave, then went to the spot above the headstone, now empty of the terrible form.

'Which one did he take?' she whispered. When Louise looked blankly at her, she said, 'He's gone. He must have taken one of them with him.'

28

THE SURVIVING FOUR ASTRONAUTS drifted silently in the Command Module. There was nothing to say, nothing to do, except wait. Nobody felt like talking. The red lighting cast deep shadows over their faces. A muted crackling came from one relay speaker, broadcasting radio conversations between the different Earth space centres. No one called Freedom.

Judith's death weighed heavily on them, all the more because it seemed she had died for nothing. Only Dawkins had been successful, bursting triumphantly back into the Command Module to announce he'd locked Vasta into one side of the space station and they had clear access to the Galley and the Accommodation Module. The terrible expression on Seerey's face and Judith's absence cut him short. Then, to make matters impossibly worse, the life support system shut down to emergency status again, another sign they'd badly misjudged Vasta's intelligence and ability. It became a waiting game once more.

Access to the extra modules gave them a bigger reserve of breathable air. It wasn't much more, but Dawkins figured it could well be the difference between a relief shuttle reaching them in time, or not. It seemed a small consolation.

There was one less person who needed to breathe.

The intercom system was left on, although Seerey moodily decided there was nothing they could do, whatever Vasta might attempt. The man was a freak, nearly invincible. He'd shrugged off the vicious head injury Seerey had inflicted. Still, they couldn't bear to turn the system down, leaving them deaf as well as blind. The strain would be too much.

So they heard the plaintive, tortured wail when it came through the intercom. It was more a cry of anguish, not anger. It made all the astronauts flinch, shocking them out of their morbid stupor.

'What in God's name was that?' Dawkins said huskily. They all looked at Seerey, who shook his head desparingly.

'She was dead, I swear it,' he whispered. 'Her neck was broken and she looked—dead.' He gestured helplessly. Words weren't enough.

Another cry filled the Command Module, then another. Lee snapped, 'Shit, can't we turn that damn thing off? I know already he's going to drive me crazy.'

'No, wait!' Frowning, Dawkins cocked his head to one side and listened. There was a low, sobbing groan. 'Did you catch that?' Dawkins asked.

They listened intently. The groan came again. 'I'm *alive?*' Seerey ventured cautiously.

'That's what I thought he said, too. But there's something else. The voice—the voice has *changed*.'

'I don't understand,' Celia said, moving closer to the intercom to hear better. 'What do you think it means?'

There was a silence, then Lee suggested, 'Multiple personalities? Could he be developing those?'

'God, I hope not. The one he's got now is bad enough,' Seerey said. It was a feeble joke, but the others had to agree. More cries came from the intercom. The last few were different.

They were clearly calls for help.

'He's got to be fucking kidding,' Dawkins growled.

'It must be a trap,' Celia said. She thought of Judith Cianta and shuddered.

But Seerey was staring at the intercom speaker, frowning in thought. He surprised them by saying, 'What if it isn't? What if he's weakened somehow—even if it is a personality change? It might be an opportunity to drive him back into the Cryogenics Module and lock him in there before he changes back.'

'No, Alex!' Celia was alarmed. 'It's *got* to be a trap. We know he's a damn sight smarter than we first thought. He's more than capable of this sort of thing. Forget it.'

Seerey sighed. 'I know, but Jesus—that sounds so real. Like he's in trouble. We could have a chance here.'

'I agree,' Lee said quietly. 'He may be a very good actor, but there's something about it which says it's genuine. He might be starting to break down.'

'This is crazy,' Celia told them flatly. She looked to Dawkins for support.

He shrugged and rolled his eyes. 'I don't know anything, any more.'

'I'm going to take a look,' Seerey decided tightly. They stared at him.

After a moment Dawkins said, 'Then I'd better come with you.'

'No, Scott. I know we live in enlightened times, but if something goes wrong, I don't what to leave two women alone up here.' Seerey waited for the expected burst of outrage from Celia or Lee. It wasn't what he anticipated.

'Then *I'll* go with you,' Celia said firmly.

'I want to go alone.'

'That *would* be stupid.'

Seerey looked at her grim expression and knew she was determined—and he was secretly glad not to be going by himself. He wasn't feeling very brave. 'Then I'll go first,' he compromised.

'Okay,' she nodded, tense.

Vasta was still crying and groaning, but the sounds were weaker, the words now impossible to understand. They used the intercom's isolation technique to determine where he was. As far as they could tell, Vasta was in the Airlock Module.

'Let's go,' Seerey said.

Dawkins opened the hatchway and gave them both a pat on the back as they went through. 'Take it easy,' he called. 'Don't take any stupid chances.'

'We won't,' Celia promised him over her shoulder. She pushed herself after Seerey, who was already halfway down the module.

They went carefully through the space station, watching the shadows for movement, expecting an attack of some sort at any moment. But as they got closer to the Airlock Module, Vasta's crying came more clearly. The two astronauts felt slightly more confident, knowing for certain where he was. Seerey slowed as he approached the access tunnel to the Airlock, trying not to bump against any equipment and warn Vasta they were coming. They both peered through the tunnel.

Vasta floated, curled into a ball, at the far end of the Airlock Module. He was alternately sobbing and crying out for help. His naked body with its ruined skin looked strangely diminished and withered in the red light. Stuff oozed out from the wound on his head. He clasped something to his chest. It was a helmet from one of the suits. As Seerey and Celia watched he held the helmet at arm's length and stared at it. Celia swore softly and put her lips close to Seerey's ear.

'He's using the tinted visor to look at his own reflection,' she whispered, awed.

'You're right,' he breathed back. 'He's *seeing* himself for the first time.' Seerey surprised her by moving into the tunnel. She quickly followed and they emerged from the other side warily, ready to retreat instantly. Still Vasta didn't acknowledge their presence. Seerey edged forward until they were level with the life support system. He jerked his head at it. 'Can you kick that back into life?' Celia was startled. Vasta must have heard him, but he didn't move.

She tried to keep one eye on Vasta as she studied the readouts. 'I can restart it normally. I can't lock it on, like Judith did. Though that didn't make any difference, anyway.' Mention of Cianta's name had Celia's gaze flicking around the module. Her heart lurched sickeningly when she saw a pair of splayed, naked legs just inside the Airlock chamber.

'Do it,' Seerey told her. 'I'll watch your back. Let's get some light in here.'

Celia quickly reactivated the life support system. The muscles in her back tensed as Vasta cried out loudly, twice, but Seerey didn't call a warning, so she kept working. When she finished Freedom once more clicked and whirred itself back into action. Normal lighting flickered to brightness in the Airlock. They waited, nervously, for Vasta to move.

He slowly turned his head towards them. A thin line of drool escaped his mouth. His eyes were glazed. The ruined skin was like an ill-fitting garment, wrinkled and bruised.

'*What have they done?*'

The voice was thin and trembling. Looking at the way his eyes searched the air in front of him, Seerey knew Vasta was nearly blind.

'Do you know who you are?' Seerey asked roughly. He had to stop and clear his throat. 'Where you are?'

'*What have they done to me?*' Vasta was either ignoring the questions or not hearing them. He looked so pathetic Celia almost felt sorry for him. Almost.

She moved closer, staring at the horrid figure. 'He's dying,' she said to Seerey, who stayed behind her. 'Whatever drove him before and kept him alive must be gone. Now he's dying, the way he should have in the first place.' She got near enough to pass her hand across the front of Vasta's face. His eyes didn't blink, but stared at an empty space beyond her shoulder. 'He can't last much longer.'

She screamed when his hand darted out and fastened around her upper arm. Vasta dropped the helmet and hauled himself close, thrusting his face into Celia's. Fetid breath washed over her as she clamped down on her shock and tried to fight back. She heard Seerey cry out, but Vasta was hissing into her face, moving his lips as though he wanted to kiss her passionately.

'*What have they done to me?*'

But he was no longer strong. With her free hand Celia shoved at his chest. She cried out in revulsion as her fingers sank deep into his skin, tearing the flesh like sodden paper. If she hadn't stopped, her fingertips would have penetrated right through to his chest cavity. It needed no effort to jerk out of his grip, but in a reflex action she lashed out with her foot and sent Vasta crashing into the bulkhead. His anguished cries were cut off and he bounced off the metal to hang limply, strands of blood drifting from the new wounds.

Celia felt stronger hands grip her clothing and haul her backwards. Scott Dawkins' voice was yelling through the intercom. Seerey was speaking urgently in her ear.

'Are you all right? Celia?'

'Yeah, yeah—I'm okay,' she told him quickly. He let go of her clothes, put an arm around her shoulder and hugged her close for a while. They gazed at Vasta, unwilling to believe it might be over.

'Christ, what happened to him?' Seerey murmured.

'I hope I never find out,' she replied shakily. Seerey gave her a squeeze and let go. He slowly approached Vasta, who hadn't moved again. Tentatively, Seerey reached out and pressed his fingers against Vasta's neck, pulling a disgusted face as the soft skin nearly parted under the pressure. After a moment he looked at Celia.

'There's no pulse. I think he's dead.'

She took a deep breath, letting it out in a trembling sigh. 'You know, I'm afraid—I think he aways was.'

29

LOUISE PICKED HER WAY around Kindling's flat one last time, but found nothing else. She found it amazing that his entire belongings fitted into just two large cardboard boxes. The furniture, the caretaker insisted, was all owned by the building. Even the television. She couldn't be bothered arguing. She signed the termination papers for the lease and paid the penalty rent in cash. The caretaker asked again what had happened to him, but Louise simply replied he wouldn't be back.

The very last thing she'd found, lying just under the bed like a favourite bedtime book, was a worn Bible. Inside the inscription read, *To Matthew. There is much in here we ignore, but you should know.* It was signed by Stewart Andrews. Louise wondered if it had been given to Kindling before the episode in the Williams' household. Uncertain whether to throw it away or keep it, she finally slipped it back on to the bare bookshelf.

There was a noise at the doorway and Czowkowski walked in. He looked different in civilian clothing. 'Is that all?' He nodded, surprised, at the two boxes.

'That's it,' she shrugged tiredly.

'Can you carry one of them? I put the car in front of the building, but I asked Bennington to sit tight. It's not the best of neighbourhoods.'

'That one's got the heaviest stuff,' she pointed. 'I can carry the other one.'

'Okay.' He picked it up and looked at her. 'Where are we taking it?'

'My place, I guess.'

He raised his eyebrows. 'Then what?'

'Can you take me back to the hospital? He might be conscious again. I'd better explain what I've done. And that he's going to be my house guest while he convalesces—whenever that might be. The surgeon said he might not be well enough to be released for months.'

Czowkowski's expression was a mixture of envy and humour. 'What happens when he's on his own two feet properly? You might have a bit of trouble getting him out of *your* house, then.'

Louise smiled. 'We'll just take one day at a time. You never know what the future will bring.'

She hefted the box and walked through the doorway. Czowkowski followed, kicking the door closed behind him.

Even as their footsteps echoed down the hallway, inside the flat the discarded Bible suddenly fell open. The paper darkened, then blackened, the edges of the pages curling. The first lick of flame was smokeless, white-hot in its centre. Then the fire started to quickly consume the dry paper. Soon, the Bible was a misshapen mound of smouldering ash.

The smoke in the air wavered, as if someone was moving through it.

30

GEORGINA HAD DISOBEYED DANIEL in one, small way. She'd kept the book—Ellen's favourite book—even though some pages were torn and angry red slashes of crayon marred others. She was glad, though. Because now, when she took it out, remembering the times she'd read it aloud to her daughter, the red slashes were beginning to make sense.

Georgina thought she could read a message. It would come to her soon.

31

THE SHUTTLE LAUNCH WENT without a hitch. For days technicians had swarmed over the tower checking for hurricane damage. The few minor problems they found were easily fixed.

The crew were fully briefed on what to expect. It had taken some time for their collective shock to subside. Two bodies, one a woman, the other some sort of gross mutation. The result of an experiment in cryogenics going wrong. Already two other crewmembers had lost their lives and a third apparently panicked and ejected with the Lifeboat—a damned expensive panic, they all agreed.

That left four surviving astronauts. A disaster.

The shuttle *Lincoln* performed its graceful manoeuvres and twenty-four hours after lift-off the gleaming superstructure of Freedom could be seen through the forward windscreen. Their movement towards the space station was almost imperceptible, as they edged towards the Airlock. Computers controlled most of the procedure. The shuttle crew could take their time and watch the view.

The Commander pointed. 'Look. These guys must be keen. With only four of them left, I'd be just sitting tight and waiting to go home.'

'What do you think he's doing?' asked the co-pilot.

He watched the bulky white figure a moment, the spacesuit brilliant in the sunshine. 'Looks like a seal check, the way he's wandering all over the place.' He went to the radio and called Freedom.

'Freedom, this is *Lincoln*. Do you want to pull in your EVA before we dock?'

There was a silence, then a puzzled voice replied, 'We have no EVA in progress, *Lincoln*.'

'Yeah?' the Commander mouthed at his companion. His eyes flicked back to the windscreen as he pressed the button to reply. Then, slowly, he released the switch again.

Impossibly, the spacesuited figure was gone.

G.M. Hague

A Place To Fear

Something's going on in the sleepy little sugarcane town of Hickory.

A disturbing light shining down by the river.

Two nasty road accidents, one after the other.

Then Jake Sanders' mother is found dead on her living room floor, her face a mask of unspeakable terror.

And no-one's seen young Ainslie McGregor since he went off on a dare to meet his best friend in the local graveyard.

Slowly, inexorably, communication with the outside world breaks down, and Hickory becomes a place to fear.

G.M. Hague

Voices of Evil

BEYOND TERROR...
A NIGHTMARE LIKE NO OTHER

A deranged Gallipoli veteran locked in a padded cell.

The grisly deaths of two beautiful young women.

An ancient charm in an old metal tin.

When journalist Brendan Craft discovers the mysterious Egyptian charm, a series of terrifying events is unleashed. Confronted with evil beyond imagining, Brendan becomes locked in a battle for his sanity. Where does a dream end and reality begin?

Death may be the only escape from the voices of evil